W9-CFG-267

BLEED FOR ME

Also by Michael Robotham

Suspect

Lost

The Night Ferry

Shatter

The Wreckage

BLEED FOR ME

Michael Robotham

Doubleday Large Print Home Library Edition

MULHOLLAND BOOKS
LITTLE, BROWN AND COMPANY
NEW YORK BOSTON LONDON

This Large Print Edition, prepared especially for Doubleday Large Print Home Library, contains the complete, unabridged text of the original Publisher's Edition.

Mulholland Books / Little, Brown and Company
Hachette Book Group
237 Park Avenue, New York, NY 10017

Mulholland Books is an imprint of Little, Brown and Company, a division of Hachette Book Group, Inc. The

Mulholland Books name and logo are trademarks of Hachette Book Group, Inc.

The publisher is not responsible for websites (or their content) that are not owned by the publisher.

ISBN 978-1-61793-706-4

Printed in the United States of America

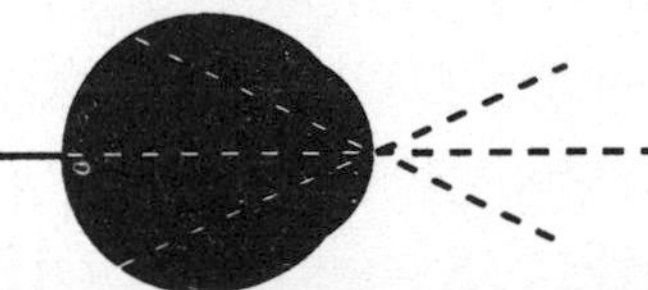

This Large Print Book carries the Seal of Approval of N.A.V.H.

For Vivien

"She was Lo, plain Lo, in the morning, standing four-feet-ten in one sock. She was Lola in slacks. She was Dolly at school. She was Dolores on the dotted line. But in my arms she was always Lolita."

VLADIMIR NABOKOV, *LOLITA*

"Everybody lies—every day; every hour; awake; asleep; in his dreams; in his joy; in his mourning; if he keeps his tongue still, his hands, his toes, his eyes, his attitude, will convey deception."

MARK TWAIN (1835–1910)

SIENNA'S DIARY

I should start by telling you my name, although it's not really important. names are just labels that we grow into. we might hate them, we might want to change them, but eventually we suit them.

when i was very young i used to hide in the dirty laundry basket because i liked the smell of my father's work clothes and it made me feel closer to him. he used to call me his "little red riding hood" and would chase me around my bedroom growling like a wolf until i collapsed into giggles. i loved him then.

when i was eleven or twelve i took a stanley knife from my father's shed and pinched a roll of flesh on my inner arm before slicing it open. it wasn't very deep, but enough to bleed for a while. i don't know where the idea came from, but somehow it gave me something i needed. a pain on the outside to match the inside.

i don't cut often. sometimes once a week, once a month, once i went for six months. in the winter i cut my wrists and forearms because my school blazer will cover the marks. in the summer i cut my stomach because a one-piece swimsuit will hide the evidence.

once or twice i've cut too deeply but each time i managed to fix myself, using a needle and thread. i bet that makes you shudder but it didn't hurt so much and i boiled the needle first.

when i bleed i feel calm and clear-headed. it's like the poison inside me is dripping out. even when i've stopped bleeding, i finger the cuts lovingly. i kiss them goodnight.

some are new cuts on virgin skin. others are old wounds reopened. razor

blades and stanley knives are best. they're clean and quick. knives are clumsy and needles don't produce enough blood.

you want to know the reason? you want to know why someone would bleed in secret? it's because i deserve it. i deserve to be punished. to punish myself. love is pain and pain is love and they will never leave me alone in the world.

every drop of blood that flows from my veins is proof that i'm alive. every drop is proof that i'm dying. every drop removes the poison inside me, running down my arms, dripping off my fingers.

you think i'm a masochist.

you think i'm suicidal.

you think you know me.

you think you remember what it's like to be fourteen.

you think you understand me.

you don't.

i bleed for you.

1

If I could tell you one thing about Liam Baker's life it would be this: when he was eighteen years old he beat a girl half to death and left her paralyzed from the waist down because she tipped a bucket of popcorn over his head.

As defining events go, nothing else comes close for Liam, not the death of his mother or his faith in God or the three years he has spent in a secure psychiatric hospital—all of which can be attributed, in one way or another, to that moment of madness in a cinema queue.

"That moment of madness" is the term his

psychiatrist just used. Her name is Dr. Victoria Naparstek and she's giving evidence before a Mental Health Review Tribunal, listing Liam's achievements as though he's about to graduate from university.

Dr. Naparstek is a good-looking woman, younger than I expected; midthirties with honey-blond hair, brushed back and gathered in a tortoiseshell clasp. Strands have pulled loose and now frame her features, which otherwise would look quite elfin and sharp. Despite her surname, her accent is Glaswegian but not harsh or guttural, more a Scottish lilt, which makes her sound gay and carefree, even when a man's freedom is being argued. I wonder if she's aware that her eyes devour rather than register a person. Perhaps I'm being unfair.

Liam is sitting on a chair beside her. It has been four years since I saw him last, but the change is remarkable. No longer awkward and uncoordinated, Liam has put on weight and his glasses are gone, replaced by contact lenses that make his normally pale blue eyes appear darker.

Dressed in a long-sleeved cotton shirt and jeans, he wears shoes with pointed toes, which are fashionable and he has gelled his hair so that it pokes towards the ceiling. I can picture him getting ready for this hearing, taking extra care with his appearance because he knows how important it is to look his best.

Out the window I can see a walled courtyard, dotted with potted plants and small trees. A dozen patients are exercising, each inhabiting a different space, without acknowledging the others' existence. Some take a few strides in one direction and then stop, as though lost, and start in a different direction. Others are swinging their arms and marching around the perimeter as though it is a parade ground. One young man seems to be addressing an audience while another has crawled beneath a bench as if sheltering from an imaginary storm.

Dr. Naparstek is still talking.

"In my months working with Liam, I have discovered a troubled young man, who has worked very hard to better himself. His anger issues are under control and his social skills are greatly improved. For the past four months he has been part of our shared-house program, living cooperatively with other patients, cooking, cleaning and washing, making their own rules. Liam has been a calming influence—a team leader. Recently, we had a critical incident when a male resident took a hostage at knifepoint and barricaded a door. It took five minutes for security to gain access to the shared house, by which time Liam had defused the situation. It was amazing to watch."

I glance at the three members of the review tribunal—a judge, a medical specialist and a lay person with mental health experience. Do they look "amazed," I wonder. Perhaps they're just not showing it.

The tribunal must decide if Liam should be released. That's how the system works. If an offender is thought to be cured, or approaching being cured, they are considered for rehabilitation and release. From a high-security hospital they're transferred to a regional secure unit for further treatment. If that goes well, they are given increasing amounts of leave, first in the grounds of the unit and later in the local streets with an escort, and then alone.

I am not here in any official capacity. This should be one of my half-days at Bath University, where I've taught psychology for the past three years. That's how long it's been since I quit my clinical practice. Do I miss it? No. It lives with me still. I remember every patient—the cutters, the groomers, the addicts, the narcissists, the sociopaths and the sexual predators; those who were too frightened to step out into the world and the few who wanted to burn it down.

Liam was one of them. I guess you could say I put him here because I recommended he be sectioned and given treatment rather than sent to a regular prison.

Dr. Naparstek has finished. She smiles and leans down to whisper something in Liam's ear, squeezing his shoulder. Liam's eyes swim but aren't focused on her face. He is looking down the front of her blouse. Resuming her seat, she crosses her legs beneath her charcoal-gray skirt.

The judge looks up. "Is there anyone else who would like to address the tribunal?"

It takes me a moment to get to my feet. Sometimes my legs don't do as they're told. My brain sends the messages but they fail to arrive or like London buses they come all at once causing my limbs to either lock up or take me backwards, sideways and occasionally forwards, so that I look like I'm being operated via remote control by a demented toddler.

The condition is known as Parkinson's—a progressive, degenerative, chronic but not contagious disease that means I'm losing my brain without losing my mind. I will not say incurable. They will find a cure one day.

I have found my feet now. "My name is Professor Joseph O'Loughlin. I was hoping I could ask Liam a few questions."

The judge tilts his chin to his chest. "What's your interest in this case, Professor?"

"I'm a clinical psychologist. Liam and I are acquainted. I provided his pre-sentencing assessment."

"Have you treated Liam since then?"

"No. I'm just hoping to understand the context."

"The context?"

"Yes."

Dr. Naparstek has turned to stare at me. She doesn't seem very impressed. I make my way to the front of the room. The linoleum floor is shining as daylight slants through barred windows, leaving geometric patterns.

"Hello, Liam, do you remember me?"

"Yes."

"Come and sit up here."

I place two chairs facing each other. Liam looks at Dr. Naparstek, who nods. He moves forward, taller than I remember, less confident than a few minutes ago. We sit opposite, our knees almost touching.

"It's good to see you again. How have you been?"

"Good."

"Do you know why we're here today?"

He nods.

"Dr. Naparstek and the people here think you're better and it's time you moved on. Is that what you want?"

Again he nods.

"If you are released, where would you go?"

"I'd find somewhere to live. G-g-get a job."

Liam's stutter is less pronounced than I remember. It gets worse when he's anxious or angry.

"You have no family?"

"No."

"Most of your friends are in here."

"I'll m-m-make new friends."

"It's been a while since I saw you last, Liam. Remind me again why you're here."

"I did a bad thing, but I'm better now."

There it is: an admission and an excuse in the same breath.

"So why are you here?"

"You sent me here."

"I must have had a reason."

"I had a per-per-personality disorder."

"What do you think that means?"

"I hurt someone, but it weren't my fault. I couldn't help it." He leans forward, elbows on his knees, eyes on the floor.

"You beat a girl up. You punched and kicked her. You crushed her spine. You broke her jaw. You fractured her skull. Her name was Zoe Hegarty. She was sixteen."

Each fact resonates as though I'm clashing cymbals next to his ear, but nothing changes in his eyes.

"I'm sorry."

"What are you sorry for?"

"For what I d-d-did."

"And now you've changed?"

He nods.

"What have you done to change?"

He looks perplexed.

"Hostility like that has to come from somewhere, Liam. What have you done to change?"

He begins talking about the therapy sessions and workshops that he's done, the anger-management courses and social skills training. Occasionally, he looks over his shoulder towards Dr. Naparstek, but I ask him to concentrate on me.

"Tell me about Zoe."

"What about her?"

"What was she like?"

He shakes his head. "I don't remember."

"Did you fancy her?"

Liam flinches. "It w-w-weren't like that."

"You followed her home from the cinema. You dragged her off the street. You kicked her unconscious."

"I didn't rape her."

"I didn't say anything about raping her. Is that what you intended to do?"

Liam shakes his head, tugging at the sleeves of his shirt. His eyes are focused on the far wall, as if watching some invisible drama being played out on a screen that nobody else can see.

"You once told me that Zoe wore a mask. You said a lot of people wore masks and weren't genuine. Do I wear a mask?"

"No."

"What about Dr. Naparstek?"

The mention of her name makes his skin flush.

"N-n-no."

"How old are you now, Liam?"

"Twenty-two."

"Tell me about your dreams."

He blinks at me.

"What do you dream about?"

"Getting out of here. Starting a n-n-new life."

"Do you masturbate?"

"No."

"I don't believe that's true, Liam."

He shakes his head.

"What's wrong?"

"You shouldn't talk about stuff like that."

"It's very natural for a young man. When you masturbate who do you think about?"

"Girls."

"There aren't many girls around here. Most of the staff are men."

"G-g-girls in magazines."

"Dr. Naparstek is a woman. How often do you get to see Dr. Naparstek? Twice a week? Three times? Do you look forward to your sessions?"

"She's been good to me."

"How has she been good to you?"

"She doesn't judge me."

"Oh, come on, Liam, of course she judges you. That's why she's here. Do you ever have sexual fantasies about her?"

He bristles. Edgy. Uncomfortable.

"You shouldn't say things like that."

"Like what?"

"About her."

"She's a very attractive woman, Liam. I'm just admiring her."

I look over his shoulder. Dr. Naparstek doesn't seem to appreciate the compliment. Her lips are pinched tightly and she's toying with a pendant around her neck.

"What do you prefer, Liam, winter or summer?"

"Summer."

"Day or night?"

"Night."

"Apples or oranges?"

"Oranges."

"Coffee or tea?"

"Tea."

"Women or men?"

"Women."

"In skirts or trousers?"

"Skirts."

"Long or short?"

"Short."

"Stockings or tights?"

"Stockings."

"What color lipstick?"

"Red."

"What color eyes does she have?"

"Blue."

"What is she wearing today?"

"A skirt."

"What color is her bra?"

"Black."

"I didn't mention a name, Liam. Who are you talking about?"

He stiffens, embarrassed, his face a beacon. I notice his left knee bouncing up and down in a reflex action.

"Do you think Dr. Naparstek is married?" I ask.

"I d-d-don't know."

"Does she wear a wedding ring?"

"No."

"Maybe she has a boyfriend at home. Do you think about what she does when she leaves this place? Where she goes? What her house looks like? What she wears to bed? Maybe she sleeps naked."

Flecks of white spit are gathered in the corners of Liam's mouth.

Dr. Naparstek wants to stop the questioning, but the judge tells her to sit down.

Liam tries to turn but I lean forward and put my hands on his shoulders, my mouth close to his ear. I can see the sweat wetting the roots of his hair and a fleck of shaving foam beneath his ear.

In a whisper, "You think about her all the time, don't you, Liam? The smell of her skin, her shampoo, the delicate shell of her ear, the shadow in the hollow between her breasts . . . every time you see her, you collect more details so that you can fantasize about what you want to do to her."

Liam's skin has flushed and his breathing has gone ragged.

"You fantasize about following her home—just like you followed Zoe Hegarty. Dragging her off the street. Making her beg you to stop."

The judge suddenly interrupts. "We can't hear your questions, Professor. Please speak up."

The spell is broken. Liam remembers to breathe.

"My apologies," I say, glancing at the

review panel. "I was just telling Liam that I might ask Dr. Naparstek out to dinner."

"B-b-but y-y-you're married."

He noticed my wedding ring.

"I'm separated. Maybe she's available."

Again, I lean forward, putting my cheek next to his.

"I'll take her to dinner and then I'll take her home. I bet she's a dynamite fuck, what do you think? The prim and proper ones, all cool and distant, they go off like chainsaws. Maybe you want to fantasize about that."

Liam has forgotten to breathe again. His brain is sizzling in an angry-frantic way, screaming like a guitar solo.

"Does that upset you, Liam? Why? Let's face it, she's not really your type. She's pretty. She's educated. She's successful. What would she want with a sad, sadistic fuck like you?"

Liam's eyes jitter back and forth like a shot of adrenaline has punched straight into his brain. He launches himself out of his seat, taking me with him across the room. The world is flying backwards for a moment and his thumbs are in my eye sockets and his hands squeezing my skull.

I can barely hear a thing above my own heartbeat until the sound of heavy boots on the linoleum.

Liam is dragged off me, panting, ranting. Hospital guards have secured his arms, lifting him bodily, but he's still lashing out at me and screaming, telling me what he's going to do.

The tribunal members have been evacuated or sought refuge in another room. I can still hear Liam being wrestled down a distant corridor, kicking at the walls and doors. Victoria Naparstek has gone with him, trying to calm him down.

My eyes are streaming and through closed lids I can see a kaleidoscope of colored stars merging and exploding. Dragging myself to a chair, I pull out a handkerchief to wipe my cheeks. After a few minutes I can see clearly again.

Dusting off my jacket, I pick up my battered briefcase and make my way through the security stations and locked doors until I reach the parking area where my old Volvo estate looks embarrassingly drab. I'm about to unlock the door when Victoria Naparstek appears, moving unsteadily in high heels over the uneven tarmac.

"What the hell was that? It was totally unprofessional. How dare you talk about what I wear to bed! How dare you talk about my underwear!"

"I'm sorry if I offended you."

"You're sorry! I could have you charged with misconduct. I should report you to the British Psychological Society."

Her brown irises are on fire and her nostrils pinched.

"I'm sorry if you feel that way. I simply wanted to see how Liam would react."

"No, you wanted to prove me wrong. Do you have something against Liam or against me?"

"I don't even know you."

"So it's Liam you don't like?"

The accusation clatters around my head and my left leg spasms. I feel as though it's going to betray me and I'll do something embarrassing like kick her in the shins.

"I don't like or dislike Liam. I just wanted to make sure he'd changed."

"So you tricked him. You belittled him. You bullied him." She narrows her eyes. "I've heard people talk about you, Professor O'Loughlin. They always use hushed tones. I had even hoped I might learn something from you today. Instead you bullied my patient, insulted me and revealed yourself to be an arrogant, condescending, misogynistic prick."

Not even her Scottish lilt can make this sound gay or carefree. Up close she is indeed a beautiful woman. I can see why a man might fixate upon her and ponder what she wears in bed and what sounds she makes in the throes of passion.

"He's devastated. Distraught. You've set back his rehabilitation by months."

"I make no apologies for that. Liam Baker has learned to mimic helpfulness and co-operation, to pretend to be better. He's not ready to be released."

"With all due respect, Professor . . ."

Whenever anyone begins a sentence like this I brace myself for what's coming.

". . . I've spent the past eighteen months working with Liam. You saw him half a dozen times before he was sentenced. I think I'm in a far better position to judge his progress than you are. I don't know what you whispered to Liam, but it was completely unfair."

"Unfair to whom?"

"To Liam and to me."

"I'm trying to be fair to Zoe Hegarty. You might not agree with me, Doctor, but I think I just did you an enormous favor."

She scoffs. "I've been doing this job for ten years, Professor. I know when someone poses a danger to society."

I interrupt her. "It's not society I'm worried about. It's far more personal than that."

Dr. Naparstek hesitates for a moment. I can almost picture her mind at work—her prefrontal cortex making the connections between Liam's words, his stolen glances and his knowledge of her underwear and where she lives. Her eyes widen as the realization reaches her amygdala, the fear center.

The Volvo starts first time, which makes it more reliable than my own body. As the boom gate rises, I catch a glimpse of the doctor still standing in the car park staring after me.

The grounds of Shepparton Park School are bathed in the spring twilight with shadows folding between the trees. Most of the buildings are dark except for Mitford Hall, where the windows are brightly lit and young voices are raised.

I'm early to pick up Charlie. The rehearsals haven't finished. Slipping through a side door, I hide in the darkness of the auditorium, gazing across rows of empty seats to the brightly lit stage.

School musicals and dance recitals are a rite of passage for every parent. Charlie's first performance was eight years ago, a Christmas pageant in which she played a very loud cow. Now she's fourteen with bobbed hair and dressed in a twenties flapper dress, having been transformed into Miss Dorothy Brown, the best friend of Thoroughly Modern Millie.

I could never do it myself—tread the boards. My only theatrical appearance was aged five in a primary school production of *The Sound of Music* when I was cast as the youngest von Trapp child (normally a girl, I know, but size rather than talent won me the part). I was small enough to be carried upstairs by the girl who played Liesl (Nicola Bray in year six) when the von Trapp children sang "So Long, Farewell." I was in love with Nicola and wanted her to carry me to bed every night. That was forty-four years ago. Some crushes don't get crushed.

I recognize some of the cast, including

Sienna Hegarty, who is in the chorus. She desperately wanted to play the lead role of Millie Dillmount, but Erin Lewis won the part to everyone's surprise and Sienna had to settle for being her understudy.

As I watch her move about the stage, my mind goes back to the tribunal hearing and Liam Baker. There are little pictures and big pictures at play. The little everyday picture is that Sienna is my daughter's best friend. The big picture is that her older sister is Zoe Hegarty, the girl in the wheelchair, who could once stand and dance and run, until Liam Baker's "moment of madness," which had been coming all his life.

The music stops and Mr. Ellis, the drama teacher, vaults onto the stage, repositioning some of the dancers. Dressed in trainers and faded jeans, he's handsome in a geekish sort of way. A fringe of dark brown hair falls across his eyes and he casually brushes it away.

The scene starts again—an argument between the play's hero and heroine. Millie plans to marry her boss even though it's obvious Jimmy loves her. The quarrel escalates and Jimmy grabs her, planting a clumsy kiss.

Erin pushes him away angrily, wiping her mouth. “I said no tongue.”

There are whistles and catcalls from backstage and the boy bows theatrically, milking the laughter.

Mr. Ellis leaps onto the stage again, annoyed at yet another interruption. He snaps at Sienna. “What are you grinning at?”

“Sorry, sir.”

“How many times have I told you to come in on the third bar? You’re half a step behind everyone else. If you can’t get this right, I’ll put you at the back. Permanently.”

Sienna bows her head glumly.

The drama teacher claps his hands. “OK, let’s do that scene again. I’ll play your part, Lockwood. It’s a kiss, OK? I’m not asking you to take out her tonsils.”

Mr. Ellis takes his place opposite Erin, who is tall for her age and wearing flat shoes. The scene begins with an argument and ends when he puts a single finger beneath her chin and tilts her face towards his, whispering in a voice that penetrates even at the lowest volume. Erin’s hands are by her sides. Trembling slightly, her lips part and she topples fractionally forward as if surrendering. For a moment I think he's going to kiss her, but he pulls away abruptly, breaking contact. Erin looks like a disappointed child.

"OK, that's it for today," says Mr. Ellis. "We'll have another rehearsal on Friday afternoon and a full dress rehearsal next Wednesday. Nobody be late."

He looks pointedly at Sienna. "And I expect everything to be perfect."

The cast wander offstage and the band begins packing away instruments. Easing open a fire door, I circle a side path to the main doors of the hall where a dozen parents are waiting, some with younger children clinging to their hands or playing tag on the grass.

A woman's voice behind me: "Professor O'Loughlin?"

I turn. She smiles. It takes me a moment to remember her name. Annie Robinson, the school counselor.

"Call me Joe."

"We haven't seen you for a while."

"No. I guess my wife does most of this." I motion to the school buildings, or maybe I'm pointing to my life in general.

Miss Robinson looks different. Her clothes are tighter and her skirt shorter. Normally she seems so shy and distracted, but now she's more focused, standing close as if she wants to share a secret with me. She's wearing high heels and her liquid brown eyes are level with my lips.

"It must be difficult—the breakup."

I clear my throat and mumble yes.

Her extra-white teeth are framed by bright painted lips.

Dropping her voice to a whisper, "If you ever need somebody to talk to . . . I know what it's like." She smiles and her fingers find my hand. Intense embarrassment prickles beneath my scalp.

"That's very kind. Thank you."

I muster a nervous smile. At least I hope I'm smiling. That's one of the problems with my "condition." I can never be sure what face I'm showing the world—the genial O'Loughlin smile or the blank Parkinson's mask.

"Well, it's good to see you again," says Miss Robinson.

"You too, you're looking . . ."

"What?"

"Good."

She laughs with her eyes. "I'll take that as a compliment."

Then she leans forward and pecks me on the lips, withdrawing her hand from mine. She has pressed a small piece of paper into my palm, her phone number. At that moment I spy Charlie in the shadows of the stage door, carrying a schoolbag over her right shoulder. Her dark hair is still pinned up and there are traces of stage makeup around her eyes.

"Were you kissing a teacher?"

"No."

"I saw you."

"She kissed *me* . . ."

"Not from where I was standing."

"It was a peck."

"On the lips."

"She was being friendly."

Charlie isn't happy with the answer. She's not happy with a lot of things I do and say these days. If I ask a question, I'm interrogating her. If I make an observation, I'm being judgmental. My comments are criticisms and our conversations are "arguments."

This is supposed to be my territory—human behavior—but I seem to have a blind spot when it comes to understanding my eldest daughter, who doesn't necessarily say what she means. For instance, when Charlie says I shouldn't bother coming to something, really she wants me to be there. And when she says, "Are you coming?" it means "Be there, or else!"

I take her bag. "The musical is great. You were brilliant."

"Did you sneak inside?"

"Just for the second half."

"Now you won't come to the opening night. You'll know the ending."

"It's a musical—everyone knows the ending."

Charlie pouts and looks over her shoulder, her ponytail swinging dismissively.

"Can we give Sienna a lift home?" she asks.

"Sure. Where is she?"

"Mr. Ellis wanted to see her."

"Is she in trouble?"

Charlie rolls her eyes. "She's *always* in trouble."

Across the grounds, down the gentle slope, I can see headlights nudging from the parking area.

Sienna emerges from the hall. Slender and pale, almost whiter than white, she's wearing her school uniform with her hair pulled back in a ponytail. She hasn't bothered removing her stage makeup and her eyes look impossibly large.

"How are you, Sienna?"

"I'm fine, Mr. O. Did you bring your dog?"

"No."

"How is he?"

"Still dumb."

"I thought Labradors were supposed to be intelligent."

"Not my one."

"Maybe he's intelligent but not obedient."

"Maybe."

Sienna surveys the car park, as though looking for someone. She seems preoccupied or perhaps she's upset about the rehearsal. Then she remembers and turns to me.

"Did that hearing happen today?"

"Yes."

"Are they going to let him out?"

"Not yet."

Satisfied, she turns and walks ahead of me, bumping shoulders with Charlie, speaking in a strange language that I'm not supposed to understand.

Although slightly taller, Charlie seems younger or less worldly than Sienna, who loves to make big entrances and create big reactions, shocking people and then reacting with coyness as if to say, "Who, me?"

Charlie is a different creature around her—more talkative, animated, happy—but there are times when I wish she'd chosen a different best friend. Twelve months ago they were picked up for shoplifting at an off-license in Bath. They stole cans of cider and a six-pack of Breezers. Charlie was supposed to be sleeping over at Sienna's house that night but they were going to sneak out to a party. They were thirteen. I wanted to ground Charlie until she was twenty-one, but her remorse seemed genuine.

The girls have reached my third-hand Volvo estate, which reeks of wet dog and has a rear window that won't close completely. The floor is littered with coloring books, plastic bracelets, doll's clothes and empty crisp packets.

Sienna claims the front passenger seat.

"Sit with me in the back," begs Charlie.

"Next time, loser."

Charlie looks at me as though I'm to blame.

"Maybe both of you should sit in the back," I say.

Sienna wrinkles her nose at me and shrugs dismissively but does as I ask. I can hear a mobile ringing. It's coming from her schoolbag. She answers, frowns, whispers. The metallic-sounding voice leaks into the stillness.

"You said ten minutes. No . . . OK . . . fifteen . . ."

She ends the call.

"I don't need a lift anymore. My boyfriend is picking me up."

"Your boyfriend?"

"You can drop me at Fullerton Road shops."

"I think you should ask your mother first."

Sienna rolls her eyes and punches in a new number on her phone. I can only hear one side of the conversation.

"Hi, Mum, I'm going to see Danny . . . OK . . . He'll drop me back. I won't be late. I will . . . yes . . . no . . . OK . . . see you in the morning."

Sienna flips the mobile shut and begins rooting in her bag, pulling out her flapper dress, which is short, beaded and sparkling.

"Eyes on the road, Mr. O, I'm getting changed."

I tilt the rearview mirror so I can't see behind me as I pull out of the parking area. Clothes are discarded, hips lifted and tights rolled down. By the time I reach the shops, Sienna is dressed and retouching her makeup.

"How do I look?" she asks Charlie.

"Great."

"Where is he taking you?" I ask.

"We're going to hang."

"What does that mean?"

"Hang, you know. Chill."

Sienna leans between the seats and adjusts the mirror, checking her mascara. As she pushes the mirror back in place her eyes meet mine. Did I have a girlfriend at fourteen? I can't remember. I probably wanted one.

We've reached Fullerton Road. I pull up behind a battered Peugeot with two different paint-jobs and an engine that rumbles through a broken muffler. Three young men are inside. One of them emerges. Sienna is out the door, skipping into his arms. Kisses his lips. Her low-waisted dress is fringed with tassels that sway back and forth with the swing of her hips.

It looks wrong. It feels wrong.

As the car pulls away and does a U-turn, Sienna waves. I don't respond. I'm looking in the rearview mirror unsuccessfully trying to read the number plate.

Julianne answers the door dressed in jeans and a checked shirt. Her dark hair is cut short in a new style, which makes her look younger. Sweet. Sexy. Her loose shirt shows hollows above her collarbones and the outline of her bra beneath.

She kisses Charlie's cheek. It's practiced. Intimate. They are almost the same height. Another two inches and they'll see eye to eye.

"What took you so long?"

"We stopped for pizza," answers Charlie.

"But I've kept your dinner!"

Julianne looks at me accusingly. It's my fault.

"I'm sorry. I forgot."

"You always forget."

Charlie steps between us. "Please don't fight."

Julianne stops herself. Softens her voice.

"Upstairs. Have a shower. Don't wake Emma. I just got her to bed."

Emma is our youngest and has started school in the village, looking tiny in her blue tunic and gray socks. Every time I see her walking out the school gate with her friends, I think of Gulliver and the Lilliputians.

Charlie dumps her schoolbag into her mother's arms and makes the stairs seem steep as she goes up to her room. Julianne unzips the schoolbag looking for school notes or reminders. She's wearing the silver earrings I bought her in Marrakesh.

"I like your hair," I say.

"Charlie says I look like a lesbian."

"That's not true."

She smiles and arranges the coats on the coatrack in the passage.

This is what our conversations are like since we separated. Brief. Polite. No deeper than a puddle. We were married for twenty years. We've been separated for two. Not divorced. Julianne hasn't asked me. That's a good thing.

We no longer shop together, go to movies, pay bills, buy cars, book holidays or attend dinner parties as a couple, but we still talk and do parent-teacher nights and family birthday parties. We talked today. I made her laugh, which is always my fallback when I've got nothing else. Humor and antidepressants are my antidotes to Mr. Parkinson, who was the third person in our marriage, the other man, who stayed with me after the separation and now is like an unwelcome relative hanging around for the reading of the will.

"How's the trial going?" I ask.

"They haven't needed me yet. They're still choosing a jury."

Nine months ago, Julianne quit her high-flying corporate job in London, to be closer to the girls. Now she's working as an interpreter for the police and the courts, occasionally getting late-night calls because victims, suspects or witnesses have to be interviewed.

They've asked her to interpret at a murder trial in Bristol. Three men are accused of firebombing a boarding house, killing a family of asylum seekers. The newspapers have labeled it a "race-hate trial" and politicians are calling for calm.

Julianne has finished tidying the hallway. I linger, rocking on my heels, hoping she might invite me to stay for a cup of tea and a chat. Occasionally, she does and we spend an hour talking about the girls, planning their weekends and itineraries. It's not going to happen tonight.

"I guess I'd better go."

"Are you going to sit outside again?" She doesn't make it sound like an accusation. "I saw you last night."

"I went for a walk."

"You were sitting out there for two hours, on the wall, beneath the tree."

"It was a nice evening."

She gazes at me curiously. "You don't have to guard us, Joe."

"I know. It was an odd day yesterday."

"Why?"

"I missed the girls."

"You're seeing them most days."

"I know, but I still missed them."

She gives me a melancholy smile and holds the door. I lean close and she lets me kiss her. I hold my cheek against hers.

Stepping outside, I walk down the path and turn. Julianne is standing motionless in the doorway, the light framing her body and creating a halo around her head that disappears as the door closes.

2

Home now is a small two-story terrace in Station Road, less than half a mile from my old life. Trains stopped running through Wellow in 1956 but there's still an old station building at the end of the street, which someone has converted into a long narrow house with a covered verandah where the platform used to be.

The tracks were ripped up long ago but it's possible to trace the route of the railway line to a redbrick viaduct with a grand arch, which is the signature photograph of the village.

My terrace is darker than a cave because the windows are so small and the rooms are full of faded oriental rugs, wobbly side tables and old-lady furniture. Charlie and Emma have to share a bedroom when they sleep over, but Emma often crawls into my bed with me, forcing me downstairs onto the sofa because her core body temperature is akin to nuclear fusion. I don't mind the sofa. I can watch late-night movies or obscure sports that don't seem to have any rules.

There are three messages on my answering machine. Message one is from Bruno Kaufman, my boss at the university.

Joseph, old boy, just reminding you about the staff meeting Thursday. Peter Tooley wants to cut the post-grad program. We have to fight this. Call me.

Clunk!

Message two. Charlie:

Are you picking me up? Remember we have rehearsal. Hey, I got a joke. There's this tray of muffins being baked in the oven and one muffin says to another, "Man, it's getting hot in here." And the other muffin says, "Holy shit! A talking muffin."

She laughs like a drain.

Clunk!

Message three is from my mother, reminding me about my father's birthday next week.

Please don't send him any more Scotch. I'm trying to get him to cut down. Oh, I almost forgot, you'll never guess who I saw in Cardiff last week. Cassie Pritchard. You remember Cassie. We

took that holiday with the Pritchards to the Lake District when you were fourteen? You and Cassie got on so well together . . .

(If memory serves, Cassie Pritchard pushed me out of a rowing boat and I almost died of pneumonia.)

. . . the poor thing has broken up with her husband in a messy divorce. Now she's on her own. I have her phone number. You should give her a call. Cheer her up. Hope the girls are well. Send them my love.

Clunk!

I hold down the erase button. Wait for the beep. The counter resets to zero.

I look at my watch. It's not quite ten. There's still time for an evening stroll to the Fox and Badger, the village pub. Collecting my coat, I step out the door and turn along the High Street.

A few minutes later I pull open the heavy door. Smell the beer fumes. The pub is noisy and energetic, full of lumpy bodies and flushed faces. Locals. Regulars. Most of them I recognize, even if I don't know their names.

There is a fireplace that must be ten

foot wide and four feet high with a box-shaped wood stove and newly chopped faggots stacked alongside. Side by side above the hearth, a fox and a badger (just their heads) peer forlornly at proceedings.

A smaller fireplace in the lounge bar has a brace of pheasants above the hearth and a sticker that reads: "If it's called the tourist season, why can't we shoot them?"

Half a dozen youngsters have taken over a corner of the lounge beneath a string of fairy lights and the pheasants. Some of the girls look underage in tight jeans and short tops. Bratz dolls grown up.

The publican, Hector, raises his eyes and pours me a Scotch. One drink won't hurt. I'll start my new regime tomorrow. Show Mr. Parkinson who's the better man.

Hector is the unofficial convener of the local divorced men's club, which meets once a month at the pub. I'm not a natural joiner and, since I'm technically not divorced, I've avoided most of the meetings but I do play in the pub's over-35s' football team. There are fifteen of us—a number that allows for frequent substitutions and prevents avoidable heart attacks. I play defense. Right back. Leaving the faster men to play up front. I like to imagine myself more in the classic European-style sweeper role, threading precision long balls that split the defense.

We have nicknames. I am known as "Shrink" for obvious reasons. "Hands" is our goalkeeper—a retired pilot who had a brain tumor—and our star striker, Jimmy Monroe, is called "Marilyn" (but not to his face). They're a reasonable bunch of lads. None of them asks about my condition, which is pretty obvious from some of my miskicks. After the game, we nurse our bruises at the Fox and Badger, sharing non-confessional personal stories. We don't confide. We never disclose an intimacy. We are men.

I finish my drink and have another, nursing it slowly. At eleven o'clock Hector signals last orders. My mobile is vibrating. It's Julianne. I wonder what she's doing up so late.

I press the green button and try to say something clever. She cuts me off.

"Come quickly! It's Sienna. Something's wrong! She's covered in blood!"

"Blood?"

"I couldn't make her stay. We have to find her."

"Where did she go?"

"She just ran away."

"Call 999. I'm coming."

I grab my coat from a wooden hook and pull open the door, breaking into a trot as I thread my arms through the sleeves. The pavement slabs are cracked and uneven under my feet. Turning down Mill Hill, I pick up speed, letting gravity carry me towards the cottage in jarring strides.

Julianne is waiting outside, a torch swinging frenetically in her hand.

"Where did she go?"

She points towards the river, her voice cracking. "She rang the doorbell. I screamed when I saw her. I must have scared her."

"Did she say anything?"

She shakes her head.

The door is open. I can see Charlie sitting on the stairs clutching her pillow. We gaze at each other and something passes between us. A promise. I'll find her.

I turn to leave.

"I want to come," says Julianne.

"Wait for the ambulance. Send Charlie back to bed."

I take the torch from her cold fingers and turn at the gate. The river is hidden in the trees, eighty yards away. Swinging the torch from side to side, I peer over the hedges and into the neighboring field.

Reaching the small stone footbridge and a wider concrete causeway, I shout Sienna's name. The road—unmade, single lane, with hedgerows on either side—leads out of the village.

Why would she run? Why head this way?

I keep thinking of when I dropped her off. The boyfriend. She skipped into his arms. Maybe there was a car crash. He could be injured too.

The beam of the torch reflects off the evening dew and creates long shadows through the trees. I stop on the bridge. Listen. Water over rocks; a dog barking; others follow.

"Sieeeeenna!"

The sound bounces off the arch of the footbridge and seems to echo along the banks of the narrow stream. They call it a river, but in places you can jump from one side to the other. Emma catches minnows here and Gunsmoke cools off after chasing rabbits.

I call Sienna's name again, feeling an awful sense of déjà vu. Two years ago I searched this same road, looking for Charlie, calling her name, peering over farm gates and fences. She was knocked from her pushbike and kidnapped by a man who chained her to a sink and wrapped masking around her head, allowing her to breathe through a rubber hose. The man was caught and locked away, but how does a twelve-year-old recover from something like that? How does she set foot outside her house, or look a stranger in the eyes, or trust anyone again?

I have never forgotten the sense of panic that tore through my soft organs like a spinning blade when I knew Charlie was missing, when I searched and couldn't find her.

A scurrying sound to my left. Footsteps on dead leaves. I swing the torch back and forth. Soft crying. I listen for the sound again. Nothing.

My left arm is trembling. Swapping hands, I move the beam of light slowly along the banks, trying to find the source of the sound, wishing it into being, solid and visible. It came from somewhere on the far bank, in the trees.

Scrambling down the side of the bridge, I slide into the water. Sinking. Mud and sediment suck at my shoes. I reach down and almost overbalance, catching the torch before it topples into the river.

Wading to the far bank, I discover brambles growing to the water's edge. Thorns catch on my clothes and skin. Head first. Crawling forward. I can't hear crying anymore.

Game birds flushed from the undergrowth explode into the clearing making my heart pound against the walls of my chest. Unhooking the last of the vines from my clothes, I stand and listen.

The weak moonlight is deceptive. The trees become people. Branches become limbs. An army marching through the darkness.

I can't find her—not in the dark. I should be fitter. I should be sober. I should have better eyesight. I should take my time or I'll walk straight past her.

The torch swings in another arc and picks up a flash of white before continuing.

Go back!

Where?

There she is! Huddled between the roots of a tree like a discarded doll. Still in her black dress. Water lapping at her bare legs. She's on the far bank. I chose the wrong side. I'm in the river now, falling rather than jumping, wading towards her, my scrotum retracting in the cold.

"It's only me, Sienna," I whisper. "It's OK, sweetheart. Everything's going to be fine."

My fingers frozen and numb, I feel for a pulse on her neck. Her eyes are open. Flat. Cold.

I put her arm over my shoulder and slide one hand beneath her thighs and another behind her back.

"I'm just going to pick you up now."

She doesn't respond. Doesn't resist. She weighs nothing, but I'm unsteady. Carrying her back along the bank, I walk blindly because I can't point the torch properly. All the while, I'm talking to Sienna, whispering between heavy breaths, telling her not to worry.

My ankle snags on a root, sending me sideways. At the last moment I take the impact on my shoulder, protecting Sienna's head.

A sudden surge of panic rips the calmness. She hasn't said a word. Hasn't moved. She might be dead. She might never be able to tell me who did this to her.

The bridge. The arch. I have to free my arm and use a sapling to pull both of us up the bank to the edge of the road. Sienna hangs limply from my other arm, a dead weight, being pulled across the ground.

"Stay with me, sweetheart. We're almost there."

One last effort, I drag her to the edge of the bridge and lever myself over the wall, holding her body to stop her tumbling back down the slope. There are torches dancing between the trees, coming towards us. Blue flashing lights decorate the sky above them.

I put Sienna down gently, cradling her head against my chest. Breathing hard.

"I told you we'd make it."

She doesn't answer. She doesn't blink. Her skin is cold, but I can feel a pulse beneath my fingers.

"There they are!" someone yells.

A powerful light illuminates every detail of the scene. I hold up my hand to shield my eyes.

"She needs a doctor."

I glance down at Sienna and notice the blood. I thought it was mud on her thighs and hands, but she's bleeding. Her eyes are open, staring blindly past me.

A paramedic crouches beside me on the bridge, taking Sienna and laying her on the tarmac with a coat beneath her head. He yells instructions to his partner. Pulse. Blood pressure. Good signs.

Another set of hands helps me to stand, holding me up, making sure I don't fall. One of them is asking me questions.

Did I find her in the water? Was she conscious? Did she fall? Is she allergic to any drugs?

I don't know.

"She's my daughter's best friend," I say through chattering teeth.

What a stupid statement! What difference does that make?

Julianne's face appears in front of me. "He's shivering. Get him a blanket."

Her arms wrap around me and I feel her warmth. She will not fail. She will not let me go.

The ambulance reverses down the hill. The back doors open. A litter slides from within. Sienna is rolled onto a spinal board and lifted on the count of three.

"We have to take you to the hospital, sir," says a paramedic.

"My name is Joe."

"We have to take you to the hospital, Joe."

"I'm all right—just out of breath."

"It's a precaution. Do you know this girl?"

"Her name is Sienna."

"You can ride with Sienna. Try to keep her calm."

Calm? She's catatonic. She's a statue.

Wrapped in a silver trauma blanket, I'm half pushed and half lifted into the ambulance. Julianne wants to come with me, but she has Charlie and Emma to think about.

The right door closes.

"Call me," she says.

The left door locks shut. A hand hammers a signal and we're moving.

"Did she take anything?" asks the paramedic.

"I don't know."

"Did she say anything?"

"No."

He shines a pencil-torch in her eyes and slips an oxygen mask over her face.

The siren wails, chasing us through the darkness. Sienna is lying completely still, her limbs muddy and pale, her stomach rising and falling with each breath.

I keep seeing her in the beam of the torch—a spectral figure with her brown hair hanging in a fringe across her face. She was looking at me as though she'd seen something terrible or done something worse.

3

It has just gone midnight and the sky is a black sponge. Police vans are parked outside the Royal United Hospital and four paramedics are kicking a coffee cup around the ambulance bay, scoring goals between the bins.

My feet move unsteadily, as though unsure of the depth of the ground. Ushered through swinging doors, I follow a young triage nurse to a consulting room. She takes my wet clothes and hands me a hospital gown and a thin blue blanket.

Then I'm left alone in the small room with a bench and an examination table covered in a sheet of paper. There are no magazines to read. No televisions to watch. I find myself reading the labels on syringes and medical swabs, making words from the letters.

Forty minutes later a doctor appears. Obese and prematurely bald, he's the sort of physician who finds the gulf between preaching and practicing healthy living one dessert too far. He examines me in a perfunctory way—blood pressure, temperature, "say aaaaah" . . .

Most of his questions are about Sienna. Did she take anything, did she say anything; does she have any allergies or sensitivities to medications?

"She's not my daughter," I keep repeating.

He makes a note on his clipboard.

"She was bleeding."

"The blood wasn't hers," he says matter-of-factly. "The police want to talk to you. They're waiting outside."

The policeman is a sergeant whose name is Toltz and he writes left-handed with a cupped wrist so he doesn't smudge his notebook.

"What was she doing at your house?"

"It's not really my house. My wife and I

are separated. Sienna turned up and then ran away."

"Why?"

"There must have been an accident. Perhaps her boyfriend drove off the road. He could be hurt."

"Why your house?"

"She's my daughter's friend. Her mother works nights. Sienna often stays with us."

The sergeant doesn't react to my sense of urgency. He wants to know where Sienna goes to school, how she knows Charlie, does she do drugs or drink alcohol?

I think about the shoplifting charge, but he's already moved onto a new question.

"Did you follow her into the woods?"

"I went looking for her."

"Did you chase her?"

"No."

Suddenly the door opens and another officer motions him into the corridor. They're whispering and I pick up only occasional words like "body" and "detectives." Something terrible has happened.

The sergeant reappears and apologizes. A detective will be along shortly to interview me.

"Can I go home?"

"Not yet, sir."

"What about my clothes?"

"They've been taken for analysis."

"Why?"

"This is a murder investigation."

Who? Her boyfriend? Someone else? The sergeant ignores my questions and tells me to wait for the detectives. His heavy boots squeak on the polished floor as he disappears down the hallway, through a set of swinging doors that flap back and forth before settling to a stop.

I look at my watch. It's after one a.m. I should call Julianne. Tell her not to worry. Reaching for my phone, I can't find a pocket. I'm wearing a hospital gown. My phone, wallet and car keys were in my jacket. Wet. Ruined.

I passed a pay phone in the accident and emergency department. I can ask Julianne to bring me some clothes.

Pushing open the door, I try to remember which way I came in. A cleaner is mopping the corridor, pushing a bucket with his foot. I don't want to step on his wet floor so I turn right, passing the X-ray department and radiology.

I must be going the wrong way. I should

go back. Ahead I see a police officer sitting on a chair in the corridor. He's young—no more than a probationary constable—with blond highlights in his hair.

"I'm looking for a pay phone."

He points back the way I came.

Glancing through an open door, I spy the same doctor that examined me earlier. He's standing beside a bed, illuminated by a low light. Sienna looks tiny in the midst of the technology around her, like a modern-day sleeping beauty under a spell. A tube taped to her right arm snakes across the sheets and rises to a bag of fluid hanging from a chrome stand.

"Can I talk to the doctor?"

"Who are you?" asks the constable.

"I brought her in."

The obese doctor hears my voice and motions me to enter.

"How is she?"

"Sedated."

The tiredness in his voice seems to drain energy from the air. A monitor beeps softly. He checks the display.

"She's dehydrated and has some bruising on her legs and back but nothing explains the semi-catatonic state. There's no sign of head injuries or internal bleeding. We're doing a toxicological screen."

Sienna's nostrils barely move as she breathes and I notice the faint tracings of blood vessels on her eyelids, which seem to flicker as she dreams. It is the face of a child on the body of a woman.

Her lips are cracked and there are scratches on her cheek. Her hospital gown has fallen open along her thigh to her hip. I want to pull it down to protect her modesty.

Gazing at her arms, I notice a network of fine white scars that run along the inside of her forearms. She's a cutter. Self-harm. Self-abuse. There is more to Sienna than meets the eye; layers that are hidden from the world. Perhaps that's why she scratches at her surface, trying to find what lies beneath.

How much do I really know about her? She's fourteen, pretty, with brown eyes and pale skin. She likes diet Coca-Cola, jelly cubes, scrambled eggs, Radiohead, Russell Brand, scary movies and has seen *Twilight* eighteen times. She's allergic to peanuts and Simon Cowell and eats crumpets by licking the bottom where the honey leaks through.

She obsesses over boy bands, *X Factor* contestants and Robert Pattinson, who she wants to marry, but only after she's traveled the world and become a famous actress.

A year ago she came to the terrace carrying a cardboard box. Her cat had caught a bird in the garden, which was still alive but could no longer fly. The tiny robin lay huddled in a corner of the box, its heart beating crazily.

"Can't you do something?" she asked.

"It's too late," I told her.

Sienna rested the box on her lap and ran her finger through the soft feathers on the robin's neck until it died. I had to unhook her fingers from the box and carry it away. By the time I came back into the house Sienna had gone. She never mentioned it again. Not a word.

I know these things because she spent so much time at our place. Sometimes it was like having a third daughter at the dinner table (and again at breakfast) because her mother worked nights and her father traveled on business and her older siblings had left home.

These are superficial details, which tell me nothing about the *real* person. Occasionally I have watched Sienna and thought I could recognize some secret sadness hidden from the world. It was as if she wore a mask to protect herself—the hardest kind of mask to notice because she had woven it from the most secret parts of herself.

When confronted with danger, people will normally fight or flee, but there is another less obvious reaction, which can be just as automatic. They freeze or close down, thinking and moving in slow motion. They shudder, they shake, they gasp, they gulp, but they cannot run or fight or scream. Something happened to Sienna—a violent event that has traumatized her.

The fat doctor turns from the drip stand. He has a name tag. Dr. Martinez.

"She's not going to wake up for another six hours."

"What about her parents?"

"Her mother is coming."

"Shouldn't you do a rape test?"

"I need her permission."

"You could test her clothes."

He glances at the constable in the corridor. "Maybe you shouldn't be here."

Sienna's eyes flutter momentarily and open. She stares at me without any sign of recognition.

"Hello," I say, trying to sound reassuring.

Her eyes close again.

4

A detective interviews me at four o'clock, wanting the facts, telling me nothing. He is not a familiar or reassuring face. He has a strange top lip that curls upwards when he speaks and gives the impression that he doesn't believe a word I'm saying.

Finally, I'm given permission to go home. I call Julianne and ask her to bring me some clothes and a pair of shoes.

"What happened to yours?"

"The police took them."

She doesn't want to leave the girls alone. Charlie didn't fall asleep until two and then only in Julianne's bed, curled up in a ball.

"What if there's someone running around the village stabbing people?" asks Julianne.

"It wasn't Sienna's blood."

"What happened to her then?"

I can't explain.

She hesitates, weighing up what to do.

"I'll get Mrs. Nutall to mind the girls. Give me half an hour."

Mrs. Nutall is our next-door neighbor. She's not technically *my* neighbor anymore, of course, which means I don't have to put up with her abusing me every time I leave the cottage. In her sixties and unmarried, she seems to blame me personally for every sin, snub or rebuff she has experienced at the hands of a man. The list must be very long.

I go to the bathroom. Wash my face. Feel a disturbing weight on my shoulders. Why hasn't Sienna's mother turned up? Surely the police have found her by now.

I hardly know Helen. We have spoken once or twice to arrange sleepovers for the girls and nodded to each other at the petrol station or in the aisle of the supermarket. Normally, she's dressed in cargo pants and old sweaters and seems in a hurry. I've met her husband, Ray Hegarty, a few times in the Fox and Badger. He is an ex-copper, a detective who earned a medal for bravery, according to Hector. Now he runs a security company and travels a lot.

Zoe was attacked six months before we arrived in the village and Liam Baker had already been convicted of GBH when I was asked to do a pre-sentence report. Some people in the village were angry that he didn't go straight to prison, but most were just happy to be rid of him.

Thirty minutes later, Julianne arrives and waits for me to change.

"I tried to call Helen," she says, adjusting my collar and doing up the buttons I've missed. "Nobody is answering."

"She's probably at work."

My left arm and leg are twitching involuntarily.

"What about your medication?"

"At home."

She holds my hand, making it go still. "Let's get out of here."

In the car, watching the sunrise. Hills lost in the morning mist. The drive from Bath to Wellow takes only fifteen minutes. We have lived in the village for three and a bit years, having moved out of London at Julianne's suggestion. Cheaper houses. Good schools. More room. It made sense. It makes less sense now that we're not together.

The locals are friendly enough. We chat over the tops of cars at the petrol station and queue for milk and bread at Eric Vaile's shop. They're decent, conservative, obliging people, but I'll never be one of them. Being single doesn't help. Marriage is a passport to respectability in a small village. My visa has been revoked.

The sun is fully up. The cottages and terraces of Wellow seem whitewashed and scrubbed clean. It reminds me of where I grew up—a pit village in the foothills of Snowdonia—although it wasn't so much whitewashed as coated in coal dust and full of mining families with lung diseases.

"Can we drive past the Hegartys' place?"

Julianne glances at me, hesitantly, her sharp fringe touching one eyebrow.

"It won't take a minute."

She turns the corner and heads down Bull's Hill. Ahead of us there are police cars, five of them. Two of them unmarked but sprouting radio aerials. They are parked outside Sienna's house, almost blocking the road. In the midst of them I notice a familiar rust-streaked Land Rover. It belongs to Detective Chief Inspector Veronica Cray, head of the Major Crime Investigation Unit. MCIU.

They must have called her at home. Woken her. There are some supermodels who won't get out of bed for less than ten thousand pounds. DCI Cray doesn't stir unless someone is dead, defiled or missing.

Julianne's knuckles are white on the steering wheel.

"Can we stop?" I ask.

"No."

"I want to know what happened."

She shakes her head.

At that moment Ronnie Cray emerges from the house and lights a cigarette. Through exhaled smoke her eyes meet mine. Diffident. Unsurprised.

We're past the house now. Julianne drives on.

"You should have stopped."

"Don't get involved, Joe."

"But this is Sienna's family."

"And the police will handle things."

There is an edge to her voice. A warning.

We've been down this road before. We've had this argument. I lost.

Three minutes later we pull up outside the terrace. The engine idles and she takes a deep breath.

"I'm going to let Charlie stay home from school today."

"That's a good idea."

Softening, she tells me to get some sleep and to call her later.

"I will."

Even before I pull out my keys I hear Gunsmoke whining and pawing at the back door. Walking along the passage to the kitchen, I unlock the side door and step into the garden, where the Labrador leaps and cavorts around my thighs, licking at my hands.

"I'm sorry I didn't come home," I say, rubbing his ears.

He frowns at me. I swear. Then he dashes to the rear gate. The rabbits are waiting. Don't I want to chase them? Hurry up.

First I need to shower and take my pills—the white one and the blue one. When the twitches are gone, I can hold my hand steady on the razor and lace up my boots. Buttons will find buttonholes and zippers will close easily. The body tremors are under control, although occasionally my left arm will launch itself upwards in my own Mexican wave.

In the six years since I was diagnosed, I have come to an understanding with Mr. Parkinson. I no longer deny his existence or imagine that I'm the stronger man. Recognizing this truth was a humbling experience—like bowing to a higher power.

My condition is not advanced yet, but every day is a balancing act with my medication, requiring meticulous timing. Too much Levadopa and I'm rocking, dipping and diving, incapable of crossing a room without visiting every corner. Too little and I grind to a stuttering halt like an engine without oil.

Exercise is recommended, which is why I walk every morning. Shuffle rather than stride. Not in all weathers. I avoid the rain. Dragging a sweater over my head, I step outside and pull the door shut. A tractor rumbles up Mill Hill Lane pulling a box trailer. The driver is Alasdair Riordan, a local farmer. His forearms are vibrating on the wheel.

"Did you hear the news?"

"What's that?"

"Ray Hegarty is dead. They say his wee girl stabbed him. Fancy that, eh?"

Breath glides out of him in a pale cloud. He shakes his head and releases his foot from the clutch, jerking into motion. This passes as the longest conversation I've ever had with Alasdair Riordan—a man of few words and fewer thoughts.

Gunsmoke has already disappeared down the hill, doing forward reconnaissance through the undergrowth, sniffing at trees and holes in the ground. When I reach the bridge I see the police tape laced around tree trunks and snaking along the banks of the river. I remember finding Sienna and carrying her this far. It seems like weeks ago. It was less than twelve hours.

In a field on the far side, Gunsmoke lopes after a skittering rabbit that is far too nimble, jinking left and right before disappearing down a hole. He did once catch a rabbit, which seemed to surprise him so much that he let it go again. Maybe he's opposed to blood sports, which would make him a curiosity in these parts.

Occasionally, he comes back to me, loping down the hill, pink tongue flapping, awaiting instructions. He gazes up at me as though I am the wisest of the wise. If only my children were so in awe of my intelligence. Reassured, he takes off again, sniffing at every cowpat and clump of grass.

Gunsmoke has made the past couple of years easier. He doesn't judge me like I judge myself. He gets me out of bed. Makes me exercise. Eats my leftovers. Babysits Emma and initiates conversations with people.

I walk for a mile across the fields, following the old railway line, before turning and retracing boot prints on the dew-covered grass. I keep thinking about Ray Hegarty, a man I barely knew.

I once saw him drawn into a fight at the Fox and Badger. Six bikers came into the bar one Friday evening just after the rugby club raffle had been drawn. Ray had won the meat tray and was sitting with his prize. The lead biker stood over his table and asked him to move.

"Plenty of spare seats," Ray replied.

The biker sized him up and liked what he saw. He was mistaken.

Leaning over the table, he casually spat

in Ray's pint of cider. Before he had time to straighten, one of Ray's hands had shot out and gripped him by the neck as the other smashed the pint glass and pressed the jagged base into his throat.

Calmly, Ray whispered in his ear, "There are six of you and one of me. Looking at those odds, I'm going to die, but here's the thing . . . you'll be dying first."

A thin trickle of blood ran down the biker's neck, over his Adam's apple, which was rising and falling as he swallowed. Another liquid trickled over his boots and onto the worn floorboards.

The scene stayed that way for maybe twenty minutes until the police arrived from Radstock. It made Ray a legend. Hector bolted a special plaque at the corner of the bar, which said, "Reserved for Ray" and guaranteed him at least one free pint every time he dropped by.

The strange thing is, when I recalled the altercation afterwards, picturing Ray Hegarty's calm hostility, I found myself feeling sorry for the bikers. It was as if the odds were always stacked against them.

Turning the corner into Station Road, I spy the battered Land Rover parked out front of the terrace. Ronnie Cray is sitting behind the wheel with her eyes closed, resting her head against the doorframe.

"Morning?"

Her eyes half open. "You shouldn't leave your door key under a rock. Second place I looked. Had to use the little girl's room. Hope you don't mind."

"You could have stayed inside."

"I don't mind the cold."

Climbing out, she shakes my hand. Holds it. Looks into my eyes. "You didn't stop earlier."

"I saw you were busy."

Her hands go to the pockets of her overcoat. She's short and round with a wardrobe of tailored trousers and men's shoes. Dark shadows beneath her eyes betray her tiredness, but there's something more.

"I've come to check on the cat," she says.

"Yeah. Sure."

Eighteen months ago the DCI dropped by unexpectedly and presented me with a box. Inside was a straw-colored kitten, part of a litter that had been born in her barn a few weeks earlier.

"I have a dog," I said.

"You need a cat."

"Why?"

"You own a dog but you need something to *own you.* That's what cats do. She'll boss you around. Run the place."

The detective put the box on the floor. It contained six cans of cat food, a bag of cat litter and two plastic dishes. Reaching inside, she pulled out the kitten, which hung over her palm like a sock.

"Isn't she a beauty? She'll keep you company."

"I don't need company."

"Hell you don't. You sleep alone. You work part-time. You're home a lot. I got all the stuff you need. She's vaccinated but you might want to get her neutered in about four months."

She thrust the kitten at me and it clung to my sweater as if I were a tree. I couldn't think of what to say except, "It's very thoughtful of you, Ronnie."

"If she's anything like her mother, she'll be a good ratter."

"I don't have any rats."

"And you won't."

"What's her name?"

"Call her what you like."

Emma named her Strawberry—"because she's colored like straw"—don't ask me to explain the logic of a preschooler.

When Charlie was kidnapped, Ronnie Cray was in charge of the police investigation. I think she blamed herself for not protecting my family. Some tragedies forge friendships. Others are touchstones for too many bad memories. I don't know what I have with Ronnie. Maybe it's a friendship. Maybe we're sharing the guilt.

Whatever the case, the detective has stayed in touch, calling me every so often to ask about the cat. Occasionally, she talks about cases that she's working on, dropping in details she thinks might intrigue me. I don't take the bait.

One night she phoned from the scene of a hostage crisis where a man had barricaded himself in a house with his ex-wife who he'd doused with petrol. Ronnie asked for my help. I said no.

Afterwards I sat up late watching Sky News, listening to the reports on failing banks, repossessions and market meltdowns, hoping the stories would stay the same. I also prayed, which is bizarre because I don't believe in God. I'm not superstitious either, yet I crossed my fingers. I *willed* things not to occur, even though that's impossible.

I sat up all night watching the news, certain that if I maintained my vigil nothing bad would happen. I didn't go to bed until the sun had come up and the beautiful TV couples were smiling brightly from their morning sofas. I had saved another life.

Cray has stepped past me into the hallway without waiting for an invitation. She shrugs off her coat and tosses it over the back of a chair. I always forget how short she is until we're standing side by side. I'm looking at the crown of her head. Her bristled hair is pepper gray.

"I saw you on TV the other week," I say. "You've been promoted."

"Yeah, I'm sleeping my way to the top." Her laugh sounds like gravel rash. "How's the shaking business?"

"Up and down."

"Is that a Parkinson's joke?"

"Sorry."

She's about to light another cigarette.

"I don't let people smoke in the house."

The lighter sparks in her cupped hands.

"I appreciate you making an exception." She inclines her head as she exhales. The smoke floats past her eyes. I can't hold her gaze.

As if on cue, Strawberry appears, walking silently into the kitchen and sniffing at Cray's shoes. Perhaps she can smell her mother. The DCI leans down and scoops up the cat with one hand, studying her eyes for answers.

"She's getting fat."

"She's part sloth."

"You're feeding her too much."

Cray drops Strawberry and watches her twist in the air, landing on her feet. The cat walks to her food bowl, looks unimpressed, and saunters off to find a suntrap.

The DCI takes a seat, ashes her cigarette in a saucer. "You don't seem very happy to see me, Professor."

"I know why you're here."

"I need your help."

"No you don't."

The statement comes out too harshly, but Cray doesn't react.

One part of me desperately wants to know what happened to Ray Hegarty, why Sienna was covered in blood, why she ran . . . At the same time I feel a swelling in my throat that makes my voice vibrate. I shouldn't want to do this again. The last time it cost me almost everything.

"You know this girl."

"She's a friend of Charlie's."

"Did she say anything to you?"

"No. She was too traumatized."

"See? You know all about this stuff."

"I can't help you."

Cray glances out the window where a swath of sunshine has cut across the field turning the grass silver.

"The man who died last night was a retired detective by the name of Ray Hegarty. He worked for Bristol CID for twenty years. He was my boss. My friend."

"I'm sorry."

She makes a quick sucking noise and her eyes glaze over. "I thought Hegarty was a prick when I first met him. He didn't want me on his team and he did nothing to stop the bullying and cruel pranks. He gave me every shit job he could find—the dirty bodies, death knocks, cleaning out the drunk tank—I thought he was trying to break me or force me out, but it was just his way of toughening me up for the bigger challenges."

Ophidian eyes blink through the smoke and her thumb passes over her lips. "He taught me everything I know. His rules. I guess I grew to respect his achievements and then to respect the man."

"I'm sure you'll work out what happened."

Anger in her eyes now, "If you're having a midlife crisis, Professor, buy a Porsche and forget about it."

"It's not a midlife crisis."

"Then what's your problem?"

"You know the answer to that."

Cray stands and hitches up her trousers. "In another lifetime I might sympathize with you, but not this one. You don't have a monopoly on fucked-up families. I've got an overweight bad-tempered son who's living with an ex-junkie and claims to be writing a book about how his parents' divorce screwed up his life even though I was pregnant longer than I was married.

"And now a man I respected is lying dead in his daughter's bedroom and the kid is so traumatized she's not saying boo to a goose. So you see, Professor, you won't get any pity from me, but I will give you some advice."

Her cigarette hisses in the sink.

"Suck it in, Princess, and put on your big-girl pants. You're playing with the grown-ups now."

5

Squeezed behind the steering wheel, the DCI sits forward so her feet can reach the pedals. Eyes ahead. Jaw masticating gum. She drives as if she's traveling at speed, even though the Land Rover can't hold fifth.

A cigarette is propped upright in her fist. She blows smoke out of the far corner of her mouth. Speaks, giving me just the facts, the bare bones. Ray Hegarty retired from the force eight years ago and set up a security business—doing alarms, CCTV cameras, patrols and personal protection. He had offices in Bristol, Birmingham and Manchester.

He had a meeting in Glasgow on Monday afternoon and stayed overnight before driving to Manchester the next day. He was supposed to stop overnight and fly to Dublin on Wednesday morning for two days of meetings but the trip was canceled. Instead he drove back to Bristol and had a late lunch with a business partner.

"Bottom line—he wasn't expected home until Friday—not according to his wife."

"Where was Helen?"

"Working at St. Martin's Hospital in Bath. Her shift started at six."

We pull up outside a house on the eastern edge of the village. Six uniforms stand guard, blocking off the street. Blue-and-white crime-scene tape has been threaded between two cherry trees and the front gate, twirling in the breeze like old birthday decorations. A large white SOCO van is parked in the driveway. Doors yawning. Metal boxes stacked inside.

Nearby, a forensic technician is crouching on the front path taking photographs. Dressed in blue plastic overalls, a hood and matching boot covers, he looks like an extra in a science-fiction movie.

Positioning a plastic evidence tag, he

raises the camera to his eye. Shoots. Stands. When he turns I recognize him. Dr. Louis Preston—a Home Office pathologist with a Brummie accent that makes him sound eternally miserable.

"I hear they woke you, Ronnie."

"I'm a light sleeper," she replies.

"Were you with anyone in particular?"

"My hot-water bottle."

"Now there's a waste." The pathologist glances at me and nods. "Professor, long time no see."

"I would have waited."

"I get that a lot."

Preston is famous for terrorizing his pathology students. According to one apocryphal story, he once told a group of trainees that two things were required to conduct an autopsy. The first was no sense of fear. At this point he stuck his finger into a dead man's anus, pulled it out and sniffed it. Then he invited each student to follow his lead and they all complied.

"The second thing you need is an acute sense of observation," he told them. "How many of you noticed that I stuck my middle finger into this man's anus, but sniffed my index finger?"

Urban myth? Compelling hearsay? Both probably. Anybody who slices open dead people for a living has to maintain a sense of humor. Either that or you go mad.

Turning back to the van, he collects a tripod.

"I never thought I'd see Ray Hegarty like this. I thought he was bloody indestructible."

"You were friends?"

Preston shrugs. "Wouldn't go that far. Mutual respect."

"How did he die?"

"Somebody hit him from behind and then severed his carotid artery." The pathologist runs a finger across his throat. "You're looking for something like a razor or a Stanley knife. It's not in the bedroom."

Cray helps him move a silver case. "When can we come inside?"

"Find some overalls. Stay on the duckboards and don't touch anything."

The two-story semi has wisteria twisting and climbing across the front façade. No longer in leaf, the gray trunk looks gnarled and ancient, slowly strangling the building. There are stacks of old roofing tiles beside the garage doors.

Two things stand out about the house. It's the sort of place that should have had a long sweeping drive—all the proportions suggest it. Secondly, it's partially hidden from the road by a high wall covered in ivy. Tall trees are visible beyond the slate roof and chimneys. The curtains downstairs are open. Anyone approaching would have seen the lights on.

"Was the door locked or unlocked?"

"Open," says Cray. "Sienna ran. She didn't bother pulling it closed."

Stepping onto the first of a dozen duck-boards, I follow her through the front door and along a passage.

"Tread lightly, she is near
Under the snow,
Speak gently, she can hear
The daisies grow."

Cray looks at me. "Who wrote that?"

"Oscar Wilde."

"Some of those Micks could write."

Orange fluorescent evidence markers are spaced intermittently on the stairs, distinguishing blood spots. A camera flashes upstairs, sending a pulse of light through the railings.

I turn and study the front door. No burglar alarm. Basic locks. For a security consultant, Ray Hegarty didn't take many personal precautions.

"Who lives next door?"

"An old bloke, a widower."

"Did he hear anything?"

"I don't think he's heard anything since the Coronation."

"Any sign of forced entry?"

"No."

"Who had keys?"

"Just the family members. There's the other daughter, Zoe. She's at university in Leeds. She's driving down now with her boyfriend. And there's Lance, who's twenty-two. He works for a motorcycle mechanic in Bristol. Rents his own place."

The sitting room and dining room are tastefully furnished. Neat. Clean. There are so many things that could be disturbed—plants in pots, photographs in frames, books on shelves, cushions on the sofas—but everything seems in place.

The kitchen is tidy. A single plate rests

in the sink, with a cutting board covered in breadcrumbs. Helen made a sandwich for lunch or a snack to take to work. She left a note on the fridge for Sienna telling her to microwave a lasagna for dinner.

Through the kitchen there is an extension that was probably a sunroom until it was turned into a bedroom. Refitted after Zoe's attack, it has a single bed, a desk, closet and chintz curtains, as well as a ramp leading down to the garden. The en suite bathroom has a large shower and handrails. On the dresser there is a picture of Zoe playing netball, balanced on one leg as she passes the ball.

Walking back along the hallway, I notice the door beneath the stairs is ajar. Easing it open with my shoe, I see an overnight bag on the floor. Ray Hegarty's overcoat hangs on a wooden peg. He came home, hung up his coat and tossed down his bag. Then what?

Something drew him upstairs. A sound. A voice.

Cray goes ahead of me, stepping over evidence markers as she climbs each step without touching the banister. The main bedroom is straight ahead. Two doors on the left lead to a bathroom and second bedroom. Sienna's room is off to the right. Ray Hegarty lies facedown on a rug beside her bed with his arms outstretched, head to one side, eyes open. Blood has soaked through the rug and run along cracks in the floorboards. His business shirt is stained by bloody handprints. Small hands.

Sienna's room is a mess with her clothes spilling from drawers and draped over the end of her bed, which is unmade. Her duvet is bunched against the wall and a hair-straightening iron peeks from beneath her pillow.

I notice a shoebox, which has been customized with photographs clipped from magazines. Someone has pulled it from beneath the bed and opened the lid to reveal a collection of bandages, plasters, needles and thread. It is Sienna's cutting box and also her sewing kit.

The untidiness of the room could be teenage-induced. I have one of those at home—messy, sullen and self-absorbed—but this looks more like a quick ransacking. A search.

"Is anything missing?" I ask.

Cray answers. “Nothing obvious. We won’t know until we interview the family.”

“Where’s Helen?”

“At the hospital with Sienna.”

Crouching beside the body, I notice blood splatters, some large and others barely visible, sprayed as high as the ceiling. A hockey stick lies near his right hand. Lacquered to a shine, it has a toweling grip in school colors.

I squat motionless in the center of the room, trying to get a sense of the events. Ray Hegarty was hit from behind and fell forward. There are no signs of a struggle, no defense wounds or bruises or broken furniture.

Turning my head, I notice an oval-shaped mirror on a stand, which is reflecting a white square of light onto the bed, highlighting the small blue flowers stitched into the sheets.

I look at myself reflected in the mirror and can also see the door behind me. Stepping over the body, I partially close the door and stand behind it. Glancing towards the mirror, I can see Cray reflected in the open doorway.

Her eyes meet mine.

"What is it?"

"This is where they stood. The mirror told them when Ray Hegarty was in the doorway."

"But there's hardly any room."

"The door was half-closed."

"Someone small."

"Maybe."

Almost immediately I remember Sienna's face bleached by the beam of the torch. There was something in her eyes . . . a terrible knowledge.

Louis Preston emerges from the bathroom, looking like a surgeon preparing to operate.

"There are traces of blood in the S-bend of the sink."

"Somebody cleaned up."

"Forensic awareness is such an important life skill," says Preston. "I blame it on American cop shows. They're like 'how-to' guides. How to clean up a crime scene, how to dispose of the weapon, how to get away with murder . . ."

Cray winks at me. "What's wrong, Preston, did some smart defense lawyer punch a pretty little hole in your procedures?"

"I got no beef with defense lawyers.

Some of my best friends are bottom-feeders. It's the juries I can't abide. Unless they see fingerprints, fibers, or DNA, they'll never convict. They want the proverbial smoking gun, but sometimes there aren't any forensic clues. The scene is cleaned up or washed by rain or contaminated by third parties. We're scientists, not magicians."

Preston scratches his nose and looks at his index finger as though he finds it fascinating.

Meanwhile, I wander across the landing to the bathroom. A wicker laundry basket is tucked beneath the sink. The toilet seat is down. The shelves above the sink are neatly arranged with toothpaste, toothbrushes (three of them), liquid soap and mouthwash. The hand towel beside the sink is neatly folded and hung over the railing.

"They tidied the place," I say out loud.

Cray appears behind me.

"Make any sense?"

"Not much."

"Did Ray Hegarty make many enemies in the job?"

"We all make enemies."

It's not an answer.

"Any skeletons?"

Her voice hardens. "He was a good copper. Straight."

A different SOCO appears at the base of the stairs. Calls to Preston. "I found a stash of porn in the shed. You want me to bag it?"

"What sort of porn?" asks the pathologist.

"Magazines, DVDs . . ."

"Anything unusual?"

"Like what?"

"Rape scenes, violent fantasies, anything involving children."

Cray stiffens in protest. Already she wants to safeguard Ray Hegarty's reputation. A murder investigation is a circus of possibilities, where the spotlight is so fierce it reveals every blemish and flaw. The victim is also placed on trial and sometimes they die all over again in the courtroom—portrayed as being somehow responsible and slandered as viciously as they were stabbed or strangled or shot.

Cray won't let that happen. Not this time. Not to her friend.

Outside, the crowd has thinned out. A few remaining teenagers are loitering on the far side of the lane, kicking aimlessly at dead leaves. A young man swigs from a lurid can. His dark hair has blond streaks cut in a ragged curtain that doesn't so much frame his face as provide him somewhere to hide.

My eyes rush to judgment. He looks familiar. Maybe it's a sign that I've seen too much of the world and now it is starting to repeat itself.

Then I remember where I've seen him. Sienna Hegarty kissed his cheek and climbed into his car. The youth is still staring at me. A fringe of hair is flicked from his eyes. He turns away and begins walking quickly.

I yell out to him and he runs, jinking between bystanders and parked cars.

Cray is still inside with Preston. I yell to the uniforms guarding the gate but none of them reacts quickly enough to stop him. The kid is forty yards ahead. Whippet thin, underfed, built for speed. I lose sight of him as he passes under the arch of the old railway viaduct. By the time I reach the same corner he's disappeared completely.

I notice a farm track on the left. It's the only possibility. Turning up the twin ruts, I keep running, feeling a weight hang around my heart and lungs. Walking hasn't made me any fitter.

Ahead, a car engine starts, rumbling through a broken muffler. The Peugeot accelerates out of a muddy farmyard, the back tires snaking in the slick puddles. He's not slowing down. I'm caught on the grassy ridge between the twin tracks with hedges on either side.

I raise my hand. He doesn't stop. At the last moment I throw myself to one side, curling my legs away from the spinning wheels.

Lying on my back, I take a deep breath and gaze at a bank of moving clouds, listening to my heart thudding.

"Are you all right?" asks a voice in a slow West Country drawl. It's Alasdair Riordan, the farmer I saw earlier.

"I'm fine."

"What are you doing?"

"Resting."

He nods, satisfied, and turns back to his tractor.

"Did you see that car?" I ask.

Alasdair pulls off his woolen hat and scratches an itch on his scalp. "Aye, I did."

"It almost ran me down."

"Aye."

"You didn't happen to get the number?"

He replaces his hat and shakes his head. "I'm not too good with numbers."

A moment later two uniforms appear. Ronnie Cray is behind them, sweating profusely.

"You all right?"

"Fine."

"Who was in the car?"

"Sienna's boyfriend."

She registers the information like a fevered prospector. "You should have left it to us."

"He ran. I chased."

"What are you—a dog?" She looks at her muddy shoes.

"I hope that kid knows how to polish."

My mobile is vibrating.

"What happened to Sienna?" blurts Charlie, close to tears.

“She’s in hospital.”

“Is she OK?”

“She’s in shock, but I think she’ll be fine.”

I can hear playground noises in the background.

“They’re saying that Mr. Hegarty is dead. They’re saying that Sienna killed him.”

“We don’t know what happened.”

“But he’s dead?”

“Yes.”

“Can I go and see Sienna?”

“Not yet.”

“Can I call her?”

“No.”

She sniffles and blows her nose. Charlie rarely cries. She bottles things up. Holds them inside. Ever since the kidnapping, I have watched her closely, anticipating problems. Is she eating and sleeping properly? Is she socializing normally? Sometimes I dare to hope the worst is over, but then the nightmares will return and she cries out, clawing the air, snatching at unseen things in the darkness. Stumbling to her room, I kneel beside her bed, stroking her forehead and talking softly. Her eyes will open, looking vacuously into space as though a terrible revelation about life has been whispered in her ear.

This was my fault, my doing, and I would flay the skin from my back if I could rewind the clock and protect her next time. I don't want to assuage the guilt. I want to change her memories.

6

Midday. Wednesday. I'm walking the same brightly lit hospital corridors, smelling the disinfectant and floor polish. Sienna's room is still under guard. Detective Sergeant Colin "Monk" Abbott, a black Londoner, is dozing on a chair with his legs outstretched and head resting on the wall. He must have pulled an all-nighter. Mrs. Monk won't be happy. I met her once at a DIY store in Bristol. She was half Monk's size, trying to control three young boys who were treating their father like a climbing frame.

Monk rocks to his feet. He could touch the ceiling.

"She awake?" asks Cray.

"Yes, boss."

"She said anything?"

"No."

A doctor comes out of the room, his white coat unbuttoned and a stethoscope draped around his neck. He's young, no more than twenty-six, lean like a greyhound, running on machine coffee and the adrenaline of residency.

"How is she?" asks the DCI.

"Physically, she's fine."

"Is there a 'but' in there somewhere?"

"Her hearing and speech seem to be functioning normally and she's responding to visual stimuli, but her heart rate keeps surging."

"She's traumatized," I say.

The doctor nods and scratches his initials on a form. "Quite possibly, but the neurologist wants to rule out brain damage. He's ordered a CT scan."

Cray opens the door. Helen Hegarty is sitting beside Sienna's bed, holding her daughter's hand. Tight-lipped and tired, she's dressed in her nurse's uniform with the pockets of her cardigan stretched out of shape. Her dyed hair is falling out of a kind of topknot and occasionally she reaches up and pats it with her hand.

The detective motions her outside. Helen kisses Sienna's forehead, telling her she won't be long.

"Mrs. Hegarty, I'm Detective Chief Inspector Cray. We've met once or twice before."

"You were at Ray's farewell."

The DCI nods gently. "That's right. I'm investigating his death."

The statement seems to wash over Helen.

"Ray was a good friend. A fine detective."

"Thank you."

"Has Sienna said anything?"

Helen shakes her head. "She woke about an hour ago. Her eyes opened and she said hello, but then she fell asleep again."

"That's a good sign," I tell her. "She's probably just trying to process things."

Helen glances at me. "You're Charlie's dad."

"Yes. Call me Joe."

Helen wipes her hands before she shakes mine. "Thank you for finding her."

Ronnie Cray motions her to a chair. Helen sits, unsure of where to put her hands. She presses them in her lap. The detective sits next to her, turning her body so they face each other, knees almost touching.

"What time did you leave the house last night, Mrs. Hegarty?"

"At about a twenty to six."

"How long have you worked at St. Martin's?"

"Four years."

"Where was Sienna when you went to work?"

"On her way home. There was a rehearsal at school. She's in the musical." Helen looks up at me. "Joe was bringing her home."

Cray turns to me for an explanation.

"But Sienna called you," I say to Helen. "She told you that her boyfriend was going to bring her home. I heard her talking to you."

A sad, crumpled smile creases her face. "She can be such a devil." As soon as the words leave her lips she regrets them. "I don't mean . . . Sienna wouldn't do anything to hurt . . . she loved her dad."

Cray interrupts her. "What do you know about this boyfriend?"

"I haven't met him, but I know he's older and he drives a car."

"Do you know his name?"

"Danny Gardiner."

"How long has Sienna been seeing him?"

"About eight months." Helen glances at me, looking for understanding. "I tried to put a stop to it because Sienna was only thirteen, but she was always sneaking out to see him. You can't lock them up, can you? Sometimes I wish I could."

"How did Sienna meet him?"

"Danny went to school with Lance—my son."

"Does he live locally?"

"Somewhere in Bath. His mother works as a tour guide."

The DCI presses her chin to her chest, choosing her words carefully. "Do you know what time Sienna got home last night?"

Helen shakes her head.

"And you weren't expecting your husband back?"

"Not until Friday."

There is a pause. I'm watching Helen's body language, looking for signs of outright deception or omission. Shy and unadorned, she strikes me as a hard worker, private and uncomplicated. She must have been a beauty in her youth, but lack of sleep and a poor diet have spun the clock forward.

A few times I've seen her walking through the village dressed in clothes that might have been bought twenty years ago. She reminded me of a factory worker during the war, when women took over men's jobs, wearing loose dungarees and oversized cardigans. It made her about as sexy as an older sister, but she went about her business with a quiet acceptance.

"Who knew your husband was coming home last night?" asks Cray.

She shrugs.

"Sienna?"

"I don't think so."

"How did they get on—Ray and Sienna?"

"Fine. They had their moments."

"Moments?"

Helen holds the cuffs of her cardigan in her closed fists. "You try to set boundaries. Kids try to cross them."

"Did your husband ever touch Sienna inappropriately? Did he ever give you any cause for concern?"

Helen's face goes through a transformation from concern to amazement and then anger.

"Not my Ray! He wouldn't do something like that."

Her features have become tighter and smaller, rushing to the center of her face.

"How dare you suggest—how dare you think . . . He hated nonces. He put them away."

Cray reaches out and touches Helen's hand. "I'm sorry. It's something I had to ask."

I know exactly what the DCI has done. Sienna is an obvious suspect who has yet to be interviewed. With one simple question, Cray has undermined one of her possible defenses—sexual abuse. Helen might change her mind later, but the impact of her future testimony will be diluted, picked apart by the prosecution, made less believable.

Cray continues to talk softly, asking if Ray Hegarty had any obvious enemies. Had he argued with anyone? Did he have any money worries?

"We have to interview Sienna, you understand?"

Helen's gaze drifts past me to the hospital room.

"You can be there or you can ask someone else—another adult to be with her. Someone like Professor O'Loughlin."

"My Sienna didn't do it . . . she wouldn't . . ."

"Detective Sergeant Abbott is going to take you to Flax Bourton Coroner's Court. Somebody has to formally identify Ray's body. Can you do that for me? I could ask one of your other children."

"No. I'll do it."

Monk steps forward and picks up Helen's handbag from the floor.

From the far end of the corridor comes the sound of a commotion, heavy boots and shouting. Lance Hegarty knocks over a young nurse who is trying to slow him down. Wearing a scuffed leather jacket and grease-stained jeans, his hair is shaved to black stubble that looks like a skullcap on his pale skin.

Monk intercepts him, hooking one arm across his chest, plucking him off his feet.

"Get your hands off me, you black bastard!"

Helen yells, “Put him down!”

Monk and Cray exchange a glance. It says more than words.

The DS releases his hold and Lance wraps his arms around his mother, stroking her hair with a tattooed hand. Then he looks at Cray, challenging her.

“What happened to Sienna? Did someone hurt her? Who did it?”

The DCI puts a hand on his shoulder. “Your father is dead. I’m sorry for your loss.”

“You’re sorry?”

“He was a fine man.”

“He was a fucking monster!”

The words seem to detonate in the enclosed space. Helen puts her hand on Lance’s chest. Fingers spread. Calming him.

Lance looks at her. “What about sis?”

Cray answers. “Sienna is going to be just fine.”

“Can I see her? Is she in there?”

Before Lance can reach the door, Monk bodychecks him.

“Get this gorilla away from me!”

The DCI rocks forward and digs a thumb into Lance’s ribs. He flinches and whines, “What was that for?”

"That's to remind you to show some respect, son."

Lance gives her a denigrating sneer before lowering his gaze. I watch from the doorway as he approaches the bed. One look at Sienna and his anger evaporates. Reaching out, he tentatively brushes his fingers across her hand lying open-palmed on the sheet.

Sienna's eyelids flutter.

"Hey, kid!"

She smiles weakly. "You've never held my hand."

"Sure I have."

"When?"

"When you were little and I took you to school."

Sienna finds it funny and squeezes his hand tighter.

"Did you hear about Daddy? I'm trying to be sad, but I'm not."

7

Three fifteen. Waiting at the school gates with dozens of mothers and grandmothers. I'm the only male here beyond the age of Huggies. I tend to stand apart because I'm not good at making small talk or remembering their names. I link mothers to their children: Jasper's mum or Sophie's mum.

One woman approaches. Young and pretty, with short auburn hair, she buries her hands in the pockets of a Barbour jacket, which looks two sizes too big for her. She's probably a nanny.

"Hello, I'm Natasha."

"Joe."

"Your Emma and my Billy are in the same class."

She's not a nanny after all.

"And you have Charlie," she adds.

"How do you know Charlie?"

"My husband teaches at Shepparton Park."

Before I can ask her husband's name,

the school bell rings and laughter and young voices fill the playground, jostling for their bags. It takes me a moment to spot Emma, whose schoolbag makes her look like a turtle walking on her hind legs.

I call her name. She raises her eyes. There's that smile.

She holds my hand—something Charlie doesn't do anymore. I loop her bag over my shoulder and shorten my stride.

"How are things, Emm?"

"Good."

"Learn anything today?"

"Mrs. Graveney said we were getting a male teacher."

"Is that so?"

"I thought the postman was going to teach us how to put letters in mailboxes."

I try not to laugh. "That's a different sort of mail."

She looks at me crossly. "I know that *now*."

We reach the terrace and Emma changes out of her uniform into a Snow White dress she has been wearing obsessively for the past two months. By now the neighbors will think she's strange, but it's not worth arguing over. I'm sure she's not going to be wearing it when she accepts her Nobel Prize.

I'm more concerned about her other "foibles," which is a polite way of describing her neuroses. Last week she launched her dinner plate across the table because a meatball "touched" her macaroni. What was I thinking, putting them on the same plate!

I have learned some remarkable things since becoming a father and I appreciate how much there is still to learn. I know, for example, that a pound coin can pass harmlessly through the digestive system of a four-year-old. I know that regurgitated chicken-flavored ramen noodles and tomato sauce will ruin a silk carpet; that nail polish sticks to the inside of a bath and too much beetroot turns a toddler's urine a neon crimson color.

There is also a mysterious person living in our house called Notme, who is responsible for leaving wet towels on the floor, empty crisp packets on the sofa and chucking buckets of toys around the bedroom. I got so sick of cleaning up after Notme that I made a dummy out of old pillows, dressed it up and hung a sign on his chest saying, "Notme."

Emma thinks it's hilarious.

When I discovered locks of her beautiful hair floating in the toilet bowl and more evidence in her bedroom, I demanded to know who did the cutting.

"Not me," said Emma.

I looked at Charlie.

"Well, it's not *me*."

I went to the dummy. "Listen, Notme, did you cut Emma's hair?"

Emma looked on nervously.

"Notme says he didn't do it," I announced.

"Did he really say that?"

"Really."

"Really?"

"Yes, really."

"Oh."

After that she confessed and took her punishment like a five-year-old.

Charlie won't be home for another hour. In the meantime I make Emma a snack and listen to her sound out words on her spelling list. Then she goes into the garden and chases Gunsmoke, wanting to tie a bonnet on his head. The Labrador lopes, stops, waits and lopes off again.

Julianne phones at a quarter past four. The trial has been adjourned. She's meeting someone for a drink and will be home at six thirty. I listen to her voice and imagine that by "home" she means coming back to me. It's a nice thought, if hopelessly optimistic.

At five o'clock I turn on the news. A blond newsreader with Bambi eyes stares unblinkingly from the screen.

A fire investigator today described how he found five bodies in a Bristol boarding house, three of them children, all belonging to the same family of asylum seekers.

The camera cuts to an equally well-groomed reporter, struggling to record a piece to camera as the wind tosses her hair.

Giving evidence at a murder trial at Bristol Crown Court, Fire Officer Jim Sherman told the jury that the house was well alight by the time the first fire crews arrived at the scene.

The family, who were all sleeping upstairs, were trapped by the blaze, except for Marco Kostin, aged eighteen, who managed to climb out of a second-floor window and jump to safety.

Fire officers discovered traces of petrol in the downstairs hallway of the

house and evidence that a fuel-filled bottle had been thrown through the front window.

The footage changes and reveals police manning barricades and forcing back protesters outside the court.

Amid extraordinary security, the three accused arrived at the court this morning where they were heckled by protesters and cheered by supporters. British National Party candidate Novak Brennan waved briefly to the crowd as he and his fellow accused, Tony Scott and Gary Dobson, were led into court. Scott and Dobson are former BNP activists with links to neo-Nazi organizations. All have pleaded not guilty to charges of murder and conspiracy to commit arson with the intent to endanger life.

Emma wants to watch something else because this is "boring."

"You might see Mummy," I tell her.

"Why?"

"She was there today."

Her brow creases and she concentrates on the TV for twenty seconds, before announcing, "Nope, I can't see her."

Losing interest, she tries to wake Strawberry, who is curled up on a chair.

Charlie should be home. I try to call her mobile but get her voicemail. Perhaps she missed the bus.

When the phone rings I'm sure it's her. Instead a male voice asks for "Charlotte's father."

My insides seem to liquefy. Nobody ever calls her Charlotte. He's a constable from Bath Police Station and he begins explaining that Charlie has been arrested for assaulting a minicab driver and failing to pay a fare.

"There must be some mistake. She's on her way home from school."

"I'm holding her student card." He reads her full name.

The rushing sound in my ears is partly relief. Mistakes can be rectified. At least she's safe.

"Where are we going?" asks Emma.

"To pick up Charlie."

I put a coat over her Snow White dress and lace up her boots. I look at my watch. Julianne should be here soon. I decide not to call her.

Bath Police Station is in Manvers Street,

just up from the railway station. It takes fifteen minutes to drive, during which I have to field Emma's questions, wishing somebody could answer mine. What on earth was Charlie doing?

I find her slouching on a plastic chair in the custody suite, schoolbag between her knees. The only other person in the room is a middle-aged Indian man holding a bloody handkerchief to his nose.

Charlie looks at me briefly and lowers her eyes to her scuffed shoes. She's been crying, but the overriding emotion is frustration rather than sorrow.

"What happened?"

Her answer comes in a rush.

"I was going to see Sienna, but I didn't have enough money. I thought I did, but it cost too much. And then he got angry." She points to the Sikh cab driver. "I was three pounds short. Three lousy pounds. I said I'd get him the money. I gave him my phone number. My address. But he wouldn't let me go."

The driver interrupts. "She called me a Paki bastard. Such a foul-mouthed girl. Truly terrible." His head wobbles.

"He had his hands all over me!"

"She broke my nose!"

"I hardly touched him."

"She's a thug."

"And you're a pervert!"

A policeman intervenes. Constable Dwyer has gelled red hair that makes his head look like it's on fire. He wants to talk to me privately. I tell Charlie to be nice and to look after Emma. She gives me a death stare—already accusing me of taking sides against her.

The constable explains the facts. The driver, Mr. Singh, picked Charlie up from school during last period after she phoned for a minicab. He dropped her outside the Royal United Hospital, where Charlie couldn't pay the fare. According to Mr. Singh, she tried to run away and he had to lock the doors. She then assaulted him.

"He has a security camera in his cab," says the constable.

"Can I see it?"

Constable Dwyer raises a hinged section of the counter and leads me to a desk with a computer. The wide-angle footage is grainy and poorly lit, shot from low on the dashboard. Instead of being focused on the driver, it is aimed at the passenger seat, revealing Charlie's legs and a flash of her underwear as she reaches for her seatbelt.

The PC fast forwards to the argument. I can hear Charlie offering to pay and giving her address. When she tries to get out of the car, he locks the doors and she panics.

"Is he allowed to imprison her?" I ask.

"He can make a citizen's arrest."

"She's fourteen!"

I glance at the computer screen again. "That's an odd place to put a camera, don't you think? What was he trying to film?"

Mr. Singh overhears the remark and takes offense.

"I'm not the criminal here!"

"Perhaps I should look at your other CCTV tapes," says Dwyer.

Mr. Singh puffs up in protest.

"I want her charged. I want compensation for my lost earnings."

My mobile is vibrating. It's Julianne.

"Where are you?"

"We won't be long."

"Is everything all right?"

What am I going to tell her?

"I'm at Bath Police Station. I'll be home soon."

"Where are the girls?" Her voice has gone up an octave.

"Charlie has been cautioned for assaulting a cab driver and failing to pay the fare."

Silence.

Maybe I should have said nothing.

"It's all right. It's under control."

Finally she speaks—her questions coming in a rush. When? Why? How?

"Stay calm."

"Don't tell me to calm down, Joe. Where's Emma?"

"She's with me."

Emma is sitting on Charlie's lap, playing a clapping game. I notice the ink stains on Charlie's fingers. She's been fingerprinted. That's ridiculous.

"What's ridiculous?" asks Julianne.

"Pardon?"

"You just said something was ridiculous."

"It's nothing. Got to go."

"Don't hang up on me."

"Bye."

I confront PC Dwyer. "Why has my daughter been fingerprinted?"

"It's standard procedure. We take DNA samples and fingerprints to confirm a suspect's identity."

"She's fourteen."

"Age isn't an issue."

"This is a joke!"

Dwyer's amiable veneer has disappeared in a heartbeat. "Nobody is laughing, sir. I ran a check on your daughter. This isn't the first time she's been in trouble."

He's talking about the shoplifting incident. I want to tell him about the kidnapping and how Charlie was trussed up in tape and left breathing through a hose. No wonder she panicked when the driver locked the doors on her. But I know Charlie is listening and I want her to forget her ordeal rather than have it brought up again.

"She had a formal caution last time," says Constable Dwyer. "This time the matter will be referred to the CPS."

Mr. Singh seems happier. His nose has stopped bleeding. I fancy punching it.

"So what happens now?"

"A court summons will be sent by post. If it doesn't arrive, she's in the clear."

I look at the driver. "What if I offered to pay your medical bills . . . and compensation?"

His head rocks and he points to his nose.

Dwyer recovers a remnant of his former

warmth. "It may not go any further, sir. Take your daughter home."

Charlie picks up her schoolbag and I take Emma's hand. Pushing through the doors, we descend the steps and follow the glow of streetlights to the car. Charlie drags her feet as though carrying bricks instead of books. Emma has fallen into a worried silence.

"Why didn't you call me?" I ask.

Charlie doesn't raise her head. "Don't blame me. If that dickhead wasn't so uptight . . ."

"Mind your language."

Emma is quick. "What's a dickhead?"

"Nobody. I'm talking to Charlie."

We sit in silence for half a mile. Charlie finally answers.

"I called the hospital but they wouldn't tell me anything about Sienna."

"So you decided to catch a cab?"

"I didn't realize how much it was going to cost."

Charlie is animated now, marshaling her arguments, defending herself.

"There were all these stories going round school. They're saying that Sienna killed her dad, that she's been arrested, that she's tried to commit suicide."

"We don't know what happened yet."

She takes a deep breath. "I saw Sienna when she came to the cottage. I saw the blood."

Emma is listening intently from her booster seat. How much does she understand?

"I don't think we should talk about this now."

Charlie won't let it go. "You're treating me like a child."

"Maybe because you're acting like one. You've been arrested. God knows what your mother will say."

"Don't tell her!"

"It's too late. She called me."

Charlie groans. "Now she'll get all sad and she'll spend days looking at me like she's a seal pup about to be hit with a club."

"She's not that bad."

"Yes she is. She's sad enough already."

Is she sad?

Julianne is standing in the doorway of the cottage as I park the car. She opens her arms for Emma, who runs up the path.

Charlie takes longer to retrieve her bag and open the car door.

"We still need to talk about this."

"Whatever."

I hate that word—"whatever." She's telling me I don't understand. I'll never understand. I'm too old. I'm too stupid. I have no taste in clothes or music or friends. I don't own the right language to talk to her. I don't dread the same things or dream the same dreams.

I'm caught in that in-between place, unsure whether I can be a father or a friend to Charlie, knowing I can't be both.

Right now she is like a separate nation-state seeking independence, wanting her own government, laws and budget. Whenever I try to avoid conflict, choosing diplomacy instead of hostility, she masses her troops at the border, accusing me of spying or sabotaging her life.

She walks up the path and steps around Julianne, going straight upstairs to her room.

Julianne calls out to me. "Did she say why?"

"Sienna."

"We'll talk about it later."

The door closes and I sit on the low brick wall across the lane, beneath the overhanging branches. Gazing at the cottage, I can sometimes make out silhouettes behind the curtains. Right now Julianne is getting Emma ready for bed. Next will come the brushing of teeth, the reading of bedtime stories, a kiss, a hug, a thirsty summons, and one final hug before the light is turned down.

I know the script. I know the stage directions. I no longer have a walk-on part.

8

It's six thirty-five. Still dark outside. Sometimes I wake like this, aware of a sound where no sound belongs. The terrace is old and full of inexplicable creaks and groans, as if complaining of being neglected. Footsteps in the attic. Branches scratching against glass.

I used to sleep like a bear, but not anymore. Now I lie awake taking an inventory of my tics and twitches, mapping my body to see what territory I have surrendered to Mr. Parkinson since yesterday.

My left leg and arm are twitching. Using my right hand, I pick up a small white pill and take a sip of water, raising my head from the pillow to swallow. The blue pill comes next.

After twenty minutes I take another inventory. The twitches have gone and Mr. Parkinson has been kept at bay for another few hours. Never vanquished. Till death us do part.

At seven o'clock I turn on the radio. The news in scolding tones:

Scuffles broke out yesterday outside the trial of three men accused of firebombing a boarding house and killing a family of five asylum seekers. Riot police were called to quell the fighting between anti-racism protesters and supporters of the accused, who have links to the British National Party.

Police have promised extra security when the trial resumes this morning at Bristol Crown Court.

The second bulletin:

A decorated former detective has

been brutally murdered in his home in a village outside of Bath. DCI Ray Hegarty, who spent twenty years with Bristol CID, bled to death in his daughter's bedroom.

Forensic experts spent yesterday at the eighteenth-century farmhouse, where they took bedding and carpets, while detectives interviewed neighbors and family members. Investigators are waiting to talk to the victim's teenage daughter who is under police guard in hospital.

The weather forecast: patchy clouds with a chance of showers. Maximum: 12°C.

Gunsmoke can hear me coming down the stairs. He sleeps outside in the laundry, an arrangement he resents because the cat sits on the windowsill almost goading him.

"A short walk today," I tell him.

I have work to do—a lecture at the university. Today my psychology students will learn why people follow orders and act contrary to their consciences. Think of the Holocaust, Abu Ghraib, black prisons and Guantánamo Bay . . .

I make mental notes as I walk across Haydon Field. I shall tell them about Stanley Milgram, an assistant professor of psychology at Yale University, who in 1963 conducted one of the most famous experiments of them all. He organized a group of volunteers to play the roles of teachers and students and then set up an "electric shock" machine. The students had to memorize a pair of words and were "punished" for any wrong answer with a shock from the machine.

There were thirty levers, each corresponding to fifteen volts. With each mistake, the next lever was pulled, delivering even more pain. If a teacher hesitated they were told, "The experiment requires that you go on."

The machine was a fake, of course, but the teacher volunteers didn't know that. Each time they pulled a new lever a soundtrack broadcast painful groans, turning to screams at higher voltages. Finally there was silence.

Sixty-five percent of participants pulled levers corresponding to the maximum 450 volts, clearly marked "DANGER: LETHAL."

Milgram interviewed the volunteers afterwards, asking them why, and was told they were just following orders. Does that sound familiar? It's the same excuse offered down the ages. The man in the white coat or the military uniform is seen as a legitimate authority figure. Someone to be believed. Someone to be obeyed.

Gunsmoke is lying in a shallow watercourse at the edge of the river where silt has formed a beach. He drinks, pants and drinks some more. Crossing the bridge, I walk up Mill Hill. The Labrador catches up, dripping water from his chin. His pink tongue swings from side to side.

As I near the terrace, I see a young woman sitting in a wheelchair. Dressed in jeans and a sweater, her dark hair is pulled back from her face into a tight ponytail.

"Mr. O'Loughlin?"

"Yes."

She raises her hand to shield her eyes from the glare, but the morning sun isn't that strong.

"I'm Zoe Hegarty."

She looks older than nineteen, with her mother's eyes and build.

"Do you want to come inside?"

Zoe glances up and down the street. Shakes her head. "I get a bit funny about being alone with men. No offense."

"None taken."

She rolls her chair to face away from the sun, resting the wheels against the low brick wall. Fumbling for a cigarette, she lights it apologetically. "Can't smoke around Mum. She doesn't like it." Turning her head, she exhales slowly.

"I heard about Liam's hearing. They're not going to release him."

"Not this time."

"But he can try again?"

"In a year."

Zoe nods. I wait for something more. Her hand shakes. She raises the filter to her lips.

"Sienna didn't kill Daddy."

"Why are you telling me this?"

"You can tell the police."

"Why don't you tell them?"

"I have. I don't think they're listening."

A car passes. She looks at it through a veil of tiredness.

"Tell me about your father."

She takes a deep breath. "It was tough being his daughter."

"In what way?"

"It was like living in some Arab country with curfews and dress regulations—home before ten, nothing above the knee." She holds up her fingers. "I wasn't allowed to wear nail polish, or go to parties. And how's this? I couldn't wear anything red. He said only sluts wore red."

"What did your mother say?"

Her shoulders rise an inch and then fall.

"Mum made excuses for him. She said he was old-fashioned."

"You think he was wrong?"

"Don't you?" She doesn't wait for me to answer. "He eavesdropped on my phone calls, opened my letters, read my diaries. I wasn't allowed to talk to boys or have a boyfriend. He thought I'd get pregnant or take drugs or ruin my reputation."

She looks at her legs. "On the night Liam attacked me I wasn't supposed to be at the cinema. I lied to Daddy and said I was studying at a friend's house. After the attack, whenever he looked at me, it was like he wanted say, "I told you so."

Her cigarette is almost finished. She stares at the glowing end, watching it burn through the last of the paper.

"Did you know that Sienna had a boyfriend?"

Zoe shrugs.

"Did she ever mention him?"

"No, but I guessed it."

"How?"

"She seemed happier. She couldn't tell me directly, because Daddy was always listening in to her phone calls and reading her e-mails."

"Was Sienna sexually active?"

She hesitates, holding something back. "I wouldn't know."

"Why did you come here today?"

"To tell you that Sienna didn't do it."

"Did she tell you that?"

"I just know."

"Was your father ever violent?"

"He had a temper."

"Did he ever touch you or Sienna?"

Squeezing her eyes shut, Zoe pops them open again. "Would it help her?"

Before I can respond, she adds, "The only reason I ask is that, in my experience, the truth doesn't always help people."

"Your experience?"

"Yes."

When did she become so cynical? I look again at the wheelchair and get my answer.

Zoe takes a deep breath as if poised to push herself off a cliff.

"It first happened when I was seven. Daddy was driving me home after I played netball. I was wearing my pleated skirt. He bought me an ice cream. He said it was dripping on my thighs and began wiping it off, pushing his hand between my legs. I kept trying to hold my skirt down. He asked me if I loved him. He said girls who loved their daddies did what they were told . . ."

She can't finish the statement, but the memory shudders through her shoulders.

"Did you tell anyone?"

"Mummy didn't believe me. She said I was making it up, but later I heard them arguing. She was screaming at him and throwing things. She broke the frame of their wedding photograph. It's still on her dresser. You can see where she's patched it up with tape.

"Later that night, Daddy came to my room, put his hand over my mouth and nose so I couldn't breathe. He held it there, looking into my eyes. 'That's how easy it is,' he said. 'Remember that.'

"From then on I knew I wouldn't be believed, so I stopped saying anything and started trying to find ways of avoiding him. I got pretty good at it—making sure I was never alone in the house with him, or in the car. I stopped playing netball. I never asked to be picked up from a friend's house or the cinema."

"Did you ever tell anyone else—a teacher, a school counselor?"

"I told my Auntie Meaghan. She and Mum had the biggest fight. Mum told her that I made up stories to get attention. Later she made me call Auntie Meaghan on the phone and apologize to her for telling lies."

I feel my breath catching. I don't want to hear any more.

"When I was thirteen, I said no to him. I had a knife in my hand. He stopped touching me after that."

"Where is your Auntie Meaghan now?"

"She died of cancer last July."

Zoe lights another cigarette. She smokes quickly. Nervously.

"Did your father ever touch Sienna?"

She closes the lighter and looks at her hands.

"When I came out of hospital after the attack, Daddy wouldn't look at me. He pushed my wheelchair up to the car door and lifted me out, but turned his face away. They set up a room for me downstairs. They had to widen the doors and build ramps. They pushed me into the room and expected me to be all excited, but I just looked at Daddy.

"Before, when I was upstairs, I shared a room with Sienna. We had bunk beds. I was on the bottom and she was on top. We were safe there because there were always two of us. Sienna thought it was so exciting, having her own room, but I had to teach her to look after herself, how to stay out of his way."

"Did he ever touch you again?"

"No. I was a wheelchair girl. A cripple. Not even he was that sick."

"What about Sienna?"

"I think she was old enough by then. He might have tried, but I think she would have fought back."

The cigarette glows as she inhales. "I sometimes wonder why people like him have children. I think my mother wanted someone else to love—other than my father. He was always a bully, bossing her around, making her fetch and carry for him. A beer from the fridge. A sandwich. A newspaper. Whenever he shouted her name she dropped everything and ran to him like a dog wanting to please her master. And all she got in return was ridicule and scraps of affection, yet she kept coming back. Surely you must get sick of being treated like a dog?"

The air has grown colder around us.

Zoe crushes her cigarette against the brickwork. Raising her elbows, she rests her hands on the wheels of her chair, rocking back and forth.

"I shouldn't have come. I'm sorry."

"You have to make a statement—tell the police about your father."

Zoe shakes her head. "That'd just kill Mum."

"What about Sienna?"

"She loved Daddy and she hated him, but she didn't kill him."

My phone is ringing. It's Ronnie Cray.

"Busy?"

"I'm lecturing today."

"This is more important."

"That's as may be, but it doesn't pay my rent."

The DCI sounds annoyed, but she doesn't raise her voice. Her tone barely alters as she suggests that my Volvo might find itself clamped in the university car park should I turn up at the campus.

"I'm pretty sure that's illegal."

"You could explain that to the clamping crew," she replies. "Those guys love a good story. They're born listeners."

Why are detectives so droll?

I consider my options.

"Since we're calling in favors here, I have a small issue you might be able to help me with."

"I'm listening."

"Charlie had an altercation with a cab driver yesterday. Didn't have the full fare. Got into a fight."

"*Princess* Charlie?"

"That's the one. She was interviewed at Bath Police Station. The driver wants to press charges."

Cray doesn't need the rest spelled out. She'll make a call.

9

The living and the dead are greeted by stainless steel: benches, basins, scalpels and scales, disinfected and polished to a dull gleam under the halogen lights.

Located in the basement of the new coroner's court, the mortuary at Flax Bourton smells like a hospital and looks like an office block. A ramp leads down from the road to an underground parking area where Home Office "meat wagons" are parked in bays.

Pushing through swing doors, Ronnie Cray walks like a sailor in search of a fight. A white coat leads the way along brightly lit corridors. The place seems deserted until a cleaning lady appears wearing elbow-length rubber gloves. I don't want to contemplate what she's been cleaning.

Another door opens. Louis Preston has his hands deep inside a butterflied rib cage. Half a dozen students are gathered around him, dressed in matching surgical scrubs and cloth caps.

"You see that?" Preston asks, adjusting a lamp on a retractable metal arm above his head.

Nobody answers. They're staring at the disemboweled body with a mixture of awe and disgust.

Preston points and raises his eyes to theirs. Still no response.

"What are we looking for, sir?" one of them asks.

"Evidence of a heart attack or otherwise."

He waits.

Silence.

"I swear you're all blind. Right there! Damaged heart tissue. You don't always find the clot, but cardiac arrhythmia can still be the likeliest cause of death."

"He suffered a heart attack," says one of the students.

"You *think*?"

Preston's sarcasm is lost on them.

"Sew him up," he says, peeling off surgical gloves. He tosses them overhead like he's shooting a basketball. Rattles the bin. Scores.

"You had something to show me," says DCI Cray.

"Absolutely."

The pathologist leads us to a glass-walled office with a desk and filing cabinets. Having collected a manila folder, he waves it above his head like a tour leader and we follow him down another corridor until he stops before a large steel door. Pulling down on the handle, he opens the door, breaking the airtight seal with a soft hiss. Lights are triggered automatically. I feel a breath of frigid air. Four cadavers are on trolleys beneath white sheets. Three walls of the room have metal drawers. Bodies lie within.

Preston checks a nameplate and tugs a handle. Another hiss as the seal breaks. Ray Hegarty slides into view on metal runners. His joints are stiff with rigor mortis and his skin marbled by lividity.

Preston pulls on latex gloves.

"He was knocked unconscious by a blow to the back of the head. The bruising and depression on the skull match the heel of a hockey stick. The blow was delivered in a chopping motion." He puts his fists together and pretends to swing an axe.

"Ray Hegarty fell forward. The killer stood over him, grasped his hair, raised his head and sliced right to left. The weapon was most likely a Stanley knife, extended about an inch, which was drawn across his neck, severing his carotid artery and jugular vein. He bled to death within twenty or thirty seconds."

I gaze at the wound, a slash of crimson that begins just below his left earlobe, cutting through muscle and cartilage.

"They were left-handed," I say.

"Most likely," says Preston. "Some people are ambidextrous."

"Sienna Hegarty is left-handed," adds Cray.

"Could a teenager have done this?" I ask.

"It's not so much a matter of strength as the sharpness of the blade," replies the pathologist.

"Is there anything else?" asks the DCI.

"Hegarty had alcohol in his system."

"How much?"

"A significant amount—it would have slowed his reaction time."

Preston opens the folder and withdraws a forensic report.

"We pulled forty-two full or partial prints from the house. Most of them match with the family. We're looking more closely at those that don't match. We collected fibers from the rug and the wound, and there might be DNA from the hand towel in the bathroom. There were old semen stains on the daughter's bed sheets and also on her underwear. The DNA results won't be back for another five days."

I can hear Ronnie's teeth grinding.

"Check them against the victim. Then run them through the national database. Tick off the boxes."

Preston slides Ray Hegarty's body from view and opens a folder of crime-scene photographs. The first shows Hegarty lying face down, his right cheek resting in a pool of blood. The image is centered on a bloody heel print beside his right knee. The second image is a close-up of Hegarty's shirt showing handprints between his shoulder blades. Another partial print was found on the right side of the doorframe.

"The tread design on the heel matches the daughter's jazz shoes. Size six."

"Sienna wasn't wearing any shoes when I found her," I hear myself say.

"We found them in the river," replies Cray.

Taking the first photograph from Preston, I study the position of the body in relation to the heel print. There is a second bloody mark on the opposite side of the body. Not a shoeprint. A knee. "Somebody knelt."

"To cut his throat?" asks Cray.

"No, afterwards."

Ronnie Cray studies the photograph and hands it back to Preston.

"So we're looking for a Stanley knife."

Preston nods.

"The daughter is a cutter. She had a shoebox full of bandages but no blade, which means she hid it somewhere else or got rid of it."

She's already convinced that Sienna was responsible.

"I don't think we should jump to conclusions," I hear myself saying. "Maybe it was self-defense."

"More like an ambush," says Cray. "She hid behind the door."

"*Somebody* hid behind the door."

"His blood was all over her."

"He was *twice* her size."

"Size had nothing to do with it."

"She's fourteen."

"I know how old she is, Professor." A sharp tone. "I hope you're not making excuses because she's your daughter's friend."

"And I hope you're not predisposed

against her because Ray Hegarty was your friend. He must have had enemies. You said so yourself."

Undisguised contempt enters her gaze. I've gone too far. Cray doesn't like having her judgment questioned publicly.

Through clenched teeth: "Do you think I want this? I can see what's going to happen. I can hear the defense warming up. They're going to trash Ray Hegarty's reputation. One of the best and bravest officers I ever served with is going to be branded a nonce, a child molester. They're going to destroy him."

"What if it's true?"

"Bullshit! There were no defense wounds. No signs of a struggle. No signs of rape."

"What about the semen on her sheets?"

"She had a boyfriend."

There's no point in arguing because Cray hasn't put a foot wrong procedurally. Meanwhile, I'm doing exactly what I tell my students to avoid—I'm ignoring the obvious answer. There's only one greater sin—embracing it.

Cray hitches up her trousers and I follow her down the corridor, noticing the scribble of purplish veins on the back of her ankles, above her drooping socks.

It's cold in the underground car park. She pulls open the car door.

"Was anything missing from the house?" I ask.

"A laptop."

"Somebody could have taken it."

"Or she could have left it at school."

We're moving. Cray has a driver, a young policewoman, who glances nervously in the rearview mirror.

"Where to, boss?"

"Trinity Road."

10

Freud said that our memories are a repository of traumatic past events, but often these are merely fantasies rather than actualities. They haven't taken place in the real world, only in our minds, which are vast storehouses for things that never existed and events that never happened. Sometimes I wonder whether my memories are real. If I try to concentrate on them too carefully, they catch in my throat and I struggle for breath.

The nightmares of my recent past involve a former soldier who was trained to unlock secrets by torturing people—a man who knew how to reach inside a mind and pry it apart as if opening the segments of a citrus fruit. This is the man who took my Charlie and wrapped her in a world of darkness.

Sometimes late at night when a car door slams or I hear footsteps on the footpath, I push back the blankets and cross the floor, carefully opening a corner of the curtain. I don't expect to see Gideon Tyler waiting for me, but I still sense he's there. Watching. Waiting.

I know why this memory has come back to me now. It's being here at Trinity Road Police Station, a redbrick fortress surrounded by closing-down sales, blighted tower blocks and crack dens. This is the last place I saw Gideon, smiling at me with a bloody froth on his lips and his tongue rolling across his teeth, painting them red. He challenged me to torture him, begged me with an unearthly smile on his face. I hated this man more than words could describe. I wanted to hurt him, I wanted him dead, but I knew it wouldn't save Charlie or my marriage.

The incident room is on the third floor. Most people take the stairs because the lift moves slower than a French tractor. Ronnie Cray's office has no photographs. No certificates. No trophies. Instead there are files stacked against every wall like she's building a child's cubby house. Perched on the windowsill is a stuffed parrot, as forgettable as a fairground prize, yet I wonder how she got it. Who in her life gave her such a gift?

Sitting at her desk, she squints as she reads a statement. She needs glasses but won't get her eyes checked because she refuses to succumb to any sign of diminishing faculties.

More than thirty-six hours have elapsed since Ray Hegarty was murdered. Detectives have gone door to door in the village, while others have tracked down family, friends and colleagues, piecing together his last movements.

Sienna is out of hospital—waiting downstairs in an interview suite.

"How should I do this?" Cray asks.

I look at the coffee in my hand, the cup is rattling in the saucer. I need both hands to hold it steady. Over the years I have had dozens of children in my consulting room, many of them damaged, vulnerable and emotionally traumatized, just like Sienna. Even though she may have killed, she has to be treated like a victim, not a perpetrator.

Cray is watching me. Waiting.

"You talk to her carefully. Slowly. Gently. She's still an ordinary frightened teenager. She may deny things at first. She will have tried to block them out. But any interview will take her back through every detail. She'll relive what happened, and that's going to increase her trauma."

"How can I avoid that?"

"Keep the sessions short. Constantly reassure her that she's doing well. Be sure of your questions, know what outcome you want, but let Sienna reveal her story in her own way. You can't treat her like an adult and hammer her with questions or you'll risk pushing her into a deep psychological breakdown.

"Be very careful about touching her. She

might be upset. You might want to comfort her, but physical contact can be very threatening to a child who has been abused."

Cray interjects. "We don't *know* that she was abused."

"You have Zoe's statement."

"Given at her second interview—not her first."

"You think she's lying?"

"I'm just telling you the facts."

The DCI doesn't want to get bogged down in claims of sexual abuse. She's an investigator, not a judge.

I tell her to avoid asking closed questions until later in the interviews, when the detail required is very specific. Until then, invite Sienna to explain. If she says something inconsistent, don't focus on it. Instead go back later. Importantly, don't ask the same question twice—she'll see it as a criticism.

"What about the crime-scene photographs?"

"Don't show her. It's too early."

Cray goes over the strategy again until she's satisfied.

"I want you in there. She's a minor. You're an appropriate adult."

"What about her mother?"

"She chose you."

"I won't hesitate to terminate the interview if you browbeat her."

Cray nods and gathers her notes. "Let's do this."

Sienna sits with her hands squeezed between her thighs and her eyes fixed on the table in front of her where a can of soft drink is beading with condensation. She's wearing jeans and a tailored shirt with dark ballet flats on her feet. The shadows beneath her eyes appear permanent.

When Ronnie Cray enters the interview room, Sienna looks at the detective's oxford brogues, polished to a shine. I can see her wondering what sort of woman would wear men's shoes, ignore makeup and shear her hair to bristle.

Cray pulls up a chair and sits directly opposite, unbuttoning her jacket. Sienna eyes her nervously.

"I'm going to turn on the tape recorder, Sienna. You can answer all of my questions, some of them or none of them, it's up to you. But if this ends up in court and you then come up with a perfectly reasonable explanation of what has really happened, the court can choose not to believe what you say, because they will want to know why you didn't give that version of events here and now in this interview.

"This is your opportunity to explain what happened. The interview is being tape-recorded and any notes I take will be kept and this information can be given to the court if needs be, whether it goes against you or in your favor. Do you understand?"

Sienna looks at me.

"You just have to say what you remember," I tell her.

"What if I don't remember?"

"Do your best."

"OK," she says, reaching shakily for her drink.

"Do you know why you're here?" asks Cray.

She nods.

"You have to speak, Sienna, otherwise we can't record your answers."

"Daddy's dead."

"Yes."

"Can you tell us about that night?"

"I don't remember."

"Just remember what you can."

"I've been trying, but it's like something wiped my memory, you know, like on those TV programs where people say they were abducted by aliens and given anal probes, which is pretty gross. I'm not saying I was abducted by aliens. I don't actually believe in little green men from outer space, although one of the doctors at the hospital looked pretty weird. He was fat and had a goatee. You never see fat doctors on *Grey's Anatomy* or *ER* and you don't see goatees. I think goatees look like women's lady parts, don't you?"

Cray looks totally perplexed. Sienna flicks her gaze from the detective's face to mine, still waiting for an answer.

"I've never thought about it," I say.

"I think about stuff like that all the time."

"Can we get back to what happened that night?" asks Cray.

"It's like I said: I can't remember. My mind doesn't want to go there. There's a door that I'm not supposed to open, because I'm not supposed to look. Mum used to hide my Christmas presents on the top of her wardrobe. I wasn't allowed to look there, but that was good stuff. This is bad."

"Bad?"

"Really bad."

DCI Cray pulls her chair forward and it makes a screeching sound. Sienna jumps as though someone has slammed a door.

"Let's talk about Tuesday, Sienna. Do you remember going to school?"

"Yes."

"You had rehearsals."

Sienna's eyes pop open. "I need to talk to Mr. Ellis."

"Mr. Ellis?"

"We have a rehearsal today. And I need to get my dress cleaned."

"You don't have to worry about that."

"If something happens to Erin Lewis, I'm her understudy. It should have been the other way around. Erin walks like a giraffe." Sienna frowns. "That sounds bitchy, doesn't it? I'm trying to stop that."

"They've postponed the musical," I tell her.

She looks relieved.

"What happened after the rehearsal?"

Sienna glances at me but doesn't answer.

"You met up with your boyfriend."

"Yes."

"Danny Gardiner."

She nods.

"How long have you known Danny?"

"A while."

"Where did you meet him?"

"He was in Lance's year at school."

"Lance is your brother?"

"Yeah, Danny used to hang out with Lance. Follow him around. They were both into cars and motorbikes."

"Where did you and Danny go on Tuesday?"

"For a drive."

"Anywhere in particular?"

"I can't remember."

Now she's lying.

Cray asks the question again, approaching it from a different angle. Sienna obfuscates and becomes deliberately vague, either covering her tracks or protecting someone.

"Do these belong to you?" Cray pulls a plastic bag from beneath the table. It contains a pair of muddy jazz shoes.

Sienna nods.

"I didn't hear you," says Cray.

"Yes," she answers.

"Do you own a Stanley knife?"

Sienna shakes her head, but instinctively covers her forearms.

"We found your box of bandages," I say gently. "You don't have to be embarrassed. What sort of blade do you use?"

"It was one of Daddy's tools. I found it in the garage."

"Where is it now?"

"It should be in the box."

"It's not there," says Cray. "Do you know where it is?"

She shakes her head and digs her right thumbnail into the back of her left hand, threatening to break the skin.

"What time did you get home on Tuesday night?"

"I don't remember."

"Did you see your father?"

Sienna shakes her head.

"But he was there?"

She nods.

"Where?"

"In my room."

I can almost see Sienna's mind begin to wander. "I used to share a bedroom with Zoe, but then she got paralyzed and Daddy moved her downstairs. I used to dream about having my own room, but now I wish Zoe were still at home and we shared a room. I'd even put up with her mess and having to share a bunk bed. When she moved out Daddy bought me a proper bed. He said we didn't need a bunk bed anymore because Zoe couldn't climb the stairs.

"Zoe and Lance hardly ever come home anymore. Zoe lives in Leeds with her boyfriend. I'm not supposed to tell anyone that because she doesn't want Daddy finding out, but I guess that doesn't matter anymore.

"When Zoe left home she gave me her favorite pair of earmuffs and her Winnie the Pooh bear, which is humongous." She holds her palm out to indicate how high. "She won him at a funfair. I can't remember what she had to do, but she's pretty good at shooting baskets. She played netball when she was at school—until the you-know-what happened. When she left home she told me I should leave too, as soon as I could. Sooner even."

"Why did she say that?"

Sienna reaches towards the table and runs her finger through the ring of condensation left by her soft drink.

"She was looking out for me."

"In what way?"

"She told me the places that were safe and weren't safe."

"What places weren't safe?"

"In the bathroom unless the door was locked, in the car at night, in the shed, on the sofa and even in my new room if I found myself alone."

Cray straightens, steeling herself, knowing she has to ask the obvious question.

"Why weren't they safe?"

Sienna lays her forehead on her arms and closes her eyes. "What did Zoe say?"

"I'm asking you. Did your father ever touch you inappropriately?"

Her voice is muffled. "Not for a long time."

"What does that mean?"

"It doesn't matter anymore."

The DCI looks at her silently, her face tired and poached-looking under the halogen lights.

"Why did you stab your father?"

Sienna's forehead rolls back and forth on her forearms. Her eyes are closed.

"He looked like he was asleep. I thought he was trying to scare me by pretending."

"Pretending?"

"To be dead."

"Why did you think he was dead?"

"He was lying on the floor."

"Did he try to attack you?"

"No."

"So why did you hit him?"

Sienna's mind suddenly switches.

"I should be sad. I've tried to cry. I rubbed my eyes really hard to make them go red. I poked them to make them water. I want to be able to cry, but I can't feel anything."

"Tell me about the knife," continues Cray.

Sienna doesn't seem to be listening.

"Do you think Daddy is in Heaven? I used to talk to Reverend Malouf. He told me God had all the answers, but I couldn't get my head around Jesus rising from the dead. If he came back, why didn't he hang around and take his show on the road? Instead he went back to Heaven and let people forget.

"Daddy used to tell people he was an agnostic, which isn't the same thing as an atheist but I don't understand the difference. Reverend Malouf tried to explain it to me once. He said an agnostic is someone who can't make up his mind and get off the fence."

"You'll have to talk to us eventually. It's for your own good," says Cray.

"Why do people say things are for my own good?" answers Sienna, fixing her gaze on the detective. There is something in her voice, so old and so tired, that takes Cray by surprise.

Sienna continues, "Mum is crying, Lance is angry, Zoe isn't here and Daddy is dead. What I do or say doesn't matter."

"Yes it does. We're giving you a chance to explain."

"No you're not."

"You're avoiding my questions."

"I'm avoiding the answers. There's a difference. You want me to remember things, but I can't."

Sienna pulls her knees up towards her, holding her shins tightly. She lets her hair tumble over her face. After a long silence, she finds a voice, small and haunted, belonging to a younger child.

"Do you know something? When Zoe got crippled she said she was lucky because Daddy stopped trying to touch her. She was his favorite, you know. The sporty one. He was proud of her."

A groan gets trapped in her throat.

Her chest convulses in a flutter of short breaths.

"I sometimes think that if Daddy'd had a choice, he would have wished it was me in the wheelchair and not Zoe."

Tears hover and her mouth opens and closes wordlessly. Suddenly she raises her hands and presses them hard against her ears.

"Can you hear something, Sienna?" I ask.

"The rushing sound."

"What's that?"

"I can't make it go away."

She rocks back and forth, digging her nails into her scalp. She's thinking about the blade. Bleeding. Clearing her mind. Finally she whispers something. I have to lean close to hear the words. It's a rhyme that she repeats over and over.

"When I was a little girl about so high,
Momma took a big stick and made me cry.
Now I'm a big girl and Momma can't do it,
Daddy takes a big stick and gets right to it."

11

The team of detectives has gathered upstairs. Jackets hang on chairs and shirt-sleeves are rolled to half-mast. It's not a big task force—a dozen at most—mostly men, midthirties, aging rapidly.

"Twelve is a biblical number," Cray tells me, when I comment on the number. "The twelve days of Christmas, the twelve tribes of Israel."

"What about the twelve apostles?"

"I wasn't going to be that presumptuous."

She picks up her notes and motions me to follow. "I'm lucky to have this many."

"Why?"

"Half my team is babysitting witnesses for the Novak Brennan trial."

That name again.

"Has someone threatened the witnesses?"

"Precautionary measure. It's a bloody circus—we've got the right-wing extremists on the one side and refugee groups on the other. I don't know who's worse."

"I think you do."

She grunts. "Look, I'm no fan of neo-Nazis or right-wing extremists, but we have a race problem in this country. We have home-grown terrorists blowing themselves up. We have gangs of teenagers killing each other with knives, Asians, blacks, whites . . ."

"Maybe that's a social problem, not a race problem."

"Makes no difference to me. I'm just sick of putting good officers in situations where every scrote and teenage scumbag on the street has a knife and a grudge."

"So where does Novak Brennan come into it?"

"He's a politician in search of a crowd. The ignorant, the uneducated, the unemployable; they listen because they want to believe their miserable lives are someone else's fault. Novak Brennan tells them what they want to hear."

"He incites hatred."

"He lances the boil."

The detectives are waiting, mostly pale and hung over. Ronnie Cray introduces me. Suddenly, my left leg stops moving and I'm stuck in front of the whiteboard.

Staring at my feet, I concentrate on making my leg lift. It looks like I'm stepping over a trip wire. They are all staring at me with solemn expressions, pitying the poor bastard.

Cray takes over, beginning the briefing. I find a chair and feel their eyes leave me. The DCI outlines developments in the investigation. Sienna's boyfriend has been interviewed. Danny Gardiner claims that he dropped Sienna on a corner in Bath just before 7 p.m. but he hasn't given police an alibi for later that night when Ray Hegarty was murdered.

Lance and Zoe Hegarty have also been interviewed. Zoe was in Leeds, but Lance is a possible suspect. He works as a motorcycle mechanic in Bristol. On Tuesday afternoon he left the workshop at five, went to the pub for an hour and then went home by himself. His flatmate was out.

"We're bringing Lance in again today," says Monk. "He's an aggressive little shit, but I don't think he's lying. He couldn't hide a hard-on in baggy jeans."

Two hours are still missing from Ray Hegarty's afternoon and telecom engineers are trying to pinpoint his whereabouts using his mobile phone. The door-to-door inquiries have thrown up several unknown vehicles in the village in the previous few days. Two motorists also reported seeing a blond-haired girl in a short dress walking down Hinton Hill at about 10:15 p.m. That's about a mile from Wellow. It could have been Sienna.

Monk picks up a spiral notebook and flips a page.

"A month ago Helen Hegarty claims she saw someone peering into the downstairs window, but they ran off before she could get a good look at them. A while later she found rocks organized in a circle in the garden bed beneath the kitchen window. The soil was compressed like someone had been crouching there. Says she told her husband. He suspected local kids."

"Any of the neighbors report similar problems?" asks Cray.

"Nope, but one of them, Susan Devlin, says she saw Ray Hegarty arguing with someone outside his house about a week ago. It was about ten o'clock at night. The car had dropped Sienna home."

"Maybe it was the boyfriend," says Safari Roy, a small tanned detective with black hair parted to reveal his scalp. Roy's nickname came from his lounge lizard clothes and his love of sunbeds.

"He drives a Peugeot," replies Monk. "The neighbor said it was a silver Ford Focus."

"Talk to her again," says Cray. "Get a better description of the driver."

Monk nods and finally asks the question on everybody's lips. "How did it go downstairs, boss?"

The DCI looks over their heads at a weak shaft of sunlight that has found a way through the building's defenses.

"She says her father was dead when she arrived home."

Glances are exchanged between the assembled.

"Our number one priority is to find the murder weapon," says Cray. "We're going to search the house again—every cupboard, crawlspace and cistern; the flowerbeds, the compost bins, the incinerator. The same goes for the river. Retrace her steps. Turn over every rock and leaf. Find the blade."

One of the officers raises his hand.

"Are we getting any help?"

"I've got twenty-four uniforms waiting downstairs and two dog teams. Make the time count. They turn back into plods at five o'clock."

I look at my watch. It's almost midday. I've missed my lecture but can still get to the university and do some work. At the same moment my mobile is singing. Julianne's number lights up the screen.

"How goes the trial?" I ask.

"We've been given the afternoon off."

"Bonus."

"You free for lunch? We can talk about Charlie."

Talk is good.

She chooses an Italian restaurant, San Carlo in Corn Street, not far from the Corn Exchange. I arrive first and take a table by the window where I can watch for her. I order her a glass of wine.

Finally she's here, dressed in a suede jacket, a scarf and a ribbed sweater. The waiters fall upon her like Elizabethan courtiers. She's a beautiful woman. Good service is guaranteed.

"Sorry I'm late," she says apologetically. "I had to make sure Marco was all right."

"Marco?"

"My witness." Her brow furrows. "He's nervous. I don't know if he's sleeping."

"Where is he now?"

"The Crown Prosecution Service has a safe house."

Her new haircut is sharp just below her jawline. I feel my mind taking a snapshot so I can study it later.

"I've decided that jury trials are one big sociology experiment. You take twelve people who don't know each other and have nothing in common and put them together for eight hours a day and then drip-feed them information, telling them not to discuss the case or read the papers or do their own research."

"You feel sorry for them."

"They saw the photographs of the fire today—three little girls and their parents—it was horrible." Julianne squeezes her eyes shut as if forcing the images to go away. They open again. "It's not what I expected, you know. The trial. The defendants. Novak Brennan doesn't look like a monster."

"There are no monsters."

"That's what you tell Emma."

"It's true."

"I know, but I expected him to be different. I feel as though he's become familiar over this past week. I've seen him every day—always immaculately dressed and polite. He nods and smiles to the court staff. He bows when the jury enters the room. He has these long lashes like a girl and the bluest eyes. Arctic blue. I can almost see the snow blowing across them. Makes you wonder."

"About what?"

"If he really firebombed that house . . . killed that family." She pauses, searching for words. "The other defendants look like thugs and bovver boys, grinning at each other and guffawing. Novak Brennan looks almost serene. He doesn't fidget or squirm. He hardly shows any emotion at all, except when he glances at his sister in the public gallery. She's been there every day."

"Which way are the jury leaning?"

Julianne shrugs. "It's too early to tell. So far it's all been about the prosecution case."

She glances at the menu, giving me an opportunity to look at her without making her feel self-conscious.

"Are you staring at me again?"

"No."

"Good. So what are we going to do about Charlie?"

"The police aren't going to charge her."

Surprise on her face. "That's great. What happened?"

"Ronnie Cray sorted it out."

"You made some sort of deal."

I don't answer. Normally, Julianne would fight against the idea, but this time she says nothing.

"How is Sienna?" she asks, switching her concern.

"In a lot of trouble."

"Did she do it?"

"I don't know. Maybe she had a reason."

Our meals have arrived. In the lottery of ordering, Julianne has again triumphed. Her choice looks healthier and more appetizing. She'll eat half and push the rest around her plate.

"So what are we going to do about Charlie?" she asks between mouthfuls.

"She made a mistake."

"She broke the law! I talked to the school counselor today and she recommended a therapist. He has a practice in Bath."

"I'm a psychologist."

Julianne puts down her fork. "You're her

father. I'm sure there is some sort of conflict of interest there."

She's right, of course, but I still balk at the idea of my daughter talking to a stranger, revealing things that she wouldn't tell her parents.

"What's his name?"

"Robin Blaxland."

"I could check him out . . . ask about him."

"And not scare him off?"

"No."

"We still have to punish her," she says.

"I saw the video of what happened. She tried to pay the driver but didn't have enough money. She only panicked when he locked the doors. I think she was frightened it was going to happen again, the kidnapping."

"She should never have gone to the hospital without our permission."

"I know. Maybe we could ground her for a few weeks."

"School and home."

"Tough but fair."

I like talking with Julianne like this—discussing anxieties and tiny victories, the happenstances of family life. Her long fingers toy with the stem of her wineglass.

"Do you want to go to dinner on Saturday night?" I ask.

"I can't."

"Why not?"

"I'm going out."

"Who with?"

"Harry Veitch."

My heart jerks like a hooked fish. Harry is an architect. Rich. Divorced. One of his houses was featured on *Grand Designs,* which I guess makes him a celebrity of sorts, or a "person of note." He has a daughter Charlie's age living with her mother. I can't remember her name.

"How long have you been . . . ?"

"We haven't."

"So this is your first date?"

"It's *not* a date."

There is an edge to her voice. She's waiting for me to say something negative. I glance at my food, no longer hungry. I didn't see this coming. Didn't even contemplate it. Harry is older than I am—by at least ten years. He's one of those big-boned former rugby players who struggle with their weight when they give up competing but never lose their self-belief.

Julianne speaks. "Harry wants to thank me for helping him choose a color scheme for one of his new houses."

"That's nice," I say.

There is a long embarrassed silence. The silence of separation. Worse—the silence of possible divorce. I can see the future flashing before my eyes. Julianne will marry Harry "big-boned" Veitch and spend her new life choosing color schemes for his McMansions. The girls will have a new father. At first they won't like him, but Harry will bribe them and make them laugh. He'll be jolly old Harry. Rich old Harry. Ho, ho, ho Harry. He laughs like that: "Ho, ho, ho."

"What did you say?" asks Julianne.

"Nothing."

"You sounded like Santa Claus."

"Sorry. So where is he taking you?"

"To a new restaurant. He knows the owner or the head chef—something like that."

"What about the girls?"

"Charlie can babysit."

"I'll do it."

Julianne arches an eyebrow. "Charlie's old enough."

"I know."

She reaches across the table and takes my hand. "You'll have to let go one day."

Is she talking about the girls or herself?

"I don't want to let go."

Her pupils dilate slightly and she releases my hand, folding her arms beneath her breasts like a teenager. I've upset her now. She changes the subject.

"Charlie says you kissed Miss Robinson."

"She gave me a peck."

"On the lips?"

"Some people peck on the lips."

"I've always found that kind of creepy," she says playfully. "It was Miss Robinson who suggested Charlie see a therapist. Apparently, some of the teachers are worried about her."

"Miss Robinson didn't mention anything."

"That's because she was flirting with you."

The silence stretches out and is far more uncomfortable than it should be after so many years of marriage.

"Did Miss Robinson mention Sienna coming to see her?"

Julianne shakes her head. “Maybe you should ask her. Take her for a drink.”

“I don’t want to ask her out.”

“She’s very pretty.”

“Yes, but . . .”

“But what?”

“She’s not *you*.”

Julianne shakes her head and drains her wineglass. “This was nice, Joe. Don’t spoil it.”

Summoning a waiter, she asks for her coat and leans towards me, accepting a kiss—a peck on the cheek, not the lips.

Almost in the same breath she hesitates, looking over my shoulder.

“Is something wrong?”

“I’m not sure.”

I follow her gaze. A man is standing on the corner, looking towards us. Pale and blade-faced, his dark oiled hair is combed back in vertical lines that cling to his scalp like the contours of a map. The tattoos on his forearms have faded with age into blue and black smears, but the most startling markings are ink lines drawn vertically down his cheeks like twin channels for his tears that extend from his lower eyelids to his jawline.

Usually, I study people instinctively, reading their body language, their clothes, their fleeting expressions, trying to understand who they are or what motivates them and what they're capable of. This time it is different. I don't want to notice this man. I want to look away. I want to ignore him.

Julianne is staring at him.

"He was in court," she says. "I saw him sitting in the gallery."

"Today?"

"Every day."

The school grounds are empty apart from a gym class running around cones on the playing fields with batches of students in the goal squares and on the halfway line. I ask at the main office for Annie Robinson and am directed to her office. The note pinned to the door says she's in the hall, painting sets for the musical.

Following a covered walkway, I pass several classrooms in the science block. Groups of students are wearing safety glasses and stand clustered around benches working with Bunsen burners and test tubes.

The main body of the hall is in darkness.

There are lights burning backstage. Nobody answers when I call. Climbing the side stairs, I step over cables and paintbrushes soaking in jars. Props are leaning on sawhorses and a large backdrop shows a Manhattan skyline with the skyscrapers in silhouette. Modern Millie meets the Big Apple.

A dressing-room door is ajar. Racks of costumes are lined up along the wall. A movement is reflected in the mirrors. Miss Robinson leans over a sink sponging paint from her blouse. Her black skirt contrasts sharply with the paleness of her skin. I can see the outline of her nipples, small and dark, through the lace of her bra.

She looks up from the running water, studying herself in the mirror. Her eyes meet mine. Pulling her shoulders back, she makes no attempt to cover her breasts.

"Can I help you?"

"I knocked. You didn't hear me."

"Obviously."

She goes back to sponging her blouse. "I should have worn an old shirt," she explains. "This is my favorite blouse and now it's ruined."

"Maybe you could soak it," I suggest.

"Are you an expert on removing paint stains?" She has a slight lisp when she pronounces her esses. "You can come in, Joseph, I'm sure you've seen a woman in a bra before."

It sounds like a question, but I can't think of anything to say.

Miss Robinson laughs and holds up the blouse to the light, sighing. "I've been painting the sets. I had a free period and thought I'd get it finished today, but it might take another session."

"I thought the musical had been postponed."

"Yes, but we're still hopeful. The show must go on—as they say."

She slips the blouse over her arms and turns to me as she does up the buttons.

"So what else can I do for you today—apart from giving you a cheap thrill?"

"You were talking to Julianne about Charlie."

"Yes."

"Is she having problems?"

"One of her teachers found her crying in a classroom. I thought it might help if Charlie talked to someone."

"A therapist."

"The school recommends a very good one."

I'm fascinated by her mouth; watching it move as she speaks. Her top lip is shaped like a stylized bird drawn by a child. Her bottom lip is fuller. I wonder what it would be like to kiss those lips. They have stopped moving and are slightly parted. Her head is cocked at an angle.

"You're staring at me," she says, covering her mouth self-consciously.

"I'm sorry. I do that sometimes."

"It's very unnerving."

"Can I ask you something, Miss Robinson?"

"Only if you call me Annie."

"Has Charlie talked to you about the separation? You see, she hasn't spoken to me or to Julianne. I thought maybe she was keeping a diary, or a scrapbook full of angry conversations in cartoon bubbles."

"She didn't say anything to me."

"It was just a thought."

"Have you asked her?"

I make a sound that could be a sigh or a murmur of agreement. "We don't have long conversations anymore."

"Maybe you should think about the therapist."

"Maybe."

Annie waits.

"Was Sienna Hegarty seeing a therapist?"

"I'm not allowed to talk about other students."

Businesslike, she makes her arguments about privacy and confidentiality. A counselor must build trust, respect personal space, protect confidences . . .

"I respect all of that, Annie, but Sienna is a murder suspect. The police think she killed her father. I know she was cutting herself. I strongly suspect she was being sexually abused. If Sienna was seeing a therapist, the police will want to talk to him."

Annie lowers her eyes, no longer certain what to do.

"Why are you here?" she asks.

"I'm trying to help her."

"Why?"

There is an accusation in her tone, a skepticism that makes her less attractive.

"Because I think Sienna is damaged and because she's my daughter's best friend."

"It's more than that."

Her eyes are fixed on mine, searching.

"Sienna was always at our place—staying for dinner or overnight, spending her weekends with us. Now I think she was avoiding going home. I should have realized."

As the words leave my lips I realize how they echo an inner voice that has been whispering to me ever since Zoe Hegarty's visit. It's as though I have a soundtrack playing in my head, along with images of a child waking each morning without seeing a world full of excitement and possibility. A child who didn't go skipping down the stairs to greet each new day; who didn't wear the bright, eager expression that said, "Hey, isn't it great to be alive!"

Annie steps closer, touching my shoulder. "You'll go mad if you try to blame yourself for this."

There is a ripple in the space between us, when I imagine kissing her or her kissing me. And I can see my hands running over her naked skin and her small dark nipples.

She steps away, faintly abashed. Whispers. "Such a ghostly girl, so pale and quiet."

"Was Sienna seeing a therapist?"

She nods.

"Did her parents know?"

"No. She wouldn't come to see me unless I promised I wouldn't tell them."

"Did she tell you what was wrong?"

Annie shakes her head. "She confided in one of the other teachers, Gordon Ellis, who urged her to talk to me." She looks around. "Gordon should be here soon. You could talk to him."

The school bell is sounding. Charlie will be getting out of class.

Annie turns back to the mirror, checking her hair and tugging at the collar of her blouse.

"I think her parents may have found out," she says.

"What makes you say that?"

"Her father came to the school and made a complaint to the headmaster."

"What about?"

"I'm not allowed to discuss it."

Excited voices drift from outside, the raucous clamor of students collecting books from lockers, preparing to go home. Annie looks at her watch. With a flourish, she picks up her paintbrush and tin of paint, heading back towards the stage.

"If you talk to Sienna, will you . . . will you . . ." She can't think of what to say. "Tell her we're missing her."

Charlie tosses her schoolbag in the back of the car and slides into the passenger seat. Her cheeks are pink with the cold and strands of hair have pulled from her ponytail. Without warning, she ducks down.

"What's wrong?"

"Nothing."

A boy walks in front of the car. His gelled hair sticks up at odd angles and his trousers hang so low on his hips I can see his brand of underwear.

Bless my little x-chromosome for giving me girls.

Charlie raises her head. Checks that he's gone. Sits up.

"Who is he?"

"No one."

"He must have a name."

"Jacob."

"Is Jacob a good or a bad thing?"

"Drop it, Dad."

"So you like him?"

"No!"

"Then why were you hiding?"

She rolls her eyes. Clearly I don't understand teenage love, which is obviously more complicated than adult love.

On the drive home I try to make conversation—asking about her day—but her answers come in single syllables. Yes. No. Good. Fine.

Finally she utters a complete sentence. "Did you see Sienna?"

"Yes."

"How is she?"

"As well as can be expected."

"What does that mean?"

"She can't remember everything that happened."

"Is that amnesia?"

"Sometimes the mind blocks things out . . . as a defense."

"Can I see her?"

"Maybe not yet."

There are so many questions I want to ask Charlie. Why was she crying at school? What's making her unhappy? Is it the nightmares? Why won't she talk to me?

"Did you know Sienna was cutting herself?" I ask.

Charlie doesn't respond.

"You knew?"

"Yeah."

"Did she say why?"

"She couldn't really explain."

"Was she unhappy?"

"I guess."

Staring out the window, she beats an edgy rhythm on her thigh.

"How did Sienna get on with her dad?"

"She said he was a Nazi."

"He was pretty strict."

"Way strict."

"Is that why she spent so much time at our place?"

Charlie nods. We're halfway home, driving through farmland that has been plowed into rich brown furrows tinged with green on the ridges. Seeded. Growing.

"What did you think of Mr. Hegarty?"

"He was OK, I guess."

"Just OK?"

"Whenever I stayed at Sienna's he got us a DVD and pizza. Sometimes he used to watch a movie with us."

"Did he ever make you feel uncomfortable?"

"Like how?"

"When you were staying at the house—

did he ever look at you, or brush against you, or say something to you that made you feel like you didn't want to be there?"

Her voice drops to a whisper and something slithers south in my chest, settling at the base of my stomach.

"Sienna always told me to lock the bathroom door. One night I was getting out of the shower and the doorknob turned, but the bolt was across. I asked who it was. Said I wouldn't be long."

"What happened?"

"The doorknob turned again."

12

Helen Hegarty holds the crumpled search warrant in her fist and steps aside. Heavy boots move with intent, going from room to room. Cupboards are opened, drawers pulled out, books feathered, CD cases pried open, rugs lifted . . .

For Helen this must seem like one more indignity added to a steaming pile—a dead husband, a traumatized family, bloodstains on her floorboards, fingerprint dust on her sills . . .

On the other side of the village, not far from the cottage, a long unbroken line of police officers shuffles across open ground. Uniformed. Silent. They call it a fingertip search, but nobody is crouching on hands and knees.

Charlie notices.

"What are they doing?"

"They're looking for something."

"What are they looking for?"

"Evidence."

DCI Cray is on the bridge, her fist clenched around a cigarette, rasping orders. She's dressed in a parka jacket and Wellingtons. They're using police dogs to trace Sienna's footsteps through the undergrowth.

Dropping Charlie at the cottage, I go back to the Hegartys' house where Helen has retreated outside, leaving the police searchers to do their worst. Pulling a cardigan tight around her chest, she lights a cigarette and ignores the stares of neighbors who have gathered to watch. Not embarrassed. Past caring.

"I didn't know you smoked."

"I confiscated them from Zoe."

Her son Lance is prowling the garden, thinking dark thoughts. The moment I step through the gate he confronts me, chest to chest, lips curled. A Union Jack tattoo flexes on his biceps.

"What are you doing here?"

"I'm just checking on your mum."

"You're working for them."

"I don't work for the police."

"Bullshit!"

Helen puts a hand on his forearm and the effect is remarkable. The frenetic energy drumming in his head seems to evaporate. Lance turns away. Paces the garden. Punches his thigh.

"He doesn't know what to do," whispers Helen. "He thinks he should be the man of the house . . . looking after us."

Something topples and breaks upstairs. She glances at the window and flinches. Then she gazes past me, as though imagining another life. Different choices.

Upstairs she has three shelves full of self-help books like *The Secret, Lose Your Friends and Find Yourself, Chasing Happiness* and *The Choice Is Yours.* Yet all this advice on forgiving herself and learning from her mistakes had simply depressed her even more with their messages of urgent hopefulness and relentless positivity.

Pulling a crumbling tissue from her sleeve, she has to squeeze it together to wipe her nose.

"Sienna didn't like you working nights."

Helen shakes her head. "We needed the money. Ray's new business took a while to get off the ground."

"That must have been hard."

"You do what has to be done."

"Did Ray and Sienna fight a lot?"

She shrugs. "They were like oil and water. One morning I came home and found her sleeping in the shed. Ray thought she'd run off."

"When was that?"

"She was eleven." Helen squints and stares past me down the lane. "Some kids want to grow up so quickly, you know. Sienna couldn't wait to get away."

"From Ray?"

"From home." She looks at me miserably. "I tried to be a good mother, but Sienna can be a terror—bunking off school, staying out late, drinking . . . I blame the boyfriend. Ever since he came on the scene she's stopped listening, you know. Now one of her teachers has made a complaint against her. Accused her of making nuisance phone calls."

"Which teacher?"

"Mr. Ellis. Teaches her drama. I told Sienna to leave the man alone."

"Why would she be calling Gordon Ellis?"

"Mr. and Mrs. Ellis have a little boy. Sienna used to babysit him, but that stopped a few weeks ago."

"Why?"

"Ray says he saw Mr. Ellis kissing Sienna one night when he dropped her home from babysitting."

"What did Sienna say?"

"She said nothing happened. She said Ray was mistaken. Mr. Ellis was just leaning across her to open the car door. Ray said she couldn't babysit anymore. It caused a huge row."

Another police car pulls up in the lane. Ronnie Cray emerges and walks quickly down the path to the front door. She signals to me, wanting me inside.

Apologizing to Helen, I follow the DCI through the house to a workshop in the back garden. An old motorcycle, partially disassembled, takes up much of the floor space. One entire wall above the workbench is hung with every tool imaginable. Beneath the bench there are clear plastic drawers containing nails, screws, brackets, nuts and bolts, as well as welding equipment and soldering irons. On the opposite wall, a series of shelves hold grease guns and cans of motoring oil. This is a proper workshop kept neatly ordered by a man who perhaps dreamed of being a craftsman but settled for something else.

Cray sits in a tall office chair with a wonky wheel. Her feet are propped on a milk crate.

"I have a hypothetical for you . . ." She laces her fingers together on her chest. "Psychologists like making excuses for people."

"We explain human behavior."

"OK, enlighten me. I can understand why a teenage girl might fight off her attacker. She might pick up a weapon. She might lash out and run off. Terrified. Traumatized. Is that true?"

"It's feasible."

"But would the same girl clean her hands in the bathroom sink and neatly fold the hand towel? Would she then take the weapon with her and try to dispose of it by throwing it from a bridge?"

I don't answer. Cray doesn't wait for me.

"Seems to me that any teenage girl who did that would be pretty clear-headed. I would even call her lucid. Maybe even calculating."

"You found the blade."

"We did."

"You searched beneath the bridge before."

"We missed it the first time. I'm charging Sienna Hegarty with murder."

There's no hint of triumphalism in her tone. Instead I sense an underlying sadness that her instincts had been right.

"What possible motive?" I hear myself say.

"She wanted him dead."

"It's that simple."

"Simple or hard, I don't differentiate, Professor. You try to understand human behavior. You try to explain it. Not me. I know we're smaller than gorillas, bigger than chimps, worse than both of them and, for all our rationality, our rules and laws, our baser drives are still straight out of the jungle."

13

Bristol Youth Court is a two-story annex in a dirty concrete building shared with the probation service and the family court. Through the vertical blinds I can see a double-decker bus rumbling past the window. The upper-deck passengers seem to float fifteen feet above the ground.

Sienna sits with a youth justice worker, whose name is Felicity and who looks like one of those solid, organized, capable girls who achieve everything with the minimum of fuss.

Normally so careful with her grooming, Sienna's hair needs washing and her fingernails are bitten to the quick. Felicity whispers encouragement to her, but Sienna might not be listening. She toys with the hem of her denim skirt. I notice a scar on her knee.

"How did that happen?" I ask.

"It was on my twelfth birthday. I fell out of a tree."

"Was it broken?"

"In three places. I don't remember the falling part. It was in the playground at school."

"At Shepparton Park?"

"Yeah. A boy called Malcolm Hogbin dared me to climb a tree. Malcolm Hogbin spent most of year seven calling me names and scrawling graffiti on my locker."

"So you took the dare?"

"Pretty stupid, huh?"

She picks at her fingernails.

Felicity leans closer and whispers. "So you understand what's going to happen today? They're going to read the charges and then your lawyer will ask for bail. The magistrates might ask you some questions. Speak clearly. Hold your head up."

"Then can I go home?"

"They have to decide."

"But I want to go home."

"Mr. D'Angelo will talk to them."

"I don't want to go back to that other place."

"Wait and see."

Sienna looks at me for support. Her whole body reacts with a start when a court usher calls her name. She holds her stomach, as though about to vomit. Taking her arm, I lead her into a room that looks more like an office than a court. The tables, benches and chairs are all on the same level and a large flat-screen TV dominates one wall, opposite a coat of arms.

Helen Hegarty is sitting in the front row next to Lance. Zoe's wheelchair is partially blocking the central aisle. Sienna gives her a little wave and a smile.

Three magistrates sit side by side at a large oak table, dressed in layman's clothes. Two women and a man, they look more like librarians than court officials.

Sienna takes a seat beside Mr. D'Angelo, her solicitor, who seems to know everyone in the room, chatting to the prosecutor and the court clerk as though swapping stories about their plans for the weekend.

The charges are read aloud, mentioning Ray Hegarty's full name and giving the time, date and place of his death. The word "murdered" brings a sob from Helen, who is somewhere behind me. Sienna seems to be shrinking under the gaze of the magistrates. I keep thinking of Alice in Wonderland meeting the Queen of Hearts.

"Is your name Sienna Jane Hegarty?"

She nods.

"And your date of birth is twelfth September 1995?"

"Yes."

"And you live at home with your mother?"

"That's right."

"Do you understand the charge?"

"Yes."

"You can sit down now, Sienna."

Then the lawyers start putting their arguments for and against bail. The prosecutor has bright red lipstick and monotone clothes. She wants Sienna kept in "secure accommodation" because of her history of "self-abuse." Mr. D'Angelo argues that she should be allowed home because of her age and her previous good record. Sienna's head swings from side to side as if she's watching a ball hit back and forth across a net.

The middle magistrate—the only man—has skin the color of putty and a wheezing voice.

"Do you want to go back to school, Sienna?" he asks.

"Yes, sir."

"What are your favorite subjects?"

"English and drama."

"If you couldn't go back to school, what would you do?"

Sienna shrugs. "Whatever I was told."

The magistrates smile.

"Do you help your mum around the house?" asks the female magistrate on the right.

"Sometimes."

"Do you do any of the cooking?"

"Not really."

The magistrate glances at a piece of paper in her hands. "You've been charged with a very serious offense, Sienna."

"I didn't do it."

"That's not what we're here for today."

"But I didn't—"

Mr. D'Angelo puts his hand on Sienna's shoulder and she flinches as though scalded. "You don't have to say anything," he tells her.

"But I want them to know."

"That happens another day."

"Why can't it be now?"

The magistrates confer, speaking in whispers that are barely audible above the hum of the air conditioning.

The senior magistrate announces their decision. Because of Sienna's history of self-harm she is to be remanded to a youth psychiatric care unit until a proper assessment can be made of her mental state.

Mr. D'Angelo stands. "Professor Joseph O'Loughlin, a clinical psychologist, is in court today. He knows the accused. Perhaps he could be heard?"

The magistrates confer again briefly.

"Professor O'Loughlin can prepare a psych report. How long does he need?"

Mr. D'Angelo turns and leans on the back of his chair, whispering, "You willing to do this?"

"I think I've just been volunteered."

"How long do you need?"

"Three weeks."

The magistrates agree and re-list Sienna's case at the Crown Court. Sienna turns to me. "Can I go home?"

"Not yet."

"Why?"

"They want to send you to a hospital."

"I've been to hospital."

"This one is different. They're worried you might harm yourself."

Sienna shakes her head.

"So I can't go home?"

"Not yet."

She grabs my wrist. "Don't let them lock me up. You have to tell them. I didn't do it."

14

Julianne has her dinner tonight with Harry Veitch. I'm looking after the girls. I shower and shave and search for a clean shirt. Eventually I'm forced to settle on something Emma bought me for Father's Day, which makes me look like Willy Wonka.

Julianne opens the door. "You really *are* having a midlife crisis."

"I ran out of shirts."

"What about the washing machine?"

"I forgot to turn it on."

"How you doing for underwear?"

"My days-of-the-week boxers will last me till Monday."

She steps back and checks herself in the hallway mirror. She's wearing a mid-length skirt and boots with a white blouse and the earrings—black pearls on silver clasps. I bought them for her thirtieth birthday.

"You don't have to babysit."

"I know. I miss them."

"I thought you might want to spy on me."

She gives the mirror her Mona Lisa smile, which annoys me.

"Unless I'm cramping your style," I say. "You might want to bring Harry back. I could leave early . . ."

She's not going to rise to the bait. Reapplying her lipstick in the mirror, she makes a popping sound. That's one of the things I have always loved about Julianne—she abides by the philosophy that the important thing about lipstick is not the color but to accept God's final word on where your lips end.

"How is the trial?" I ask.

"They seem to waste so much time arguing over what evidence is admissible and not admissible. The jury gets sent out. The judge makes a ruling. Then they troop back in again."

She adjusts her hair. "Stacey Dobson gave evidence yesterday. She's the sister of Gary Dobson—one of the accused. The day before the firebombing she made a complaint to the police that she'd been raped. She said four men had lured her into a van and taken her to a house. They were asylum seekers and she named Marco Kostin."

"And they raped her?"

"No, she made it all up. She and Marco were sweet on each other. They'd been out a few times."

"Why would she make up a story like that?"

"Stacey thought she was going to get into trouble for staying out late. Her parents were angry. They called the police and Stacey was too frightened to recant. Eventually she told the truth, but Marco's house was firebombed the next night."

"As payback."

"That's what the prosecution is arguing."

Julianne notices Charlie sitting at the top of the stairs and quickly changes the subject. "The girls have eaten. There are leftovers if you're hungry." Raising her voice slightly, "Charlie should be doing her homework."

She glances up the stairs again. Empty now.

A car pulls up outside. Harry drives a black Lexus, which he replaces every year. Julianne grabs her handbag but stops before she reaches the door.

"My pashmina—I left it on the bed."

"I'll get it."

"No, I'll go."

She hurries upstairs while I watch Harry get out of his car and adjust his trousers, touching his hair. The Lexus lights up from every corner as the central locking engages.

He rings the doorbell. I don't want to talk to him but Julianne hasn't returned.

"Harry."

"Joseph."

A touch of concern appears in his eyes, like a slight fever.

"Julianne won't be a moment. She's getting something upstairs."

"Right. Good." He rocks on his heels. "This is a little embarrassing."

"Why?"

"Well, you know . . . you being here."

"It's still my house, Harry."

"Of course."

I step to one side, allowing him in, trying to sound relaxed and friendly, when in reality I want to take a swing at his jaw or sink my fist into his stomach, which looks soft and flabby.

Maybe I should warn him about Julianne's little foibles—how she likes dunking chocolate biscuits in her tea and how she always has to wear something blue, and that when she plays Monopoly she insists on being the boot.

Harry hasn't asked to see the owner's manual. He doesn't know that she likes having her feet massaged and hates having her earlobes licked. That she thinks all professional sport is manufactured drama with overpaid actors and trying to explain the offside rule with salt and pepper shakers, silverware and a loud voice is not going to make it any easier for her to understand.

Why should I? Why should I give him any help at all?

Harry's hair is neatly parted on the right and I can smell his aftershave.

"She's great, isn't she?" he says, referring to Julianne.

I can't believe it. He wants to talk about my wife. When he's known her for twenty-six years and been married to her for twenty—then we can talk.

"She shouldn't be long," I say. "She's just taking her medication."

"Medication? Is she ill?"

"No, of course not, not really." I lower my voice. "She doesn't like to talk about it. Upsets her." I glance up the stairs. "You could do me a favor."

"What's that?"

"Don't let Julianne order dessert. See if you can talk her out of it. It's the sugar. She craves it but she shouldn't have any. Too much and . . ."

"What?"

I hold a finger to my lips. "It's not a big deal—just keep her away from the dessert trolley."

Harry nods. "I will. Definitely."

He looks positively grateful, eager to help. I should feel guilty. Jealousy is a terrible thing. I know all the psychological triggers. The fear of losing control, the fear of loss, the fear of abandonment, neglect and loneliness . . . But the most destructive thing about jealousy is that it kills what it values—the love you want to save won't survive the constraints of jealousy. There is no entitlement. Love is either equal or a tragedy.

Julianne appears. The pashmina is wrapped around her shoulders. She smiles at Harry and looks at me questioningly.

"Is everything all right?"

"Fine."

"Don't let Emma stay up too late."

"I won't."

"That was pretty weird," says Charlie, appearing on the stairs again. She's dressed in her flannelette pajamas, a pair so stretched at the waist they hang on her hips. "Did you want to hit him?"

"Why would I want to hit Harry?"

"Isn't that what boys do when they're jealous?"

"No, not always. Hardly ever. And I'm not jealous."

"So you're OK?"

"I'm good."

She gives me the same sort of questioning look I got from her mother. Leaning against the wall, I close my eyes and try not to picture Julianne and Harry in the car, in conversation.

"So what do you think of Harry?" I ask.

She shrugs. "He's OK, I guess. He cooks Coca-Cola-flavored chicken and has a cool car."

"Coca-Cola-flavored chicken?"

"It tastes better than it sounds." She hesitates, tugging at her bottom lip with her front teeth. "He's not a loser, Dad."

At that moment I feel something stretch and break inside me. Not something vital or essential, but a single strand that floats broken in the wake of Charlie's words.

Emma wanders out of her room. She wants a story. This will mean reading two stories and making a third one up involving stuffed animals and the "tickling spider" that lives in my pocket.

Later, when she's finally asleep, Charlie and I watch a movie which isn't age appropriate according to the British Board of Film Classification, but a few swear words and a token fight won't scar her emotionally. The elephant in the room is Sienna. Charlie hasn't mentioned her but I know she wants to ask.

The credits are rolling. She stares at her feet.

"Kids were talking yesterday."

"At school?"

"Yeah."

"What were they saying?"

"That Sienna has been charged with murder."

"That's true."

Charlie shakes her head adamantly. "She didn't do it."

"You don't know that."

"Yes, I do. She was scared of her dad. She didn't like him. But she wouldn't kill him."

"People don't always do what we expect."

I'm thinking of Julianne and not Sienna.

Charlie hikes up her pajamas. "Are you going to help her?"

"There's nothing I can do."

"Yes, you can."

"It's not as simple as that."

"But you know people." She wipes her eyes with the sleeve of her pajamas. Still they shine. "You can find the person who did it."

"I'm not a detective."

I know what she's suggesting, but she's asking too much.

"You're tired. Go to bed. Get some sleep."

I hear the stairs creak as she climbs them. She pauses on the landing, speaking in a stage whisper.

"Goodnight, Dad."

15

Perched on the edge of the Bristol Channel, surrounded by nineteen acres of grounds and ringed by trees and an iron-spiked fence, Oakham House is called a Regional Secure Unit. In the old days it would have been an asylum or a special hospital, but no matter what label they assign it now, the stigma remains.

Walton, the nearest village, is half a mile away, Bristol another ten. That's the one abiding feature governing the construction and placement of any psychiatric unit—out of sight, out of mind. It has been that way for more than two hundred years.

Sienna is sitting at a window with one leg propped on the sill, hugging her knee, while her other leg dangles to where her toes brush the floor. She's wearing a dress that is too big for her and a shapeless woolen cardigan. A strand of dark wool has pulled from the sleeve and she worries it with her fingers, rolling it back and forth under her palm.

Condensation has misted the window. She reaches out and draws her finger through it. Outside, the Bristol Channel is dotted with whitecaps, which my father calls "white horses," although I've never understood why.

I stand in the doorway of the lounge watching Sienna. Her movements are almost exaggerated in their slowness and everything about her body language seems to be passive and resigned.

I say hello and she rewards me with a huge smile.

"I thought you'd come."

"Why's that?"

"I just knew. I was sitting here thinking how nice it would be to talk to someone, and here you are."

The statement is so matter-of-fact that I can almost believe she willed me into being. She reaches into the pocket of her cardigan and pulls out three small fruits with dark orange skin.

"Do you know the difference between a tangerine and a clementine?"

I shake my head.

"Tangerines aren't as sweet." She hands

me one. "Fresh fruit is really good for you. It will help you with that."

She motions at my left hand where my thumb and forefinger are pill-rolling. I fight the urge to put the hand in my pocket.

"So why do you shake?"

"It's nothing."

Sienna looks disappointed. "That's your first lie."

"How do you know I'm lying?"

"I can tell."

I press my thumb into the tangerine. The skin peels easily, filling the room with citrus smells.

"I want to talk about what happened the other night."

Almost immediately I sense her mind trying to flee. No longer looking at me, she squeezes the peel in her fist.

"I know you're scared."

"I want to go home."

"I know, but first you have to answer some questions. The court wants me to prepare a psych report."

"What does that mean?"

"They want to know if you're likely to hurt yourself or hurt someone else."

"I wouldn't."

She turns to the window again, as though frightened of missing someone arriving.

"I can't *make* you talk to me, Sienna, which means you're in control of this conversation. I'm not going to get upset or irritated if you don't say anything. I'm not going to get angry or annoyed. The very worst that can happen is I walk out of here and say you weren't able to speak to me."

I can see her visibly relax. She pops a segment of tangerine into her mouth and crushes it between her teeth.

"So, tell me how you're feeling."

"Lonely. Homesick."

"You've been charged with the most serious crime imaginable."

"I didn't do it."

"You told the police you wanted him dead—you wished for it."

"That's not the same thing. That's just using words." Her rope-like curls sway against her cheeks. "Robin says I'm supposed to separate bad memories into colored's and whites—just like the washing—and run them through the machine. Wash them away. Put them on a heavy wash and spin cycle. I laughed when he told me that, but Robin makes it sound so normal."

"Who's Robin?"

"My therapist."

Robin Blaxland. Annie Robinson arranged for Sienna to see him.

"Did you talk to Robin about your father?"

"Sometimes."

"Will you talk to me?"

Again she shrugs.

I ask her to sit on the sofa, lean back and close her eyes. Breathe deeply.

"Feel your nostrils opening slightly as you inhale. The air feels cooler as you breathe in and warmer as you breathe out. Feel the change in temperature. How your breath fills your lungs."

"What are you going to do?"

"I'm just going to talk. If I ask you something that upsets you, or makes you frightened, I want you to raise your right hand. Just lift your fingers a little and I'll know to stop. That's our special signal."

Sienna nods.

"Let's start at the beginning. Where were you born?"

"Bristol."

"You're the youngest."

"Yeah."

"How old is Zoe?"

"Nineteen."

"And Lance?"

"Twenty-two."

Sticking to closed questions, I gently draw out her history, which takes a long time because her answers are devoid of detail. Sienna talks about school—her favorite subject is English, her favorite teacher is Mrs. Adelaide. I ask about other subjects and other teachers.

An odd detail emerges. An omission. She doesn't mention Gordon Ellis, her drama teacher, yet the musical is all she and Charlie have talked about for months. They have sung into hairbrushes and danced in front of the mirror.

I take her back to Tuesday and the rehearsal.

"Do you remember getting into trouble with Mr. Ellis?"

"Yes."

"Mr. Ellis was quite hard on you."

"I'm used to it."

"Do you like him?"

"He's OK."

"You babysit his little boy."

"Sometimes."

"How do you get home afterwards?"

"He drops me."

"Did your father ever argue with Mr. Ellis?"

Sienna's hand rises. She doesn't want to talk about it.

"You don't want to talk about your dad or Mr. Ellis?"

Sienna's hand rises again. As promised, I change the subject and ask her instead about Danny Gardiner.

"Where did you meet him?"

"It was ages ago. He went to school with Lance."

"But you hooked up with him?"

"Yes."

"When was that?"

"Early last year."

"Does he pick you up after school sometimes?"

She nods.

"Where do you go?"

"The cinema or the mall or just for a drive."

"Where did you go after Danny dropped you off last Tuesday?"

"Nowhere."

"You mentioned your therapist, Robin. Is that where you went on Tuesday?"

"No."

"Where then?"

Her fingers begin to rise.

"You don't want to tell me."

She nods.

"Who are you protecting, Sienna?"

"No one."

I back off again, asking her instead about later that night.

"What time did you get home?"

"About ten thirty."

"Did someone drop you?"

"I caught the bus to Hinton Charterhouse and walked the rest of the way."

Two motorists reported seeing a blond-haired girl in a short dress walking down Hinton Hill on the night of the murder.

"That's a two-mile walk."

She doesn't reply.

"Were there lights on in the house?"

"I don't remember."

"Think back. Put yourself outside the house again. It's late. You're tired. You've walked home. You step through the gate. What do you see?"

"A light in the hall."

"Is that unusual?"

"Mum normally leaves it on."

"Where is your key?"

"In my schoolbag."

"Can you see yourself getting the key out, unlocking the door?"

She nods.

"You're opening it."

"Yes."

"What do you see?"

"I look on the phone table to see if there are any messages on the answering machine or letters for me. Mum sometimes leaves me a note."

"What about this time?"

"No."

"What do you see?"

"The door under the stairs is open. Daddy's overnight bag is inside. Unzipped. I see his shaving gear and dirty clothes."

"How does that make you feel?"

"He's not supposed to be home until Friday."

"Does that bother you?"

"I don't like being alone with him."

"What else do you see?"

"A light at the top of the stairs."

"What about downstairs?"

"I can hear the TV."

"What are you thinking?"

"If I can get to my room I'll be OK. There won't be a scene. I can lock the door and go to bed and he won't bother me."

"How does he bother you?"

Her fingers rise and fall. She doesn't want to talk about it.

"What happens next?" I ask.

"I creep up the stairs, trying to be quiet. The fourth step has a squeak. I step over it."

Her breath quickens.

"What is it?"

"I hear something."

"What do you hear?"

"A toilet flushing, then a tap running . . . in the bathroom."

"You're sure?"

"He's upstairs. I have to hurry."

"Where were you?"

"At the top of the stairs. My room is just there. I have to be quick. I have to get inside."

Her hands go to her mouth.

"What?"

"I'm falling."

"Down the stairs?"

A long pause. "He's lying on the floor . . . Daddy. Not moving. I'm on top of him."

Her whole body is shaking.

"What do you see?"

"Blood. Everywhere. The floor is wet. I'm sitting in it. I try to scream, but no sound comes out. And I'm wiping my hands over and over, but I can't get it off."

"Can you hear anything?"

"A rushing sound in my head—it's like the wind only louder and it fills every space and blocks out every other sound. I can't make it stop."

Sienna covers her ears.

"Is there someone else in the house, Sienna?"

She's not listening. I hold her face in my hands, making her focus on me. "Is there someone in the house?"

A whisper: "Yes."

"Can you see who it is?"

"No."

Fear floods her eyes. Suddenly, she's on her feet, trying to run. I catch her before she can take more than two steps, wrapping my arms around her, lifting her easily. She's fighting at my arms, her legs pumping. Mucus streams from her mouth and nose.

"Shhh, it's OK. You're safe. You're with me."

Slowly the fear evaporates. It's like watching an inflatable-pool toy spring a leak and sag into a crumpled puddle of plastic. I put her back on the sofa and she curls her knees to her chest, closing her eyes. Spent. Raw.

The interview has taken three hours but Sienna can tell me nothing more. Her emotions can't be detached from her memories. I risk traumatizing her if I keep pushing.

Whoever killed Ray Hegarty was still in the house when Sienna came home. SOCO found blood in the S-bend of the sink. The killer was cleaning up. Wiping the blade clean.

An intruder? A robbery gone wrong? There were no signs of forced entry, yet Sienna's laptop is missing. Far more expensive items were untouched.

Ray Hegarty wasn't expected home until Friday. Helen Hegarty worked nights. Sienna spent most evenings alone. Whoever killed Ray Hegarty was inside the house. Waiting.

Who were they waiting for?

16

The journey to London takes just over two hours by car. I leave after the morning peak and arrive before midday, pulling into a side street off Fulham Palace Road where I'm held to ransom by a parking machine.

Walking back to the main road, I head towards the echoing shadows of Hammersmith flyover past empty shops and "For Lease" signs. London is bleeding. It's like a virus that is spreading from the top down. No job is secure enough. No mortgage small enough.

London has changed in the past two years. People have changed. I thought it would be something violent and shocking that altered this city—an outrage like the July 7 bombings or our version of 9/11—but it was something else: a financial meltdown, a banking crisis triggered on the far side of the world by poor people who couldn't repay their loans.

As I get near the Thames I can smell the

mud flats and brine. I'm visiting a friend—a former detective inspector with the Metropolitan Police called Vincent Ruiz, who retired five years ago.

Broad like a bear with a busted nose and booze-stained cheeks, Ruiz has had three marriages and three divorces. World-weary and fatalistic, I sometimes think he's a walking, talking cliché—the heavy-drinking, womanizing ex-detective—but he's more complicated than that. He once arrested me for murder. I once rescued him from himself. Friendships have flourished on less.

We've arranged to meet at a pub on the river, not far from where he lives. The Blue Anchor is tucked in the shadows of Hammersmith Bridge where patrons can watch the rowers skim across the water and tourist boats chug west towards Hampton Court.

Whitewashed with a blue trim, the pub has nautical paraphernalia on the walls and Van Morrison on the sound system. Ruiz is waiting at the bar. He's a big man with big hands. One of them is wrapped around a pint glass.

"Professor."

"Vincent."

"A shirt like that deserves a drink."

It's another of Emma's choices.

"What would happen if I had matching trousers?" I ask.

"I'd have to make a citizen's arrest. Don't look at me like that—I don't make the rules."

Ruiz is in a good mood, telling jokes and stories. We shoot the breeze about family and rugby. He's on the committee of his local rugby club, which had a winning season.

We've spent a lot of meals like this but mostly when Julianne was still with me. Ruiz would flirt with her shamelessly and call her high maintenance, while she treated him like a naughty schoolboy who refused to grow up.

We order. The waitress suggests the special, a vegetarian lasagna. Ruiz tells her he didn't fight his way to the top of the food chain to be a vegetarian. He orders the rump steak. Medium rare. Mashed potatoes with butter not oil. Pepper sauce on the side.

The waitress turns to me. Her name is Polly.

"I'll have the Ploughman's."

She looks relieved. Ruiz orders another beer. He's dressed in casual trousers and a sweatshirt. I seem to remember him making a promise when he left the Met that he would never wear a tie again unless it was to a rugby dinner or a funeral.

"So how's Julianne?"

"She's interpreting—working on a big trial."

Ruiz waits for something more, sensing it, but I don't want to talk about Ho-ho-ho Harry Veitch.

"So why are you really here?"

"I need your help."

"You're in trouble."

"No."

I tell him about Sienna and her father, trying to keep the emotion out of my voice by sticking to the facts. Even so, I can hear myself defending her, putting the best possible spin on the evidence.

Ruiz keeps his head down as he listens.

"What makes you so sure she's innocent?" he asks.

"She says she didn't do it."

"Everybody lies."

"There was somebody else in the house.

They stood behind the door in the bedroom. They were waiting."

He looks straight through me, keeping his thoughts to himself. "Any other suspects?"

I mention Sienna's boyfriend Danny Gardiner and her brother Lance, who had no alibi for the night of the murder.

"Are we talking about Sugar Ray Hegarty?" asks Ruiz. "Worked out of Bristol CID?"

"You knew him?"

"We helped each other out once or twice."

"What was he like?"

"Old school."

"Fair?"

"And hard."

Ruiz gazes into his pint, as if saying a silent prayer. "Typical, isn't it? You survive a career like his and all the terrible shit happens after you're out. I remember his daughter getting crippled by that sadistic fuck—what was his name?"

"Liam Baker."

"Yeah, him."

Ruiz wants to know the details of Ray

Hegarty's death, taking down correct spellings and looking for inconsistencies. Sienna's laptop is missing and her room had been searched.

"Anything else taken in the house?"

"Nothing."

I can see his mind working. What could a teenage girl have on her computer that was worth stealing?

"What about the son?"

"Lance didn't get on with his father, they were always fighting, but I don't think he could have done this."

"Why?"

"Cutting someone's throat is personal. It's hands-on. It takes courage. Anger. Lance was frightened of his old man."

Ruiz nods.

"You might want to take a look at a schoolteacher: Gordon Ellis."

"What's his story?"

"He teaches music and drama at a secondary school. Lives locally. Married. One child. I think Sienna confided in him; she might have told him about the abuse, but when I mentioned his name, she clammed up and wouldn't talk about him."

"You hit a raw nerve?"

"It might be nothing. About ten days before the murder, Ray Hegarty had an argument outside his house with someone who dropped Sienna home. The police haven't been able to ID the driver, but it could have been Gordon Ellis. Sienna used to babysit for Ellis and according to Helen Hegarty, Ray saw the two of them kissing. Sienna denied it, but Hegarty made a complaint to the school. I don't know if the two events are related, but Gordon Ellis has since accused Sienna of harassing him with phone calls."

Ruiz pats his pockets and his coat rattles. He used to be a smoker, but now he sucks on boiled sweets that will rot his teeth instead of his lungs.

"Who's heading the investigation?"

"Ronnie Cray."

"She still rolling her own tampons?"

Political correctness is not one of Ruiz's strong suits. He once told me that being politically correct was like pretending you could pick up a dog turd by the clean end.

"I thought you weren't going to help the police out anymore," he says.

"This is different."

"Meaning?"

"Sienna Hegarty is Charlie's best friend."

Ruiz nods and leans back as our meals arrive. Tucking a paper serviette into his collar, he rubs his knife and fork together and tucks in. As he chews he mulls over the information.

"So I'll run a few checks. See what I can find out." Then he puts on a West Country accent. "Maybe I'll drive down your way and spend a few days in your neck of the woods."

"I'll tell all the single women in town what a stud you are."

"I believe that memo has already been sent."

The rest of our lunch is spent swapping stories of family and trying to outdo each other in the dysfunctional relatives stakes. In truth, whenever I talk to Ruiz I don't feel so badly about my own parents. His mother suffers from dementia and lives in a nursing home. The only thing she remembers with any clarity is the war and every embarrassing detail of Ruiz's childhood, which she repeats in a megaphone voice whenever he visits her.

"Do our children talk about us like this?" he asks.

"Probably."

My mobile is vibrating. I pull it out and stare at the screen, not recognizing the number.

"Professor O'Loughlin?"

"Yes."

"You might remember me—Dr. Martinez. I treated Sienna Hegarty when they brought her into hospital."

A pause. In the background I can hear the sound of the hospital PA system.

"You asked me about a rape test and I said I couldn't perform one without her parents' permission."

"Yes."

"There was evidence of rough sex, which might have been rape. And there's something else. She miscarried."

The statement fizzes inside my brain like an aspirin disappearing in a glass of water.

Dr. Martinez continues, "She must have lost the fetus on the night she came in."

"How many weeks was she?" I can't recognize my own voice.

"I ran a blood pregnancy test for levels of hCG. The hormone level doubles every two days for four weeks after conception. Given her levels and the amount of blood we found on her clothes, I'd say she was in her first trimester—at least four weeks, no more than ten."

He stops talking. The silence stretches out.

"Are you still there?" he asks.

"Yes."

"I'm not sure if I've done the right thing, but since you'd asked . . ."

"Thank you, I appreciate that."

He's about to hang up when something occurs to me. "Would she have known?" I ask.

"She was late. Most women know their cycles."

There was no evidence of a pregnancy test found at the house, but Sienna would most likely have destroyed the test kit.

Closing the phone, I stare at the screen as the light fades. Ruiz is watching me from the opposite side of the table.

"She was pregnant," I whisper. "She miscarried on the night of the murder."

"Can they do a paternity test?"

"Not without the fetus."

17

Just south of Reading, I pull into a motorway service center and park among the long-haul trucks and tourist coaches. Hiking across the parking lot, I enter a brightly lit lobby full of fast-food outlets and shops.

The men's room is cavernous but I still have to queue for a urinal. The men around me are truckers in plaid shirts or football strips hung over beer guts. One of them hauls up his jeans and saunters off like a man who has marked his territory.

My left hand is trembling. My bladder won't do as it's told. I stand and stare at the wall. Someone has scrawled a message in marker pen above the urinal: *"Express Lane: five beers or less."*

Nothing is happening. The queue is getting longer.

"Are you gonna piss or just piss me off?" says a trucker with a wallet chained to his belt.

"I'm sorry. I won't be a moment."

He grunts and says something to the

person next to him. They laugh. It's not going to happen now. That's one of the problems with my medication. I used to piss like a racehorse. Now I squirt and dribble.

Outside the restroom I put in a call to Trinity Road Police Station. Ronnie Cray is in a meeting. Monk answers her phone. Certain people don't match their voices, but Monk's comes from deep in his chest and seems to rumble down the line as if he's standing in a tunnel.

"Danny Gardiner?"

"What about him?"

"Did you interview him?"

"Yes."

"Sienna was pregnant."

I can hear Monk exhale slowly.

"The boss isn't here."

"Can you take me?"

Monk hesitates momentarily. We'll meet at Danny Gardiner's house.

I have the rest of the journey to consider the implications of Sienna's pregnancy. I think back to the afternoon I collected her and Charlie from school. Sienna had seemed distracted and upset. I thought she was annoyed about the rehearsal and being made to stay behind. Even so, she skipped into her boyfriend's arms, kissing his lips, sliding her hand down his back.

Danny Gardiner told police that he'd dropped Sienna on a street corner in Bath only thirty minutes later. Where did she go? Three hours are missing from the timeline.

Danny lives with his mother in Twerton on the western outskirts of Bath where most of the older houses are clustered around St. Michael's Parish Church. The newer estates have encroached onto farmland and already I see white pegs marking out more plots of land.

Monk is waiting in an unmarked police car.

"What did Cray say?"

"Nothing."

"You didn't tell her."

"I'm doing you a favor."

Nobody answers the door. Monk knocks again. Then we wait. The sky is low and gray, smelling of woodsmoke and rain.

A white hatchback pulls into a parking space ahead of us. A woman in her fifties emerges, dressed in a tour guide's uniform. She collects a bag of groceries from the boot and walks to the house, cursing as she drops her keys.

"Mrs. Gardiner?" I ask.

"Who wants to know?"

The door swings inwards and a long-haired dog that could have a head at either end dances around her stockinged legs, yapping.

She turns, waiting for an answer.

"We're looking for Danny."

"He's talked to you lot already."

"Not to me."

Her blue-gray eyes examine me quickly and then settle on Monk, gazing at him as though he's sprouted from magic beans in her front garden. "Lordy, your mother must have gone cross-eyed having you. How tall?"

"Six-four last time I measured."

"I think you've grown since then, love. You should have played basketball."

"Yes, ma'am."

She has stepped inside the hallway. The house smells of damp dog, air freshener and dope. Mrs. Gardiner lifts her shopping bags over the threshold, using one hand to hold the collar of the dog.

"I haven't seen Danny since yesterday."

"His car is outside," says Monk.

"Must have taken the bus," she replies.

"That's too bad. We'll have to tow the car. Forensic boys want to pull it apart. Tell him we'll put it back together again . . . best we can."

Two beats of silence follow before Danny bursts out of a bedroom, barefoot, bare-chested, wearing low-slung jeans. Marijuana smoke wafts in his wake.

"Not me fucking car! I just finished paying it off."

Danny reaches the front door and bounces off Monk's chest.

"The car's fine. We just need to ask you a few questions."

"I answered your questions."

"More of them."

"Fuck off!"

Mrs. Gardiner clips him around the ear. "Mind your language."

Danny nurses the side of his head where three studs decorate the cartilage above his ear.

"I suppose you'd better come in then," says Mrs. Gardiner. "Carry them bags, Danny."

We follow her along a hallway into a tired-looking kitchen, with red-painted cupboards and a fridge that doubles as a notice board. She begins unpacking her groceries while Danny pulls a bottle of soft drink from a bag. She tells him to get a glass. He rolls his eyes.

"What's he done now?" she asks Monk.

"We want to ask him about his girlfriend."

"A girl? That's all he thinks about—girls. You should see the state of his bed sheets."

Danny gives her a murderous look.

"Lazy, just like his dad. Spends his time tinkering with cars. Not really a proper job, is it?" Mrs. Gardiner sizes Monk up again. "How tall you say you were, Detective?"

"Six-four."

"I've got a job for you. Won't take a minute."

"I'm needed here."

"Don't take two of you to talk to Danny. Call it a community service."

Mrs. Gardiner is halfway down the hall, motioning to him to follow. Monk glances at me, hoping to be rescued, and then reluctantly accepts his fate.

Danny relaxes now that his mother is no longer orbiting.

"Do you remember me?" I ask.

Danny shakes his head.

"I saw you outside Sienna's house last Wednesday morning."

He screws up his face. "Wasn't me."

"You legged it when I tried to talk to you. Almost ran me down in that car of yours. That's one of the problems with having a distinctive-looking car, Danny. You think it makes a bold statement, but it sticks out like a turd in a punchbowl."

Danny is working his tongue around his cheek as though counting his teeth. His hair sticks up at odd angles and I can see traces of pimple cream dabbed on his forehead. For all his brazen defiance, he doesn't look particularly tough or aggressive. He has small hands. Delicate features.

"Tell me about Sienna Hegarty."

"What about her?"

"Is she your girlfriend?"

"She's a friend."

"She's underage."

"So what?"

"How old are you, Danny?"

"Twenty-two."

"Don't you know any horny girls your own age?"

"I get my share."

"So why Sienna?"

"Listen, I'm not shagging her, OK, and if she says I am then she's a lying cow. We're mates."

"Mates?"

"Yeah. We hang out together. I drive her around the place. Drop her off."

"And what do you get in return?"

He shrugs.

"Come on, Danny, I wasn't born yesterday. You're trying to tell me that you hang out with a hot-looking fourteen-year-old because she's a mate."

"Yeah, well, I figured one day, you know . . ."

"One day?"

"She might pay out, you know. When she's legal?"

"You're lying."

"No."

"Sienna was pregnant. You knocked her up."

"No fucking way!" His voice grows shrill. "I just take her places. Drop her off. I'm not shagging her. Haven't touched her."

"No?"

"It's true."

"Either tell me the truth, Danny, or Detective Abbott is going to search your room.

He'll find your hash and your porn magazines and whatever else you're hiding. Then he'll take you down to the station and put you in a cell downstairs with the drunks and the perverts and the drug addicts. Do you know how long a night lasts in a place like that? By morning you'll be an old man."

Sweat pops out on Danny's forehead and runs down the side of his nose. He's trying to look like he doesn't care, but I can see his mind working.

"I saw you with Sienna last Tuesday. Where did you go?"

"We drove around for a while, then I dropped her off."

"What time was that?"

"Seven."

"Where did you drop her?"

"In town."

He names a street corner on Lower Bristol Road.

"Why did she want to go there?"

Danny shrugs. "That's where she told me to drop her. She had the address on a piece of paper."

"And you just drove away?"

"Yep." One of his feet is jiggling up and down.

"Where did you go?"

"A mate's place."

"For how long?"

"I kipped on his sofa. I was there all night."

"What's your mate's name?"

Danny reacts as though scalded. "What difference does that make? He's just a mate."

Something about the response borders on panic. Danny's eyes have clouded over and his hands are pressed to the top of his thighs. There is something slightly effeminate about the pose. In that instant I suddenly see him clearly. I pull my chair closer and tell him to relax.

"I don't want to know your friend's name, Danny. It's not important."

He visibly relaxes.

"Sienna is a pretty girl," I say. "Did you tell your mates you were doing her?"

Danny doesn't answer.

"It's important to have a girlfriend, isn't it? Otherwise your mates might think you're not interested in girls."

He blinks at me.

"I mean, it must be tough—being a mechanic. All those girlie calendars in the workshop, the wolf whistles, the banter about Page Three girls; it's a job for blokes."

"What do you mean?"

"Your mates think you're doing her, don't they? They're in awe of you. Lucky bugger, they say, but I think Sienna just pretends to be your girlfriend."

Excuses clot in the back of Danny's throat.

"I think you arrange to pick her up and she's all over you, putting on a good show for your mates. That's when you tell them you need some privacy."

"I don't know what you're on about."

"Sure you do. You're both trying to hide something. You have a boyfriend . . . and so does Sienna."

Danny leaps to his feet. His chair crashes to the floor. "I'M NOT QUEER! IT'S A LIE! YOU TAKE THAT BACK!"

He's pleading with me, his face twisting in suffering. I pick up the chair and tell him to sit down. He slumps over his knees, staring at the floor.

"Listen, Danny, I don't care how many boyfriends you have. Just tell me about Sienna."

Pressing his lips tightly together, he contemplates what to do. He can hear his mother laughing in the front room. He glances sidelong at the door.

"She was seeing someone else," he mutters.

"Who?"

"I don't know. I just dropped her off."

"Did you always drop her at the same place?"

"No, it was different each time."

"And then what happened?"

"I drove away."

"You're lying."

"Piss off!"

"You were curious. It's human nature. You didn't just leave her. You wanted to know who she was seeing."

Danny chews the inside of his cheek. "Yeah, well, maybe once."

"What happened?"

"I hung around; parked up behind some trees. I saw a car pull up and Sienna got inside."

"Who was driving?"

"An old dude."

"Who was he?"

"Fuck knows!"

"But you saw him."

"Not up close. He was midthirties, maybe older."

Ancient.

"What sort of car was he driving?"

"A Ford Focus. The five-door two-liter estate. Silver."

"You remember the number?"

"Yeah, I tattooed it on my foreskin so I wouldn't forget."

Danny laughs and decides he's going to remember the line and use it on his mates in the workshop.

"Would you recognize the driver again?"

"I'd recognize the car. I'm good with cars."

No longer anxious, Danny picks up a butter knife and begins scraping a speck of dirt from beneath his thumbnail. He has a habit of nodding his head as though he's agreeing with himself.

"This day you watched and waited, what happened?"

"The old dude made Sienna duck down. I figured he wanted a blowjob, you know, but they just drove off."

"What about last Tuesday—did you see his car?"

"Nah. I just dropped her."

"So you didn't see the guy who picked her up?"

Danny shakes his head.

"What were you doing at Sienna's house next morning?"

Danny hesitates for a beat too long. I don't give him time to make excuses.

"Listen very carefully to me, Danny. I'm happy to let your secret life stay secret, but not if you lie to me."

He looks at me sheepishly.

"I tried to call Sienna, but she wasn't answering. I was driving home from my mate's place and I went by Sienna's house—hoping I might see her. Place was crawling with coppers."

"Why did you run?"

His shoulders rise and fall. "I didn't want to get involved."

The age-old story.

Danny lets out a low, whistling breath. "They said her old man had his throat cut. Never seen a dead body—not one like that. What did he look like?"

Outside: darkness. The wind has freshened and a beech tree groans in protest from a corner of the garden where the moon is hiding in the branches.

Monk leans on the car. "Get what you wanted?"

"Sienna was seeing someone else. Somebody older. There must be evidence: e-mails, text messages, letters . . . we have to search Sienna's room."

"It's been searched," says Monk.

"Yes, but her laptop was missing and her mobile was damaged in the river. We'll need to retrieve her messages from the phone company database and her Internet server.

"Sienna does some babysitting for her drama teacher, Gordon Ellis. According to Helen Hegarty, Ray saw this teacher kissing Sienna in his car when she was being dropped home. He made a complaint to the school."

"When was this?"

"In the week before the murder. Ellis could be the person Ray Hegarty was arguing with outside his house. You should find out what sort of car he drives."

Monk scratches his unshaven jaw with his knuckles. "The boss is going to say you're muddying the water."

Is that what I'm doing?

"I'm trying to understand what happened."

"What if she's guilty?"

"What if she's not?"

Monk seems to think carefully, as though taking a conscience vote. He's a family man who worries about his own children. He's also a realist and knows how the truth can be manipulated, ameliorated and negotiated away at every stage of an investigation and trial. That's the reality of modern policing. Overworked, underpaid and unappreciated, investigators are forced to cut corners and paint over their mistakes. Usually, with a little luck, the facts fall into place and the right person goes down. And even if the system fails, detectives can normally sleep peacefully at night because the defendant was probably guilty of something equally terrible. Truly innocent people very rarely go to jail. That's the theory. It's normally the practice. Then someone like Sienna Hegarty comes along.

On the drive home I listen to *PM* on Radio 4, Eddie Mair analyzing the events of the day.

Jury members broke down in tears today as they were shown photographs

of a Ukrainian family including three young children who perished in a fire-bomb attack on a Bristol boarding house.

Two of the children, Aneta and Danya Kostin, aged four and six, were found huddled in a second-floor bedroom. Their eleven-year-old sister Vira perished on the first-floor landing, near to where their parents' bodies were discovered. All were overcome by smoke after petrol was allegedly poured through the letterbox and petrol bombs were thrown through the windows.

Neighbors told Bristol Crown Court of hearing windows breaking and seeing a white Ford transit van leaving the scene moments before flames were spotted on the ground floor of the building. A forensic expert also presented fingerprint evidence linking one of the three accused, Tony Scott, to a petrol container used in the attack . . .

I turn off the radio. Crack the window. The cold air helps me concentrate.

Parking the car outside the terrace, I walk down the hill to the cottage and sit outside on a stone wall in the shadows of low branches. The lights are on downstairs. A TV flickers behind the curtains.

Something pushes me up the path. My finger hovers over the doorbell.

Julianne opens the door a crack. “Hello?”

“Hi.”

“Is everything OK?”

“Fine. I just thought I’d drop by. How are you?”

“I’m good.”

There is a pause that stretches out in my mind, becoming embarrassing.

Julianne opens the door wider. “Do you want to come in?”

I step past her and wait for her to close the door. She’s been watching TV, but the sound is now turned down.

“Where’s Charlie?” I ask, glancing up the stairs.

“Babysitting.”

“Who is she looking after?”

“A little boy in Emma’s class.”

Julianne curls up in an armchair by the fire. A book lies open on the armrest. A cup of tea is empty on the table next to her.

“How was your date with Harry?” I ask.

She holds up her hand and rocks her

palm from side to side. “So-so. I discovered that he’s rather controlling.”

“How?”

“I asked for the dessert menu and he made such a fuss.”

I feel a stab of guilt. “That’s very odd.”

Julianne pushes hair back behind her ears. “I doubt you came here to talk about Harry.” She smiles and effortlessly takes repossession of my heart.

“Sienna was pregnant,” I say, which is definitely a conversation starter.

Julianne blinks at me. “Who?”

“I don’t know.”

We’re both thinking the same thing. What if it had been Charlie? What would we do?

Julianne grows pensive. “I walked past the Hegartys’ house today and I saw the curtains closed and I started thinking about Sienna. She was always here, Joe, staying for dinner, sleeping over, curled up on the sofa with Charlie.” She takes a deep breath. “Then I started thinking about how angry I’ve been at you, and some of the things I said.”

She raises her eyes to mine, filling me

with a sense that all her remembered anger, grief and impatience are gone.

"We haven't lost someone, Joe. We have two wonderful daughters. We're very lucky."

"I know."

Her ocean-gray eyes are shining. "I don't know if I should tell you this."

"What?"

"There are nights when I miss you so much I cry myself to sleep and other nights when I realize that loving you took every ounce of energy and more. I didn't have enough . . . I'll never have enough."

"I understand."

"Do you?"

"Let me come back."

She shakes her head. "I'm not strong enough to live with you, Joe. I'm barely strong enough to live without you."

"Why?"

"Because you're not always going to be here."

A stray lock of hair falls from behind her ear. She tucks it back again. For a moment I think she might cry. The last time I saw her tears was two years ago, in her hospital room where rain streaked the windows and it felt as if the clouds were crying for me.

"I don't love you anymore," Julianne told me blankly, coldly. "Not in the right way—not how I used to."

"There isn't a right way. There's just love," I said.

What do I know?

Now she's smiling sadly at me. "You're so good at analyzing other people, Joe, but not yourself."

"Or you."

"I hate it when you analyze me."

"I try not to. I prefer you to be a magnificent enigma."

Julianne laughs properly this time.

"I'm being serious," I say. "I don't want to understand you. I don't want to know what you'll do next. I want to spend the rest of my life trying to solve the mystery."

She sighs and shakes her head. "You're a decent man, Joe, but . . ."

I stop her. No statement that begins that way is ever a harbinger for anything good. What if she's clearing the decks before telling me that she's going to marry Harry Veitch?

"Tell me something honest," I say.

Julianne presses her lips into narrow unyielding lines. “Are you saying I tell lies?”

“No, that’s not what I meant. I just want to talk about something important.”

“This isn’t a necessary conversation, Joe.”

“I like it when we talk about the girls. It makes me feel like we’re still a family.”

“We can’t live it over again,” she whispers sadly.

“I know.”

“Do you? Sometimes I wonder.”

18

On Tuesday afternoon I park the Volvo outside a house made of weathered stone with a slate roof. The small square front garden is divided by strips of grass between flowerbeds where gerberas are pushing through the loam searching for sunlight.

Grabbing my overcoat from the passenger seat, I walk up the front path and give the doorbell a short ring, putting on my friendliest professional demeanor. Nobody answers. Ringing the bell again, I press my ear to the wooden door. Canned TV laughter leaks from inside.

Retreating down the steps to the front window, I try to peer through a gap in the curtains into the murky twilight of a living room. The TV is a flickering square. I can just make out a blurred outline of someone sitting on the sofa. Perhaps they didn't hear the doorbell.

This time I knock loudly and listen for footfalls or muffled voices or the sound of someone breathing on the other side of the door.

Nothing.

I'm about to leave when I hear a voice from the rear garden. Gordon Ellis appears from the side of the house. He's dressed in tracksuit bottoms and a Harlequins rugby shirt. A fringe of chestnut hair falls across his forehead. He brushes it aside.

"Hello."

"Hi. Were you waiting long? I was out back."

"No, not long."

He looks at me closely. "Have we met?"

"I'm Charlie O'Loughlin's father."

"Of course you are." He offers his hand: a killer grip. "Call me Gordon."

"Joe."

He's carrying a hoe, which he rests against his shoulder.

"Charlie is a great kid."

"Thank you."

I glance at the front door. "I don't want to interrupt . . . if you have a visitor."

"Nope, it's just me. Natasha has gone shopping. I was just doing some chores. Almost finished. Do you mind if we talk out back?"

I follow him along the side path where a rusting bicycle is propped against the fence, alongside recycling bins. The long narrow garden has a sandbox with toys, a vegetable patch and a small greenhouse. At the far end there is an old stable block, now a garage, which backs onto a rear lane.

Through an open side door I notice a silver BMW convertible. Ellis follows my gaze.

"You're wondering how a teacher can afford a car like that?"

"It did cross my mind."

"Natasha's family is loaded. You could say I married well." He looks a little embarrassed. "We met at school. I didn't know she was rich. Honest."

He laughs and begins turning soil in the vegetable garden, swinging the hoe over his shoulder and driving the blade into the compacted earth.

"I'm running late with this. I should have planted a month ago."

Glancing at the house, it looks less welcoming from this angle with small, mean windows. From somewhere on the street side I hear a door close. Ellis hears it too. His eyes meet mine.

"What can I do for you, Joe?"

"I want to ask you about Sienna Hegarty."

He swings the hoe again. "A terrible business!"

"You were close?"

"She's one of my students. She's in the musical."

"I saw the dress rehearsal last Tuesday. You were very hard on her."

"Sienna was distracted. She forgot her lines. Her timing was off. I know what she's capable of." He pauses and wipes his forearm across his forehead. "You didn't come here to discuss the musical."

"No."

"Why are you here?"

"I'm trying to help Sienna. I'm a psychologist. I've been asked to prepare a psych report for the court."

"How can I help?"

"I talked to Sienna a few days ago. I asked her about school—general questions about her favorite subjects and teachers. When she listed her teachers she left you out."

"You make it sound like she failed an exam."

"She grew agitated when I mentioned your name. She didn't want to talk about you. Can you think of a reason?"

"No."

"Nothing occurs to you?"

The hoe is poised above his head with his fists gripping the handle. "Why are you really here, Mr. O'Loughlin?"

First names have been dropped.

"Miss Robinson, the school counselor, said it was you who encouraged Sienna to come and see her. Did Sienna tell you what was troubling her?"

Ellis relaxes a little. He takes a small packet of tissues from his pocket and wipes the corner of his lips. Gazes past me at the treetops.

"Sometimes you can tell when a child is struggling. Sienna was quiet. Anxious."

"You saw this?"

"It was a day last summer. We'd just started back at school after the holidays. It was hot and nobody was wearing a sweater except Sienna, which I thought was odd. Then I noticed a smear of blood on her palms, which had run down from her wrist. She kept her arms folded so nobody would see. She'd cut herself and was still bleeding."

"Did she say why?"

"No. And she wouldn't go to the infirmary. So I collected some bandages and slipped them into her schoolbag. She didn't say anything, but I think she knew it was me."

"Did you report the incident?"

"No, but after that I kept an eye on her. She joined the drama club. Over time she grew to trust me. We talked."

"What about?"

"She was having problems at home with her father."

"What sort of problems?"

"Do I have to spell it out, Mr. O'Loughlin? I encouraged Sienna to see the counselor.

And when she didn't want to see a therapist, I helped convince her."

"She trusted you?"

"I guess."

"Why was that?"

He blinks, suddenly angry. "Maybe I was willing to listen."

"Did she tell you she was being abused?"

"No. I just knew it. You teach for long enough and you learn to recognize the signs."

Resting the hoe against the fence, he picks up a rake and begins smoothing the soil, breaking up the larger clods and creating channels for drainage. Across the fence, a neighbor is pegging her washing, the whites, sheets and towels.

Gordon returns her wave.

"Sienna needed my help. I wish I could have done more." The words seem to catch in his throat.

"Did you know that Sienna was pregnant?"

Ellis pauses for a moment, the rake suspended in midair. Tension ripples across his shoulders. Then he exhales and shakes his head.

"I know she had a boyfriend."

The neighbor has finished with her washing and is calling her dog. "Here, Jake, c'mon boy. C'mon, Jake."

Ellis is staring at me now, resting the rake handle on his shoulder.

"Did Sienna have a crush on you?"

"Yes."

"You admit it?"

"It happens."

"It doesn't worry you?"

"On the contrary—I take it as a compliment. It's a sign that I'm doing my job pretty damn well."

"Doing it well?"

"You've got to understand the process of teaching. If I do my job properly I can change the way a student thinks about himself or herself. It's a process of seduction, but it's not about sexual conquest. It's about creating an interest and a passion where none previously existed. It's about getting students to want something they didn't know they wanted."

"You make them fall in love with the subject?"

"I make them feel excited, energized, provoked and challenged."

"So you encourage crushes?"

"Yes, but not to feed my ego. Instead I

turn the focus back on the student. I encourage them to use their newfound curiosity and passion, to run with it, indulge it, let it take them places . . ."

"And what happens when a student sexualizes their crush?"

"I take a step back. Let them down gently. Sienna didn't get a crush on me because she wanted to be *with* me but because she wanted to be *like* me. I brought out her best. I made her feel special. This has nothing to do with physical attractiveness. It's a meeting of minds."

He makes it sound so obvious that nobody could dispute his logic. He's a passionate teacher, possibly a brilliant one, but what adolescent girl knows the difference between seduction and persuasion, love and infatuation?

"Did you know Ray Hegarty?"

"We met once or twice."

Ellis looks at the garden with a weary smile. "If I don't get these planted soon, we won't have vegetables for the summer."

A sharp gust of wind scatters his words.

"How is Sienna?"

"She's traumatized."

"Is the baby . . . ?"

"She miscarried."

He nods sadly and raises his eyes to the pearl-gray sky. "That may have been for the best."

Something rises in my stomach. Burns. I swallow hard and find myself saying goodbye, retracing my steps across the lawn to the side path.

Out of the corner of my eye I notice the garage again and the sports car.

"What sort of car does your wife drive?" I ask, turning to Ellis.

He gives me a wry smile. "Natasha's not really interested in cars. They just have to get her from A to B."

"So what does she drive?"

"A Ford Focus."

19

Sometimes we know things even if we don't *know* we know them. Maybe all we have is a fluttering sensation in our stomachs or a nagging sense of doubt or an unexplained certainty that something has happened.

Call it intuition or perception or insight. There is no sixth sense—it is a simple mental process where the brain takes in a situation, does a rapid search of its files, and among the sprawl of memories and knowledge it throws up an immediate match, a first impression.

That's why on trivia nights it's often best to go with the first answer that pops into our heads, because that initial thought is based upon a subconscious cue; a knowledge that cannot be articulated or defended. Ponder the same question for too long and our higher brain functions will begin to demand proof.

The trick is to train your mind to pick up the cues. Trust your first response. My gut tells me that Sienna Hegarty didn't kill her father. My gut tells me that she's protecting someone. My gut tells me that Gordon Ellis knows more than he's letting on. My gut tells me that there was something between them—teacher and student—a friendship that crossed a boundary.

For the past four days I have wrestled with this problem, going back over the details of Sienna's interview and Ellis's reaction. Another image keeps coming back to me: Gordon Ellis onstage during the rehearsal, looking into the eyes of a teenage girl, putting his finger beneath her chin, tilting her face towards his. She wanted to be kissed . . . wanted to surrender . . . he wanted control.

I can see Ellis's eyes traveling from the girl's dilated pupils over her flushed cheeks, down her exposed neck, across her underdefended body. Was it the look of a practiced manipulator or a committed teacher? Was it a predator's leer or a harmless piece of theater?

It's Saturday morning in Bath. I'm sitting in Café Medoc, overlooking Pulteney Bridge and the riverside path running north past the Bath Library arcade. The weir is downstream, turning brown water into foam. Ducks paddle above the falls as if waiting for a ramp to be delivered.

Annie Robinson takes a seat and puts her brightly colored hippie shoulder bag at her feet. She's wearing a quilted jacket over a shirt and thin woolen tights.

"I didn't think you'd call me, Joseph O'Loughlin."

"Why?"

"You looked so embarrassed when you last saw me."

"I wasn't embarrassed."

She laughs. "I seem to remember you didn't know where to look."

Coffees are ordered. Delivered. Spooning foam from a cappuccino, she holds the spoon in her mouth.

"You don't give a girl much notice. Normally, I wouldn't agree to a date when someone rings me on the same morning. Did someone else stand you up?"

"It's not really a date," I say, and then backtrack. "I mean, I wanted to see you socially, but I didn't think of this as one—a date, I mean . . ."

Again she laughs, her eyes dancing.

"Don't worry, Joseph O'Loughlin, I won't be offended if we don't call it a date."

Annie seems to find my full name amusing. "So tell me," she says, "since we're two friends meeting socially—what do you do for a living?"

"I'm a clinical psychologist and please call me Joe."

"Is that what your wife calls you?"

"Yes."

"Then I shall call you Joseph. Do you have a practice?"

"Not anymore. I lecture at the university. Part-time."

She nods as though satisfied. "Do you find the weekends are the hardest?"

"Hardest?"

"Being alone. When I'm at work it doesn't matter because I'm busy, but the weekends are lonelier."

"How long has it been?" I ask.

"Three years since we separated. Ten months since the divorce. I held out hope until the very end. How about you?"

"No divorce yet."

"Oh, I thought, you know . . . I didn't realize." There is a squeak in her voice.

"Were you always a school counselor?" I ask, trying to rescue her.

"I used to teach history. My father said it was the perfect subject because there was always more to teach."

"Even if it repeats itself?"

"Because we never learn."

She smiles and a dimple appears on her left cheek, but not the right.

The sun has come out. Reaching into her bag, she takes out a pair of sunglasses.

"That's a very colorful bag."

"My ex-husband gave it to me when we were still married. It was stuffed full of lingerie, most of which was totally obscene and not sexy at all. Don't even try to get me out of my good old Marks and Spencers striped pajamas."

"I wouldn't try."

She feigns surprise. "Am I *that* undesirable?"

"No, that's not what I meant. I just . . . I mean . . . I wouldn't force you out of them . . ."

She laughs prettily and then convinces me to share a slice of "death by chocolate" cake because a "true gentleman would share some of the guilt."

"So why did you call me, Joseph?"

"How well do you know Gordon Ellis?"

"Why?"

"I'm interested."

She licks her spoon. "We were at college together during teacher training—back in the days when we were young and committed to the cause."

"What's he like?"

"Too handsome for his own good."

She says it in such a matter-of-fact way that I feel a twinge of jealousy.

"Is he popular?"

"Very. Particularly with the senior girls—he sets their little hearts aflutter. Some of the really presumptuous ones pass him notes or make excuses to rub up against him. Gordon has to be very careful."

"Has he had problems?"

She looks at me doubtfully. "Why are you so interested?"

"I think Sienna Hegarty has a crush on him."

"She wouldn't be the first or the last."

"What if it went further than that?"

Annie's head tilts to one side. "Sexual misconduct—are you making an accusation?"

"It's a hypothetical question."

"A dangerous one. Rumors spread very quickly. Careers can be ruined."

"This is just between us."

She toys with her earring, rubbing it between her thumb and forefinger.

"The school has procedures to deal with sexual misconduct."

"Internal procedures?"

"Usually. Most incidents rarely get beyond a harmless crush and misplaced affection."

"And when it does?"

"The school accepts responsibility. The teacher is quietly suspended, sacked or transferred without any fuss."

"Or damaging publicity."

Annie doesn't disagree.

"Maybe you don't remember being at school, Joe, but classrooms are like sexual Petri dishes, full of hormones and sexual tension. I've had my share of admirers. When I was at school I fancied Mr. Deitch, who taught English and PE. We used to go and watch whenever he was on the track because he wore Lycra running shorts just like Linford Christie. He had an impressive lunchbox."

"I get the picture."

She laughs. "Did a teacher break your heart too?"

"Miss Powell—she taught French and had done some modeling in Paris. I saw her shopping one day and made up a story about how she'd been buying sexy underwear. My mates were so jealous. Anyway, the story got back to her and she sent me to see the headmaster. I had to write an essay on why women shouldn't be treated as sex objects."

"You poor boy."

"It wouldn't have happened to a girl."

Mock surprise. "You're blaming *me* now."

"No. Never. But tell me, how do you guard against it—teenage crushes?"

"I avoid meeting students outside of school or having them in my car. I don't play favorites. I avoid situations where I'd be alone with a particular student. I don't accept gifts or give them. I avoid physical contact. I leave the classroom door open. I don't write notes or e-mails that could be misinterpreted."

"It's a minefield."

"Yes and no."

She runs a finger around the top of her coffee cup. "I can usually tell when a student has a crush on me—the lovesick looks and excuses to stay late or arrive early."

"And then what?"

"I find a way of distancing myself. I let them down gently. I maintain the boundaries."

Annie raises her eyes and holds her gaze on mine. I can feel myself blink and color come to my throat.

"Is that why you asked me here—to talk about Gordon?"

"Yes and no."

"Oh well, as long as you're paying." She laughs gaily. "You wouldn't even recognize Gordon if you saw photographs of him as a kid."

"Why?"

"He was a real Billy Bunter. Overweight and short-sighted with crooked teeth and a face like a pizza."

"How do you know?"

"I once met his mother. She came to college to make sure he was looking after himself. She had photographs of Gordon as a youngster. You've got to give him credit for remaking himself. He lost the weight. Got his teeth straightened. Worked out. It helped that he grew to be six-two."

"Did you know Natasha?"

"Who?"

"Gordon's wife. She must have been around."

"What makes you say that?"

"Gordon said they met at school. I thought she must have been around during his college years."

Annie shakes her head.

"He had loads of girlfriends at college.

He went out with a friend of mine, Alison, for about three months."

"Did you date him?"

She shrugs. "He's not really my type." She pauses. "You're very nosy, Joseph. Are all psychologists like that?"

"We're interested in people."

"Are you interested in me?"

"Of course."

It's the right answer. Suddenly she stands and suggests we go for a walk. Crossing Argyle Street, we follow Grand Parade through Bath City Park. Annie hooks her arm through mine. Her shoulder bag swings gently against our hips. It's nice to flirt and banter with a pretty woman. Julianne and I used to be like this, teasing each other, making observations, righting the wrongs of the world.

"So what made you decide to become a counselor?" I ask.

"It's probably the same reason you became a psychologist. I wanted to make a difference. Why did you decide to lecture?"

"I'm not really sure. I'm not certain that psychology *can* be taught."

"Why?"

"Clinical work is very instinctive. It's about listening to people and sharing the burden. Making them feel as though someone cares."

"What made you give it up?"

"A really effective psychologist is someone who commits. Who goes into the darkness to bring someone out. Years ago I told a friend of mine that a doctor is no good to a patient if he dies of the disease, but that wasn't the right analogy. When a person is drowning, someone has to get wet."

She pauses and turns to me.

"You got tired of getting wet?"

"I almost drowned."

We have reached North Parade. Canal boats are moored on the opposite bank. Someone is cooking on deck, dicing carrots and tipping them into a bubbling pot on a gas burner.

"Thank you for the coffee and cake, Joseph."

"I hope you didn't have too far to travel. I didn't even ask where you lived."

"Are you inviting yourself home?"

"No, not at all . . . I was just . . ."

She's laughing at me again.

"I'm glad that I'm such a source of amusement."

"I'm sorry. I'll make it up to you at dinner." She says it quickly. Nervously.

I take too long to answer.

"Don't let me push you into anything," she says. "I'm not usually this forward."

"No. I mean, yes, dinner would be great."

"Are you sure?"

"I'm sure. It's just that I haven't been invited to dinner by a woman since . . . since . . ."

"Maybe you should stop counting."

"Good idea."

She pecks me on the lips.

"So it's dinner. How about Monday night?"

"Sure."

And then as an afterthought, she says, "About Gordon Ellis and Sienna . . ."

"Yes."

"I'll try to find out if anyone complained to the school."

"Thank you."

20

Charlie has a football game for her district team. Watching teenage girls play a competitive team sport is completely different from watching boys. There is no diving, feigning injury, flying elbows or cynical fouls. Body contact tends to be completely accidental and should one of the girls get injured twenty-one players will stand around her asking, "Are you OK?"

Charlie is getting less interested in football as she gets older. There seems to be a moment in adolescence when girls abandon sport as being either too sweaty or too much like hard work. Maybe they discover boys. Why can't they discover schoolwork?

I wander along the sidelines, occasionally yelling encouragement, which Charlie hates. I'm also not allowed to dissect the game afterwards or comment on how she played.

Julianne comes along sometimes, which is nice. She chats to the other mothers, sipping thermos coffee and rarely following the action unless a penalty is being taken or a goal has been scored.

She didn't come today. I offered. She declined.

Keeping one eye on the game, I try to call Sienna's therapist again. I've left three messages. Robin Blaxland hasn't answered any of them. He has an office in Bath, not far from the Jane Austen center.

I always find it ironic that Jane Austen is Bath's most famous former resident—yet she reportedly hated the spa town. She lived in Bath for six years and didn't write a word in that time, but that hasn't stopped them naming streets, festivals and tearooms after her.

At half-time I call Ruiz. He's outside, puffing slightly.

"Are you jogging?"

"Yeah, I'm running the New York marathon."

"How's it going?"

"I'm in Scotland."

"Why?"

"Gordon Ellis used to teach in Edinburgh."

"Is that important?"

"Might be."

He's not going to tell me anything else.

That's the thing about Ruiz—he's a man of few words and those "few" are chosen like the boiled sweets he carries around in his pocket.

"I need a favor," I tell him.

"I'm still working on the last one."

"I need a home address for a psychotherapist called Robin Blaxland. He was treating Sienna Hegarty."

"Give me an hour."

Ruiz hangs up and I go back to watching the game.

The full-time whistle signals a narrow defeat. Charlie sits on the rear tray of the Volvo and unlaces her muddy boots. She slips tracksuit bottoms over her shorts and puts her boots into a plastic bag.

"You want a hot chocolate?"

"Nope."

"Hungry?"

"Not particularly."

She examines a blister on her big toe. Her nails are painted dark purple and she's wearing a silver ankle bracelet.

"That's new."

"Sienna gave it to me."

"Why?"

"She didn't want it anymore."

"It looks expensive. Where did Sienna get it?"

Charlie's eyes fix on mine. "You think she stole it."

"I never said that."

"It was a year ago, Dad. One time. You want to see a receipt? I'll ask her."

She turns away. Disgusted.

Nicely done, I think. Charlie is changing out of her strip on the backseat.

"Can I get my navel pierced?" she asks.

"No."

"Erin got hers pierced last summer."

"That makes no difference."

"How about a tattoo?"

"Definitely not."

"What if it's a really small tattoo on my ankle?"

"When you're eighteen you can tattoo your entire body."

I know she's rolling her eyes. Holding her foot, she examines her blister again. I have plasters in a first-aid kit. Taking off the wrapping, I get her to hold her foot still.

"Can I ask you about Mr. Ellis?"

Charlie looks at me defensively. "What about him?"

"Does he play favorites?"

"What do you mean?"

"Does he seem to favor particular students?"

"I guess. Some girls flirt with him."

"Does he flirt back?"

"Not really."

Charlie pulls a sock over her foot. "Why are you so interested in Mr. Ellis?"

"It's nothing."

"I'm not stupid, Dad. You never talk about nothing."

Another game is about to start. The teams are warming up, doing short sprints and passing drills.

"What do you think of Mr. Ellis?" I ask.

"He's cool."

"What makes him cool?"

"You can talk to him. He listens."

"About what?"

"Stuff."

"What sort of stuff?"

"Stuff. Problems. It's like he understands because he's been there."

We've all been there, I feel like saying.

"Gordon doesn't judge us. He doesn't look down on us. He doesn't treat us like children. And if anyone has a problem, he says they should come and see him. He's a good listener."

"You call him Gordon?"

"Yeah, he lets us, but only during drama classes."

"Do you ever talk to him?"

Charlie's shoulders rise and fall. The gesture says all I need to know.

"Was Sienna close to Mr. Ellis?"

"She used to be."

"What happened?"

"He started picking on her. Criticizing her. Saying she wasn't trying hard enough. Sienna didn't seem to mind. I don't think she cared."

"That surprises you?"

"Yeah, I guess. It's not like her."

A whistle blasts and the game is under way. Charlie watches the action, aware that I'm studying her profile. Normally she complains when I look at her like this—accusing me of trying to read her mind.

"Was Sienna seeing Mr. Ellis outside of school?"

"She used to babysit for him. He has a little boy. Billy. He's adorable."

Charlie doesn't understand what I'm asking.

"Was Mr. Ellis Sienna's boyfriend?"

Charlie's head snaps around. "What gave you that idea?"

"Sienna was seeing someone outside of school. Not the boyfriend she claimed to have. Somebody older."

She laughs. "And you think it was Mr. Ellis?"

"What's so funny?"

"You're right. It's not funny. It's tragic. Gordon said this might happen."

"What might happen?"

"He said that people sometimes make up stories because they're jealous or they're hurt. It happened at his last school. He had to leave."

"He told you that?"

"Yeah."

"Did he say what happened?"

"He said one of the girls made a complaint and said that he'd kissed her. She took it back but it was too late. The school told him he had to leave."

Why would Gordon tell Charlie something like that?

She goes back to looking at the game.

"Sienna was having sex," I say.

"So?"

"You knew?"

A shrug. Indifferent. "A lot of girls are having sex, Dad. Maybe not the full monty, but they're doing plenty of other stuff."

Glancing at me sideways, she checks to see if I'm shocked. The silence stretches out, punctuated by the scoring of a goal and celebrations on the sidelines.

"You want to ask me, don't you?" A slight smile plays on her lips. My daughter is challenging me. Every fiber of my professional being says I shouldn't rise to the bait. I should end the conversation now. But a small pilot light of parental concern flares in my chest. I have to know.

"Are you having sex, Charlie? I don't mind. What I mean is, I'd be a little worried. You're underage. Too young."

She shakes her head. Disappointed. Proven right.

"Can we go home now?" she asks.

"You haven't answered my question."

"Here's the thing, Dad. I can say no and I *could* be lying or I *could* be telling you the truth. That's a fifty-fifty chance of disappointing you. Or I could say yes and definitely disappoint you. The odds aren't in my favor, so I figure I'll just say nothing."

"I want you to answer."

"And I want another horse."

"What's that got to do with anything?"

"We both want something we're not going to get."

She tosses her ponytail over one shoulder and gazes at me resolutely. "I'm a good kid, Dad. Trust me."

And that's it—end of conversation. I drive her home, aware more than ever before that she is her mother's daughter and equally mysterious.

21

Robin Blaxland lives in a semi in the shadows of St. Saviour's Church in Bath. After dropping Charlie at the cottage I drive back into town, pulling up outside a neat front garden, glowing under the streetlights.

I ring the bell. Three children open the door, shoulder to shoulder. The eldest is about eight. She has glasses, milky white skin, red hair and freckles—the Royal Flush of embarrassing attributes for a child.

Her younger brothers look alike enough to be twins.

A woman follows them down the hall, wiping her hands on an apron. Three pregnancies past her optimum weight, she has a pretty round face and the same red hair as her daughter.

"Can I help you?"

"I'm looking for your husband."

"Of course, just one moment. Janie, go and get your daddy."

Janie scampers up the stairs. The two boys stare at me. One has a bruise on his forehead and a sticking plaster above his eye.

"You're in the wars."

"He ran into a tree," says his brother. "It was sooo funny."

"Shush," says their mother.

I notice suitcases in the hallway. One of them is open and still being packed.

"Are you going somewhere?" I ask.

"Skiing. We leave in the morning."

"Where are you going?"

"Italy."

"The Dolomites?"

She mentions a resort that I haven't heard of before.

Her husband appears on the stairs. Robin Blaxland is three sizes smaller than his wife and is wearing braces that cross at his back and are clipped to his trousers. He blinks at me from behind frameless glasses.

"I'm Joseph O'Loughlin. I left messages for you. You didn't get back to me."

He blinks again. "How did you get this address?"

I lie to him. "From the school."

"I didn't know the school had my private address."

"Yes."

Blink. Blink.

"I wanted to talk about Sienna Hegarty."

"I couldn't possibly comment on a patient."

"You heard what happened?"

"Yes, of course, but our sessions were private. It's a matter of patient confidentiality."

"I'm preparing a psych report on Sienna for a bail hearing."

Blink. Blink. The information is being processed.

"You're a psychologist?"

"Yes."

Finally he steps back, inviting me upstairs to his study on the first floor. I can hear the children being called to dinner by his wife.

"What branch of psychotherapy do you specialize in?" I ask.

"I studied under a Jungian."

"Dream analysis?"

"Among other things. I also offer hypnotherapy and cognitive behavioral therapy. How is Sienna?"

What should I tell him? She's confused. Frightened.

"She hasn't been entirely forthcoming. There are three missing hours in the timeline. Was she with you that afternoon?"

"No."

"You don't have to check your diary?"

"The police have already asked me that question."

He sits up very straight in his chair as though posing for a photograph.

"Who organized for Sienna Hegarty to come and see you?"

"Her school counselor."

"Annie Robinson?"

"Yes."

"How often did she come?"

"Once a week."

"When did you last see her?"

"Nearly three weeks ago. She missed our last appointment."

"What day was that?"

"After school, Monday at four thirty."

"Did Sienna normally come on her own?"

"Yes. I think she caught the bus."

"What about the first time she came to your office?"

"A male teacher brought her in. I think his name was Ellis."

Mr. Blaxland wants to cross his legs but the office is so small our knees are almost touching. He has psoriasis on his joints. I can see the flaking skin on his elbows below his folded shirtsleeves.

"What did Sienna talk about?"

"We covered all the areas of her life: her family, her friends, how she felt about things."

"She was cutting herself."

"Yes, we were looking at different coping mechanisms."

"Did Sienna ever talk about her father?"

"Of course. They didn't get on particularly well."

"Did she say why?"

"They fought. She felt he was too hard on her . . . too strict. He frightened her. Sienna had a recurring dream in which a dark-haired man came into her room. She didn't see his face and sometimes he didn't have physical form, but she knew he represented something evil, hovering over her."

"And she used the term 'evil'?"

"Yes. Why?"

"It just seems unusual."

Was it Robin Blaxland's terminology or Sienna's?

"What else can you tell me about this dream?" I ask.

"The most recurring feature was her belief that she was awake and conscious, but unable to move, unable to turn on the light, or to call for help. She talked of being 'caught' in the dream and hearing a 'rushing sound' in her ears."

"A false awakening?"

"Just so."

Sienna had mentioned the "rushing sound" when I spoke to her at Oakham House.

"Could she recognize this man?"

"No, but it was a manipulative figure."

"Could the dark-haired man be her father?"

"I don't know if this dream figure related to a real person or even a compilation of several real people. Perhaps it reflected some part of Sienna's own personality—a darker side."

"How often did she have these dreams?"

"Every night, she said. Sometimes she woke and discovered her bedroom had been ransacked. Clothes and belongings were spread across the floor."

"Did she ever tell you she was being sexually abused?"

He hesitates. "No, but I suspected as much."

"You didn't report your concerns?"

"I had no proof," he says defensively.

From the chair where I'm sitting I can see along a hallway to an open bedroom door—a child's room with an alphabet chart on the wall and toys spilling from a chest.

"Did Sienna ever talk about school?"

"Of course."

"What about her teachers?"

Mr. Blaxland drums his fingers on his knee. "Nobody in particular."

"What about Gordon Ellis, her drama teacher?"

"He was obviously very concerned about her."

"Did she talk about having a boyfriend?"

"Yes. I got the impression he may have been a little older."

"Why?"

"She talked about going away with him for the weekend. I thought it was odd because she was so young."

"Did she say where?"

He shrugs. "I don't know if it happened. Sienna was the sort of girl who often said things to shock me."

"Did you know she was pregnant?"

Genuine surprise flares in his eyes. Blink. Blink. In that moment I catch a glimpse of something. Disquiet. Embarrassment. He had missed a truly important detail.

"Did you tape your sessions, Mr. Blaxland?"

"No."

"Did you take notes?"

"I have always found it more useful if I concentrate completely on what my patient is saying. I sometimes make a note afterwards."

"But not always?"

A slight recoil but not in his eyes. "No."

I scan his face, looking for a hint that he's hiding something.

"Perhaps you could make your notes available to me . . ."

"I've made myself available. That should be sufficient."

There are footsteps on the stairs. Mrs. Blaxland glances through the stair rails. "Your dinner is getting cold, Robin."

"I'm sorry," I say, rising slowly. "Thank you for your time."

Collecting my coat at the front door, I pause.

"How much?" I ask.

"Sorry?"

"Your sessions—how much did you charge Sienna?"

"My standard rate—forty-five pounds for fifty minutes."

"Where did she get the money?"

"I have no idea."

It's after eight and the day is ending, but I feel as though I've accomplished something. The temperature has dropped even further and beads of dew have formed on the parked cars. All except one—a dark colored four-wheel drive parked further down the street.

The windows are tinted and I can't see anyone inside until I fumble for my own keys and notice a watch face illuminated on a wrist. The driver is checking the time.

I pull out and turn right into London Road. The traffic is heavy until I reach the outskirts of Bath. The radio is playing. Evening talkback. Brian Noble. "The voice of the Lord" is his catchphrase and sums up his general attitude to his callers.

. . . the Home Secretary this week labeled Bristol one of the five worst crime "hotspots" in Britain, but I'm pleased to report that the Old Bill has responded magnificently, announcing a blitz—not on crack dealers or armed robbers, but on drivers who don't wear seatbelts.

We have Muslim imams in this country preaching hatred and violent jihad, yet our police are issuing speeding tickets and seatbelt fines.

And what else are our finest doing? They're standing outside Bristol Crown Court failing to protect people from being pelted with eggs and abuse.

Now whether you agree with the views of Novak Brennan or not, he deserves to be able to walk into court without being egged by thugs and vandals who call themselves anti-racism protesters or refugee advocates. Shame on them . . .

Headlights loom in my rearview mirror. Large. Close. Flashing on high beam. Someone in a hurry.

I slow down. Move to the side. They stay behind me. Maybe there's something wrong with the Volvo. The taillights might not be working. I could be blowing smoke. None of the warning lights are showing. My temperature gauge is normal.

We're bumper to bumper. I touch the brakes. He won't back off. High-beam lights fill my mirrors, making it hard for me to see the road.

Unconsciously, I'm accelerating, trying to pull away. A long sweeping left-hand corner is followed by a right-hand bend where Combe Hay Lane passes through a copse of trees. There's nowhere to pull over.

I'm traveling too fast, gripping the wheel too tightly, my eyes smarting at the brightness, seeing phantoms leaping from the ditches and from behind trees. I try to remember what lies ahead. There's a farm track on the left with a turning circle for tractors. It's two hundred yards away. I'll pull over. Let the car pass.

We're inches apart. I touch the brakes. Indicate. I don't want him crashing into me. The nearside tires leave the asphalt and dig into the softer edges. I almost lose control and wrench the wheel to the right. The Volvo fishtails and veers wildly across the road, heading for a ditch. I have to correct again.

Ahead I see the approaching lights of a car. The headlights behind me suddenly disappear. As the oncoming car passes, I see a vehicle for a brief moment in the rearview mirror. Big and boxy, it could be a Range Rover. Black. Just a driver—he must have turned off his headlights.

He flicks them on again and the high beam blasts my corneas burning a white spot that won't go away.

The Volvo leans heavily on the bends and surges over dips. The trees and hedges are like passing shadows. I've missed the farm track. There's a turn-off to Combe Hay a hundred yards ahead. I can't make the turn at this speed.

Fifty yards. Forty. I hit the brakes hard. Swing the wheel. Brace for the impact. The Volvo skirts the far ditch but makes the turn and skids to a halt on loose gravel. I expect to see the Range Rover shoot past, but instead it makes the same maneuver, far more expertly, stopping twenty yards behind me.

Shouldering open the door, I scream at his idiocy, my heart pounding. Shielding my eyes against the brightness, I take three steps towards the car. There's no response. The doors remain closed, the engine running.

"What's your problem?" I yell.

No response.

I glance at the Volvo. Nothing appears to be wrong. The taillights are working.

Hesitating, I can think of a dozen reasons why I shouldn't move any closer. I'm alone. I'm unarmed. I don't have a tire iron to take out his fucking windows.

Finally, I take a step back, reach into the car and pull out my mobile.

"You see this? I'm calling the police."

The waiting car rocks forward suddenly and stops. What's he doing?

I start punching in 999, glancing at the glowing screen. At the same moment, the car accelerates in a roar of horsepower and spinning wheels. It's heading straight for me.

I don't have time to run. I throw myself across the seat and pull my legs inside as the driver's side door is ripped from its metal hinges with a crunching finality.

The sudden backdraft blows dust around the interior of the Volvo. Then there's silence. No sound except my breathing.

I climb out and look down the empty road. My crumpled car door is lying thirty yards away in the ditch. The Range Rover has gone. Walking across the road, I retrieve the door, loading it in the back of the Volvo. Then I put in a call to Ronnie Cray.

"Sounds like something out of *Duel,*" she says.

"Duel?"

"Spielberg's first classic. This ordinary guy—Dennis Weaver—is driving through the desert and he gets terrorized by this big truck that's like the Freddy Krueger of trucks."

"Are you taking this seriously?"

"Yeah. Course. Did you get a number?"

"No."

"Did you get a make?"

"It looked like a Range Rover. Black."

"Did you get a description of the driver?"

"I couldn't see anything."

"Not much I can do. Where were you going?"

"Home."

"Where were you coming from?"

"I was talking to Sienna Hegarty's therapist."

"You think it's connected?"

"Maybe. What do you think?"

"It was probably just a joy-rider, winding you up."

"What about my car door?"

"You're insured. Make a claim."

She's about to hang up. "Hey, Professor, maybe you should stop asking so many questions."

22

Swinging my legs over the side of the bed, my feet argue for a moment, curling inwards and not wanting to press flat on the rug. I have to concentrate, forcing my toes to the floor, then my heels. Slowly the spasms ease and I can reach the bathroom.

The mirror is cruel this morning. I pull at the skin beneath my bloodshot eyes and examine my tongue. For the past two nights I have had a black Range Rover with blazing headlights chasing me in my dreams. Each time I've woken with my heart pounding and my fists clenched on an imaginary steering wheel.

Strawberry is weaving between my bare legs, nipping at my toes, wanting to be fed. I follow her downstairs and fill her bowl, listening to the sound of Gunsmoke beating his tail against the back door and whining with excitement. At least one creature celebrates my getting up each morning.

The phone rings. Ruiz shouts to be heard above aircraft noise.

"Hey, Professor, you ever wondered why when you park in a totally empty airport car park someone always comes and parks next to you?"

"It's one of life's great mysteries."

"Like pigeons."

"What's so mysterious about pigeons?"

"They're always the same size. You never see baby pigeons or old-age pigeons."

"You don't get out enough."

"I'm just a thinker."

The jet has passed. A boiled sweet rattles against his teeth. "Hey, there's someone I want you to meet."

"Where?"

"In Edinburgh."

"Who is it?"

"I'll explain when you get here."

A part of me wants to resist the idea. I don't want to travel. I want to stay close to home—particularly after what happened two nights ago—but I set Ruiz on the scent and he wouldn't ask if it weren't important.

"I'll book a flight and get back to you."

Firstly, I call Bill Johnson at the local garage and ask him to pick up the Volvo and find me a new door. I tell him that I'll leave the keys under the seat. Hanging up, I turn on my laptop and go online to book a flight to Edinburgh. Finally, I call Julianne and ask if I can borrow her car.

"What's wrong with yours?"

"It doesn't have a door."

"Why?"

"It's a long story."

I can imagine her eyes rolling towards the ceiling in a well-worn expression of un-surprise.

"One more thing—I'm going away tomorrow. Just for the day. I won't be back in time to pick up Emma."

"I'll get one of the other mothers to take her home."

"Are you sure?"

"I'm sure."

Fifteen minutes later, I let myself into the cottage. Breakfast dishes are rinsed in the kitchen sink. Julianne's car keys are on the mantelpiece. I'm about to leave when I remember that I wanted a photograph of Sienna. Charlie used to have one pinned to the corkboard above her desk. I hope she won't mind me borrowing it.

I climb the stairs and open her bedroom door, which has a "Do Not Disturb" sign with a note written underneath: "That means you, Emma!" Given that Emma can't read yet, it seems rather superfluous, but I'm sure the message has been passed on orally.

Charlie's pajamas are pooled on her unmade bed. Her desk is near the window. Her laptop is open. I scan the corkboard and spy a strip of passport-sized photographs taken at a photo booth. Charlie and Sienna are sitting on each other's laps, pulling funny faces. The last picture is of Sienna leaning towards the lens as though reading the instructions, unsure if the camera is going to flash again.

Elsewhere the notice board is decorated with Post-it notes, pictures, newspaper clippings and reminders. One snapshot shows Charlie and Sienna on a Ferris wheel at the Wessex Show. It was published on the front page of the *Somerset Standard*.

Charlie's laptop is "sleeping." I press the spacebar and the hard drive begins spinning. The screen illuminates. I know I shouldn't be doing this. I should respect her privacy. At the same time, I keep thinking of Sienna and her secrets and of Charlie crying at school and of our post-game conversation on Saturday.

Clicking open the history directory, I scan through the websites Charlie has been "surfing." Most of them I recognize: her Facebook page, iTunes, YouTube, Twitter . . .

She has set up a profile on MSN, a message application that allows her to communicate with friends online. There are no text conversations recorded. Charlie must have ticked a box in the settings to delete old messages.

I look at her Facebook page—the photo albums. There are shots of her last school camp, a friend's party, our weekend in the Lake District, chasing Gunsmoke through the garden after he stole one of her trainers. Some of the photographs make me smile. Others tug at unseen strings in my chest.

Opening a new "album" I discover two photographs where I don't recognize the context. Charlie is lying on a large bed, playing with a young boy. Dressed in a T-shirt and jeans, she is lying on her front, resting on her elbows. The collar of the T-shirt dips open at her neck, revealing little yet I still find it disconcerting.

The next image shows her lying on her

back with the little boy balanced on her knees. I wonder who took the shots. Someone she felt comfortable with. Someone she trusted.

Looking at them, I can imagine Charlie as a young woman, a mother, married with a family. It's strange because, normally, I still picture her as being a little girl in her Dalmatian pajamas and red cowboy boots, putting on "shows" in the garden.

Clicking off the site, I close the lid of the laptop, sending it back to sleep.

Shepparton Park School. Mid-morning. The headmaster Derek Stozer is a tall, slope-shouldered man with a lumpy body and the makings of a comb-over. I've only met him twice—including at a prize-giving day when he mumbled through his formal welcome speech and made fifteen minutes last longer than a wet weekend in Truro.

His secretary, Mrs. Summers, is like an over-protective wife who dotes on him.

"You should have called for an appointment," she says. "He's a very busy man."

"Of course, I'm sorry."

"What's the nature of your inquiry?"

"It's personal."

She blinks at me, expecting more. I smile. She's not happy. Leaning across her desk, she whispers into an intercom. Eventually, I am escorted down a carpeted corridor, past honor boards and trophy cabinets.

Derek Stozer rises from his chair and hitches his trousers before shaking my hand.

"Professor O'Loughlin, how can I help you? Is this about Charlotte?"

"No."

"Oh?" He gazes at me along his nose.

As soon as I mention Sienna Hegarty his mood changes and he mumbles something that might be "terrible business" or could be "ermine fizziness." He points to a chair and resumes his own.

"I've been asked to examine Sienna and to prepare a psych report for the court. In the course of interviewing her family, I became aware that Ray Hegarty made a complaint to the school a week before he died. I believe it related to a member of your staff. I've since learned that this same member of staff has complained about harassing phone calls from Sienna."

The headmaster doesn't react immediately. After a moment of reflection, he clears his throat. “From time to time parents and students have issues with teachers. It’s not uncommon.”

“Mr. Hegarty claimed he saw this particular member of staff kissing his daughter.”

There is a longer silence. Mr. Stozer stands and stretches his legs, wandering between the window and his desk, clasping his hands behind his back.

“Mr. Hegarty was mistaken. I have talked to the member of staff involved, who assures me that nothing untoward occurred. This member of staff admitted failing to appreciate that a student had developed a crush on him. It was a harmless infatuation. The member of staff immediately distanced himself from the girl and submitted a report.”

“Did he kiss her?”

“No, that’s not what happened.”

“What *did* happen?”

“I am led to believe that the girl tried to kiss him. He spurned her advances and reported the matter immediately. I was aware of the incident before Mr. Hegarty raised it with me.”

“Sienna was his babysitter.”

"And he should never have allowed this. It was a mistake. He admitted as much. It was a failure of judgment."

"You investigated?"

"Of course."

"Did you talk to Sienna?"

"I organized an internal review of the staff member's actions and performance. I delegated the task to a senior member of staff—the school counselor."

"Miss Robinson?"

"She's trained to talk to students about delicate issues."

Why didn't Annie tell me any of this?

Mr. Stozer continues: "Sienna denied anything had happened. She said her father was mistaken."

"And you believed her?"

"Yes, Mr. O'Loughlin, I believed her. And I believed Mr. Ellis and I believed Miss Robinson."

The last statement is delivered with far more authority than I thought Stozer capable of.

"I don't see what relevance any of this has," he adds. "Sienna Hegarty was a model student. She wasn't being bullied.

She wasn't struggling academically. She enjoyed coming to school. She was a healthy, happy teenager—"

"If Sienna was so healthy and happy, why did Miss Robinson suggest she see a therapist?"

"Many young girls experience problems when they go through adolescence—I'm sure I don't have to tell you that. I'm led to believe that Sienna Hegarty was having difficulties at home."

"But not at school?"

"If you're trying to suggest that her state of mind or her actions had anything to do with this school, I would take serious issue . . ."

He doesn't finish the statement but the steel in his voice seems to stiffen his resolve. Marching to the door, he turns and says, "I have a staff meeting to attend, Professor. If you have any more questions I suggest you put them in writing to the school governors."

When I cross the river, I don't turn onto Wells Road but continue along the south bank until I reach Lower Bristol Road. Keeping to the inside lane, I drive slowly and try to pick out the signs on the cross streets.

Danny Gardiner said he dropped Sienna on the corner of Riverside Road and Lower Bristol Road. I pull up a little past the intersection, parking in the forecourt of a used-car dealership. A balmy wind, smelling of the river, sends litter swirling in the gutters.

There are shops and businesses on both sides of the road—a video store, a fish and chip shop, a British Gas showroom, a hairdresser, a florist, sex shop, a minicab office and an off-license. According to Danny Gardiner this was the first time he'd ever dropped Sienna here.

"Spare some change, guv?"

A stick-thin black man in a woolen hat holds out his hand with a fingerless glove. Nearby is a shopping trolley of his possessions. I fumble in my pocket. Find a pound. He looks at the coin as though it's an ancient artifact.

"You lost?" he asks.

"No."

"You have a good day."

"You too."

Stepping around his shopping trolley, I

push open the door of the hair salon. A young woman in her midthirties is washing a customer's hair in a sink.

"Excuse me."

"What do you want, petal? I don't do men's hair."

Moving closer, I show her a passport-sized photograph of Sienna. I've folded the strip of images so that only one is showing.

"Have you seen this girl?"

She dries her hands on a towel and studies it for a moment.

"Who is she?"

"A friend of my daughter's."

"Is she missing?"

"She's in trouble. Do you work on Tuesdays? She was here a couple of weeks ago—about six o'clock, wearing a black dress."

The hairdresser shakes her head. "Don't remember her."

"Thanks anyway."

I step outside. The flags are snapping above the car dealership. Next door at the florist shop, a dark-haired woman in jeans and a flannel shirt is moving buckets of flowers, arranging them to best effect. I show her Sienna's photograph but she says that she closes early on Tuesdays.

"Maybe you've seen her on other days?"

"I don't think so," she says, looking at me suspiciously.

I move from business to business, hoping somebody might remember Sienna. She looked quite striking in her flapper dress, still wearing her stage makeup. The sex shop is closed up, barricaded behind metal shutters. A sign says it opens late, seven days a week.

Next comes the minicab office on the corner, which is little more than a waiting room with half a dozen plastic chairs and a control booth behind a plywood partition and small glass window. A woman is waiting. Dressed in a long overcoat and high-heel shoes, she's young. Pretty. She's wearing too much makeup and has lipstick on her teeth.

The controller is on the phone. Morbidly obese, he has three chins and has to sit two feet from the desk to accommodate his stomach.

He meets my gaze. Keeps talking.

". . . yeah, the skinny faggot wanted three-to-one . . . yeah . . . fucking dreaming, I told him so . . . yeah . . ."

He screws a finger into his opposite ear and examines his fingertip.

". . . that's my point, Gaz, you can't trust the fuckers . . . you got to show them who's boss, you know . . . otherwise someone's gonna get seriously fucked up . . . later, Gaz."

He hangs up. Talks on the two-way radio.

". . . yeah, Stevo, it was George Street . . . number eighteen . . . bottom buzzer."

The controller looks past me at the young woman. "Five minutes, love." His gaze lingers on her short skirt and her rangy legs. I can almost smell his torpid lust.

Finally, he turns to me and we reciprocally decide to hate each other.

"I'm looking for this girl. You might have seen her a couple of weeks ago. Tuesday, late afternoon."

I slide the photograph through a gap in the glass security screen. The controller holds the photograph up to the light like he's looking at a high-denomination banknote.

"Who is she?"

"A friend of mine. I'm trying to help her."

"A friend? How are you trying to help her?"

"She's in trouble. Have you seen her?"

I want to take the photograph back. I don't want him touching it.

"Can't say I have," he wheezes. "But if you leave it with me I'll ask some of the drivers." He pushes a scrap of paper towards me. "Jot down your name and number. I'll call you if I come up with anything."

"I can't leave it with you. I don't have any more photos of her."

The obese controller has unfolded the strip of shots and now he's studying the pictures of Charlie and Sienna together. He runs his thumb over Charlie's face.

"So who's this other girlie?"

"Nobody important."

A smile extends across his face. "I'm sure that *she* thinks she's important."

"Just give it back to me."

Again that same predatory leer. Pinching the strip of photographs between his thumb and forefinger, he extends his arm towards me. I have to tug it once, twice, three times before he lets it go.

A car pulls up outside, the engine running.

"That's your car, love," says the controller.

The woman rises and straightens a skirt beneath her coat, checking out her reflection in the darkened front window. I hold the door open for her but she doesn't acknowledge me. It's as though she's trying hard *not* to be noticed despite how she's dressed.

The minicab driver gets out of the car and opens the door for her. He's wearing jeans and a long-sleeved T-shirt with a slogan on the back: "Happy Hour—Half-Price Sex."

When he turns I can see his pale, narrow face and the tattoos running down his cheeks like black tears dripping from his chemical green eyes. It's the same man I saw standing outside the restaurant when I had lunch with Julianne.

The minicab controller interrupts my thoughts. "He's got a photograph. He's looking for a girl."

The driver doesn't answer, but takes a step towards me. Every instinct tells me not to show him Sienna's photograph, but he takes it from me, cocking his head to one side and studying the image as though committing her face, her hair, her budding body to memory.

Then slowly he raises his face to mine. I can smell his aftershave and something else, lurking beneath.

"What's this girl to you?"

"It's not important."

"Really? Try me."

"No, that's OK."

I reach out for the photograph.

"Maybe you should leave this with us," he says. "I'll keep an eye out for her."

As he says the words, he raises two fingers to his face and traces the dripping tattoos down each cheek, dragging his flesh out of shape. Something inside me shudders.

"Forget I asked," I say. "I'm sorry to bother you."

"No bother. What's your name?"

"It doesn't matter."

"Yeah, it does. You should leave your name and number—in case she turns up."

He's in front of me now. What is that smell? Reaching out, I take the strip of photographs from his fingers, not wanting to touch him. Lowering my gaze, I step around him and keep walking, not looking back. I don't want to think about this man. I don't want to know his name or where he lives or what he's done.

The minicab pulls away from the curb and accelerates along the street past me, carrying the sad-eyed girl and the crying man. As I watch the car turn the corner, a voice inside my head is whispering that I've been wrong. This is bigger and darker and more complex than I imagined.

23

Annie Robinson opens the door. She's wearing a yellow dress and her hair is pinned up in a messy, casual way that probably took her an hour to achieve. I feel the coolness of her lips on mine and can almost taste the brightness of her lipstick.

"You came."

"What did you expect?"

"I just thought you might find an excuse."

"Why?"

"I can be rather pushy. I wasn't always,

but when you're pushing forty and you're a notch below Bambi in the beauty stakes, you either grab your chances or languish in boredom listening to your girlfriends talk about Botox injections or their latest diet."

Her voice tails off. She pours me a glass of wine. Her glass is almost empty. She refills it.

"When I get nervous I talk too much—I'm doing it already."

"You're being charming."

"I should just be indifferent. Men find indifference sexy."

Annie looks at me for confirmation, but I don't know how to answer her.

"It's true," she says. "Why do twenty-five men in a bar always chat up the single prettiest woman when the odds of success are so poor and she's probably not going to want to go home with any of them? Meanwhile every other single woman in the bar is wondering what they have to do to get some attention."

Annie lives in a listed Georgian terrace converted into six flats and backing onto the old Kennet and Avon Canal in Bath. Her flat is on the ground floor and has a walled garden with trellises and a small patio dotted with terra-cotta pots.

After giving me a tour of the garden, she points to the sofa and we sit, sipping wine. In the next breath she puts her arms around my neck and pushes her stomach against my thigh, kissing me urgently, wetly. Next thing she's pressing my hand between her thighs, grinding her crotch against my knuckles and I'm reacting like a man dying of thirst who has crawled a hundred miles across a desert just to be here.

The kiss continues as Annie pulls me up. Standing and kicking off her shoes, she edges me towards the bedroom. Breathlessly, we topple backwards onto her bed and she lands on top of me with a grunt.

"Ow!"

"What?"

"Your elbow."

"Sorry."

Annie slips her fingers beneath the elastic of her knickers, pushing them over her thighs. I try to negotiate the zipper of her dress.

"My hair! It's caught! Don't move."

She sits up on my thighs, reaching behind her to loosen the zip.

"It's jammed."

"I'm sorry."

She laughs. "We're hopeless."

"It looks a lot easier in the movies."

"Maybe we should start again."

"I'll just use your bathroom."

Rolling off the bed, I escape for a moment, feeling the cold tiles through my socks. The bathroom is nicely renovated, with a wall-to-ceiling mirror. There are shelves of shampoos, pastes, powders and moisturizers, which she appears to be stockpiling.

I study myself in the mirror. My mouth is smudged with her lipstick. How long has it been? Two years without sex: more of a drought than a dry spell. I've crossed the Sahara. I've forgotten how to drink.

She'll be under the covers now, waiting for me, which is depressing rather than exciting. I look at my penis and wish it were bigger. I wish it would boss me around more often and stop me rationalizing things.

I'm not a perfect human being. I know more about feelings than I do about the physical world. It's easier for me to understand passion than to experience it.

Annie has brought another bottle of wine and glasses to the bedroom. She's also wearing lingerie, lying self-consciously, trying to show herself to best effect. I take off my clothes and lie down next to her. She doesn't let my doubts linger, taking my hand and pulling me next to her. Her tongue moves against my teeth.

Then she straddles me, squeezing me between her thighs, her breasts against my chest. I run my hand down her back and trace a finger over her curves. She lifts her hips, wanting me to touch her, but I glide my finger away moving higher and then drifting lower again.

"Don't tease me," she whispers, her voice vibrating.

I let my fingers sweep across her mound and she traps my hand beneath her, grinding her pelvis against my knuckles. Her lips are pressed to my ear, whispering what she wants.

I feel a familiar stirring. You don't forget. It's like falling off a bike or falling off a cliff or falling for someone. Even so, my lack of practice is quickly apparent. And I mean *quickly*.

Annie doesn't mind. We have all night, she says. The next time is slower, more deliberate, less urgent, better, and for just a moment all the loneliness and thoughts of Julianne leave my memory and the only sound in the room is the squeak of bedsprings under our weight and the gentle slap of Annie's stomach against mine. I cry out involuntarily, more like a woman than a man, lost in the smell of her hair and the beating of her heart.

I leave Annie sleeping, breathing softly. All men hope to do that. She looks like a child curled up in the disordered bed, one arm covering her eyes. There is a tiny mole on her shoulder blade; her upper lip more prominent than the lower; her eyebrows are shaped; she makes a soft humming noise as she sleeps and the soft swell of her stomach is strikingly feminine.

Creeping through the house, dressing quietly, I let myself out. It's an odd feeling, having slept with someone other than Julianne, to have touched and tasted another human being. I don't know what I feel. Relief. Guilt. Happiness. Loss.

I still have Julianne's car. Her traveling make-up bag is in the pocket of the door and I imagine I can almost smell her shampoo on the headrest.

In between the sex, Annie had told me about her divorce and how her husband and his lawyer had stitched her up, crying poor and hiding assets.

"I was married for six years and four months and couldn't get pregnant," she told me. "We tried. My husband had an affair with his secretary, which sounds so boring when I say it—like a cliché. That's my life—a cliché."

"I'm sure that's not true," I said.

I wanted to ask her about Gordon Ellis. Annie knew about Ray Hegarty's allegations. She conducted the internal investigation, yet she didn't react when I mentioned Gordon and Sienna. Was it natural caution, or confidentiality, or was she protecting a colleague?

Another bottle of wine was opened. Annie drank most of it. She apologized for being so maudlin. "I don't know why I'm telling you all this, spilling my secrets."

"You don't have to explain."

"Really? Are you sure?"

I wasn't sure but I said yes and Annie continued, wanting to tell me everything; to share her secrets, funny stories and her bad decisions. It should have been intimate. It felt more like a therapy session.

I once had a patient who believed that the clock ran faster for her than anyone else. She was a university student and she was convinced that her exam time was concertinaed and that "her clock" would speed up, giving her less time, which is why she could never finish.

The same clock ran slower for other people, she said. Annie acted like that. The world had conspired against her and she wanted me to know that it wasn't her fault.

24

The flight from Bristol Airport to Edinburgh takes just over an hour and I'm on the ground before 8 a.m. Ruiz is waiting for me in the lounge, leafing through the pages of the *Scotsman*.

"Do you think if I got enough people to vote we could get London declared part of Scotland?"

"Why?"

"Well, the Scots get more of our taxes than anyone else. They've got better health care, free prescriptions and no student fees. I could be a Jock, as long as I didn't have to eat sheep's guts and support the Scottish rugby team."

"They are pretty terrible."

"Total rubbish."

He tosses the paper on a seat. "Come on."

"Where are we going?"

"Breakfast. I'm famished. I ate Chinese last night—gave me thunderous wind. Not even the Scots can fuck up breakfast."

Ruiz leads me to his hire car. Something small and compact. He continues to spout his theories on Scottish devolution as we pull into the morning traffic and head towards Edinburgh. The sunrise is pink and misty, leaving tentacles of fog clinging to the valleys where church spires seem to float like islands in rivers of white.

Parking near the old city walls, Ruiz leads me through a maze of alleys until we reach the Royal Mile. The buildings are made of slate-gray stone and look as though they've risen directly from the earth.

It's twenty years since I've been to Edinburgh. Julianne and I came up for the "Fringe" with a crowd of university friends.

We camped in tents and it rained for a week, but we filled our boots with satire and comedy.

Ruiz chooses a café, which looks positively medieval. Most of the patrons are tourists carrying video cameras and city guides. Taking a table near the window, he orders a full breakfast with extra sausages, toast and a pot of tea.

"Do you know what that stuff does to your arteries?" I ask him.

"Do you have a chart? I love charts."

The waitress is a big-boned Polish girl with bleached hair and a nose-stud. I order the poached eggs on sourdough toast on her recommendation. Ruiz looks at me as though I've asked to be castrated.

Once she's gone, he takes out his battered notebook and rests it on the table.

"Hey, you want to hear a Scottish joke?"

"Maybe you should avoid Scottish jokes."

"Nonsense. The Jocks have a great sense of humor. Look at Gordon Brown."

The tea arrives and he opens the silver pot and jiggles the bag impatiently. Then he unhooks the rubber band holding his notebook together.

"You want to ask the questions?"

"No, you talk."

He starts with Ray Hegarty. His security business was solvent, the tax returns up to date, with no major debts or lawsuits. Ray was the public face of the company, a bona fide hero, decorated for bravery after he rescued two children from a flooded storm-water drain.

His son, Lance, left school at sixteen, signed to play football for Burnley. A knee injury ended his career before he turned eighteen. Initially, Lance tried to find work as an assistant coach, but then he trained as a motorcycle mechanic.

"The kid has had some problems. Two years ago he was arrested and deported from Croatia with twenty other hooligans after England played a World Cup qualifier. He also has convictions for racially aggravated assault and low-range drink driving."

Breakfast is served. Ruiz tucks a paper napkin in the collar of his shirt and scoops baked beans onto a corner of toast.

"I came up with nothing on Danny Gardiner. Kid's clean."

"You still haven't told me what I'm doing here."

Ruiz gives me a wry smile. "You were right about the schoolteacher."

"Gordon Ellis?"

"Yeah, but he wasn't always called Ellis. He used to be Gordon Freeman, but three years ago he took his mother's surname and became Gordon Ellis."

"Is that important?"

"It helps if you're running away from something."

Ruiz is going to tell me the story in his own time. He slurps a mouthful of tea and dabs his lips with a napkin.

"What do you know about his wife?"

"Natasha?"

"Yeah."

"Ellis said they met at school. Childhood sweethearts."

"Well, he wasn't lying."

"Meaning?"

"Natasha's maiden name is Stewart. She was thirteen when Gordon Ellis started teaching at Sorell College. It's a private girls' school here in Edinburgh."

"She was his student?"

"Music and drama. I put in a call to the headmaster and set off a dozen alarm bells. Twenty minutes later I had a plummy-voiced solicitor on the phone telling me to ever so politely fuck off.

"According to her school yearbook, Natasha left in year nine, Gordon Ellis transferred a year later. She claimed to be nineteen when they married, but her proper birth certificate puts her at three years younger than that."

"How old is she now?"

"Officially, she's just turned eighteen."

"Maybe they hooked up after they both left the school," I say.

"OK, but why lie about Natasha's age on their marriage certificate?"

I think back to my meeting with Natasha outside the school. She was picking up Billy, who is Emma's age.

"But she has a son?" I say.

"Not her boy," replies Ruiz. "That's where it gets really interesting."

Wiping his plate clean with a half-slice of toast, he consumes it in two mouthfuls and finishes his tea. Then he pulls fifteen quid from his wallet. Leaves it on the table.

"You still haven't told me what I'm doing here."

"We're meeting a family. They're called the Regans. They don't live far."

"Why am I meeting the Regans?"

"They have a daughter, Carolinda, who was married to Gordon Ellis."

"He's been married before?"

"Exactly."

"Divorced?"

"Not exactly."

"What then?"

"According to Gordon Ellis, Caro packed her suitcase and took off. Happens all the time. Some people don't like waking up every morning and seeing the same old face on the other pillow, day in, day out. Depresses the shit out of them."

"You're such a romantic. So why did she walk out?"

"She escaped into the arms of a secret lover, according to Ellis, only nobody has ever met the gentleman in question."

"I don't understand."

"Caro hasn't been seen since. She hasn't contacted her family, hasn't touched her bank account, hasn't used a credit card, or applied for welfare, or visited a doctor, or picked up a speeding ticket, or lodged a tax return, or traveled overseas. She hasn't sent her kid a Christmas card or a birthday card. Lothian and Borders

Police launched an investigation, but it petered out. They couldn't prove Caro was dead and they couldn't find any evidence of foul play."

Ruiz doesn't have to explain the inference. People disappear all the time. Housewives reach the end of their tether and take the grocery money and a taxi to the nearest station. Battered wives flee brutality. Children escape abuse. Dodgy businessmen flee the auditors. Criminals change their names and buy villas on the Costa del Sol.

Ruiz is talking and walking. We weave between narrow alleys and lanes, passing historic pubs, tourist hotels and gift shops with racks of postcards and shelves full of souvenirs.

Gordon Freeman (now Ellis) was born in Glasgow in 1974, the son of a portrait painter and a nurse. His father died of lung cancer when Gordon was fourteen. He and his mother moved to Edinburgh where he went to six different schools in four years.

After finishing his A-levels, he studied drama at Keele University and played some minor TV and theater roles before turning to teaching. He settled in Edinburgh. Married a local girl. He was handsome, popular and well respected. And then something happened.

Ruiz has stopped outside a large slate-gray house, converted into flats, rising so suddenly from the footpath that the building appears to be leaning out over the street.

"Here we are," he says, pressing the intercom.

A woman's voice answers and the door unlocks automatically. Climbing the stairs, I hear a door open above us. She's waiting on the landing—a heavy-set woman in a floral dress and cardigan.

Philippa Regan wipes her hands on her dress. Her copper-tinted hair is permed into a mess of tight curls that match the color of her red-rimmed eyes. She shakes us each by the hand and invites us into the kitchen, apologizing for the cold. Turning up the thermostat, she listens as the boiler burps and groans consumptively.

"Ah cannae get warm anymore. That time of year."

Used teabags have solidified in the sink and a dripping tap rings the same note over and over.

She offers to make tea but doesn't seem

to have the energy. At the same time she glances at the sitting-room door, which is slightly ajar. I can hear the sound of a TV.

"The professor wants to ask you a few questions about Carolinda," Ruiz explains. "I told him that you haven't heard from her in a long time."

Again Mrs. Regan glances at the door.

"Do you have any children, Professor?"

"Two. Girls."

Her generous bust expands as she sighs. "Ah know my Caro is dead. Ah know who killed her, but Coop doesn't like me talking about it."

She presses the heels of her hands against her eyes.

"What happened to Caro?"

"She didn't come home. She went to get something for her supper and didn't come back. That's what Gordon told us, the murdering bastard!"

The kitchen table shudders beneath her elbows.

"Ah never trusted him—even when she married him. Ah could tell he was trouble—always looking for something better. Someone better. He treated Caro like a dog he'd rescued from the pound; expecting her to be grateful just because he married her."

Mrs. Regan is going to say something else but the words don't make it past the lump in her throat. She begins again.

"Vincent says you're a psychologist, Mr. O'Loughlin." She motions to the door. "Talk to him. Talk to mah Coop."

"What would you like me to say?"

"He's nae sleeping and he drinks all day. Ah'm not sure what to do anymore."

My heart strikes a beat for every one of hers.

Over the years I have seen countless people overwhelmed by loss. Each of us reacts differently. Some husbands and wives look straight into each other's eyes without needing words, while others are like strangers sitting in a dentist's waiting room. Some men want to beat someone so badly they can't walk right for a month. Others drink themselves into oblivion. Some pretend nothing has changed.

I can picture Coop and Philippa Regan lying side by side in bed at night. Still as corpses, peering at the ceiling and wondering if their daughter might still be alive. That's the great tragedy of a missing person. The dead are farewelled, mourned and given a resting place. The missing float in a kind of limbo, leaving family and friends to wonder and hope.

Ruiz pushes open the sitting-room door. It's dark inside. The blinds are drawn. "It's only me, Coop, come round for a chat."

The reply is thick with phlegm. "Ah'm nae in the mood."

Mr. Regan is sitting in an armchair, his tattooed forearms resting horizontally at his sides. I can't see his face in the gloom, but a soiled singlet is stretched over his barrel chest.

The flicker of a television throws shadows across the room. He's watching old home movies. On screen, a young girl, barely three, is playing under a sprinkler, running in and out of the spray. The sound is turned down.

Mr. Regan raises a glass to his lips. The dark fluid turns to amber as it passes in front of the light.

"This is Joe O'Loughlin, he's a friend of mine, Coop," says Ruiz. "He's come to ask about Carolinda. Maybe he can help."

"He cannae bring her back, can he?"

"No," I reply, feeling a strong impulse to

turn and go back down the stairs, along the street, back to the car; as far away as possible.

Coop reaches for a bottle at his feet and refills his glass. His tattoos seem to move in the light from the television, becoming animated and telling stories of drunken nights, tattoo parlors and hangovers.

Ruiz takes a seat opposite him. "It's early to be drinking."

Coop doesn't answer. I move further into the room and sit in an armchair beside the TV. Coop gazes past me at the screen, which reflects in his eyes.

"I wanted to ask about Caro."

"Ah'm listening."

"What was she like?"

Coop takes a ragged breath and seems to hold it inside.

"Ah wanted a wee lad," he says finally. "Ah was sure Caro were going to be a boy. Came as a shock when she came out. Thought something had gone wrong. 'It's a bonnie lass,' Ah said, and Philippa she says, 'Are you sure, Coop?' Ah looked again just to be certain."

The home movie has changed and Caro is singing into a pretend microphone, wearing one of her mother's dresses, which keeps slipping off her shoulders.

"Ah watched her grow," says Coop. "Ah counted her smiles, her steps. She were ten months old when she took her first steps from this chair to that one where you're sitting. She were always in a hurry. Ah couldn't get her to slow down. Even when she married, Caro did everything in a hurry. Didn't like her choice, never trusted him, but Caro loved him. Ah paid for the wedding. Rented a posh place for the reception. Walked her up the aisle. She were a bonnie bride."

Coop looks at me, questioning. "It was mah wee girl's wedding, but Gordon shoved us away in a corner, treated us like dirt because we weren't rich or well connected."

"When was that?"

"Seven years ago now," replies Coop. "Caro weren't the same girl after that. Gordon did something to her."

"What did he do?"

He shrugs. "Ah cannae say for certain, but he took away her smile."

He turns his glass slowly in his hand.

"When a bairn loses both parents they become an orphan, but they don't have a name for parents who lose a child."

"No."

"Sometimes Ah pray. Ah'm not very good at it. Ah pray that he didn't leave her body somewhere cold. Ah pray Caro's in Heaven, which is somewhere she believed in. Cannae say that Ah do."

The TV screen flickers and new images appear. Caro, aged about ten, riding on a Ferris wheel. Every time it circles close to the ground she waves at the camera, holding her dress between her knees to stop it blowing up.

"What's your name?" asks Coop.

"Joe."

"Ever wondered, Joe, whether the pain of losing a child is equal to the happiness of becoming a father?"

He doesn't wait for an answer.

"There's nae fucking comparison. Becoming a father is about that first step, that first smile, that first word, that first time she rides a bike or climbs a tree or goes to school, her first dance, her first date, her first kiss. You add all those moments together—every birthday, Christmas, every dream—and there's nae fucking comparison.

"When you have a child you think your

life means something, you know. It's not like you've cured cancer or captained Scotland, but you've had a kid. You've left something behind."

His voice has begun to shake and his chest heaves. He bites down hard on his fist.

"You want to know the worst thing?" he says, struggling to get the words out. "Ah'm angry with her, with Caro. Ah want to scold her, ground her, send her to her room. Ah want to tell her she cannae go out. Ah want to stop her growing up, leaving home, getting married.

"Ah'm angry because she took over our lives—our day began and ended with hers—we planned her schooling, her holidays, her future. What future? For all that love and pain, this is what we get! What's the fucking point?"

"You'll think differently one day, Coop."

"What should Ah be thinking?"

"About your wife out there in the kitchen."

He nods, looking chastened.

"Ah used to feel guilty about loving Philippa less after Caro were born."

"You loved them both."

He nods. The image changes again. Caro is grown up, sitting up in a hospital bed, cradling a newborn baby. Hair is plastered to her forehead, but she's smiling through her tiredness.

"That's our lad, Billy," says Coop, motioning to the screen. "We don't get tae see him anymore. Gordon will nae bring him home and he won't let us take Billy for a holiday. We're his grandparents. He shouldn't be allowed to keep him from us."

"How old was Billy when Caro disappeared?"

"Almost two. Caro dropped round to see us the day before Billy's birthday. She had to sneak over because Gordon didn't like her coming round here."

"Why?"

Coop shrugs. "Ah think he wanted to control her."

"Did she tell you that?"

"Ah could see it."

"When Caro disappeared, what happened?"

"Gordon said she just up and left him. Walked out. He told the police that Caro had a lover, but that were a lie."

Coop's whole body jerks and the Scotch spills over his fingertips. He licks the liquid from his hand and wrist.

"Did the police interview Gordon?"

"Aye."

"Do you know the name of the officer in charge?"

"Frank Casey. He's retired now."

The TV screen flickers and new images appear. Caro, aged about thirteen, is riding a pony that seems impossibly large, cantering between jumps, and she waves as she passes the camera. Coop's whole body rocks forward as she approaches each jump, as if he's riding with her.

It's the emptiness inside him that's the hardest. The voice he'll never hear again. I have almost lost a child. I have almost lost a wife. I can imagine it. I can remember each moment with a clarity that overwhelms the senses. Words get trapped in my windpipe. Sweat prickles. Guts twist.

People who lose children have their hearts warped into weird shapes. Some try to deny it has happened. Some pretend it hasn't. Losing friends or parents is not the same. To lose a child is beyond comprehension. It defies biology. It contradicts the natural order of history and genealogy. It derails common sense. It violates time. It creates a huge, black, bottomless hole that swallows all hope.

We leave the flat. Ruiz walks ahead of me, fists bunched, as though wanting to hurt somebody. I'm still thinking about what Coop said about life leading somewhere or meaning something. Mine doesn't. I am living in a kind of limbo, a lull in proceedings. I am waiting for my wife to have me back—when I should be seizing every day and living it like it could be my last.

I'm like a guy stranded in a traffic jam, who wonders what the holdup is and whether anyone is hurt and if I'll make it home in time to watch *I'm a Celebrity, Get Me Out of Here*.

Instead I want to be the guy who looks at a pretty woman on the footpath and imagines making love to her; the guy who embraces life and lives it on fast forward; the guy who kisses often, hugs shamelessly and treats every day like the briefest of love affairs.

Why can't I be *that* guy?

25

We're driving out of Edinburgh towards the coast. Ruiz is playing music on the car stereo, something bluesy with rolling guitar chords that rattle the speakers in the doors. Closing my eyes, I can picture endless fields of sugarcane in the American South rather than bleak Scottish hillsides. Opening them again I see the wind lifting white plumes from the waves and trees that are bent and twisted like arthritic old men.

"You thinking about Caro Regan?" he asks.

"I'm thinking about Gordon Ellis."

"He strike you as the killing kind?"

"Not until now."

My mind goes back to the murder scene. Ray Hegarty wasn't expected home that night. Ellis could easily have known that Helen Hegarty worked nights and that Sienna was on her own. Knowledge and opportunity are not enough to place him in Sienna's room or put a weapon in his hand.

"What are the chances?" I say out loud.

Ruiz glances at me. "The chances of what?"

"Ray Hegarty saw his daughter kissing Gordon Ellis and complained to the school. A week later he's dead. A coincidence?"

"Coincidences are just God's way of remaining anonymous."

"You don't believe in God."

"Exactly. An affair with a schoolgirl is a motive for murder. It could destroy his career and end his marriage. A man like that had a lot to lose."

"Is it enough to kill?"

"I've seen people kicked to death for fifty pence and a packet of pork scratchings."

Forty minutes later we pull through stone gates into a shooting club. Cyprus trees line the long drive. Flags flap noisily against flagpoles. Workmen are erecting scaffolding around a stone clubhouse that clings to the hillside like a limpet on a rock.

Frank Casey is mid-sixties with white wispy hair that spills from beneath a woolen cap and the sort of wide blue eyes that deepen with age. We watch him break open a shotgun, plug two shells in the chambers and snap it closed again before tucking the gun against his shoulder and gazing along the barrel.

"Pull!"

Two clay discs launch into the air flying left to right. The shotgun leaps in his hands and each disc disappears in a cloud of dust that disperses in the wind.

Casey pulls yellow earmuffs to his neck and turns, cracking the shotgun again. Most of the shooting bays are empty.

"Do Ah know you?" he asks.

"I used to be a DI in the Met. Vincent Ruiz. This is Joe O'Loughlin."

Casey shakes our hands. "How long you been out?" he asks Ruiz.

"Five years."

"Ah been out two. Hypertension was going tae put me in a box. Should have done it sooner. My wife wouldn't agree. She's going off her head, having me around."

His accent is a blend of Glaswegian and something less harsh on the ear. Reaching into his pocket, he produces a small silver flask.

"Fancy a wee snort?"

"I'm good," says Ruiz. I shake my head.

"Suit yourselves." Casey tips up the flask and swallows noisily.

"So what can Ah do for you gentlemen?" he asks, resting the gun over his forearm.

"We wanted to ask about Gordon Ellis," I say. "He used to call himself Gordon Freeman."

"Aye." Casey studies me momentarily over the top of his flask. "Ah did know a man called Gordon Freeman, but why would you want tae talk about him?"

"You handled the investigation into his wife's disappearance."

"Aye, Ah did."

"We're looking into a murder down south. A teenage girl is accused of killing her father."

"And you think Gordon Freeman is involved?"

"He's a possible suspect."

Casey's eyes keep returning to Ruiz as he speaks. "So this is not an official police request?"

"No. We're investigating this on behalf of the young girl who's been charged."

Casey presses his thumb to the center of his forehead. "How old is the wee lass?"

"Fourteen."

He nods knowingly. "Do you fish, Vincent?"

"No."

"How about you, Joe?"

"No."

"The thing with fish, you see, is they exhibit two drives—fear and hunger. The large eat the small. They even eat their own—starting with those youngsters that are nae paying attention at fish school. Know what Ah'm saying?"

The answer is no, but I don't want to interrupt him.

"Gordon Freeman, or whatever he calls himself—he eats the young. He finds the weakest and picks them off. The youngest and the prettiest and the happiest—he devours them bit by bit."

Two more shooters have walked down the path from the clubhouse. They take a bay at the far end of the range and put on vests with pockets for shotgun shells.

Casey presses his hand to his lower spine as though relieving himself of a sharp pain in his back.

"Gordon is the one that got away. The one Ah wish Ah'd caught."

He glances at Ruiz, his face suddenly tired and his eyes shivering.

"We found Caro's car parked at the railway station. A suitcase was missing from the house wi' some of her clothes, but she didnae leave a note or tell her family.

"It took the Regans three months before anyone took them seriously. By that time the trail had gone cold. The CCTV footage wasnae kept, so we had tae rely on witnesses. We interviewed passengers on the trains and filmed a reconstruction—had an actress wearing Caro's clothes and put it on TV—but naebody came forward."

"What did Gordon say?"

"He claimed Caro was having an affair and had run off with her boyfriend."

"So what do you think happened?"

"Me? Ah think Caro Regan is dead. Mah guess is he weighted down her body and dumped it in an abandoned pit. Countryside is dotted with them—old silver mines and coalmines—we dinnae have a register of all of them." His mouth constricts to a pucker. "We tried to break him. We pulled him in, followed him, pieced together his movements, but came up with fuck-all. The bastard has ice water in his veins. He's a genuine fucking sociopath, you know what

Ah'm saying? Clever. No remorse. Two years after she disappeared, Gordon applied for a divorce."

"He had a new girlfriend."

"Aye."

Casey takes another swig from his flask.

"There's no way Caro Regan would have left home without her son. It was Billy's birthday the next day. She'd bought him a rocking horse. What mother leaves her son the day before his birthday?"

Casey closes his eyes. His eyebrows are so pale they're almost invisible.

"Ah didnae get to meet Caro Regan, but Ah think Ah would have liked her. Ah talk to her sometimes, you know, in mah head. You probably think Ah'm mental."

"Only if she talks back," I tell him.

He grins. "When Ah talk tae Caro, Ah ask her where she is now, but she doesn't know the answer. Maybe that's what they mean by Purgatory—trapped between Heaven and Hell. Ah knew her mother, you know. Philippa was a fine-looking girl when she was younger. You wouldnae know it now, but take mah word for it."

There is a click in his throat and an exhalation of breath like he's blowing out a match. He raises his face to the sky. Sniffs at the air.

"Gordon had a caravan. We found the receipt for when he bought it, but we couldnae find it."

"Maybe he sold it," says Ruiz.

"It's still registered in his name."

"Is it important?"

Casey shrugs. "We turned over every rock and shook every tree."

"What did Ellis say?"

"He told us he lost the van in a poker game. Gordon likes playing the cards and he likes the horses. Spread betting—the work of the devil. Word is that he skipped town owing a loan shark called Terry Spencer fifteen grand.

"Terry is a reasonably easygoing lad, but he lost patience and sent one of his boys looking for Ellis to remind him of his fiscal responsibilities—know what Ah'm saying? Stan Keating took a flight down south to Bristol and visited Ellis; roughed him up a wee bit, poured acid on his motor, the normal stuff.

"About a fortnight later Stan was back in Edinburgh, drinking at his regular boozer in Candlemaker Row, when a guy turned up looking for him—an Irishman with weird tattoos on his face. He asked after Stan, who was sitting not twelve feet away, but the barmaid was old school and didnae say a thing.

"For the next hour the Irishman waited, drinking orange juice and doing a crossword puzzle, cool as you like. Stan was watching him and making phone calls, arranging reinforcements—two brothers, the Lewis twins, good wit' iron bars.

"Eventually, the Irishman gets sick of waiting. Stan follows him outside where the Lewis twins are waiting. 'You looking for me?' he asks, taking off his gold watch and rolling up his sleeves. The Irishman nodded. 'You got fifteen seconds tae state your business,' says Stan.

" 'You paid a visit to a schoolteacher.'

" 'What's that got to do wi' you?'

" 'You made a mistake.'

"Stan gives a glance over his shoulder at the twins. Smiles. In that split second he discovered the truth about the Irishman. A silver knuckleduster spiked with half-inch nails crushed his windpipe. It was three against one. They didnae stand a chance.

The Irishman drove the knuckleduster into one twin's jaw and took out the other twin with a telescopic baton that broke both his arms.

"The fight lasted less than thirty seconds. Stan and the twins were on their knees, foreheads bent to the ground, whimpering. Stan's voice box couldnae be repaired."

The skin on Ruiz's face flexes against the bone. "How did Gordon Ellis get a friend like that?"

Frank Casey shrugs his shoulders. "Ah wouldnae want one."

"So what about Terry Spencer?"

"He got his money eventually. Ellis's new family probably stumped up the cash, but that's just a theory."

"And Stan Keating?"

"He drinks in the same pub, but he don't say much anymore. Ah guess you could call him a man of few words." Casey rises from the bench and extends his hand. "Ah know Ah shouldnae say this, but Ah'm glad Gordon Ellis isn't mah problem anymore. Ah hope you have more luck than we did."

Resting the shotgun over his shoulder,

he shuffles up the cinder path to the rest of his retirement.

It's mid-afternoon. Bobby's Bar has a dozen or so drinkers inside and the nicotine-addicted at an outside table. The retired, the unemployed and the unemployable—old men in quilted jackets with awful teeth. It's like a horror film: *Night of the Unsmiling Granddads.*

A plaque on the wall tells the story of the place. John Gray, an Edinburgh policeman, died of tuberculosis in 1858 and was buried in the adjacent yard. His dog, a Skye terrier called Bobby, spent the next fourteen years guarding his master's grave until the dog died in 1872. There's a statue of Bobby on a plinth outside—another monument to our desire to erect monuments.

The barmaid tries not to react when I mention Stan Keating's name, but a small twitch in the corner of her mouth tells me she's lying. Ruiz is already ordering a pint so as not to waste the trip. He hands the barmaid a fiver and waits for his change. Bottles of spirits are like glass organ pipes above his head.

Collecting his pint, he joins me at a table and surveys the bar. A lurid computer game winks and squawks in the corner trying to woo punters into competing unsuccessfully.

"You know the problem with banning smoking in pubs?" he asks, sucking an inch off the top of his Guinness.

"What's that?"

"The smell."

"Of smoke?"

"Of farts."

I wait for an explanation.

"Take a whiff of this place. Disinfectant and farts. Lager farts and Guinness farts and cider farts. When people could smoke, you couldn't smell their farts. Now you can."

"Farts?"

"Yeah."

He takes another huge swallow and wipes his mouth. Then he nods over my shoulder. Further along the bar, one drinker sits on a stool studying a racing guide. A cravat is wrapped around his neck, making him look like an aging fifties film star.

I sit on the barstool next to him. "I'm looking for Stan Keating."

He doesn't answer. His jacket has holes in the elbows and his nose is a roadmap of broken capillaries. The racing guide is ringed with red pen marks.

"I wanted to talk about Gordon Ellis," I say. "Maybe you know him as Gordon Freeman."

The barmaid answers, "He can't talk."

I turn to her. "I just need to ask him a couple of questions."

"Good luck with that," she says, polishing a glass. "Mr. Keating doesn't like being disturbed."

"Maybe he should tell me that."

Keating reaches for his pint glass and raises it to his lips. The cravat on his neck slips, revealing a scar that extends from his Adam's apple down his throat until it disappears beneath the fabric.

"He *can't* talk," says the barmaid, "unless he's got his machine."

"What machine?" asks Ruiz, who has taken a stool on the opposite side.

She holds her hand to her neck and silently moves her lips.

Keating lowers the glass and continues reading the form guide.

"You're not deaf, though, are you, Stan?"

says Ruiz. "I'll buy you a drink." He motions to the barmaid. "Same again."

Keating takes his hand slowly from his pocket. I see the dull gleam of steel as he presses a pencil-shaped device to his neck.

"Tell them to fuck off, Brenda."

The words have a buzzing metallic quality, like listening to a Stephen Hawking interview without the pauses between the words.

Brenda wipes a rag along the bar. "You heard him, gentlemen."

Keating lowers the device and goes back to his newspaper.

"Maybe you don't understand our motives," says Ruiz. "We're investigating Gordon Ellis. We know about his first wife. We know about his gambling debts."

Keating doesn't respond. He folds the paper and looks at the clock behind the bar.

Ruiz tries another approach. "You got children, Stan? I got two. A boy and a girl. Twins. They're grown up now, but I still worry about them. Joe here has two daughters. Still young. Gordon Ellis is a nonce. He preys on schoolgirls."

Keating shifts slightly and reaches for a glass, finishing the dregs before placing it carefully down again.

He prods the amplifier into his neck again, aggressively this time. "Ah used to sing. Nothing professional, like, just around the piano in pubs and clubs. Ah'd warm up the crowd before the main act. Ah sung Dean Martin stuff and Bing Crosby. Do you remember Dean Martin?"

Ruiz nods.

"That boy could croon, drunk or sober, but he preferred to be drunk."

Keating pauses and takes a gurgling breath. His eyes meet mine in the mirror behind the bar. "Ah cannae sing nae more."

"Who did this to you?"

"Go home. There's nae point coming here."

"What are you afraid of?"

The statement hits a nerve and Keating's nostrils quiver as he sucks in a breath. His ears are like cauliflowers pressed to his scalp.

"Fuck you," he says, mouthing the words silently.

At that moment the door opens and a

young woman appears wearing low-cut blue jeans, sockless trainers and a tight-fitting gray T-shirt that rides up to show a strip of smooth abdomen. Her hair is held back with a band and a toddler perches on her hip sucking on a biscuit.

"Come on, Dad," she says. "I'm running late."

Stan Keating folds his paper and turns on his bar stool, finding his feet. His daughter is gazing at Ruiz and me. A breath of concern clouds her eyes.

Keating points to the men's room.

"Hurry up then," she says.

He pushes through a door and disappears from view. The woman talks to Brenda behind the bar, consciously ignoring us.

"Who did that to him?" I ask.

She looks from my face to Ruiz and back again. "Are you coppers?"

"I used to be," says Ruiz. "We're trying to help your father."

"Let me guess—he won't talk to you, so now you're asking me?"

"Has he ever mentioned someone called Gordon Ellis?"

"Never heard of him."

She picks a sodden crumb of biscuit off her chest and wraps it in a tissue. Shifting the toddler on her opposite hip, she tucks the tissue into the tight pocket on her jeans. She's not wearing a wedding ring.

"How old is your little one?" I ask.

She eyes me suspiciously. "Just gone two."

"What's his name?"

"Tommy."

"Must be hard."

"What do you mean?"

"Being a single mum, looking after Tommy and keeping an eye on your dad. Does he live with you?"

"Yeah." She's anxious now. "Who are you?"

"I'm trying to help a girl who's in a lot of trouble. She's not much younger than you. Still at school."

"What's that got to do with us?"

"Your dad went to collect a debt from a man called Gordon Ellis and that's how he got hurt. We're trying to find out who did it."

The toddler is growing heavy in her arms. She sets him down, holding tight to his hand. Then she looks over my shoulder towards the men's room.

"My dad fought in the Falklands with the Paras. Battle of Goose Green."

"Second Battalion?" asks Ruiz.

She nods. "They gave him a medal and a piece of paper. What good is that?"

"He fought for his country."

"You know he never stops talking about it—the Falklands. Two months out of his whole friggin life and he can't forget it. Doesn't want to." She looks from face to face. "Sometimes I think he wishes he'd never come back."

The door to the bathrooms swings open. Stan Keating nods goodbye to Brenda. The machine touches his neck and he looks at his daughter. "Let's go."

I talk to her urgently. "Gordon Ellis preys on underage girls. I'm trying to help one of them."

"That's nothing to do with Dad."

"Who did this to him?"

She fingers a silver chain around her neck. "He's never said."

Keating is already out the door. Reaching down, she picks up her little boy whose hands go around her neck.

"We heard it was an Irishman."

She shrugs. "I wouldn't know, but he calls him something in his sleep."

"What?"

She draws two fingers down her cheeks leaving white lines that fade to pink on her smooth skin.

"The Crying Man."

26

Sitting in the departure lounge at Edinburgh Airport, I gaze out the terminal window where sheets of rain sweep across the tarmac. Men in yellow rain jackets are walking beneath the fuselage of a jet, loading luggage and food trolleys.

My flight to Bristol leaves in forty minutes. Ruiz has to wait another hour to get to London.

"You want one of these?" he asks, offering me a boiled sweet from a round flat tin.

"No, thanks."

One of the lollies rattles against the inside of his teeth. He tucks the tin into his jacket pocket. Some people have smells and some have sounds. Ruiz rattles when he walks and creaks when he bends.

I tell Ruiz about going to the minicab office and seeing an Irishman with tattoos that looked like tears. The same man had been outside the restaurant when I had lunch with Julianne.

"How does Gordon Ellis get protection from someone like that? He's a secondary-school drama teacher, not a gangster."

"He's a sexual predator."

"Yeah and nobody likes a nonce. Not even hardened crims can abide a kiddie fiddler. Ellis wouldn't last a month inside. Someone would shank him in a meal queue or hang him from the bars."

"Maybe the Irishman doesn't know he's a nonce."

I watch a jet land in a cloud of spray and recall a patient of mine who was so scared of flying she tried to open the door of the plane and jump out. It turned out that she wasn't scared of flying (or crashing). She was claustrophobic. Sometimes the obvious answer fits perfectly, yet it's still wrong.

"How is Julianne?" asks Ruiz.

"Fine."

"You're still talking?"

"We are."

"You bumping ugly?"

"She's started seeing someone else. An architect."

"Is it serious?"

"I don't know."

Silence settles around us and I begin thinking about Harry Veitch. When Julianne and I were together, we used to crack jokes about Harry and the way he always insisted on tasting the wine at restaurants, describing the tannins and bouquet. Maybe I was the one who told the jokes, but I'm sure Julianne smiled.

Then I think about last night with Annie Robinson. For years I couldn't imagine getting up the courage to show my naked body to another woman. Now it's happened and I don't know how to feel.

I want to ask Ruiz if it gets any easier. Marriage. Separation. Possible divorce. He's been there, done that, bought the T-shirt. At the same time I want to avoid the subject. Live in denial.

"On the day she left me, Julianne said that I was sad; that I'd forgotten how to enjoy life. I looked at Coop today—how he'd stopped living after his daughter disappeared, how he'd given up—and I wondered if maybe Julianne was right about me."

"You're not like Coop."

"I keep expecting things to go back to the way they were."

"It won't happen. Take it from me."

"You don't think she'll take me back?"

"No, I'm saying it'll never be the same."

"You're still seeing Miranda."

"That's not the same thing. She's an ex-wife with benefits."

"Benefits?"

"Perfect breasts and thighs that can crush a filing cabinet."

I shake my head and laugh, which I shouldn't because it will only encourage him.

Instead he grows serious. "Do you know what makes a good detective, Prof? We're the suspicious ones. We believe that everybody lies. Suspects. Witnesses. Victims. The innocent. The guilty. The stupid. Unfortunately, the very thing that makes us good detectives makes us lousy husbands.

"When I was married to Miranda, she put

up with my moods and my late nights and my drinking, but I know she lay awake sometimes wondering what doors I was kicking down and what lay on the other side. All she ever really wanted was to have me walk through *her* door—safe and whole.

"I think maybe she could have lived with the uncertainty if I didn't leave a part of myself behind every time. We'd be at a restaurant, or a dinner party, or watching TV and she knew I was thinking about work. It got so bad that sometimes I didn't want to go home. I used to make up excuses and stay in the office. That's your problem, Joe—you can't leave it behind."

I want to argue with him. I want to remind him I no longer have a home to protect or pollute, but Ruiz would just slap me around the head for being pessimistic and defeatist. It's one of the things I've noticed about him since he retired—he's become far more pragmatic. He can live with his regrets because one by one he has set them to rights or laid them to rest or made amends or accepted the things he cannot change. When you've been shot, stabbed and almost drowned, every day becomes a blessing, every birthday a celebration—

life is a three-course meal occasionally seasoned with shit but still edible. Ruiz has learned to fill his boots.

"If you want my advice," he adds, "you need to keep getting laid."

"What do you mean?"

"It's pretty self-explanatory."

"You think sex will cure me?"

"Sex is messy, sweaty, noisy, clumsy, exhausting and exhilarating, but even at its worst . . ."

He doesn't finish the statement. Instead he looks at me closely. "So who is she?"

"Who?"

"Your bit on the side."

I want to deny it, but he grins, showing me the boiled sweet between his teeth.

"How did you know?"

"I wasn't born yesterday."

"Is it written on my forehead?"

"Something like that. Who is she?"

"I'd rather not talk about it."

"Suit yourself."

We lapse into silence. I'm thinking of Annie Robinson. I can still see the freckles on her shoulders and feel her breath on my face. One arm lay across my chest and her breasts were pressed against my ribs.

I always feel empty after sex, sad and happy at the same time.

"Hey, did I tell you," says Ruiz, "I heard a guy being interviewed the other night on one of those sex-therapy shows. The interviewer asked him to describe in one word the worst blowjob he ever had. You know what he said?"

"What?"

"Fabulous."

Ruiz's face splits into a mess of wrinkles and his eyes glitter. We're laughing again. He's happy now.

Wind buffets the plane as it takes off and rises above the clouds. Rain silently streaks the windows.

By the time I get home it's after nine. The house is dark. Quiet. Opening the front door, I turn on the hall light and walk through to the kitchen expecting to hear Gunsmoke thumping his tail against the door.

He must be in the laundry. Perhaps he didn't hear me. Opening the back door, I call his name. He doesn't come bounding down the path, licking at my hands. The old rubber mattress he uses is unoccupied.

Retrieving a torch from the laundry, I search the yard. Maybe he dug a hole beneath the fence or somebody could have opened the back gate. When he was a puppy he got out of the yard and went missing for a day. One of the neighbors found him sitting by the bus stop, waiting for Charlie to get home from school. He must have followed her scent.

A noise. I stop moving and listen. It's a soft whimpering sound from the direction of the compost bin. The torch beam sweeps cautiously across the ground and picks out something shiny in the grass. My fingers close around it—the tag from Gunsmoke's collar.

I call his name. The whimpering grows louder.

I see him then. His front legs are hogtied and his neck is pinned to the tree by an arrow that sticks out at a right angle. Torchlight gleams on his matted fur, slick with blood.

His head lolls forward. Instead of eyes he has weeping wounds. Acid or household cleaner has been poured across his face, dissolving fur and flesh, blinding him permanently.

Dropping to my knees, I put my arm around his neck, cradling his head, trying to take pressure off the arrow which is holding his body upright. How in God's name is he still alive?

He swings his head to the left and licks my neck. A groan deep inside reveals how much he must be hurting.

Gunsmoke, my dog, my walking companion, my housemate, my hopeless guard dog . . . Why would someone want to hurt him?

Leaving him for a few moments, I go to the shed and pull out a hacksaw from the box beneath the bench. Gently, I put my hand between the Labrador's body and the tree, feeling for the arrow. Then I use the hacksaw to cut through the shaft.

Wrapping Gunsmoke in a blanket, I carry him through the house to the car.

What car? The Volvo is still at the workshop.

On the verge of tears, I sit on the front step with the Labrador's head on my lap. Fumbling for my mobile, I call directory inquiries and ask for an animal hospital. The nearest one is in Upper Wells Way, about three miles away. I count the rings and then it clicks to an answering machine—a recorded message gives the business hours and an emergency number.

I don't have a pen. I repeat the number to myself, trying not to forget it.

I hear it ringing. A woman answers.

"I need your help. Someone shot my dog."

"Shot him?"

"With an arrow."

"Hold on, I'll get my husband."

I can hear her calling to him and he shouts back. Under my breath I'm whispering, "Please hurry. Please hurry. Please hurry."

"This is Dr. Bradley. Can I help you?"

I try to speak too quickly and start choking on a ball of saliva that's gone down the wrong way. I'm coughing in his ear.

"Is there a problem?" he asks again.

"The problem is someone tortured my dog and shot him through the neck with an arrow."

Questions need answering. Where is the arrow now? How much blood has he lost? Is he conscious? Are his eyes fixed and dilated?

"I can't see his eyes. They poured something caustic into them. He's blind."

The vet falls silent.

"Are you still there?"

"What's your address?"

Dr. Bradley is on his way. I lean my head back on the door and wait, feeling for Gunsmoke's heartbeat. Slow. Unsteady. He's in so much pain. I should put him down, end his misery. How? I couldn't . . .

Growing up I was never allowed to have a dog. I was away at boarding school most of the time so my parents couldn't see the point. I remember one summer finding a Jack Russell cross trapped on a ledge above the incoming tide. We'd rented a house near Great Ormes Head, overlooking Penrhyn Bay, and after lunch one day my sisters took me for a walk to the lighthouse.

I ran on ahead because they were always stopping to pick wildflowers or to look at the ships. I heard the dog before I saw it. I lay on my stomach and peered over the edge of Great Orme, holding on to clumps of grass in my fists. Foaming white water spilled over jagged rocks, swirling into the crevices and evacuating them again. Grassy banks divided the crumbling rock tiers, which dropped at irregular intervals to a narrow shingle beach. On one of the lower tiers, I noticed a small dog, huddled on a ledge about twenty feet above the waves. He had a white face with black markings like a pirate patch over one eye.

I ran back to the holiday house. My father, God's-Personal-Physician-in-Waiting was enjoying an afternoon siesta, sleeping beneath *The Times* on a hammock in the garden. He didn't appreciate being woken, but came grudgingly. My pleas for him to hurry washed over him like water.

The girls had gathered on the headland, talking over each other and offering advice until my father bellowed at everyone to be quiet while he tried to think.

Towropes were collected from the garage and a harness fashioned from an old pair of trousers. I was the lightest. I was to go down the slope. My father wrapped the rope around his waist and sat with his back to the headland, bracing his legs apart, digging in his heels.

"Go down slowly," he said, motioning me onwards.

It wasn't the thought of falling that scared me. I knew he wouldn't let go. I was more worried about the dog. Would it bite me?

Would it squirm out of my arms and fall into the waves?

The Jack Russell did none of these things. I could feel it shivering as I opened the buttons of my shirt and pushed it inside. I yelled out and felt the pressure on my waist. The rope dragged me upwards while I clung to tufts of grass and used rocks as footholds.

The Jack Russell was soon tearing around our garden, chasing after ribbons and balls. I wanted to keep him. I figured I'd earned the right. But my father sent two of my older sisters into Llandudno where they put up notices in the cafés and at the supermarket and the post office.

Two days later an old woman came and collected her dog, whose name was Rupert. By then, emotionally if not technically, he belonged to me. She offered a reward—ten pounds—but my father said it wasn't necessary.

The woman drove away with Rupert and later she left a bag of turnips and a marrow on our doorstep. I hated turnips. Still do. But my father made a big point of me eating them. "You earned them," he said. "It's your reward."

Gunsmoke's head has dropped off my lap. His tongue touches my hand but he doesn't have the strength to lick it.

A van pulls into Station Street, moving slowly as it searches for a house number. The name of the pet hospital is painted on the side, beneath a cartoon dog with a bandaged head and a paw in a sling.

Dr. Bradley opens the rear doors. Grabs his bag. The sight of Gunsmoke catches him by surprise. Something else in his eyes: uncertainty.

He crouches next to me, puts a stethoscope on Gunsmoke's chest. Listens. Moves it. Listens again. His eyes meet mine, full of a sad truth. All I need to know.

"You couldn't have saved him," he says. "His injuries . . . it's best this way."

His hand touches my shoulder. A lump jams in my throat.

"Do you want me to take care of the body?"

"No. I can handle it. Thank you for coming."

The van does a three-point turn. He waves goodbye.

Grunting with the effort, I lift Gunsmoke in my arms and carry him through the house again, setting him down on the old rubber mattress he uses as a bed. Then I take a shovel from the shed and clear the leaves near the compost bin, picking out a spot between the flowerbeds.

I don't know how long it takes to dig the grave. A couple of times I stop and lean on the shovel. My medication is wearing off and my left side keeps locking up, sending me sideways. I'm fine if I keep digging, but as soon as I stop it begins to show. When the hole is deep enough, I wrap Gunsmoke in his favorite blanket and lower him down, almost collapsing on top of him when I overbalance.

"Too many treats, old friend, no wonder you couldn't catch those rabbits."

I'm not a prayerful man or a believer in an afterlife for animals (let alone humans) so there is nothing to say except goodbye before I shovel the first clods on his body. When I finish, I scatter leaves across the turned earth and put the shovel back in the shed. Then I go inside and pour myself a drink and sit at the kitchen table, too tired to climb the stairs, too angry to sleep.

27

The cold wakes me before dawn. Stiff. Sore. Trembling. I brush my teeth and splash hot water on my face and manage to shave. I won't walk this morning. It doesn't seem right. Instead I medicate and make coffee, sitting at the kitchen table, listening to Strawberry crunch her cat food.

If Gordon Ellis was having an affair with Sienna someone must have known. There would have been clues: e-mails, text messages, handwritten notes passed between them.

My answering machine is flashing. There are three messages.

The first is from Bill Johnson at the garage:

I found a door for the Volvo at the wrecker's yard. It's never going to close properly, but it should do the job. You have to nudge it with your hip. You can pick it up any time.

Clunk!

Annie Robinson.

Hi, Joe, it's Annie. She leaves a long thought-organizing pause: *I don't have your mobile number. I had a nice time the other night. I hope you did too. Call me when you get home. It doesn't matter if it's late. Bye.*

Clunk!

Message three. Annie again.

Hi, again. I looked into that thing you mentioned . . . about Gordon. I found a few photographs from college. Hey, I was thinking about cooking dinner to-night. I promise I really will cook this time. Seven thirty or earlier. You choose. Let me know if you can't make it.

Clunk!

Just after eight, I shower and dress in casual clothes before walking up the hill to Emma's school. The children are arriving, muffled up against the cold. Emma will be among the last. She sleeps like a teen-ager, cocooned in a duvet, ignoring every summons. I can picture Julianne dragging her out of bed and pulling clothes over her sleepy head.

Further along the street I see Natasha Ellis pull up in her Ford Focus. She lifts Billy from his booster seat and slips a rucksack over his shoulders. He's wearing a woolen hat, pulled down over his ears, and carrying a faded Tigger. They walk hand in hand to the gate. Natasha crouches and hugs him and Billy solemnly hands her the soft toy. Then he turns and runs to a group of friends.

"Mrs. Ellis?"

She turns at the sound of my voice.

"Hello. It's Joe, isn't it?"

"Yes."

"Please call me Natasha. Nobody calls me Mrs. Ellis. Makes me feel ancient."

"You're certainly not ancient."

She laughs brightly. "Gordon calls me Nat—but that makes me sound like a bug. Don't you think?"

She's wearing skinny-legged jeans, boots and a turtleneck sweater. Her cheeks are blushed with the cold.

"I was hoping we might talk."

"I hope there's nothing wrong."

"Do you know Sienna Hegarty?"

Natasha raises her eyebrows. "Of course. She used to babysit for us. I heard what happened. What a shock! I can't believe she'd do such a thing."

"I'm trying to help her."

"That's good. That's the nice thing about village life—people support each other. Don't you think?"

Her eyes cut sideways to me and lips part slightly. She wants to leave. My left hand is tapping against my thigh. A nervous gesture.

"How long have you been married?"

"Nearly two years."

"Happy?"

"That's an odd question."

"I'm sorry. You must miss not having your family around. You're from Scotland, aren't you?"

She drops into an accent. "Just a wee lassie from Edinburgh."

"Gordon told me you were childhood sweethearts."

She smiles fondly. "It's funny really. He tells people we were at school together, but that's just because he wants people to think he's younger than he really is. He was a teacher at my school. We met up after I'd left. I saw him at a rugby game."

"Gordon plays?"

"Oh, Heavens no! Gordon isn't the sporty type. He watches."

"You must have been very young."

"Eighteen."

She's lying to me.

"That's quite an age difference. What did your parents think?"

"Oh, they love Gordon."

"So Billy's not your son?"

"No, Gordon was married before. His wife left him . . . walked out on Billy. Gordon still can't understand why."

Her eyes shift from mine and she gazes along the road.

"Did you know Ray Hegarty?"

Her face clouds with concern. "Not really. I might have spoken to him on the phone when I called to arrange for Sienna to look after Billy. I don't know if I would have liked him, you know—is that an awful thing to say, I mean, now that he's dead?"

"Why wouldn't you have liked him?"

"He sounded like a bully. Some of the things Sienna said . . ."

"She talked about him?"

"Yeah."

"Saying what?"

Natasha's voice drops to a whisper, "He was very controlling. He wanted to choose the clothes she wore and to stop her seeing her boyfriend. I think he used to beat her . . ." She hesitates. "And there might have been worse things. That's why we had her babysit so often. We even let her sleep over. Have you seen Sienna? Is she all right?"

"Holding up."

Natasha nods and raises her hand, brushing hair from her eyes.

"Did you know that Ray Hegarty made a complaint to the school about your husband?"

Color fades in her cheeks and her features tighten. For a moment I think she's going to deny everything or plead ignorance, but her mind works quickly.

"I blame myself," she says.

"Why's that?"

"I should have seen how close Sienna was getting to Billy . . . and to Gordon. She had a crush on my husband. One night when Gordon dropped her home, she tried to kiss him."

"Is that what Gordon told you?"

"That's what happened." Steel in her voice. "Gordon was very upset. He told her parents and the school. She couldn't babysit for us after that. That's why we use Charlie."

"Pardon?"

"That's why Charlie has been babysitting Billy. She's lovely. Billy adores her. Is there something wrong?"

I can't answer her. The photographs on Charlie's Facebook page; she was lying on a bed playing with a small boy. Billy. I replay the scenes as though I'm looking through the camera lens, watching my daughter, seeing how she responds.

I'm staring at Natasha. Sometimes I don't realize how Parkinson's can lock up my features, creating a living mask. It's making her uncomfortable. She edges away from me, moving towards her car.

"Your husband argued with Ray Hegarty."

A flash of anger sparks in her eyes. I can see a pulse beating in her neck and her hands are opening and closing nervously on her car keys.

"You'll have to talk to Gordon."

"Was he home that night?"

"Yes."

"You sound very sure."

"It was my birthday. He bought me flowers and made me dinner." She unlocks her car, fumbling with the keys, almost dropping her purse.

"Your birthday—that's lovely. How many candles did he put on your birthday cake?"

Her head turns and she peers at me with a cold fury that lays something to waste inside of me. Her voice comes out in a dry rasp.

"Stay away from my family!"

28

Julianne and Emma turn the corner. Emma is wearing a woolen hat with earflaps that tie under her chin.

Tugging at her mother's arm, she complains that she'll be late.

"And whose fault is that?" says Julianne. "Next time, get out of bed when I tell you to. And get dressed . . . and eat your breakfast . . . and brush your teeth . . . and put on your shoes."

Emma spies me and runs into my arms. I try to lift her above my head and get about halfway. She's getting too big to be thrown into the air.

Julianne wants to know what's wrong, but she doesn't ask. She'll wait until Emma is in school. We both get a hug goodbye and a wave at the gate. Emma milks every moment, turning and waving, turning and waving.

"What's up?" asks Julianne.

"I didn't know Charlie had been babysitting for Gordon Ellis."

The statement sounds too much like an accusation. Straight away, she raises her defenses.

"What's the problem?"

"I don't want Charlie in his house. I don't want her alone with him."

"You're not making any sense."

"We can't talk here."

Pulling her further along the street, away from the school, we stop at a picnic table near the green, overlooking the church. A car with a blown muffler rumbles around the corner and I feel my heart race.

"OK. Now what's this about?"

I tell her about my trip to Edinburgh, about Caro Regan's disappearance and Gordon Ellis marrying a former student, a schoolgirl, and moving away.

"Natasha Ellis is barely eighteen. She was sixteen when she married and only thirteen when she met Gordon."

"What about Billy?"

"He's not Natasha's son. Caro Regan disappeared the day before Billy's second birthday. That was four years ago. She hasn't contacted her family or tried to see Billy, or applied for welfare or withdrawn money from an account. The police think she's dead."

Julianne's fingers rise to her face, partially concealing her mouth.

"And they think Gordon . . . ?"

"Yes."

"Does the school know?"

"Ray Hegarty saw Gordon Ellis kissing Sienna and made a complaint to the school, but the allegation was dismissed because Sienna denied it. I talked to Mr. Stozer on Monday but he called it a misunderstanding and a harmless schoolgirl crush. He's wrong. I think Gordon Ellis was sleeping with Sienna."

"You said she was pregnant!"

"Yes."

"You have to tell the police."

"I need Sienna to confirm it."

Julianne turns her head and glances back towards the school. Her tone softens. "Are you sure you're right about this?"

"Even if I'm wrong, I don't want Charlie going anywhere near Ellis."

"Do I stop her going to school?"

"No."

I hesitate, not wanting to frighten her. How much should I say? Should I tell her that someone ran me off the road—or about what happened to Gunsmoke? This is why she left me. Every time I get involved in a case like this the stakes become too high.

"Are you taking your medication?" she asks, looking at me closely.

"Yes."

A hand reaches towards me and her fingers brush against my cheek. Then she steps closer and puts her arms around me, pulling my head to her chest. I stay very quiet, listening to her heart beating. Then suddenly step back, breaking contact with her.

"What's wrong?" she asks.

"Nothing."

"Have I upset you?"

"I'm fine. I just don't think we should . . ."

"Should what?"

She's waiting. I can't look at her face.

"Every time you touch me it feels as though you're leaving me all over again."

"That's not my fault, Joe."

"I know."

She looks at my expression and understands that something has altered between us. Turning her head, she gazes at the bare limbs of the oak trees in the churchyard.

"I have to go. I'm due in court. You're going to fix this."

"I'm going to try."

She spins and walks away, stepping around the puddles. Perhaps it's my imagination, but I think I glimpse a flash of wetness in her eyes.

29

Oakham House looks different today, blurred at the edges and bleached into monotones like an old black-and-white film. A sea mist is shrouding the whitecaps and obscuring where the sea meets the land. Only the pine trees stand out darkly, bedraggled and scabrous, like a silent army massing on the ridges, ready to invade.

I get lost trying to find the same lounge as before. Sienna is in her favorite place, sitting on the windowsill.

Elsewhere in the same room, an overweight teenager with apple cheeks moves between pieces of furniture, picking lint from the sofas and rearranging the cushions. He has a leather helmet on his head, strapped beneath his chin. Another youth is playing chess with himself, moving his chair to the opposite side of the table before making each move.

The one cleaning reaches the game and unexpectedly picks up the white queen, polishing it with his rag.

"For fuck's sake, Trevor, leave my queen alone."

Trevor sheepishly replaces the piece and grabs another. The player tries to retrieve it, chasing him around the table.

"Do that again and I'll deck you, Trevor."

Sienna has continued staring out the window. Her shoulder blades look like stunted wings beneath her clothes. She turns at the sound of my voice and gives me a tired smile. Then she spends a moment watching the chase until Trevor is cornered and surrenders the chess piece.

"Trevor is our resident clown," she explains. "The rest of them are mad, but he's just an idiot."

"Why doesn't he speak?"

"He doesn't have a tongue. He bit it off." She leans closer and whispers, "They say his entire family died in a plane crash and Trevor was the only survivor. They found him strapped in his seat surrounded by dead people. Imagine that. You can see what it's done to him." She twirls her finger close to her ear.

"Why does he wear a helmet?"

"To keep his brains from falling out."

She makes it sound so obvious.

Trevor goes back to dusting and rearranging pillows. Sienna swings her legs off the windowsill and sits on a sofa.

"Do you want to play poker? Nobody else will play with me."

"Why?"

"Because I always win."

"You sound very confident."

"It's true. People try to bluff me, but I can tell."

She separates her knees and pushes her dress between them to form a hammock. My left arm swings of its own initiative and almost hits her. Sienna flinches.

"What was that?"

"Just a tremor. No need to worry."

"You could be a really good poker player—all that twitching and squirming. People wouldn't know if you had four aces or sweet FA."

I laugh out loud and her face brightens. Then she shrugs and tilts her head. "I like you."

"Why's that?"

"You're kind of broken."

The statement rattles something in my chest.

"I'm not the one in here."

Again she shrugs. "Do you have a cigarette?"

"You're too young to smoke."

"It's not for me. I can swap a cigarette for other stuff."

"Such as?"

"Cans of drink and chocolate bars and stuff."

On the far side of the lounge Trevor has stopped in front of the TV and is singing along to a commercial for a breakfast cereal.

"I thought you said he bit off his tongue."

Sienna looks at me sheepishly. "It's a miracle."

She quickly changes the subject. "Are you going to get divorced?"

"I'm here to talk about you."

"Charlie wants you to get back together."

"I know."

"Why did you separate?"

"It's complicated."

"The shaking business?"

"No."

"Why?"

"Julianne didn't like who I'd become."

Now the TV is showing a reporter on the steps of Bristol Crown Court. The camera cuts to a police helicopter flying low over the courthouse and images of police on horseback forcing back protesters.

Sienna glances at the screen. "Is that where I'm going?"

"Yes."

"I didn't do anything wrong."

"It would help if you told the truth."

"The world is full of liars."

"That's not an excuse."

Her skin is so translucent I can see the veins running down her neck.

"Did you know you were pregnant?"

Her eyes widen. Something sparks inside them. Fear. Shock. She looks at me with unexpected coldness.

"I'm not pregnant."

"But you were. The doctors can tell."

Holding my gaze for a moment, she calculates her next move, before slumping back onto the sofa.

"Who was the father? I know it wasn't Danny."

She pulls strands of hair across her forehead and down between her eyes.

"It doesn't matter anymore."

"Who are you protecting?"

"No one."

"Tell me about Gordon Ellis."

Sienna hesitates.

"I babysit for him. Gordon has a little boy, Billy. He's such an angel. You should see him sleeping. He has a Tigger that he takes everywhere with him. He's chewed off Tigger's tail and ears so that it looks like a genetic mutant, but Billy guards Tigger like nobody's business. I made Tigger a new tail and sewed it on. Billy didn't say a thing. It's like he thought Tigger had always had a tail and it had never been chewed off."

Sienna doesn't want to stop talking because she fears the next question. Eventually she has to draw breath.

"Did Gordon Ellis rape you?"

"No!"

"Was he the father?"

She doesn't answer.

"Were you sleeping with him?"

Again she remains silent, but her reaction is one of defiance. She's not ashamed or embarrassed.

"Do you love him?"

"Yes." A whisper.

"Tell me how it started."

"You wouldn't understand."

She is still toying with her hair, pulling it along her nose, making herself cross-eyed.

"Explain it to me."

"You're going to say bad things about Gordon. I know what you're thinking. You think he's done something wrong."

"I'm trying to help you."

"No, you're not. You're trying to break us up. You're trying to drive him away!"

She spits the words, turning them into

accusations. Lashing out with her foot, she kicks a chair, sending it skidding across the polished floor, where it cannons into the wall. Sienna shrinks at the noise and looks up at me apologetically.

"How old are you?"

"Forty-nine."

"Do you think there is a proper age for people to fall in love?"

"I think you have to be old enough to understand what love is."

"My mum said that some people never understand love."

"That may be true, Sienna, but some relationships are wrong. Gordon Ellis is your teacher. It's against the law."

She smiles to herself. "You don't understand. It's going to be all right."

"Why?"

"Because love always finds a way."

"Where is he, this person who loves you so much? He's left you here to take the blame."

"No, he hasn't. He's going to rescue me."

"He denies having any relationship with you."

"He *has* to do that."

"He says you're a foolish infatuated teenager who imagined it all."

"He *has* to say that."

"Did you know that Gordon was married once before? His first wife disappeared. Billy's mum. She walked out, according to Gordon, but she hasn't been seen since. She hasn't contacted her parents or friends. She hasn't tried to see Billy. Don't you think that's strange?"

Sienna has fallen silent.

"Gordon met Natasha when she was still at school. She was about your age. He was her teacher."

"This is different."

"How is it different?"

"He loves me."

"Did he tell you that?"

She doesn't answer.

"Did he tell you that he was going to leave Natasha, but only when you're older?"

"You don't understand him."

"Oh, but I do. I've seen a lot of sexual predators."

"TAKE THAT BACK!" she screams, on her feet. "YOU DON'T KNOW HIM LIKE I DO. HE COULD HAVE ANY GIRL HE WANTS, BUT HE CHOSE ME."

Her words come in a hot rush of snot and tears.

"NOBODY HAD EVER CHOSEN ME. NEVER. NOT ONCE."

From the far side of the room, the chess player looks up and puts a finger to his lips, asking for quiet. Sienna pulls a face at him and then shrugs, her anger dissipating into a sullen silence. Resuming her seat, she squeezes her hands between her thighs. Her narrow chest rises and falls.

"I know exactly how he made you feel."

She doesn't respond.

"Do you remember the first day he smiled at you? He wasn't like the other teachers. You thought he was handsome. Charming. That's why you blushed when he looked at you and laughed when he told you jokes. You flirted with him. It was innocent. And he reciprocated. He asked about the book you were reading. Talked about your acting. I bet he commented on your curls. You said that you wanted straight hair, but he said he liked your curls and that straight hair was boring.

"Soon you found excuses to spend time with him, hanging back after class or arriving early. You could talk to him. He listened.

You told him about your father, your problems at home, how lonely you felt once your brother and sister had gone. You talked about not belonging in your family—how you felt like you'd been adopted. Did you cry on his shoulder? Did he tell you that he understood?"

"Stop it," she whispers.

"Pretty soon you were sneaking looks at each other in class and sharing private jokes that none of the other students understood. Gordon left small presents in your locker, treats that he knew you'd find. He found excuses to brush against you and to bend over your desk in class. It felt sweet, exciting, not at all weird or wrong."

"Please stop."

"I bet he asked about your boyfriends. Teased you. 'If only I were twenty years younger . . .' He said you were beautiful. He made you *feel* beautiful. You weren't just another student and he wasn't just another teacher. It was more than that. He didn't treat you like a child. And when he put his hands on your shoulders, or whispered something in your ear, your heart was beating faster than a kitten's."

Sienna won't look at me now. Head

bowed, I can see only the top of her scalp and faint traces of dandruff along the parting.

"He was grooming you, Sienna. He knew you were vulnerable."

"It wasn't like that," she groans.

"You went to his house to babysit and you saw him with Natasha and Billy. He drew you into the warmth of his family and you saw how close they were. You envied what they had. You wanted to be just like Natasha."

Her head rocks from side to side in denial.

"And then one night Gordon kissed you and held you and told you how much he loved you, but it had to be a secret. Nobody could know. Not yet. Not ever. His face was close and his lips were pushing against yours. His tongue was there, lapping at the space between your teeth. He didn't want sex. He took things slowly, touched you, praised you, his breath in your ear. 'You want this. You need this. You'll like this. Nobody understands what we have . . . Let me show you how special you are to me. And you can show me how special I am to you.'"

A tear lands on Sienna's clasped hands. It hovers on her knuckles and then slides between her fingers.

"Afterwards you felt ashamed and embarrassed, but Gordon made you feel as though you were being prudish and uptight. When you didn't want to do it again, he got cold and sarcastic, but then he apologized. 'You don't understand how much I love you,' he said. 'How I'd die if you stopped loving me.' "

Another tear slides down her cheek.

"Soon you were meeting him after school and on weekends. Sometimes you stayed the night when you babysat and he would sneak into your room. Did he ever take you away?"

She gives a slight nod of the head.

"But you had to be careful. There could be no notes or text messages or phone calls. You always spoke face-to-face and you were careful not to be seen alone. You met him that Tuesday afternoon? Where did he take you?"

"I can't tell you."

"Why?"

"He'll punish me."

"He can't reach you."

She lifts her head. Eyes on mine. Flecks of gold in the brown.

"He can *always* reach me."

The drive home is through a water-streaked windscreen beneath a sky that looks like torn wallpaper. The wipers slap open and closed. Red taillights flare and fade ahead of me. My Volvo has been repaired but looks like it's been coupled together in a breaker's yard and customized with knocks, bangs and squeaks.

The radio playing: news on the hour.

A false rape allegation made by a teenage girl could have triggered a fire-bombing in which a family of asylum seekers died, a court was told today. A teenage girl claimed to have been abducted and sexually assaulted by four Ukrainian men, but later admitted having made up the story because she was frightened of getting into trouble from her parents for staying out late.

The prosecution alleges that the fire-bombing of a Bristol boarding house was a payback attack for the alleged rape. Five people died, all members of the same family, including three sisters

aged four, six and eleven. The lone survivor, Marco Kostin, jumped to safety from a second-floor window.

Stacey Dobson, aged seventeen, gave evidence that she'd spent the previous afternoon and evening with Marco Kostin, but later made up a story of being dragged into a van and sexually assaulted by four asylum seekers. Several men, including Marco Kostin, were arrested but subsequently released without charge.

Twenty-four hours later, Marco Kostin's house was firebombed while he and his family slept. Three men, including British National Party candidate Novak Brennan, have pleaded not guilty to charges of murder and conspiracy to commit murder with the intent to endanger life.

Brennan allegedly drove the van used in the attack and was later seen celebrating at a bar where one of his co-accused boasted he had been to a "Russian barbecue."

Parking beneath a dripping oak, I run to the door of the terrace, dodging puddles and sheltering beneath my coat. The key turns and the door opens. Even before I step across the threshold I sense a change. It's not so much a foreign smell as a variation in the air temperature or the pressure. Perhaps I left a window open upstairs. Maybe I'm disconcerted because Gunsmoke isn't outside, thumping his tail against the back door.

Gently, I place my wallet and car keys on a side table and glance along the passage to the kitchen. There are two doors off to the left. The first opens into the lounge. Nudging it with my foot, I reach for the light switch. Nothing is moved, missing or disrupted.

The gas fireplace has a decorative poker on a brass stand. I pick up the polished brass bar and weigh it in my hand. Backing into the hallway, I move to the next door, the dining room. Empty.

Again I pause and listen.

Edging along the hallway, I approach the kitchen. Through the window I can see the vague outline of the trees in the garden and the edge of an eighteenth-century brick millhouse next door. A flash of lightning fills in the details. The sink, the kitchen table, three chairs . . . Why not four?

"Come on in, Professor, it's just me," says a voice. Gordon Ellis has been sitting in darkness. He rises to his feet and swivels to face me. "The door was unlocked. Hope you don't mind."

I'm still holding the poker in my hand. "I didn't leave the door unlocked."

"My mistake," he says. "I found the key under a rock. I'd be more careful about where I hid it next time."

He's wearing denim jeans and a dark shirt with faint traces of dandruff or powder on the front. A carmine-colored scratch weeps on his right cheek, below a bruise. Ellis sniffs and rubs his nose with the palm of his hand. I can see the dilation in his pupils, which are working hard to retain the light.

"What were you going to do with that?" he asks, motioning to the poker.

"Wrap it around your head."

"I didn't take you for a violent man."

"You're trespassing."

His lazy half-smile slowly widens. "Do I frighten you?"

"No."

"It's all right to be afraid."

"I'm not afraid."

Moving slowly, he carries his chair to the table. "Do you mind if I sit down?"

"Yes."

"That's not very polite."

"What do you want?"

"I want you to stop harassing my wife."

"I asked her some questions."

"You were out of order. I don't want you going near her again."

"Does she know about Sienna Hegarty?"

Ellis closes his eyes as though meditating. "What's that young girl been saying?"

"That you were having sex with her."

"She's lying."

"Why would she do that?"

"She's embarrassed and she's angry. She tried to kiss me one night after she babysat my boy. I pushed her away and spoke to her harshly. Maybe I hurt her feelings."

"That's not what Sienna says."

"Like I said, she's lying."

He's a cocky bastard. I want to wipe the smug grin off his face.

"You once told me that teaching was a process of seduction. You seduced your students into learning. You seduced Sienna into bed."

"No."

"She was special to you."

"All my students are special."

"Yes, but some are more precious than others. Every once in a while, a girl emerges from the pack and you take a special interest in her. She's not the best or the brightest or the most beautiful—but she has something that makes her attractive to you. Some weakness you can exploit or an arrogance you want to punish."

Ellis shakes his head. "It's her crush, not mine."

"I bet you can remember the first time you saw Sienna. You noticed her from a distance at first—coming through the gates or walking in the corridor. She stood out from the other girls. She was confident. Highly sexualized. Flirtatious. At the same time there was something vulnerable about her. Damaged. You thought maybe she was being abused at home or bullied at school. You recognized her potential as a plaything."

"I recognized her potential as a drama student."

"Sienna didn't even realize that she was being seductive. Young girls often don't.

They pretend. They practice. They make mistakes."

"I nurtured her. I know the boundaries."

"That's right. You kept telling yourself that you were just doing your job. Pastoral care is so important. She talked about her problems at home . . . the unwanted attentions of her father. You comforted her. Patted her knee. Squeezed her hand."

Ellis bristles. "I don't have to listen to this."

"You began finding ways of getting her alone—isolating her somewhere quiet, somewhere private, somewhere you could show her how much you cared, how you understood, how you wanted to protect her."

"You're sick!"

"You told her she was beautiful. She believed you."

"She's lying. There isn't one shred of evidence to support her story."

"At first I couldn't understand how you managed to keep it a secret. And then I remembered seeing you criticize Sienna during the rehearsal. That's how you removed suspicion—you picked on her, you punished her and she played along."

"You're a pervert!"

"Oh, I'm not the sick one, Gordon. I know

all about you. I know *how* you did it. I know *why* you did it. You were the fat, four-eyed kid at school, who got teased and bullied and ridiculed. There's one in every playground. What did they call you? Lard-arse? Butterball? How much toilet water did you swallow, Gordon? How many people laughed at you?"

Ellis is no longer sitting. He's an inch taller than I am. Younger. Fitter.

"I bet there was *one* girl at school who didn't laugh at you. She was nice. Friendly. Pretty. She didn't tease you. She didn't call you names."

"Shut up!"

"You really liked her, Gordon. And you thought she might like you."

Ellis takes a step out of the shadows into the half-light spilling from the hall. "I told you to shut up!"

"One day you decided to tell her how you felt; ask her to be your girlfriend. Did you write her a note or send her a Valentine? Then what happened? She laughed. She told the others. She joined in the tormenting."

Ellis rocks forward, his neck bulging and fists clenched.

"That's why you target the nice girls, Gordon, the popular ones, the princesses. You're preying on the girls who wouldn't look at you at school when you were overweight and short-sighted—the ones who laughed the loudest. You want to punish them. You want to tear them apart. Living things. Young things. I know about your first wife. I know what you did to her. That scratch on your cheek—did Natasha get angry with you? Did she accuse you of seducing another schoolgirl? She should know—"

"Don't talk about my wife!"

"Sienna was pregnant. She was carrying the evidence inside her—the proof. That's why you tried to kill her."

His eyes lock onto mine. Ropes of spittle are draining from the corners of his mouth.

"You're not very good at this, are you?" he says, laughing drily.

"This is not a game."

His eyes leave mine momentarily and focus on the fire poker in my fist. His nostrils flare and partly close.

"You want to know?" he whispers, challenging me. "You *really* want to know?"

"Yes."

A strange twisted light appears in his eyes.

"Yeah, I fucked her. I fucked her every which way, in her pussy, in her arse." He steps closer. "And guess what, Joe? I fucked your little darling. Charlie was begging for it and I made her bleed. She was moaning under me, saying, 'Fuck me harder, Gordon, fuck me harder.' "

What happened next is something that I can't explain. My vision blurs and the room swims. My fist is holding the poker, which swings savagely, backstroking Ellis across the side of the head. The back of my hand scrapes against his unshaven skin and his mouth leaves a streak of saliva across my knuckles.

His head snaps sideways and I hit him again from the right, sending him down. Ellis tries to curl into a ball but I beat his arms and his spine and his kneecaps and shins. With each blow I can feel the metal bar reverberating in my fist, sinking all the way to his bones.

"This is for Charlie," I yell, "and this is for my dog!"

He raises his head from the floor and gazes at me uncertainly.

The poker clatters to the floor. Lifting Ellis by the front of his shirt, I drop him to a sitting position on a chair. His bladder has opened on the floor. My hand is streaked with his blood.

Instead of cowering, he turns his face to mine. Through bloody teeth, he grins. "How do you feel?"

I don't answer him.

He says it again. "I fucked your princess, how do you feel?"

I knot my fist in his hair and wrench back his head.

"I don't believe you."

He smiles. "Yeah, you do."

30

The holding cell reeks of vomit and urine and sweat. It's a smell that can instantly transport me back to another place and time—a different police cell scrawled with comparable pictures of genitalia and profanities aimed at the police and homosexuals.

Sitting on a wooden bench, I lean my head against the wall, listening to doors clanging, toilets flushing and inmates either sobering up or kicking off incoherently down the corridor.

My skin feels dead to the touch and my chest aches as though I'm breathing into lungs full of wet cotton. Opening and closing my right hand, I wonder if anything is broken.

A drunk is sleeping on the bench opposite. He stole my blanket and tucked it beneath his head, but I'm not going to fight. Now he's snoring, ending each breath with a long raspberry fluttering of his lips.

I don't know the time. They took away my wristwatch, along with my belt and shoelaces. Occasionally, there are footsteps outside and the hinged observation flap opens. Eyes peer at me. After several seconds, the hatch shuts and I go back to staring at the ceiling light, contemplating the bad luck and bad choices that have brought me here. Where did it come from—the violence that rose up inside me?

I am an intelligent, rational, civilized man, yet the blood on my shirt says otherwise. What I did was stupid. Reckless. Wrong.

Yet I don't regret it. I don't feel sorry for myself. I could have killed him. I *wanted* to kill him.

Taking off my shirt, I roll it into a ball and put it beneath my head, resting my arm across my eyes.

I can hear Ronnie Cray's voice before she arrives like an elephant entering a phone box. I expect her to have me released. Instead I'm taken from the holding cell to an interview suite. She pulls up a chair. "Were you trying to kill him?"

"I don't think so."

"You might want to rephrase that."

"OK. No."

"He says there was no provocation. He says you harassed his wife and when he came to complain you attacked him."

"He broke into my house."

"There was no sign of forced entry."

"He found the key."

"He said you invited him inside."

"This is ridiculous! Ellis seduced Sienna Hegarty. He was grooming other girls." I can't bring myself to mention Charlie. "His first wife disappeared four years ago. Her name was Caro Regan—"

"I know all about Caro Regan," says Cray.

The statement silences me.

"Don't look so surprised, Professor, and don't treat me like some wet-behind-the-ears probationary constable who doesn't know shit from Shinola. I checked on Gordon Ellis the moment his name came up in the Hegarty investigation. I pulled his file and I interviewed him."

"And what?"

"He had an alibi. Natasha Ellis says her husband was home all evening."

"She's covering for him."

"Maybe."

"I talked to Sienna. She was seeing Ellis."

"Did she name him?"

"I'm naming him."

"You and I both know that's not the same thing. Unless she makes a statement, there's nothing I can do."

"She's fourteen."

"Teenage girls develop unhealthy infatuations with teachers all the time. Sometimes they convince themselves it's love. Sometimes they convince themselves it's reciprocated."

"She was pregnant. Ellis was the father."

"Can you prove that?"

"No."

"So it's a theory. That's the difference between you and me, Professor. I deal in facts and you deal in theories. We checked Ellis's DNA against the semen stains found on Sienna Hegarty's sheets. No match. And you asked DS Abbott to look at her e-mail accounts and phone server. There wasn't a single e-mail or text message either to or from Gordon Ellis. No love letters or notes or photographs. Nobody saw them together or overheard them talking . . ."

"Danny Gardiner saw them."

"And Ellis will say he was taking Sienna to see her therapist."

"Ray Hegarty complained to the school."

"It was investigated and discounted."

"This is bullshit!"

Cray rises from her chair and paces the room. "You're going about this all wrong, Professor. I know that Gordon Ellis is a human toilet—maybe he deserved a beating—but you're too close."

"Meaning?"

"Sienna is your daughter's best friend. You're emotionally involved."

"You think I'm being irrational."

"You just beat a man half to death."

"Someone ran me off the road. Someone killed my dog. Someone has been following me."

Even as the words come out, I realize that I'm sounding paranoid rather than making my case.

Cray shrugs, blinks. "So you pissed someone off. I can see how that might happen. You're being charged with malicious wounding."

"He broke into my house!"

"He was unarmed and you used unreasonable force."

She turns towards the door and bangs twice.

"You want me to tell your wife or can you handle that yourself?"

"Don't do me any favors."

My sarcasm grates on her. "Suit yourself. You'll appear in court in the morning. Get yourself a lawyer."

The drunk is talking in his sleep, arguing with his addiction. Lying on my wooden bench, I can taste my self-loathing. I've been fingerprinted, photographed and had my buttocks pried apart in a strip search. I have joined the faceless, uneducated and inept, locked up in a police cell, humiliated and belittled. If ever there was a benchmark to indicate how far my life has unraveled, this is it.

Gordon Ellis was sleeping with Sienna and Ray Hegarty found out. Did that warrant killing him? Motives come in all shapes and sizes. Maybe Sienna and Ellis organized the killing together. Both had reasons to want Ray Hegarty out of the way.

The weight of the day is like a fever and my mind keeps drifting. Every part of me seems to ache with exhaustion, even the roots of my hair. Sleep is a blessing.

At some point in the hours that follow, my head and arms begin jerking uncontrollably. My medication has worn off and Mr. Parkinson, a cruel puppeteer, is tugging at my strings and twisting my body into inhuman shapes.

Hammering on the cell door with the flat of my hand, I wait. Nobody responds. The drunk rolls over and tells me to be quiet. I hit the door again.

I can feel my limbs jerking and my body contorting in a strange dance, without music or any discernible rhythm. My head dips and sways, my arms writhe, my legs twitch, moving constantly. The drunk opens one eye and then the other. Wider. He scrambles away and stands in the corner. Crossing himself, suddenly religious.

"What's wrong with you, man? You having a heart attack?"

"No."

"You possessed."

"I have Parkinson's."

The hatch opens. A young constable peers into the cell.

"He's fucking possessed," yells the drunk.

"I need my pills," I explain.

"Get him out of here! He's scaring me."

"I have Parkinson's."

The young constable tells me to sit down. "We're not allowed to issue medications."

"They're prescribed . . . in my coat."

"Step back from the door, sir."

"You'll find a white plastic bottle. Levodopa."

"I'll warn you one more time, sir, step away from the door."

With every ounce of willpower, I stop myself moving. I can hold the pose for a few seconds, but then I start again.

"A phone call. Let me make a phone call."

The young constable tells me to wait.

Ten minutes later he returns. I'm allowed a call.

The first name in my head is Julianne's, but nobody answers. Charlie's voice is on the recorded message. It beeps and I start to speak but realize I don't know what to say. I put down the receiver and call Ruiz.

"What's up, wise man? You sound like shit."

"I'm in jail."

"What did you do—forget to take back a library book?"

"I beat up Gordon Ellis."

I have to wait until he stops laughing.

"I'm glad you think it's funny."

"I have visions of handbags at ten paces."

"I need your help. My pills. The police won't let me have them. I can't function."

"Leave it with me."

I go back to waiting and writhing and being watched by the drunk. If I lock my left and right ankles together I can sometimes get my legs to remain still. But making one part of me stop means the energy finds somewhere else to spasm.

An hour passes and the young constable unlocks the door. He has a glass of water and my bottle of pills. I can get the tablets on my tongue, but keep spilling the water. I swallow them dry and sit on the bench, waiting for the jerking to subside.

"Your lawyer is on his way," says the PC.

"I don't have a lawyer."

"You do now."

Two hours pass. I'm taken upstairs to an interview suite. Even before I arrive I recognize the profanity-laden south London accent of Eddie Barrett, a man who can make a smile seem like an insult. Ruiz must have called him.

Eddie is a defense lawyer with a reputation for bullying and cajoling witnesses and juries. Years ago he earned the nickname "Bulldog," which could be due to his short body and swaggering walk, or his passionate embrace of all things British. (He has "Land of Hope and Glory" as his ringtone and is rumored to wear Union Jack underwear.)

"Well, well, look who got himself arrested—the Hugh Grant of the head-shrinking profession. Should I call it a profession? I guess if it's good enough for prostitutes . . ."

Like I'm in the mood for this.

Eddie reads my expression and tells me

to sit down. Taking a seat opposite, he splays his thighs like his bollocks are the size of grapefruit. “Let’s make this quick, Britney, I’m missing out on my beauty sleep. I hope you didn’t make any admissions . . . sign any statements.”

“No.”

“Good. Are they treating you OK?”

I nod and glance at his watch. It’s after midnight. He must have driven down from London.

“OK, here’s the plan, Oprah. Your case is listed for the morning. We won’t plead. I’ll make an application for bail, which should be a formality. Do you have any savings?”

“Not really.”

“Family who can put up a surety?”

“My parents, maybe.”

“Good.”

Eddie starts making notes on a pad. He asks me about Julianne and the girls, my job and whether I’m involved in any charities.

“Have you ever been arrested?”

“Once. It was a misunderstanding.”

Eddie rolls his eyes and scrubs out a note.

"Can't you get this stuff dismissed?" I ask.

"You didn't piss in a phone box, Professor."

"He broke into my house."

"And you tried to remove his head."

"Surely we can cut a deal?"

"In case you haven't noticed, Dorothy, we're not in Kansas anymore."

Eddie stands and readjusts his hanging bits before tossing his raincoat over his arm.

"Is that it?"

"For now."

"Don't you want to know what happened?"

"Right now, I want to find a king-sized bed, a twelve-ounce Porterhouse and a minibar. You'll be paying for all of them."

Picking up his briefcase, he lifts the flap and inserts the notepad before doing up the buckle.

"By the way, the guy you hit needed thirty stitches and a blood transfusion. I hope he had it coming."

31

Bristol Crown Court looks almost white-washed in a burst of sunshine grinning through a gap in the clouds. Resting my forehead against the window of the police van, I watch clusters of shivering workers smoke cigarettes in doorways.

The van has to stop at a police checkpoint. Barricades have blocked off either end of the street, guarded by officers in riot gear standing almost shoulder-to-shoulder. Protesters, carrying placards and banners, have been funneled onto the footpath and kept well away from the entrance to the courthouse.

Glancing ahead, I can see another group at the far end of the street forming a makeshift honor guard for a larger prison van. Some of the crowd are carrying political posters and placards with slogans about "taking back our country." They're a strange mixture of shaven-headed youths with tattoos, middle-aged men in zip-up jackets and pensioners still wearing war medals. Among them is a woman with a baby in a sling and a grandmother carrying a picnic basket and vacuum flask.

My eyes pick out a familiar face in the crowd. It takes me a moment to place it. Lance Hegarty is in the front row, taunting refugee advocates and pro-immigration protesters. The crowd surges forward, trying to follow the prison van. The police link arms and force them back.

A woman yells, "We love you, Novak!"

Someone else shouts, "It's a stitch-up! A state fucking conspiracy!"

TV crews and reporters record the moment, filming from the safety of no man's land, between the groups of protesters.

Large wooden doors swing open and the prison van pulls down a narrow concrete ramp. The prisoners disembark and walk single file into the bowels of the building.

I'm driven down the same ramp and forced to wait as the doors close behind us. A police officer takes me inside to a holding cell. Other prisoners have lawyers to talk to. I can't see Eddie Barrett anywhere.

"O'Loughlin," yells a guard. "You're second up."

Twenty minutes later I'm being led down corridors and upstairs before emerging directly into the courtroom. The dock is set off to one side and separated by glass partitions. Opposite is an empty jury box. Half a dozen lawyers in black robes and horsehair wigs are standing at the bar table like crows hovering around roadkill. Eddie Barrett is not among them.

A hush falls over the courtroom as the judge arrives, climbing three steps to the bench. The bailiff calls the courtroom to order. Judge Spencer is in attendance, looking down from his enormous leather chair like a headmaster who has summoned miscreants to his study. His round face is blotched with blood vessels that break across his nose and cheeks in a claret-colored blush.

"If it pleases Your Honor, my name is Mellor, I appear for the Crown. We have an application for bail and two matters for mention. If we can dispense with them first you can proceed with the trial."

The judge turns to the clerk. "Has the jury been informed?"

"Yes, Your Honor."

At that moment Eddie Barrett pushes

through a heavy door and swaggers to the bar table.

"Barrett for the accused, Your Honor."

"Have you had an opportunity to talk to your client, Mr. Barrett?"

"I have, Your Honor."

Eddie's hair is still wet from the shower and one untucked shirttail flaps up and down as he pulls out a chair.

"We're happy to waive the reading of the charge, Your Honor, and won't be entering a plea at this time, but we do wish to discuss the issue of bail."

Nobody has addressed me or even acknowledged my presence.

Mr. Mellor speaks.

"The prosecution doesn't object to bail, Your Honor, but we will be seeking a substantial surety and other guarantees. This was a savage, unprovoked assault, which has left a young schoolteacher with severe facial injuries. The victim is still in hospital and may require plastic surgery."

Eddie is on his feet. "My client was defending himself and his property after an intruder entered his house illegally."

"The victim was unarmed."

"He was trespassing."

"The injuries are horrific."

"I haven't seen a medical report."

Judge Spencer interrupts. "You'll get your chance to speak, Mr. Barrett."

Eddie holds up his hands in surrender, his short blunt fingers pointing to the ceiling.

"Carry on, Mr. Mellor."

"Thank you, Your Honor. The prosecution will also be seeking a protection order. The defendant has threatened and harassed Gordon Ellis and his wife. We ask the court to order that Mr. O'Loughlin not approach either of them at their home or their places of work . . ."

Unshaven and exhausted, I can barely keep up with the arguments and feel no emotion other than abject humiliation. Eddie Barrett is waxing lyrical, describing me as a fine, upstanding member of the community, a university professor, married with two daughters . . . an unblemished record . . . close ties to the community . . . a history of public service . . . blah, blah, blah.

No mention of the separation.

"This is a case of a home invasion. The defendant found an intruder hiding in his house. It was dark. He was frightened. He acted to protect himself and his property."

Eddie pulls out a handkerchief and waves it like a white flag. It's a nice touch.

"This is an outrage. A travesty. To incarcerate a man whose privacy has been violated. A man who has selflessly served the community . . ."

Judge Spencer raises his hand. "All right, Mr. Barrett, you've made your point. Save the speeches for the trial."

At that moment I sense I'm being watched and glance over my shoulder. The public gallery is deserted but there is a blind spot to the right of the main doors, an area of shadow big enough to hide a person.

Someone pushes through the door, throwing light into the dark corner. Julianne is watching me. Her hair is brushed back from her face, the fringe falling diagonally across her forehead. She's wearing a dark trouser suit she bought when she worked in London.

I raise my hand, but she turns away and pulls open the door.

Judge Spencer has finished. Eddie Barrett signals me to the edge of the dock.

"Can you raise twenty thousand?"

"That's a lot."

"It could have been worse."

"Call Ruiz. He'll know what to do."

This time I'm placed in a different holding cell. Three men sit on separate wooden benches against the walls. All of them are wearing suits, but only one of them leans forward to stop the jacket from creasing.

I recognize them from photographs. The nearest is Gary Dobson. Next to him is Tony Scott and sitting slightly apart from them is Novak Brennan. I know what I've read about them. Scott is six foot tall, shaven-headed, a veteran football hooligan who has served time for assault and robbery. Dobson is shorter, stockier and ten years younger with convictions for car theft, drug possession and assaulting a police officer. Both men drank at the same pub and were activists for the BNP.

Brennan was a party candidate at the recent council elections. He narrowly missed winning a seat on Bristol City Council because the Labour Party withdrew its candidate and urged its supporters to vote for the Liberal Democrat, ensuring the BNP couldn't win the contest.

Brennan looks younger in the flesh, with barely a line on his face. His trademark thick dark hair is brushed back from his forehead and he has laughter lines around his eyes. Unlike his fellow accused, his suit doesn't look like a straitjacket.

Scott and Dobson acknowledge my arrival by making eye contact. Brennan is picking at his manicured nails, elbows on his knees. I take the bench opposite. The walls have been recently painted. Without the graffiti I have less to read and more time to think.

I find myself staring at Brennan. His eyes lift and meet mine, locking onto a place inside my head. I glance away, staring at the floor.

I'm holding my breath. When I realize, I exhale too quickly.

"How's the trial going?" I ask.

The three of them are staring at me now.

"I just got bail," I explain. "I'm waiting for someone to post it."

"Big fucking deal," says Scott, shaking his head.

Brennan continues to stare at me as if he's trying to examine my conscience.

"Congratulations," says Dobson, who

seems happier to talk to someone. "What *didn't* you do?"

He laughs.

Brennan takes a moist paper cloth from a small travel pack in his pocket and begins carefully wiping his fingers one by one, almost polishing his fingernails.

"You must be getting sick of being in that courtroom," I say.

He raises a forefinger, signaling me to stop. "Do you know the first lesson you learn in a place like this?" he asks.

"No."

"You learn to keep your mouth shut just in case the person they put in the cell with you is a snitch who's going to claim later that he heard you say something you didn't say."

His accent is slightly Irish. The North. Belfast maybe.

"I'm not a snitch."

"Oh, so you brought references did you?"

"No, I mean . . ."

"Best you not say anything."

I nod and he goes back to cleaning his hands.

Julianne told me that he didn't look like a monster. I wanted to tell her that they rarely ever do, bad people. They don't have a rogue gene or a tattoo on their foreheads and, despite what people seem to think, you can't "see it in their eyes."

A few minutes later Brennan, Scott and Dobson are led upstairs and their trial resumes. Julianne will be there. Her witness gives evidence today. The survivor.

32

Two hours later I step outside the crown court registry office alongside Ruiz, who posted my bail.

"Where did you get twenty grand?"

"It doesn't matter."

"You put up your house."

"More fool them—it's falling down."

"I don't know how to thank you."

"Just make sure you turn up for the hearing or I'll track you down myself and kill you."

We've spent the last hour waiting for the paperwork to be approved while I recounted what happened yesterday—first with Sienna, and then Gordon Ellis. As I told him the story, I could see every turn in the road, every dip and curve, every fuckup. When I reached the point where Ellis claimed to have slept with Charlie, I could feel the temperature rise in Ruiz.

"It's not true," he told me. "Charlie's too bright for that."

"I know. I wish I could have been thinking more clearly at the time. Instead I wanted to kill him."

"Yeah, well, don't go publicizing the fact."

We're standing on the steps. The street outside is empty except for police and a handful of protesters who have stayed behind. Ruiz unscrews the lid from his sweet tin and pops a boiled lolly on his tongue.

"You medicated?"

"I'm all right."

"You should get some sleep."

"I have to talk to Julianne. She's working today. Translating."

I glance towards the courthouse and try to push away the memory of her watching me standing in the dock. The look she gave me. Blank. Empty.

"Which court is she in?"

"The Novak Brennan trial."

Ruiz seems to taste something in his mouth that turns sour and unpleasant. He spits the sweet into the gutter where it shatters against the concrete.

"What's wrong?"

"Nothing."

"You know Brennan?"

"Yeah, I know him. We go way back."

"I just spent an hour in a holding cell with him."

"Then you might want to shower."

Planting his hands in his coat pockets, Ruiz stares indolently into the pearl-gray sky, but his gaze has turned inward, replaying past events in his head. Clearing his throat, he begins talking about his years in Northern Ireland when he was seconded to work with the Royal Ulster Constabulary, monitoring intelligence on IRA terror cells operating on the British mainland but controlled from Belfast.

"A prostitute called Mae Grace Brennan died of a drug overdose in a bedsit on the Antrim Road in 1972. It was just after Bloody Friday. She was dead two days before the neighbors broke into her flat. They found Novak and his sister living in filth. Novak was three, Rita only nine months. The baby was so undernourished she had bleeding sores on her buttocks and back. Novak could barely walk.

"Brother and sister were made wards of the court and fostered. A Methodist minister and his wife adopted them, but the die was cast early when it came to Novak. He had behavioral problems which saw him expelled from school and given counseling from the age of seven. When he was ten he killed the family cat by throwing it against a wall after it scratched him. Four years later, he beat up the minister's wife so badly that she had to be hospitalized.

"The family gave up and Novak and Rita were taken back into care. Four months later they ran away and finished up on the streets of Belfast. It was 1983, just before I started my secondment.

"That December the IRA set off a car bomb outside Harrods and killed six people—three of them coppers. I knew one of them. Inspector Stephen Dodd. He died on Christmas Eve. We were trying to trace the men responsible and the trail led to Belfast."

Ruiz registers the passing of a police car. The windscreen catches the light like a camera flash and two men in uniform watch us as though we're middle-aged suicide bombers.

"What happened to Novak and Rita?" I ask.

"They lived on the streets, in squats, deserted factories and freight cars. Then Novak came up with a honey-trap scam. Rita used to dress up in a short leather skirt and boob tube, wandering up Adelaide Street, drawing attention from the johns. She lured them into a dark alley, unzipped them and got on her knees. That's when Novak crept forward and tapped Rita on the shoulder, aiming a knife at their soft bits and demanding money.

"He stole wallets, credit cards, sometimes clothes. Later he graduated to blackmail by taking Polaroids and threatening to post them home if the john didn't stump up more cash. Nothing shakes money from a tree like a photograph of an underage girl giving a married man a blowjob.

"Soon they had plenty of cash and rented a place. Set up house. Stayed clear of the social. It seemed like a perfect setup."

"What happened?"

"Rita attracted the wrong customer one

night. A biker by the name of Nigel Geddes plucked her off the street before Novak could intervene. Geddes took Rita to a gang party where she was raped every which way by at least a dozen bikers. When they discovered she was a virgin they laughed. What were the chances, eh?

"They dumped Rita back on the street, bleeding internally, with cigarette burns that turned to weeping sores. Novak lost it completely. The only constant in the shit-storm he called a life had been his little sister and he had made a promise to himself that he'd protect her.

"So while Rita was still in hospital, being looked after by social workers, Novak bought himself a .25 caliber automatic handgun for eighty quid from an IRA gunrunner called Jimmy Ferris. The Ferret.

"I know what you're thinking. You're thinking a kid like Novak, with his history of violence and his hair-trigger temper, would go all Dirty Harry and shoot a place up, but it didn't go down like that. Novak didn't walk into that clubhouse guns blazing. He watched and he waited. He followed the bikers, making a note of their faces, their routines, where they lived . . .

"The first mark made it easy. He left a bar in Short Strand with a young girl in tow. The pair walked into a dimly lit parking garage. By the time Novak turned the corner, the biker had the girl on her knees.

"It was a familiar scene. Novak tapped her on the shoulder and she pulled back in fright. The biker opened his eyes and the pistol slipped between his lips.

"Novak told the girl to get lost. He waited until she disappeared before he looked back at the biker whose shrinking wet penis was still hanging outside his pants.

"The girl heard him begging for his life. Apologizing. Novak counted down from three and pulled the trigger. Because it was a low-caliber weapon the bullet didn't make a clean entry and exit. Instead it ricocheted around the inside of his skull, turning his brain to pulp.

"Novak used the guy's shirt to wipe the saliva and blood from the barrel of the gun. Two hours later, he killed a second biker. This time the guy ran into a school and hid in a toilet block. Novak found him in one of the stalls and shot him four times, but only after he'd kicked him unconscious.

Novak slipped on the muck and left a neat handprint on the floor. That's how the police eventually caught him, but not before he'd killed eight more times.

"One by one he tracked down the men who'd raped Rita. Nigel Geddes was the last. By then Geddes knew he was being hunted so he fled to Liverpool and changed his name, but Novak caught the ferry to Holyhead and slept rough in the streets of Anfield for two months until he found his man. Geddes was shooting up in a squat in Everton and Novak helped him find a vein and then an artery. Bled him dry.

"The police caught up with Novak when he stepped off the ferry in Belfast. He didn't say a word during the interviews. He wouldn't speak to the social workers or child psychologists. The bloody handprint saw him charged with one of the murders, but investigators didn't have enough evidence to pin the others on him.

"When Novak's barrister stood up at the bar table, he told the jury that Novak had been sexually assaulted by the biker, who mistook him for a rent boy. The jury believed the story and the prosecution accepted a manslaughter plea. Novak was still a minor so he was sent to a youth prison and served barely four years."

Ruiz doesn't look at me for a reaction. Nor does he editorialize with his own body language. This is history now. Indisputable.

The clang of metal on metal makes him turn. Across the road an overloaded skip sits beneath a forest of scaffolding pipes. Workmen are dismantling the framework around the Guildhall. Another pipe drops from a height, bouncing onto the cobblestones.

"How do you know this stuff?" I ask.

"Nigel Geddes was part of the IRA cell that set off the Harrods bomb. He'd been under surveillance for nearly two years."

"But if you're right—if Novak Brennan was convicted of manslaughter—why hasn't it come out?"

"He was still a juvenile. He can't be named. Juvenile records are sealed. Anyone tries to publish a detail like that and they risk going to prison."

Ruiz doesn't sound too bothered by the fact. If anything, I sense a grudging admiration for Novak.

"So what's your take on this?" I ask.

"The guy loved his sister."

"Meaning?"

"It means Novak Brennan has the capacity to care about people, just like the rest of us."

"So what happened to him afterwards?"

Ruiz shrugs. "He changed and he didn't change. He studied for his A-levels in prison and moved to England when he got released. I think he went to university in the Midlands. Then he set about making his fortune, using the same basic technique that he and Rita had employed, only on a much bigger scale."

"He blackmailed people."

"He took advantage of their weaknesses."

"So when did Novak Brennan become a pin-up boy for the neo-Nazis?"

Ruiz shakes his head. "No idea."

"You think he's genuine?"

"All politicians have an agenda."

"And Rita?"

"She's still around. Never married. Dotes on him."

Julianne mentioned that Novak had a sister.

We push through a revolving door into the foyer of the Crown Court where security guards are x-raying bags and searching visitors with a body scanner. Ruiz has to unload his pockets as we pass through.

The marbled foyer is dotted with barristers and clerks. A spiral staircase rises to the upper floors. The daily court listings are pinned on a notice board behind glass. Novak Brennan is on trial in Court One. It's the same courtroom and the same judge that heard my bail application.

Seats in the downstairs public gallery are being kept clear. We're directed upstairs to a balcony area, overlooking proceedings. Ruiz slips in behind me, easing the door closed with a trailing hand.

Below us in the courtroom, the jury is seated along one wall closest to the witness box. On the opposite side of the room, Novak Brennan, Tony Scott and Gary Dobson are side by side in the dock, behind a glass screen. There are more lawyers now. Each defendant has one.

Julianne is sitting on a chair between the witness box and the jury, looking calm and businesslike, yet I can tell she's nervous because she's playing with the charms on her bracelet. Usually, when I picture her, she is the same young woman I met in 1983 after an anti-apartheid rally in Trafalgar Square. She is still beautiful—with a voice that can make an offer of coffee seem like an invitation to sex—but she has changed in the past two years. She's grown weary. Perhaps I'm to blame for that too.

A new witness has been summoned: Marco Kostin. There is a murmur in the courtroom, a frisson of anticipation that runs like an unseen current from the press benches to the jury box. Every trial has a main act—the moment when it can swing one way or the other. It could be a witness, a piece of evidence, a brilliant closing argument or an excoriating cross-examination. This is the main act. Marco Kostin. The survivor.

After a few moments he appears, walking with a slight pigeon-toed gait, following the court clerk to the witness box. Tall and gangly, he seems younger than eighteen, with large eyes and long lashes that would look almost feminine except for his thick adult eyebrows. Putting his left hand on the Bible, he raises his right hand and promises to tell the truth, the whole truth and nothing but . . .

Julianne translates the oath and nods to Judge Spencer, who addresses the jury.

"Ladies and gentlemen, I apologize for the delay this morning but there were other cases for mention and certain points of law that had to be addressed. This witness requires a translator because his English is limited. I know this makes it more difficult and time-consuming, but both Miss Scriber and Mr. Hurst have agreed to keep their questions short and to give the witness extra time to answer."

Miss Scriber QC is a pinch-faced woman with pencil-thin eyebrows and a body rendered featureless by her black robes. She asks Marco for his full name and age and then asks where he was born. Occasionally Marco answers without the need of Julianne, but mostly he waits for her to translate each question.

Over the next twenty minutes he reveals how his father, Vasily Kostin, had been a Soviet "Liquidator" sent to clean up the Chernobyl Nuclear Plant after the disaster in 1986. He drove a bus and helped evacuate people from the town of Pripyet. On one of these journeys he met

Olga and they married two years later. Their first child Oles was born without a brain and lived for only a few hours. Then came Marco and his sisters, Vira, eleven, Danya, six and Aneta, four.

The family arrived in the UK fourteen months ago and spent two months in an immigration detention center before being released into the community. The local authority provided them with housing and vouchers for food and clothing. Marco enrolled at a language school and the family prayed at a local church.

"Why did you come to the UK?" asks Miss Scriber.

"We wanted to start a new life."

"What were you told?"

"They said we couldn't stay, but we were lodging an appeal."

Miss Scriber brings Marco to the week of the fire.

"How well do you know Stacey Dobson?"

"She is a friend."

"Is she your girlfriend?"

Marco dips his eyebrows. "I see her sometimes at the bus stop. We catch the same bus. She jokes about my English."

"Did she flirt with you?"

Marco looks at Julianne for a translation of "flirt."

"She is a nice girl. Friendly. I have not met many English girls."

Marco reveals how they spent a Saturday afternoon together. They went to the movies and then to an amusement arcade. Later he walked her home.

"Did you kiss her?"

"Yes."

"Did you have sex with her?"

Marco lowers his gaze and murmurs something. Embarrassed.

Miss Scriber asks the question again.

"Yes."

"Did you abduct Stacey Dobson?"

"No."

"Did you sexually assault her?"

"No."

Miss Scriber glances at her notes. "Have you ever met Gary Dobson?"

"Yes."

"When did you meet him?"

"He was at the police station when I was taken there. He shouted at me."

"What did he shout?"

"Bad words."

"Do you remember those words?"

"He said: 'You're dead! You're fucking dead!' "

"Is the man who uttered those words in the court today?"

Slowly Marco raises his right arm and points towards Gary Dobson, who sits a little straighter in the dock with a crazy beaming smile on his face. There are cheers from the gallery. Judge Spencer calls for silence. For a moment the jury seems more interested in what's going on above them, but the first question about the fire focuses their attention again.

Marco describes having dinner with his family. His mother had made his favorite meal and they said a prayer because Marco was home after spending the night in a police cell. After dinner Marco read a bedtime story to his two youngest sisters and turned off the light in the girls' bedroom.

He slept at the top of the house in a small loft room accessed by a narrow set of stairs. Photographs of the house and a floor plan are projected onto a white screen. Marco points out each of the bedrooms. His sisters slept on the first floor at the rear of the house. His parents were in the main bedroom overlooking the street.

He was woken just after midnight by the sound of breaking glass. At first he thought someone had shattered a bottle on the footpath outside. He looked out the window and saw a white Ford van in the street. Two men were running. The door opened. The interior light showed a third man behind the wheel.

"Did you recognize this man?"

"Yes. I had seen his photograph in the newspapers."

"Do you know this man's name?"

"Novak Brennan."

"Is he in the court?"

Again Marco points to the dock. Novak Brennan looks completely relaxed, with one leg propped on the other at right angles, revealing a pale shin beneath his trouser cuff.

"What did you see next?"

"The van drove away."

"And then?"

Marco reaches for a glass of water, spilling a few drops. He mops up the spill with his sleeve, concerned that he'll get into trouble. The judge tells him not to worry.

Miss Scriber repeats her question. "What did you do after you saw the van drive away?"

"I went back to my bed and closed my eyes, but I smelled smoke. I got out of bed and opened my door, but there was smoke everywhere. I had to crawl on the floor . . . feel my way down the stairs. I saw flames in the hallway near the door. We could not get out this way."

"Where were your sisters?"

"I heard them coughing. They were in a bedroom next to Mama and Papa. I could hear windows breaking . . . my mother screaming."

"What did you do next?"

"I crawled to my sisters' room. I couldn't find them. I kept calling and feeling for them. Aneta was under the bed. Danya beneath the window. I carried them. I told them not to breathe."

"What about Vira?"

"She was in the hallway. I don't know how she got out. She was calling for Mama and Papa but I could not hear them anymore."

Marco raises his eyes. The courtroom is so quiet I can hear the tremor in Julianne's voice as she translates. Marco recounts how he climbed back to the loft bedroom carrying his youngest sisters. He tried the window, but it could only be wound open six inches. Marco held up his sisters so they could breathe. They took turns but it wasn't enough. Vira panicked and tried to run downstairs.

"I heard her fall," Marco says, the words catching wetly in his throat. "She did not answer me when I called to her. I hope she died with no pain . . ."

A juror sobs. There's nowhere to hide from the raw, numbing emotion in Marco's voice. He describes how he used a suitcase to bash at the window, swinging it upwards into the reinforced glass until the hinges broke and he kicked it clear. He wanted to lift Danya out onto the roof, but the pitch was too steep.

Instead he pulled the bed beneath the window and climbed out. Leaning back through the hole, he told Danya to lift Aneta, the four-year-old, so he could pull her up . . . but she wasn't strong enough.

"She tried, but she couldn't breathe. She couldn't see . . . I couldn't pull them out. I couldn't go back . . . Aneta called to me.

Danya was on her knees. They couldn't breathe."

Marco gulps a breath as if trying to help them still. Judge Spencer asks him if he'd like a break.

Glancing along the row of seats in the gallery, I notice a woman sitting alone, head bowed, holding something in her lap. She's dressed in layers of mismatched clothes with clumpy shoes and woolen tights. As she rocks gently back in her seat, I see that she's clutching a battered teddy bear with a ribbon around its neck. A mascot.

Someone's mother, I think, perhaps one of the defendants'. Brennan's mother died of a drug overdose, according to Ruiz, yet I can see a fleeting resemblance in the shape of her face and her narrow lips.

The truth drops into the stillness. This must be Rita, Novak's sister.

Strands of hair fall across her face and I find myself trying to find her eyes in the shadows, wondering how much she remembers from the streets of Belfast at the age of twelve. Her face has a haunted look that I've seen before in children's homes and consulting rooms. Beaten. Broken. Cautious. Young rape victims don't wear the soft, gentle, confident expressions that say, "Isn't it great to be me." Instead they are eternally vigilant, but not even that can save them from hurt. It's in their faces.

Judge Spencer has ordered a recess. He stands and the courtroom follows. Novak Brennan turns from the dock and makes eye contact with Rita. Something passes between them, less of a smile than an understanding. It's as though Novak has touched her in some way, squeezing her shoulder or patting her hand. Her face flushes with affection. Novak is led away.

At the same moment a door opens in the public gallery. A man appears, waiting for Rita. Tall with slick black hair that gleams under the overhead lights, he's dressed in a leather jacket and jeans, but it's not his clothes that make him stand out. The bones of his face are like metal scaffolding beneath his skin and inky tears drip from his eyes and down his cheeks.

This is the man Stan Keating described. The man I saw at the minicab office and outside the restaurant. Ruiz has seen him too. Although he doesn't physically react, I can almost sense him mentally stepping back and shrinking slightly.

The door closes. They've gone.

Ruiz hasn't moved.

"You going to follow him?" I ask.

He shakes his head. "I'll find out who he is."

"And then what?"

"I'll try to leave him alone."

33

I once had a patient, an actor, who invited all his family and friends for a drink on his eighty-second birthday at a pub near Vauxhall Bridge in London. "The drinks are on me," he said, putting money on the bar, along with a letter addressed to the gathering.

At some point during the evening, he slipped away and a fisherman found his body next morning floating in the Thames.

He'd written:

> I didn't like the thought of spending my last years lying in bed, surrounded by my children and grandchildren feeling they must

> sit by my old wrecked body until my last gasp.
>
> So I hope you will understand and raise a glass and give me a cheer for catching the tide tonight.

There's something noble about an exit like that, but I doubt if I'd have the courage or the conviction. Somebody still had to find his body and retrieve it—strangers who didn't deserve a shitty day.

I used to think I wouldn't care about losing control of my body, as long as my mind remained strong. A psychologist losing his mind is like a painter losing his sight or a composer his hearing. You could call it a tragic irony, but only if you believe in fate or that God has a sick sense of humor.

Right now I feel as though my mind is slipping. My emotions have been manipulated and my reason distracted. It's like watching a magician using sleight of hand, cleverly drawing my attention away so that I don't see the "palm" or the "ditch" or the "steal."

I can make a connection between Gordon Ellis, Ray Hegarty and Sienna, but I don't know what glue holds them together.

And where does the Crying Man come into this, or Lance Hegarty? Someone killed my dog. Someone ran me off the road. Gordon Ellis gave me a strange look when I mentioned Gunsmoke. It was like he didn't understand.

I have to go back to the beginning and question everything, but right now I'm too tired to think. I'm dirty, unshaven, exhausted and I want a shower. I want a bed. I want to square things with Julianne and Charlie.

Ruiz drops me at the terrace and does a three-point turn, heading back into Bristol. Seeing Novak Brennan again has reignited something inside him—an instinct that never leaves a detective, even a retired one.

Opening the door of the terrace I get a flashback of last night. The reminders are smeared across the kitchen floor—a trail of blood showing where Gordon Ellis sat holding his head, where he pissed his pants, where he grinned at me with his bloodstained teeth. Filling the sink with hot soapy water, I begin mopping and rinsing, twisting the towel and watching the pink wash run between my fingers.

The answering machine is flashing:

Bruno Kaufman:

Joe, this is beyond the pale. You've now missed two lectures and two staff meetings—do you want to keep this job? Your students are complaining that you're not answering their e-mails. Call me. Have an explanation.

Clunk!

Annie Robinson:

Listen, you prick! I'm not some pimply-faced teenager sitting by the phone. I'm old enough to deserve some respect. If you don't want to see me, fine! But at least have the decency to call or tell me to my face. Thanks for nothing!

Clunk!

I wince. It's not like I'm ducking to avoid a bullet or a rock, it's an internal shudder—the sort of wince you get when you spend a night with a woman and don't follow it up.

Annie isn't the first woman to produce this reaction in me. That dubious honor belongs to Brenda, a girl my parents employed to clean our house one summer when I was home from boarding school. I saved up my pocket money so I could look at Brenda's breasts. She charged me fifty pence a time and double if I wanted her to lift her skirt and pull her knickers up tightly, leaving little to my imagination.

Brenda lived in the local village and had a brother, Jonathan, who was my age. It was Jonathan who first told me about the mechanics of sex, but it wasn't until Brenda gave me a personal guided tour of female anatomy that I believed it was possible for Tab A to fit into Slot B.

I wince when I think of Brenda because of the sadness in her eyes and because five years later, I teased and cajoled and promised that I loved her as she slipped her knickers down in the backseat of a car (which the ever-willing girl had done many times before) and allowed me to lose my virginity. Brenda wanted to be close to someone and this was the only way she knew how.

Annie Robinson is sweet, well-meaning, good-natured and slightly damaged—or maybe I should say bruised. The sound of her voice makes me wince. It tells me everything I need to know.

At three o'clock I pick Emma up from school. She has a sticker on her jumper that says "Best Counter."

"I can count to sixty-one," she announces proudly.

"That's very good, but what comes next?"

"Sixty-two."

"So you can count higher."

"I can, but the teacher wanted me to stop. I think she was getting bored."

When I laugh, Emma gets cross. She doesn't like people laughing unless she understands why.

As soon as she gets to the terrace she goes looking for her Snow White dress.

"It's in the wash," I tell her.

"When will it be out of the wash?"

"Not for a long time."

"You can put it in the dryer."

"It will shrink."

She looks at me doubtfully and then opens the washing machine. "You haven't even started."

"I've been busy."

Eventually she searches through the dirty washing until she finds the dress and puts it on, ignoring the chocolate and Bolognese stains.

Charlie arrives at about four, dropping her bag in the hallway.

"How are things?" I ask.

"Guess."

She blows a strand of hair from her eyes, but doesn't look at me.

"What's wrong?"

"Let me think. That's right, my father is an idiot, that's about it."

"That's not very polite, Charlie."

"I was going to call you an arsehole, so 'idiot' is far more polite."

Slumping angrily onto the sofa, she picks up the remote and flicks aggressively through the channels without taking any notice of what she's ignoring.

"I can explain."

"It's all over the school. You beat up Mr. Ellis and put him in hospital. He's everyone's favorite teacher—which makes me as popular as swine flu. I'm going to have to leave school, leave the country, change my name."

"I think you're overdramatizing this."

"Am I?" I can hear the hated tone in her voice.

"Gordon Ellis said things about you."

"What things?"

"It doesn't matter."

"Yes, it does. Tell me!"

"He said that he'd slept with you."

"And what—you believed him and beat him up! I babysat his little boy, Dad. I didn't sleep with anyone—that's just stupid. Gordon wasn't even there . . ."

"Don't call him Gordon."

She shoots me a look.

"I know things about him, Charlie."

"And you don't trust me—is that it?"

"That's not it."

"So what were you doing—defending my honor?"

"It wasn't like that."

Charlie looks at me dismissively.

"What's going to happen when I bring a boyfriend home? Are you going to beat him up too? Maybe you want to beat up my football coach—he's a bit of a lech. And what about the creep on the bus who's always perving at me? You could beat him up."

"Don't be ridiculous."

"I'm not the one who's being ridiculous. I'm starting to understand why Mum left you."

The statement cuts through the hard spots, right to the soft center where it hurts the most. Charlie senses that she's gone too far, but she doesn't take it back, which hurts even more.

Brushing past me, she pulls on her coat.

"Where are you going?"

"Out."

"Where?"

"Away from you."

The door closes and I tell myself that she'll forgive me eventually and grasp what happened. And then I realize that I don't want her to understand. I don't want her to know what Gordon Ellis said and how much I wanted to kill him. I want to *stop* her knowing things like that.

"Can I watch TV?" whispers Emma.

She's standing in the doorway. How much did she hear?

"Come on in, Squeak, I'll find you something to watch."

A few hours later I take Emma for a walk, looking for Charlie. Letting myself into the cottage, I find her riding boots missing from the laundry. She's across the lane in Haydon Field where she stables her mare in the barn.

Slipping inside, I watch as Charlie throws a quilted pad on Peggy's back, smoothing it down. I help her lift the saddle from the railing and set it in place. Charlie ducks under Peggy and buckles the strap, pulling it tight.

Inserting her boot into the left stirrup, she swings herself upwards and looks down at me.

"I'm sorry for what I said."

"I deserved it."

A braided ponytail hangs beneath her riding hat. "You don't have to worry about me and boys."

"Why's that?"

"I have a horse."

She laughs, kicks her heels and bolts away, thundering across the field, her hair flying and jodhpurs clinging to her young body. In every sense she's getting further and further away from me.

34

Norman Mailer said there were four stages in a marriage. First the affair, then the marriage, then children and finally the fourth stage, without which you cannot know a woman, the divorce.

That night Julianne visits me and hands me the papers. I've just taken two sedatives and drunk a large Scotch, desperate to sleep. The alcohol and the Valium are starting to work when she appears, pushing past me at the front door and striding into the kitchen. She spies the bottle of Scotch and it seems to confirm her suspicions.

Calmly and dispassionately, she tells me about her decision. She wants me to understand that she has thought this through very carefully. She might use the term "long and hard" but my mind is fuzzy. I feel as though I'm floating on the ceiling, looking down at myself, hearing myself trying to explain.

"Gordon Ellis broke in here and said things about Charlie—terrible things—I just sort of snapped."

"Snapped?"

"Yeah."

"You don't snap, Joe. You never snap."

"I know, but this was different."

"Did you want to kill him?"

I hesitate. "Yes."

She is quiet a long time, staring into space, her lips pressed into thin straight lines. I keep waiting for her to speak. "Is that how little you think of us?"

"What?"

"Is that how little we mean to you?" I can see anger climbing into her face. "You tried to kill someone. What if you're sent to prison? What sort of father will you be then? We're not living in the Middle Ages, Joe, men don't challenge each other to duels. They don't bash each other's heads in."

She flicks hair from her eyes. I can see the twin furrows above her nose. Charlie has them, too. I want to defend myself, but the drugs have turned my brain to treacle.

Julianne sighs and hands me the divorce papers. "It's time to move on, Joe."

"What does that mean exactly?"

"What does what mean?"

"Moving on. You see, I don't think we move at all. We run up and down on the spot and the world moves under us. Days, weeks, months, pass beneath our feet."

"So you're saying we're like hamsters on a wheel?"

"Going nowhere."

Julianne scoffs at this and tells me to grow up. Looking at her hands more than my face, she asks me to sign the papers, saying something about it being both our faults. We got engaged too young and too quickly—six months and three days after our first date.

"This isn't about love anymore, Joe. You joke about your Parkinson's. You pretend nothing has changed. But you're sadder. You're self-absorbed. You obsess. You monitor every twitch and tremor. You're like an archaeologist piecing together his own remains, finding bits and pieces but nothing whole. It breaks my heart."

Her face is drifting in and out of focus. I concentrate on the tiny vein pulsing on her neck just below where her hair curls and touches her skin. Her heart never stops beating. Mine feels like it's slowly breaking or grinding to a halt like an engine without oil.

I remember our wedding day, standing at the altar, saying, "I do." After we kissed I wanted to punch the air and yell, "Hey! Look at me! I got the girl."

On my side of the congregation were doctors and surgeons and my mates from university. Julianne's side was full of her hippie friends, painters, sculptors, poets and actors. My father called them the "Three P's"—potheads, pissheads and pill-heads.

"Are you listening to me, Joe?" she asks.

"Can we talk about this tomorrow?"

"There's nothing else to talk about."

"Please? I'm exhausted. I just need to sleep."

She nods and stands. I feel unsteady on my feet.

"Don't hate me, Joe."

"I could never do that."

She puts some dishes in the sink and tells me to go upstairs to bed.

"Stay with me," I ask, "just for a few minutes."

"I don't think that's a good idea."

My fingers touch her hair and I want to press my body against hers and put my lips against the pulsing vein in her neck. She opens her mouth to say something but changes her mind.

"Stay."

"I have to go."

"Just five minutes."

"I can't."

"Why?"

"If I stay it will only make things worse."

"For you or for me?"

"For both of us."

As she opens the door, I see Annie Robinson on the doorstep about to ring the bell. Her eyes go wide and she rocks unsteadily on her feet.

"Oh!"

"I'm just leaving," says Julianne. "Annie, isn't it?"

Annie giggles nervously. "I'm sorry—I laugh when I get embarrassed. It also happens when I drink." She leans forward and whispers, "I've been to the pub."

"That's OK," says Julianne.

Annie looks at me accusingly. "I left messages for you."

"I'm sorry. I've been really busy."

"Were you busy ignoring me or just beating up Gordon Ellis? I was coming round to slap you in the face, but now I'm too drunk."

"I wasn't ignoring you."

"Maybe I'll just puke in your garden instead."

Julianne looks even more uncomfortable.

Annie stumbles slightly and Julianne

has to steady her. Annie apologizes. "Don't mind me—I made the mistake of fucking your husband."

Julianne flinches.

Annie giggles. "This is pretty surreal, isn't it?"

That's not the word I'd use, but I'm not going to quibble. Succumbing to the pills and booze, I can barely keep my eyes open.

Julianne steps around Annie and hurries down the street, disappearing quickly from sight.

"Can I see you tomorrow?" I ask.

Annie's nostrils flare and her voice changes. "You're an arsehole!"

"I've been told that already today—or maybe I was an idiot. I can't remember now. I'm just so tired."

"Are you still sleeping with your wife?"

"No."

I can't see Annie clearly anymore. She says something about feeling ashamed and humiliated.

"I only came round to give you some information."

"Information?"

"About Gordon Ellis—we were at university together, remember? I was looking through some of my old photographs and I found something."

I'm reading her lips.

"There was someone else in one of the photographs. I only recognized him because he's been in the papers. He was one of Gordon's mates. They shared a house."

"Who?"

"Novak Brennan."

35

The South Bristol Crematorium and Cemetery is perched on a ridge overlooking Ashton Vale where rain clouds are threatening. Umbrellas hover above the mourners and beads of water cling to the panels of the hearse like costume jewels stuck on a black dress.

Ray Hegarty has a guard of honor and six police pallbearers. Ronnie Cray is among them, resplendent in her full dress uniform, sitting alongside the Deputy Chief Constable and a handful of other top brass.

Some of the regulars from the Fox and

Badger have come to pay their respects, including Hector the publican and his daughter Susanne. The villagers are sitting together behind Helen, while the other side of the chapel is taken up by retired or serving police officers. Annie Robinson is also here, looking hung over despite the dark glasses and bright lipstick.

Helen Hegarty is just visible in the front pew, between Lance and Sienna, who has been allowed out of Oakham House for the funeral. Zoe's wheelchair is partially blocking the central aisle, squeezed between the coffin and the pews.

Watching Sienna through the bowed heads, I can tell she's lost weight and isn't sleeping. She knows that people are staring at her, wondering whether she killed her father and why she did it. Pulling her coat tighter around her shoulders, she sinks down, trying to disappear completely.

The silence is a miasma, weighted with the inaudible breathing. I wish someone would play some music. Anything would be better than shuffling feet and seats creaking beneath buttocks.

High above us a tiny bell jangles once, twice, three times and the music starts. A hymn sung by a Welsh choir, played through the sound system.

I don't like funerals. I know how stupid that sounds, but it's not because of the bleedingly obvious. Whenever I come to a place like this I can't shake the idea that death is something that can be transmitted like a disease or inhaled like a spore. What if it sprouts inside me like that Russian guy who inhaled a seed and had a fir tree growing in his lungs? What if I'm witnessing a dress rehearsal of my own fate?

When the service is over, the pallbearers carry Ray Hegarty's coffin through a guard of honor to the graveside. Draped in a flag, it bears a framed photograph of a young man in a PC's uniform, clear-eyed, square-jawed, ready to take on the dark side.

Sienna follows the coffin, glancing up occasionally as though looking for someone among the mourners. She makes eye contact with Annie Robinson and looks away.

Helen Hegarty moves with sure steps and dry eyes. Perhaps she is saving her tears for a less public occasion or has shed enough by now. Her long hair is unpinned and I notice how gray she has become and how the twin notches between her eyebrows have grown deeper.

The wind has sprung up, slapping the artificial grass against the side of the coffin. Words of comfort are ripped away and carried across the cemetery. Hats are held in place. Coats flap against knees. In a different part of the cemetery I spy a couple crouching to replace flowers at a child's grave. A vase and a picture frame are cemented to the base of the headstone to stop them blowing away. A favorite toy has been pinned beneath wire like a butterfly in a display case.

Afterwards I intercept Ronnie Cray as she walks towards the parking area.

"I want to apologize for my conduct the other day."

She doesn't answer. Her eyes are stained by the wind.

"I feel as though I've let you down," I add.

Still she doesn't speak.

"I guess this is a bad time."

She sighs. "You're one of the good guys, Professor, but you're heading for a serious fall. I can't afford to be associated with someone like you."

"I understand." I feel like I've swallowed a bubble of air. "Can I just ask you one question—is there a link between Novak Brennan and Ray Hegarty?"

Her eyes narrow. "Are you suggesting Ray was bent?"

"No."

"Why ask the question?"

"I saw Lance Hegarty outside the Crown Court. He was with Brennan's supporters."

"I guess the lad is entitled to have his opinions," she replies. "Is that all you want to ask me?"

"Gordon Ellis went to university with Novak Brennan."

"That's a statement not a question."

"Ellis got into trouble with a bookmaker. Owed him a lot of money. The bookmaker sent someone to remind Gordon of his responsibilities. The messenger spent three months in hospital and now talks through a hole in his throat."

"Gordon Ellis beat him up?"

"No, but I've seen the man who did. He's been looking after Rita Brennan during the trial."

"The sister?"

"Yes."

I describe the tattoos on his cheeks, like black tears. Cray seems to be sucking on the information like it's one of Ruiz's sweets.

"Is that it?"

"I think it's worth investigating."

"First you were trying to convince me that Sienna was the intended victim. Now you're telling me that Novak Brennan organized a hit on Ray Hegarty. Why would he do that?"

"I just want you to keep an open mind."

"Oh, I know all about keeping an open mind, Professor. Yours is so open that all your ideas fall out. I've just got to be careful not to step in them."

The funeral is over. Mourners are blown back to their cars by the wind. No wake has been planned. Ronnie Cray and her colleagues will no doubt retire to a watering hole and raise a glass to Ray Hegarty—swapping anecdotes about him and contemplating their own mortality.

Sienna is being allowed home for a few hours. Her chaperone is a mental health nurse with gelled hair, stovepipe jeans and a skinny black tie. His name is Jay Muller and his handshake—a brief pressure and release—tells me nothing.

"Call me Jay," he says. "You're a psychologist?"

"Yes."

"You're doing the report on Sienna?"

"That's right."

Jay claps his hands together as though he's won a guessing game. I ask him how Sienna has been coping.

He leans closer, about to share his professional opinion. "Sleep is the problem. False awakenings. She dreams of waking up only she can't move or make a sound. She describes being trapped in her body, unable to call out or press the emergency bell. Then there's the 'screaming' in her head."

"Screaming?"

"It's more like a rushing sound, she says, but it's deafening."

"Has she mentioned her father?"

"Nothing."

"Can I see her today?"

Jay has a habit of picking at the corners of his lips as though scraping away food encrusted there. "I got no problem with that, as long as Mrs. Hegarty agrees. I'm taking Sienna back to Oakham House at six."

On the far side of the parking area, Lance Hegarty leans against the side of a black limousine, smoking a cigarette. Sienna is somewhere inside behind tinted glass while Helen and Zoe are outside the chapel saying goodbye to the Deputy Chief Constable.

Walking up the slope towards Sienna, I prepare to confront Lance. The last time I saw him he was hurling abuse outside the Crown Court.

"You've got some damn nerve, coming here," he says, stepping in front of me and pushing his face into mine. His eyes are flecked with tiny red veins. "You're working for the police."

"Wrong."

"You got her locked up."

"I'm trying to get her out."

Lance spits a gob of phlegm near my shoe.

"I saw you yesterday," I tell him. "You were outside the Crown Court. I didn't have you pegged as a neo-Nazi thug."

"I'm a patriot."

"The last refuge of the scoundrel."

Lance doesn't understand the reference. "You know nothing about me."

"That's where you're wrong. You left school at sixteen and signed to play football for Burnley, but a knee injury ended your career. Two years ago you were arrested and deported from Croatia after a World Cup qualifier. Seven months ago you bashed a Pakistani student because you saw him kissing a white girl. You're a thug, Lance. And you're a racist. I know you're angry. You're pissed off that you couldn't protect your sisters from your father. You're angry at yourself because you didn't stand up to him, the bully, the abuser. But what frightens you most, Lance, is the nagging little voice in your ear that keeps saying you're just like him."

Blood rises. Fingers close into fists.

"I'm *nothing* like my father."

For a moment I think he's going to hit me, but the car window glides down. Sienna's eyes have a strangely androgynous cast. White headphones are plugged into her ears, leaking a tinny hiss.

"We need to talk," I say.

She nods her head to the beat of the music. "I'm sick of talking."

"I still have questions."

"Nothing matters anymore." Her voice is flat, almost devoid of emotion.

The window is gliding up. Unless I say something now, I'll lose the opportunity.

"I have a message from Charlie."

The window stops. Sienna pulls the earphones from her ears. "Is she OK?"

"She misses you."

"I miss her too." Her tongue flicks out and withdraws, moistening her bottom lip. "Tell her I'm sorry."

"You could tell her yourself."

Sienna pushes the earbuds back into place, flooding her mind with music. The window glides to a close.

Helen Hegarty has finished saying her goodbyes. The compassion and sympathy have worn her down and I can almost see her mask slipping as she pushes Zoe's wheelchair towards the car. She wants this day to finish.

"I was hoping I might drop round to the house . . . to talk to Sienna."

"She's only home for a few hours."

"I know."

Helen glances at the limousine and sighs, "She won't talk to me. Maybe she'll talk to you."

I help Zoe into the car, lifting her easily. She puts her arms around my neck, holding me tightly, making it easier for me to carry her. She sits alongside Sienna, taking her hand. Sienna doesn't react.

Having folded the wheelchair and placed it in the boot, I watch the limousine being driven away, stunned by how much misfortune can befall one family. A crippled daughter. A slain father. A racist son. A child charged with murder. There is no truth in the cliché that luck evens itself out. Maybe in games of chance, but not in real life.

An arm slips through mine, hooking around my elbow. It is such a familiar touch that I expect to see Julianne.

"I'm so sorry about last night," says Annie Robinson. "I shouldn't have turned up like that. I don't know what I was thinking."

"It's not your fault."

"You didn't call me."

"I didn't call a lot of people."

"You're angry."

"It's been a difficult few days."

She brushes her cheek against mine. "Come and see me. I'll show you the photograph of Gordon and Novak Brennan."

36

Helen Hegarty unlatches the front door and I follow her through to a kitchen that smells of sugar and citrus peel. She is making jam. Saucepans bubble on the stove and sterilized jars rest upside down on dishcloths on the table.

The steam has straightened strands of her hair, which are plastered to her forehead. She wipes her hands and glances at the ceiling. "Sienna is upstairs. She's packing some things."

"You're on your own?"

"Zoe and Lance have gone into town."

I climb the stairs and tap gently on Sienna's bedroom door.

"Don't come in," she says, sounding startled.

"It's me."

"Can you come back later?"

"No. I'll wait."

Pressing my ear to the door panel, I hear drawers being closed and a window opening.

"I really don't want to talk to you today."

"Why?"

"I'm not feeling well."

"I'm sorry to hear that. Let's talk about it."

"I'm getting changed. Won't be a minute."

The door eventually opens and Sienna spins away from me, crawling onto her bed and sitting against the wall, drawing up her knees and tugging her dark skirt tight over them. The room is tidier than I remember. The bloodstained rug has gone and the floorboards have been scrubbed clean.

Walking to the window, I glance outside, wondering if someone might have been with her. The garden is below. Sienna used to brag to Charlie about climbing out the window and shimmying down the rainwater pipe while her parents thought she was studying upstairs. A gnarled cherry tree has been cut back so its branches don't scrape against the wall.

"It must have been tough today."

Her shoulders rise and fall.

"You thought he might come, didn't you?"

She doesn't answer.

"Mr. Ellis was never going to come, Sienna. He says you made it all up."

No answer.

"Now he's complained to the school that you've been harassing him. He wants you suspended."

Sienna tilts her face and glares at me. "I don't believe you."

Behind her head I notice a torn strip of wallpaper curling like a roll of parchment. Beneath is an older layer with nursery rhyme characters. Little Bo Peep is visibly searching for her lost flock.

"I don't want to fight with you, Sienna. I just want to understand."

"You can't. You're too old. You don't know what it's like to . . . to . . ."

"Be in love?"

"Yes."

"I know you believe your feelings, Sienna. You believe he loved you. Tell me how it started."

"And then you'll leave me alone?"

"If you help me understand."

"Remember I told you how I got the scar

on my leg?" she whispers. "Malcolm Hogbin dared me to climb a tree and I fell out."

"Yes."

"Mr. Ellis was the first teacher to reach me. He carried me to the infirmary and got me a blanket and called the ambulance. Then he sat talking to me and told me really lame jokes until it arrived. 'Don't laugh or it'll hurt more,' he said, and he wouldn't let me look at my leg because the bone was sticking out. I remember wondering if he saw me fall. My dress flew up which meant he probably saw more of me than he should have, but having Mr. Ellis see my underwear didn't creep me out like I thought it might.

"They had to put metal pins in my leg and I was in plaster for three months. Mr. Ellis signed my cast. He drew a bird and signed his name.

"Why a bird?" I asked him.

"Because birds can fly, which you obviously can't."

"I remember looking at his long fingers as he signed his name. He had such nice hands. And when he talked he had this deep round voice that rolled out of his mouth and burst in my ears. He said I could call him Gordon, but only when we were alone."

"You started to babysit Billy?"

She nods and smoothes her skirt over her knees. Her bruised-looking eyes now look sleepy.

"I missed six weeks of school, but Gordon helped me catch up. I know you think he's done something wrong, but it wasn't like that. He made me feel lovely. Grown up. Special."

"How old were you when he made you feel grown up?"

"We were just sitting in his car and he put his finger beneath my chin. Suddenly his lips were right there, pushing against mine."

She won't look at me. Her forehead is resting on her knees.

"I knew about sex. Lance kept magazines in his room and I once saw him and Margo Langdon going at it like nobody's business in Simpson's barn. Margo was on her back and Lance had his pants down and his backside was going up and down on top of her. I remember because Lance started whimpering and shaking and that's when Margo turned her head and she looked straight at me."

"How old were you when you had sex with Gordon?"

"Thirteen."

"That's against the law."

"Juliet was only thirteen when she fell in love with Romeo. Gordon told me that."

"Romeo wasn't forty."

"That doesn't matter. True love doesn't wait."

She says it defiantly, parroting the words that I'm sure Gordon whispered in her ear when he took her.

"I wish you could understand," she explains. "You don't know how wonderful he makes me feel. He could have had any girl he wanted, but he chose me."

"He's married."

"He was going to leave Natasha when I finished school. He doesn't love her. He loves me!"

I produce a photograph from my pocket, holding it between my thumb and forefinger.

"Remember I told you that Gordon had been married before? Her name is Carolinda Regan. Everyone called her Caro. She's Billy's proper mother. Nobody has seen her in three years."

"What about Natasha?"

"Gordon met her at school—just like he met you. She was about your age."

Sienna chews at her bottom lip leaving a carmine mark that slowly fades. Hugging her knees more tightly, she grimaces as though in pain. Her bare feet are tucked beneath the bedspread.

"You told me that Gordon took you away for a weekend. Where?"

"I don't know exactly. It was during the summer. Natasha was in Scotland visiting her folks."

"Where was Billy?"

"He came with us. We took him for a trip to the seaside. Gordon has a caravan. I told Mum that I was spending the night with Charlie."

"This caravan—is it near the beach?"

"I think so. I can't remember much of anything. The whole weekend is a blur. I know we left on Friday afternoon and I can remember coming home. Gordon said I slept most of the time. He said it was food poisoning."

"Is that the only time you went away?"

She nods. He eyelids are half closed. She forces them open.

"Did anyone ever see you with Gordon outside of school?"

"I don't think so. Mostly we stayed in the car or went somewhere private. Sometimes I slept over when I was babysitting. I stayed in the spare room, which is next to where Billy sleeps. Gordon would sneak in and spend a few hours with me."

"What about Natasha?"

"She was sleeping. I was scared she might wake up, but Gordon said that wouldn't happen."

"Why?"

"He mentioned something about sleeping pills."

Sienna's skin has grown ashen and beads of sweat prickle on her upper lip.

"Did you ever tell anyone about Gordon?"

"He made me promise."

"Did anyone suspect—someone at school, a friend?"

Her head rocks from side to side and then stops. "Miss Robinson asked me."

"What did she ask you?"

"If I was spending time with Gordon outside of school."

"When was this?"

"Late last year."

"You're sure?"

"Yes."

"Tell me where you went on that Tuesday—after Danny dropped you in town."

Sienna shrugs. "It doesn't matter anymore."

"Did you meet up with Gordon? Did he take you somewhere?"

Sienna's line of vision sweeps past me as though watching something terrible approaching. Something she has to escape from. She wants to run but I need her here. Gently gripping her shoulders, I make her meet my gaze.

"You don't have to be frightened, Sienna. I'm going to protect you."

"I didn't kill Daddy."

"Show me. Prove it to me. Where were you?"

Tears hover at the edges of her eyelids.

"With Gordon," she whispers.

"Gordon says he wasn't with you. He's given a statement to the police. He has an alibi. Natasha has backed him up."

"They're lying."

"He's letting you take the blame, Sienna. Just tell me where you went after Danny dropped you off."

"Gordon wanted me to do something for him."

"What was that?"

Her mouth opens, but she can't bring herself to tell me. I wait and she tries again. The words come slowly and then in a rush as though she wants them gone, forgotten, buried.

"Gordon said he was in trouble, but I could help him. I just had to do this one thing for him and everything would be OK. I'd prove myself. He'd know I was the one. Then we could be together."

"What sort of trouble?"

"He didn't say."

"What did he want?"

She shakes her head, embarrassed, ashamed.

"I had to visit someone and do what he asked."

She puts the heel of her hand against her forehead. There are patches of color on her throat as if someone has wrapped an invisible rope around her neck.

"What did you have to do?"

"I had to sleep with him," she whispers.

There is a tingling in my chest like a heated wire is being pressed against my heart.

"Who was he?"

"I don't know his name—some old guy who lived in a big house." Her voice starts to break. "I was dropped off and picked up later."

"Who dropped you off?"

"Gordon and another man."

"Another man?"

"His eyes looked like they were bleeding."

"Where did they take you?"

"I don't know. It was a big house. Old. It smelled funny." She rocks forward, breathing through her mouth. "It was horrible. I had to have . . . I had to let him . . . he did things to me. Gordon said it would prove how much I loved him."

I can hear the wetness in her throat as she swallows. At the same time, a shudder goes through her body like tension leaving a metal spring.

"What happened afterwards?"

"Gordon drove me back to his house but we couldn't go inside because Natasha was home. He said it turned him on—knowing what another man had done to me. He took off my clothes and we had sex in the car but he was rough. He hurt me. I told him to be careful."

"Did you tell him you were pregnant?"

"Yes."

"What did he say?"

"He swore and shoved me away. He was yelling at me, saying I'd tricked him, saying I got pregnant on purpose. He told me to get rid of the baby. An abortion. That's when I ran away. I ran home."

Sienna looks at me blankly, too numb to cry. Touching her upper arm with my palm, I feel the coolness of her skin. She leans against me, pushing her face under my chin. Motionless in my arms, she remains curled up, her skirt pulled tight over her knees.

The patchwork quilt has slipped down, uncovering her feet. A dark stain runs over her right foot. It looks like a birthmark or a lesion. Then I notice that it's shining and viscous, soaking into the sheet beneath her.

"What have you done?" I whisper, unhooking my arms and raising her skirt up her calves and over her knees, which are slick with blood.

Sienna's eyes are closed as though she's fallen asleep, but she's still conscious.

"Don't tell Mum," she murmurs.

Twin lacerations on her inner thighs are swollen and leaking. She has cut from the edge of her panties towards her knees, probably using a razor blade wrapped in a tissue.

I glance around the room. Where did she hide her implements?

"You need stitches."

"I'll be OK."

"You need to go to hospital."

"It doesn't matter anymore."

Her eyes are closing.

"Have you taken something, Sienna?"

She doesn't answer. I shake her gently. "Did you take something?"

In a sing-song voice, "White pills, yellow pills and long green pills."

"Where did you get them?"

"I stole them," she sings. "From the trolleys and from bedside tables."

She's talking about Oakham House.

Flinging open the door, I yell down the stairs, "Call an ambulance!"

Sienna opens her eyes just long enough to give me a pitying look. "They're never going to let me out now, are they?"

I grab her top sheet and rip it into bandages to wrap around her thighs. I need to know what she took. What drugs?

Sliding sideways down the wall, Sienna rests her head against a pillow and mumbles, "He told me not to write a note. He said too many suicides spend too much time composing letters, trying to find words. 'You could die of old age, trying to write a note,' he said. 'You just have to do it.'"

"Who told you that?"

"He said to do it like Juliet, but I couldn't. So I did it like Romeo."

37

Gordon Ellis is laughing at me, mocking me with his bloodstained teeth and reptilian smile. I keep picturing Sienna's bloody thighs and seeing her eyes roll back into her head.

Hurting him won't be sufficient. I want to feed him broken glass. I want to see spittle fly from the corners of his mouth. I want to see him suffer like she's suffering.

After following the ambulance to the hospital, I continue driving. Sick. Dry-mouthed. Fists clenched on the wheel. A mantra playing in my head: "She's just a kid. A child. He used her. He poisoned her mind."

Rage consumes me. Rational thinking has been replaced by a single linear idea that runs on tracks like a bullet train, hurtling towards a single destination.

Parking the Volvo, I push open the groaning door and walk to the rear. Pulling out a tire jack, I slam the boot closed. Sienna's face is melting in front of me. Her eyes are closing. Her thighs are sticky.

Julianne is divorcing me. My eldest daughter thinks I'm a failure. My life's going to shit, but I should have stopped this. I should have seen this coming. Predators like Ellis don't stop. They never relinquish control. They invest too much time and effort in grooming a victim.

Bounding over the gate, I walk towards the house. Tunnel vision. Halfway up the path and Ruiz appears in front of me. I try to step around him but he won't let me pass. His lips are moving, but I can't hear what he's saying.

Then I feel my left arm being twisted up my back, followed by the searing pain that spreads from my shoulder socket to the base of my spine. His leg swings into the back of my knees and I stagger forward crashing into a garden bed.

Ruiz falls with me, knocking the wind from my lungs. I try to roll away, but he wraps his arm around my neck in a choke-hold.

"Enough now!" he warns me, squeezing my neck.

"S'OK."

"Concede."

"OK."

A bubble of exhaustion breaks inside me. Rage leaks away.

"I'm going to let go," says Ruiz.

"OK."

His arm slips away. He pulls me up to my knees, but I don't have the strength to stand.

"What are you doing here?" I ask.

"I could ask you the same question."

"Sienna took an overdose. She tried to kill herself." I stare at my muddy hands. "Ellis told her to do it. He wants her dead."

"How?"

My throat swells. "I don't know. She told me that Ellis could always reach her. I didn't believe her."

Ruiz drags me to my feet. "So you decided to confront Ellis. You came here to give him another beating—or were you gonna kill him this time?"

He pushes me away in disgust. "What sort of idiot . . . you couldn't count your balls and get the same answer twice. You're on remand. I lodged my house as surety. You're not allowed within a thousand fucking yards of Gordon Ellis and yet here you are—breaking the law. They can lock you up. Forget about that—they can take away my house!"

"I'm sorry."

He shoves me in the chest, pushing me towards the car. "Get in the fucking car."

"I didn't think . . ."

"Do as you're told."

I glance at the house. Natasha Ellis is standing at the window, holding the curtains aside. She looks like a child looking outside at a rainy day. We've made a mess of her garden.

Ruiz opens my car door. "Get inside and drive."

"Where?"

"The hospital."

"What about you?"

"I'll follow."

"What were you doing here?"

"Watching Gordon Ellis."

I start the engine and pull away from the curb. By the time I reach the end of the street, Ruiz's Mercedes is in my rear mirror, a 280E with two-tone wheels and a bright red paint job. Think pride. Think joy.

My anger has subsided but the black hole survives within me, still and even, sucking in the light. Ellis can't get away with this. He can't destroy another life.

The air in the hospital feels dirty and recycled. Ruiz has gone to get tea at the canteen, leaving me sitting at a table, staring at spilled sugar and an old coffee ring.

Sienna is in a stable condition. Doctors have pumped her stomach to get rid of any pill fragments and given her activated charcoal to bind the drugs in her stomach and intestines, reducing the amount absorbed into her blood.

She overdosed on TCAs—antidepressants that are the drug of choice for treating depression. The lethal dose is eight times the therapeutic dose, which makes it a risky drug to have around someone like Sienna.

Shutting my eyes, I let exhaustion slide over me like a prison blanket. My mind wants to curl up and sleep. Maybe I can wake up without any blood on my hands.

Gordon Ellis did this. It was classic grooming behavior. He drew Sienna close and then pushed her away, constantly keeping her off balance. He praised her then belittled her, withheld his affection and then doled it out in token amounts until she began to question herself. She surrendered her body and then her self-esteem. She slept with someone because he told her to. She took an overdose because he told her to. This was the ultimate demonstration of his control and of his arrogance.

Normally a predator focuses on the weak, but Ellis wanted a challenge. He chose someone adventurous and outgoing, a risk taker. He took a bright, vibrant young teenager and bent her, broke her, remade her and then broke her again.

Ruiz has returned. He puts a mug of tea in front of me and begins spooning sugar.

"I don't take any."

"You do today."

He wants to hear the story. I start at the beginning and tell him about the funeral and visiting Sienna. As the details emerge, so do the questions. Ellis has a caravan somewhere down the coast. It could be the same caravan he had in Scotland when his wife disappeared. The police could never find it.

Sienna couldn't remember where they went. She said that she slept most of the weekend and Gordon told her that she had food poisoning. Most likely he drugged her. He could also have drugged Natasha when he had sex with Sienna in their house. Sedatives, barbiturates, date-rape drugs, what did he use?

Ellis covered his tracks. He didn't leave notes or send text messages or e-mails. When he picked Sienna up after school she had to hide beneath a blanket on the backseat and turn off her mobile. He dropped her off at her therapy sessions with Robin Blaxland and picked her up again afterwards.

Helen Hegarty appears in the canteen. She's wearing a beige jumper and slacks.

Leaving Ruiz, I make my way between the tables, standing uncomfortably as she searches her handbag for tissues.

"How is she?"

Helen's eyes focus past me. The skin around her mouth twitches. "They put her in a coma. They say it's going to help her."

Lance Hegarty comes out of a nearby men's room. He shoves me into a table. Obscenities and spittle roll off his tongue. "Are you satisfied? You won't be happy until she's dead."

Ruiz moves swiftly to intercept, stepping between us.

Lance's lips pull back from his teeth. "Who the fuck are you?"

Ruiz speaks softly. "Lower your voice, son, and show people some respect. I'm asking you nicely."

"Fuck you!"

Lance swings a punch from his waist but Ruiz has been expecting it. Knocking it aside with his left arm he sinks a short sharp jab into the softness of the younger man's belly. The anger in Lance's eyes changes to surprise. He doubles over, winded, and Ruiz lowers him into a chair, apologizing to Helen.

"Maybe you should go," she says helplessly.

Lance squeaks, still trying to suck in a breath.

We retreat, leaving mother and son in the empty cafeteria. I can hear them arguing as the lift door closes behind us.

"Other people's families," mutters Ruiz.

"What about them?"

"They should serve as a warning."

38

Ronnie Cray closes the barn door and drops a plank of wood into place. She's dressed in jeans, a checked shirt and Wellingtons that are caked in mud. I hear horses inside. Smell them.

"So this is what you do in your spare time?"

"Yeah, I shovel horseshit."

She wipes her hands on her jeans and then eyes Ruiz, who has never been top of her dance card.

"Mr. Ruiz."

She's calling him "mister" for a reason—letting him know that he no longer has a police rank.

"DCI."

"You're looking older," she comments.

"And you're looking great. That's the benefit of going braless—it pulls all the wrinkles out of your face."

"Now, now, children, play nice," I tell them.

"I'll be nicer if he tries to be smarter," says Cray.

The DCI lights a cigarette, cupping her hands around the flame. The lighter clinks shut and I catch a whiff of petrol.

"The place is looking good," says Ruiz, trying not to be sarcastic.

Cray looks around. "It's a dump."

"Yeah, but you're doing it up."

"That's one of the great traps of buying a place like this. You see all the space and get excited, imagining beautiful lawns and gardens, but then you spend every week-end removing tree stumps and rocks."

"When you're not shoveling shit," says Ruiz.

"Exactly."

Cray pushes a wheelbarrow to the side

of the barn and tosses a bucket of vegetable scraps to the chickens.

"On my mother's side I have several generations of women shaped to pull plows. My father's side was a family of pen pushers—delicate as Asians. In the genetic roll of the dice, I got the agricultural build."

She carries the bucket towards the house. "I guess you gentlemen better come inside."

Scraping mud from her boots and kicking them off, she ducks through a doorway as though imagining herself to be two feet taller. The kitchen is full of French provincial furniture and has copper-bottom pots hanging from the ceiling. A tan cat stretches, circles and resettles on a shelf above the stove. This is the champion ratter that Cray told me about, Strawberry's mother.

"Make yourselves comfortable," she says, washing her hands. "This had better be a social call. It's Saturday and I'm off-duty."

Neither of us answers.

"You want a drink?"

"I thought you'd never ask," says Ruiz, eyeing the row of liquor bottles on top of the cupboard. "Scotch and a splash of water."

"I'm offering wine."

The DCI pulls an open bottle from a shelf and cleans two wineglasses with a paper towel.

"How about you, Professor?"

"I'm OK."

Ronnie is not the most social of women, which could have something to do with her low regard for people and even lower expectations. Most of her life is a mystery to me, although I know she was married briefly and has a grown-up son. She doesn't hide the fact that she's gay, but neither is it open for discussion. I suspect there have been women in her life who got under her skin and into her heart, but now she seems to be closed off, anchored to her memories like a lone sailor who looks out of place on dry land and is only happy on her own.

Lighting another cigarette, she sucks hard into her lungs as if concerned that fresh air without tobacco smoke might damage her health.

"Sienna Hegarty overdosed yesterday afternoon," I tell her.

"Where did she get the pills?"

"She stole them from the meds trolley at Oakham House."

Cray glances at my left hand. My thumb and forefinger are brushing together, rolling an imaginary pill between them.

"That's not why you're here."

"I talked to Sienna. She admitted sleeping with Gordon Ellis when she was only thirteen. She was pregnant with his child."

"Will she make a statement?"

"Yes, I think so. There's something else: Gordon Ellis organized to meet Sienna on the afternoon Ray Hegarty died."

"Natasha Ellis gave him an alibi."

"And you believe her?"

"No, but it means that we have to *prove* otherwise."

"Danny Gardiner dropped Sienna on a corner on the Lower Bristol Road, near a minicab office. From there she was taken to an address—she can't remember the location—and Ellis gave her instructions."

"What sort of instructions?"

"She had to sleep with someone."

Cray looks at me incredulously. "He pimped her!"

"Gordon Ellis told her it was the final proof that she loved him."

Cray wipes her face with her sleeve and wrinkles her nose as though smelling an odor rising from her armpit. "Who was the john?"

"She doesn't remember the address and she didn't get a name."

"So we just have *her* word for it?"

I borrow a piece of paper and a pen and begin jotting down names and drawing lines between them. Sienna, Gordon Ellis, Caro Regan, Novak Brennan and the Crying Man—all of them can be linked by one or more acts of extreme violence.

Cray doesn't react. She stubs out the cigarette and reaches for another. "You'll have to excuse me if I don't stop the presses, Professor." She flicks the bottom of the packet and a cigarette pops out. "Forty years ago my father changed the spelling of our surname because he didn't want anyone knowing we were related to Ronnie and Reggie Kray. He was their first cousin. Never met them. But he didn't want to be associated with a couple of psycho gangsters."

"I don't get your point."

"Some links are completely harmless. It's like six degrees of separation—we're all linked by only a few steps."

Ruiz reacts, "What sort of bullshit response—"

She cuts him off. "Let me finish. You're probably right about Gordon Ellis—the man got rid of his first wife and married one of his students—but trying to tie him to Novak Brennan is stretching things too far. MI5 has been investigating Brennan for six years. They've infiltrated local right-wing organizations and neo-Nazi groups, surveilled meetings, bugged phones, tailed cars and taken photographs. The name Gordon Ellis has never come up."

"Ellis and Brennan went to university together."

"Fifteen years ago."

"What about the Crying Man?"

"He's your bogeyman—not mine. Stan Keating didn't file a police report. Nobody else has complained about this guy."

Cray takes the harshness out of her tone. "If Sienna Hegarty makes a statement I'll investigate it personally. That's a promise. But you and I both know what happens next. It's Sienna's word against

Ellis's, and he has an alibi. If we charge him with sexual assault, Sienna will have to give evidence. She'll be cross-examined by his barrister. Her personal life will be scrutinized. Her character will be dissected. Wait till he gets to the murder charge she's facing . . .

"Don't look at me like that, Professor, I'm giving you the good news. A word in the right ear and Ellis gets suspended and investigated by Social Services, the Education Trust and his own union. He'll have a child protection team crawling up his arse and he'll spend the next two years fighting his way clear of them. And even if he wins, there won't be a school in the country that'll risk employing him."

Cray reaches across the table and puts her hand on mine. My arm stops trembling.

"If I were you, Professor, I'd take a step back from all this. You're facing serious charges and you shouldn't be talking to Sienna Hegarty. The CPS called me yesterday. You can forget doing a psych report. They've appointed someone else. If you really want to help Sienna, tell her to get a good lawyer and to cut the best deal she can."

"She needs protection."

"I'll put a guard on her room."

"She's suicidal."

"We try to prevent deaths in custody."

Everything Cray has said makes perfect sense but still I want to rail against it. I'm all for making the best of a bad situation, but this smacks of surrender, not compromise. Lawyers can be pragmatic and so can detectives, but the victims have to live with the outcome.

As we walk away from the house I shake myself, trying to rid myself of the conversation. My worst dread is that it may be contagious.

39

Sunday morning, on the Spring Bank Holiday weekend. Ruiz is still asleep in the spare room. His feet are sticking out from beneath a Night Garden duvet and a pyramid of stuffed animals that collapsed during the night. I can picture him wrestling teddy bears in his sleep and subduing them with his breath.

I make coffee and breakfast. The smell wakes him and he appears downstairs wearing just his Y-fronts and a singlet.

"I thought you'd be a boxer man," I tell him.

"What's wrong with these?"

"They're man briefs."

"They're Y-fronts."

"If you say so."

He looks at himself over his stomach. "I've always worn Y-fronts."

"Good for you."

"They're comfortable."

"I'm sure they are. A lot of body builders and cowboys wear them."

Ruiz gives me a pitying look. "You're a weird fucker."

"Where are you going? I got breakfast ready."

"I'm getting dressed."

While we eat he talks me through what he did yesterday afternoon after we left Ronnie Cray's farm. He began by staking out the minicab company—hoping to get a glimpse of the Crying Man.

"He didn't show up, but something occurred to me while I was watching the place. A lot of the drivers were picking up young women dressed to the nines—short skirts, high heels, lots of face paint. They'd drop these girls at an address and then wait for them."

"For how long?"

"An hour—sometimes more."

"And you have a theory?"

"Smells like sex."

"Escorts."

I think back to the girl I saw waiting at the minicab office when I was showing Sienna's photograph around. Mid-twenties and dressed to kill, yet unsmiling and cold. I've seen the look before in my consulting room and when I've lectured groups of prostitutes about staying safe on the streets.

Ruiz takes the last rasher of bacon from the pan. "Sienna was dropped on the same corner. Maybe it was a commercial transaction—somebody ordered a young girl and the escort service provided one—courtesy of Gordon Ellis."

"But what does Ellis get out of it?"

"Money. Favors."

"He's interested in schoolgirls not prostitutes."

"What then?"

I think about Sienna—the stolen pills, the suicide attempt—there isn't a court in the land that will grant her bail after what's happened. Gordon Ellis reached her once and could risk it again because Sienna is so vulnerable and easy to manipulate. She's also his weakest link.

Ruiz licks his fingers. "I still don't understand how he did it."

"Did what?"

"How did Ellis get to Sienna? She was in a secure unit."

"Maybe he called her."

"Phone calls are monitored and can be traced. Visitors have to be registered."

"So if he didn't call and didn't visit . . . ?"

I run through the events in my head again. When Ray Hegarty was found dead in Sienna's room, the only thing missing was her laptop.

"What about her e-mail account?"

"The police checked her service provider."

"So she used someone else's computer . . ."

Even before I finish the sentence, I realize what I've missed.

"Grab your coat," I tell Ruiz.

"Where we going?"

"To see Charlie."

Julianne answers the door and kisses Ruiz on each cheek, telling him he needs to shave. Emma squeaks in surprise and demands the big man's undivided attention like a jealous girlfriend.

Charlie is still in bed. She won't surface until at least eleven, citing mental fatigue and exhaustion from too much schoolwork. I send Emma upstairs to wake her.

"What if she won't wake up?"

"Jump on her head," says Ruiz.

A few minutes later I can hear Charlie yelling at Emma. Something is thrown. Something falls with a bump.

Ruiz calls from the bottom of the stairs. "Front and center, young lady, you don't want me coming in there to get you."

Charlie goes silent.

Ruiz resumes his seat at the kitchen table. Julianne has offered to make him breakfast and he's going to eat a second one.

"So I hear you're getting a divorce," he says, making it sound like she's buying a new car.

The statement lands like a rock in a still pond. Julianne looks at him suspiciously and continues cracking eggs into a bowl. "We've been separated for more than two years."

"You both have to consent."

Julianne switches her gaze to me. Accusingly. "It's really none of your business, Vincent," she says.

"If you're too embarrassed to talk about it . . ."

"I'm not embarrassed."

"Maybe you should change the subject," I tell Ruiz.

"So you don't love him anymore?" he asks her.

Julianne hesitates. "I don't love him like I used to."

"Jesus Christ, there's only one sort of love."

"No there's not," she says angrily. "You don't love a child the same way as you love a husband or you love a friend or you love a parent or you love a movie."

"So what is it you don't love about him?"

Julianne is beating the eggs like she wants to bruise them.

"I don't want to talk about this."

Ruiz isn't going to let up. "He's still in love with you."

"Yes," says Julianne. "I know."

"And that doesn't make any difference?"

"It makes the world of difference. It makes it harder."

"I *am* in the room," I remind them.

"Yes," replies Julianne. "Please tell Vincent to leave this alone."

He raises his hands. "OK, but just answer me one thing—is it because he's sick?"

I feel myself cringe. Julianne stiffens. It's as though the air has been sucked out of the room and we're sitting in a vacuum.

No longer beating the eggs, she whispers, "I know what you're trying to do, Vincent, but I don't need *you* to make me feel guilty. I feel guilty enough already. What sort of wife abandons her husband when he's sick? I know that's what people are saying behind my back. I'm a hard-hearted bitch. I'm the villain."

"That's not what I said."

"Everyone loves Joe. He makes people feel special. He makes everyone feel as though they're the only person in the room. I used to get so jealous—I used to wish someone would say something nasty or cruel about him. It was terrible. I hate myself for that."

Julianne won't look at me now.

"You don't know what it's like—watching him crumble, knowing it's going to get worse, knowing I can't help him."

"You're wrong," says Ruiz, softening his tone. "I watched my first wife die of cancer."

"And look what happened!" says Julianne. "You ran off the rails. You abandoned the twins and went off to Bosnia. You're still trying to make it right with them."

The hurt flashes in Ruiz's eyes. I never met his first wife, but I know she died of breast cancer and that Ruiz nursed her through her final weeks and months. Days after her death, he quit his job and went to Bosnia as a UN peacekeeper, leaving the twins with family. He couldn't bear to be around anything that reminded him of Laura, including his own children.

Julianne wants to take the comment back. "I'm sorry, Vincent," she says softly. "I'm just trying to hold myself together—for the sake of the girls."

Charlie appears, still in her pajamas, her hair tousled and bed-worn.

"Morning, Princess," says Ruiz. "Do I get a hug?"

"No."

"So you're not my girlfriend anymore?"

"As if!"

"Maybe if I were twenty-five years younger?"

"Try fifty."

Everybody laughs—even Charlie, who slouches on a chair and puts her elbows on the table. "Why is everyone shouting?"

"We're not shouting," replies Julianne. "We're having a discussion."

Julianne asks if she wants some eggs. Charlie shakes her head.

"Did Sienna ever use your computer?" I ask.

"I guess. Sometimes."

"Do you know what sort of stuff she was doing?"

"Why?"

"I'm trying to find out what sites she visited or if she sent any messages to people."

Charlie puts two slices of bread into the toaster.

"So you want to look at my computer?"

"Yes."

"But you're not spying on me?"

"No."

Then she shrugs. "I got nothing to hide."

After she butters her toast, I follow her upstairs to her room where she munches noisily in my ear as the laptop boots up. She once described her bedroom as being "designer messy," as though she dropped clothes with artistic intent.

"Do you remember the last time Sienna used it?"

"When she slept over."

It was probably a weeknight. I search through the history directory, going back to before Sienna's arrest. I recognize some of the sites—Facebook, Bebo and YouTube. There are some music pages and Google searches.

"Are these *your* searches?" I ask.

"I think so."

"Can you see anything unusual? Something you wouldn't have called up."

Scrolling through the history directory, she runs her finger down the screen. One site comes up regularly: Teenbuzz.

"What's that?"

"It's a chat room. Loads of my friends use it."

"Sienna?"

"Sure."

"What's your username?"

She looks at me sheepishly. "Madforyou."

"What about Sienna's?"

"She's Hippiechick."

The site has a variety of different chat rooms with names like "Just Friends," "Young at Heart" and the "Chillout Room." Some are forums on music, movies or relationships, but all come with a list of warnings, advising users not to give out personal contact details, addresses or to use their real names.

- You are strongly advised to NEVER meet anyone that you know just from the Internet.

- Predatory, threatening, harassing and illegal behavior will not be tolerated. The police will be contacted and offenders prosecuted.

"How often did Sienna use the chat room?"

"Pretty much every day."

Charlie can see where I'm going with this. "It's really safe, Dad. We're not stupid—we're not going to tell people where we live. We just chat."

"Did Sienna have any favorite people she chatted with?"

Charlie falters. "I guess."

"Who?"

"There was this one guy, Rockaboy."

"What do you know about him?"

She shrugs. "They used to meet."

"Where?"

"In a private chat room."

"They were alone?"

"Chill out, Dad, it's not like you can get pregnant typing messages to someone."

"Did you ever chat to this Rockaboy?"

Charlie brushes hair away from her eyes. "Sometimes."

"Did he say anything about himself?"

"You're not supposed to do that."

"He must have given some clues."

She sits cross-legged on her bed, balancing her plate on her knee. "He likes some of the indie bands like Arctic Monkeys and The Kooks. He doesn't like school very much."

"Did he like the same music as Sienna?"

Charlie frowns. "How did you know that?"

"What about his favorite subject at school?"

"Drama."

Feeling uncomfortable, Charlie changes the subject. "Are you coming Tuesday night?"

"Where?"

"To the school musical."

"I thought it was postponed."

"Mr. Ellis has decided to go ahead. We're giving one performance only. Jodie Marks is going to play Sienna's role. Do you think Sienna is going to mind?"

Charlie doesn't know about the suicide attempt and I'm not going to tell her. It can be something else she blames me for later.

"Can I go see her?" she asks.

"Not today."

Side by side we walk up the hill, filling the silence with our breathing. Ruiz limps slightly on his shorter leg—the legacy of a high-velocity bullet that tore through his upper thigh leaving a four-inch exit hole. A second bullet amputated his wedding finger. That was five years ago when he was found floating in the Thames, bleeding out, without any memory of the shooting.

Ruiz survived the bullet and the memories coming back. Some people are meant to prevail. They stay calm and collected under extreme pressure, while others panic and unravel. We each have a crisis personality—a mindset that kicks in when things go badly wrong. True survivors know when to act and when to hold back, choosing the right moment and making the right choice. Psychologists call it "active passiveness"—when doing something can mean doing nothing. Action can mean inaction. This is the paradox that can save your life.

"Ellis used an Internet chat room to reach Sienna," I say.

"How did she get access to a computer?"

"She must have borrowed one at Oakham House. It could also explain why her laptop was stolen that night."

"He's covering his tracks."

Above us the sun radiates through thin gauze-like cloud, but still seems bright enough to snap me in half. Even before I reach the house I notice the unmarked police car. DS Abbott and Safari Roy are sitting on a low brick wall, eating sandwiches from grease-stained paper bags.

Monk chews slowly, making us wait.

"We had a complaint," he says. "Natasha Ellis says you turned up at her house on Friday. Is that true?"

Before I can answer, Ruiz interrupts. "It was my fault, Detective. I went to see Gordon Ellis."

Monk looks at him doubtfully. "Why was that?"

"Sienna Hegarty had taken an overdose and was in hospital. She said that Gordon Ellis had taken liberties with her."

"Liberties?"

Ruiz can make a lie sound noble. "Yes, sir. Liberties. I was angry. I may have done something I regretted if it weren't for Joe. He stopped me and calmed me down."

Monk's not buying a word of it. He turns his gaze to mine. "So let me get this straight, Professor. The only reason you were outside Gordon Ellis's house was to prevent a disturbance?"

Monk wants me to agree with the statement.

Ruiz pipes up, "That's what happened."

"I'm asking the Professor," says the DS, waiting.

I look at Ruiz and then at Safari Roy, who is nodding his head up and down slowly.

"Yes," I say, "that's what happened."

Monk opens the lid of a rubbish bin on the footpath and drops his sandwich wrapper inside.

"Mrs. Ellis must have been mistaken." He lets the statement hang in the air. "If she'd been correct we would have had to arrest you, Professor, for breaching a protection order."

I don't reply.

"Sienna Hegarty is being interviewed tomorrow and we're going to investigate her allegations. I'm sure you wouldn't want to impede or jeopardize our inquiries."

"No."

Monk seems satisfied, and signals to Safari Roy, who has dripped egg yolk onto his tie and is trying to wipe it off with a handkerchief.

An electric window glides lower.

"Have a good day, gentlemen," says Monk. "Mind how you go."

40

Annie Robinson isn't answering. I press the intercom again and give her another few seconds before walking back to my car. A horn toots. Annie is pulling into a space. She has bags of groceries.

"If you're busy . . ."

"No, you can help me carry these."

She drapes me in plastic bags and I follow her inside. She's wearing shrunk-tight jeans, leather boots and a concha belt that dangles below a fitted black shirt. My eyes are fixed on her denim-clad thighs as she walks ahead of me. I remember them wrapped around me and I get that feeling again.

Annie unlocks the door and leads me through to the kitchen, where she begins unpacking the bags, talking constantly.

"I know I said I was sorry about the other night, but I really mean it. I *never* do things like that."

Does she mean she never gets drunk or never knocks on a man's door and abuses him for ignoring her?

"It's a little blond of me, don't you think?"

"Maybe just your roots showing."

She smiles back at me. "Have you eaten?"

"I'm fine."

"Sit down. Have lunch."

She heats up two small quiches and opens a plastic bag of washed salad leaves. She's used to cooking for one, buying pre-packaged, ready-made meals.

I look around the flat.

"This is a nice place."

"Rented. I couldn't afford it otherwise. I can't really afford it now, but I've spent my entire life waiting for things. I don't do that anymore. The only point of waiting is if you have something worth waiting for. That's a *good* kind of waiting."

"I didn't know there were different sorts of waiting."

"Oh, there are. That's the mystery." She laughs and her thin blond hair sways.

"Let's eat in the garden." She points through the glass doors to a small round table inlaid with blue and white tiles. She sets out two forks and knives, two plates and two napkins.

"Do you ever think about your ex-husband?" I ask.

She's drizzling dressing on the salad. "No."

"Not at all?"

"David Robinson. There you go—that's the first time I've said his name in months. I did think of changing back to my maiden name when we got divorced, but I couldn't be bothered getting a new passport and driver's license."

Annie is about to light a candle. "Is this too much?"

"Probably."

"OK, no candle."

She opens the oven door. They're still not ready.

"You mentioned a photograph of Gordon Ellis and Novak Brennan."

"Yes. Come look."

I follow her into the bedroom where she pulls out an old photograph album from the shelf in her wardrobe. We sit side by side on her bed, leafing through the pages.

"That's me there," she says. "I'm with my friend Jodie and that's Heidi and her boyfriend Matt. You see Gordon? He's with Alison. They went out for about three months and then he started dating Jodie. She's the blonde. They went out for almost a year. The longest of anyone."

Jodie's hair is cut short and she has a long slender neck and big eyes.

"She looks about twelve," I say.

Annie laughs. "Jodie was always getting carded when we went out."

She turns the page. "There's Gordon again."

He is wearing a trench coat cinched at the waist, which he probably bought from a charity shop because he thought it made him look urbane and cool. Instead he looks like he's dressed in his father's clothes.

The photograph was taken at a party.

Ellis is grinning at the camera with his arms draped around Jodie and Annie, his out-spread fingers suspended above their breasts. There's nothing wolfish about the pose, but he's a man who knows what he wants.

"This is the photo I was talking about," she says, pointing to another image taken in the same series. A person hovers at the edge of the frame, trying to avoid the camera—a younger Novak Brennan with longer hair and fewer lines. His face is partially obscured by Annie's raised arm holding a beer glass. Only one eye is visible and the camera flash has turned it red.

"Did you know him?" I ask.

"I didn't remember him at all until I saw the picture. I think he shared a house with Gordon. They were always hanging around together."

"But if you were friends with Gordon . . ."

"He dated my girlfriends, remember?"

"Where were these taken?"

She shrugs. "Some party. You're not supposed to remember them—that's the whole point of college."

Annie turns more pages of the album. There are photographs of a holiday in

Turkey, Annie in a bikini, lying on the deck of a sailing boat. She looks good.

"You don't want to see these old things," she says, not closing the page immediately.

We're sitting close enough for her breast to brush against my forearm.

"Maybe those quiches are ready," I suggest.

Annie cocks her head, having read the signal.

"Do you have to be somewhere?"

"I promised I'd take Emma to the park."

It's a lie. Annie knows it.

"Well, at least have something to eat."

She leaves me in the bedroom. I keep turning the pages of the album. There are more photographs from college. Foundation Day celebrations. Theater productions. A charity car rally with a customized VW beetle. A black-tie dinner on a bridge.

Gordon Ellis features in several more images, often in the background. One particular shot stands out because two girls are dancing in the foreground. Behind them, to one side, Ellis can be seen kissing a girl on a sofa, twisting her head towards his. Both their mouths are open, an inch apart, and he looks like a bird about to deposit food in a chick's beak.

The glass coffee table in front of them is littered with drug paraphernalia and traces of white powder in smudged lines.

I study the girl on the sofa. Gordon's hat obscures most of her face, but she has a small dark mole on her shoulder blade, just below her neck. I have kissed that spot. Felt her pulse quicken beneath my lips.

Annie calls from the kitchen. Taking the photograph with me, I slip it onto the table next to her plate. She glances at it but says nothing. Instead a strange transformation seems to take place. Rising from her chair, she walks around the garden, examining the shrubs and new blooms.

"It's not just the parties you forget," she says. "A lot of things about college are best left alone."

"You're kissing Gordon Ellis."

"I'm snogging him, to be exact."

"Why didn't you tell me?"

"I dated him twice. That's as far as it went."

Annie sighs and her eyes grow brighter

as though a generator is spinning inside her.

"What about Novak Brennan—how much more do you know about him?"

"He had a reputation on campus for dealing."

"Dealing?"

"Hash. Ecstasy. Speed. Cocaine. Novak could get it. He was always very mysterious. People said he'd been to prison, but I don't know if that's true."

Annie takes the photograph and tears it into pieces, letting the scraps fall into the garden. She keeps her face turned away from mine.

"Why didn't you tell me?"

"The past is the past."

The chemistry of our conversation has changed. Annie picks up her wineglass, her hand trembling slightly. The quiches are growing cold.

"Sienna tried to commit suicide on Friday. She took an overdose."

Annie doesn't react. Dissected by the afternoon sun, the skin on her face looks coarse and grained.

"Is she going to be all right?"

"She's out of danger. Before she went

to hospital she told me something that puzzled me."

"What was that?"

"She said you asked her if she was seeing Gordon Ellis outside of school. It was late last year."

Annie holds the glass to her lips for a beat. Her eyes meet mine over the rim, a private thought buried within them.

"I heard she was babysitting for him."

"You suspected something?"

"I thought it was inappropriate."

"But you didn't say anything to the school or to Sienna's parents."

A sharper edge in her voice. "You think I covered it up."

"I think you knew. I think you protected Gordon. I want to know why."

She puts down the wineglass. All remaining warmth has gone.

"It's time you left."

"Explain it to me, Annie."

"Go now or I'll call the police."

Taking my coat from the lounge, I walk to the front door. Annie unlocks it for me. I want to say something. I want to warn her about getting too close to Gordon Ellis because everything he touches begins to rot and perish. Suddenly she grasps my forearms through my shirt and plants a kiss on me, hard but not mean, whispering into my mouth.

"That's what you're missing."

41

The problem with secrets and lies is that you can never tell which is which until you dig them up and sniff. Some things are buried for safekeeping; some are buried to hide the stench; and some are buried because they're toxic and take a long time to disappear.

Annie Robinson lies as easily as she kisses. I can still taste her. I can see her eyes beneath her fringe, awkward and sad. I see a woman ready to surrender completely—to freefall into love, if only to escape the memories of a bad marriage.

Thirty minutes later I'm almost home. My mobile is chirruping. Ruiz.

"I've found the freak with the tattoos."

"Where?"

"I was watching the minicab office, thinking he was never going to show, thinking I got better things to do, thinking about how I'm retired and I'm too old for this shit . . ."

"OK, OK."

"Anyway, he finally turned up and picked up a girl. He took her to a hotel in Bristol. Fancy place. Dropped her off. Waited downstairs while she did her horizontal polka with some suit on a business trip. Afterwards he dropped her at a train station and drove to a gaff off the Stapleton Road—a bed and breakfast hotel called the Royal. Place needs a facelift or a bulldozer. Now he's in a pub around the corner. I'm sitting outside."

"Do we know his name?"

"Mate of mine—shall remain nameless—ran the number plate. It's an Audi A4 registered to a Mark Conlon. Lives in Cardiff. Nameless is running a full computer check. He should have something in a few hours. You want to join me? I'm not fronting this freak alone."

I don't think we should front him at all.

Thirty minutes later I knock on the steamed-up window of his Mercedes. Ruiz unlocks the doors and I slide inside. Sinatra is singing "Fly Me to the Moon." Takeaway wrappers litter the floor.

Ruiz offers me a cold chip.

"I've eaten."

"Yeah, but what were you eating? Is that lipstick I see? You've been knobbing your schoolteacher friend while I've been out here freezing my bollocks off."

"It wasn't like that."

"Shame. Is there lipstick anywhere else?"

"You have a one-track mind."

"When you get to my age it's the only track worth playing."

We're outside an ugly modern pub with redbrick walls, small windows and harsh lines. Streetlights reflect from the wet black pavement. Ruiz takes a sip from a thermos mug.

"You been inside?"

"Not yet."

Glancing at the pub I ponder the wisdom of this. We don't know anything about Conlon except that he put three men in hospital and one of them now speaks through a hole in his neck.

"Novak Brennan was supplying drugs at university. Ellis might have been one of his dealers."

"Who told you that?"

"Annie Robinson."

Ruiz rolls down his window and tosses the dregs of his tea. "Novak always knew how to spot a gap in the market."

The pub door opens. Light spills out. Two men step onto the pavement. Conlon is the taller of the two. He's wearing dark jeans and a hooded sweatshirt. The second man is older with a receding hairline and a stiff military bearing. He's dressed in a beige raincoat, carrying an umbrella like a walking stick.

Conlon glances down the street. For a moment he seems to be looking directly at us, but it's too dark for him to see anyone inside the Merc. Conlon reacts to something. He grabs the man by the lapels and pushes him hard against the side of a car. The older man is nodding. Scared.

Conlon shoves him away and gets behind the wheel. The Audi pulls away.

"You want to follow him?" asks Ruiz.

The older man is walking towards us.

"Wait! I want to see who this is."

Reaching below the dash, Ruiz pops the bonnet. Climbing out, he unhooks the latch and the bonnet hinges open. The man has almost reached us. The streetlight reflects from his bald patch and his umbrella clicks on the pavement with each second step.

"Hey, guv, you wouldn't happen to have any jumper leads?" asks Ruiz. "I can't get a spark out of this thing."

The man barely pauses. Looking flustered and feverish, he mumbles a reply and keeps walking. He's in his fifties with a solitary band of graying hair that warms the top of his ears. I know him from somewhere.

"Is there a garage nearby?" asks Ruiz.

The man stops and turns. "Perhaps you should call the AA." His accent is public school. Genteel. Erudite.

"Not a member," says Ruiz. "Always thought it was a waste of money. Isn't that the way?"

"Quite," says the man, turning again. His eyes meet mine. I see no hint of recognition.

"Well, you have a nice evening," says Ruiz.

His umbrella swings and clicks as he walks away.

Ruiz shuts the bonnet and slides back behind the wheel.

"Now there's a turnup." He glances in the rearview mirror.

"You recognized him."

"Didn't you?"

That's the thing about Ruiz: he doesn't forget. He has a memory for names, dates, places and faces—for the victims and perpetrators—going back ten, twenty, thirty years.

"I know I've seen him somewhere," I say.

"You saw him on Thursday."

And then I remember . . . Bristol Crown Court . . . he was sitting in the front row of the jury box. The foreman.

Ruiz has found my father's birthday present—the bottle of Scotch I forgot to wrap or to send. He cracks the lid and pours a generous amount over ice before settling the bottle on a table in the lounge where it can keep him company.

We sit opposite each other, listening to the ice melting. Ruiz once told me that he didn't talk politics anymore, or read newspapers, or watch the *News at Ten*. One of his ex-wives had accused him of opting out of public debate. Ruiz told her that he'd served his tour of duty. He'd manned the barricades against outraged pacifists, anti-globalization protesters, poll-tax rioters and hunt saboteurs. He had fought the good fight against the violent, corrupt, treacherous, hypocritical, cowardly, deviant and insane. Now it was time for others to take up the battle because he had given up trying to save or change the world. He simply wanted to survive it.

"What did we just see?" I ask.

"We saw evidence of jury tampering."

"Maybe it was a chance meeting?"

"It's against the law to approach a member of a jury."

"He's one of twelve."

"He's the *foreman!*"

"Yeah, but he's not Henry Fonda and this isn't *Twelve Angry Men.* You need ten jurors for a majority verdict."

"What about a hung jury? You need three."

"Maybe they have three."

"So there's a retrial and they do it all again with a different jury. That doesn't help Novak."

"So what do you suggest?" I say.

"We have to tell someone."

"The judge?"

Ruiz almost chokes. "You're joking. He'll abort the trial. That poor kid giving evidence will have to go through it all again."

"Maybe he'll just dismiss the foreman. The jury can still deliberate. Eleven is enough."

Ruiz stares at the fireplace. "Maybe we should talk to a lawyer."

He gives Eddie Barrett a call. Puts him on speakerphone. It's a bank holiday Monday and somebody is going to pay for Eddie's fifteen minutes—probably me. His voice comes through like a fog-horn.

"You two bumboys are getting a reputation. You're like Elton and David without the wedding. I thought you'd retired, Ruiz."

"On holidays."

"Try Benidorm next time, or Jamaica. Get yourself some black bootie. What do you want?"

"I got a hypothetical," says Ruiz.

"I hate fucking hypotheticals. Don't you fairies ever deal with real situations?"

"We weren't boy scouts like you, Eddie."

"Dib fucking dob. What's your hypothetical?"

Ruiz pitches the question: "You're at trial. You discover the foreman of the jury meeting up with an acquaintance of the defendant. This particular acquaintance has a history of violence. And this particular defendant has a history of getting away with murder. What do you do?"

"Am I the defense or the prosecution?"

"Does it matter?"

"Sure it fucking matters."

"You're neutral."

"Could it be an accidental meeting?"

"Doubtful."

Eddie sucks air through his teeth. "The trial is probably fucked but the judge might just cut the foreman loose. Warn the jury. Keep going."

"So you'd tell the judge?"

"Nah, I'd tell the police."

"Will you help us?" I ask.

Eddie laughs. "Now *there's* a fucking hypothetical!"

42

Tuesday morning, sunny and warm—the forecast said rain. The roads are quiet on the drive to Bristol. Ruiz has one hand on the wheel and an elbow propped on the window.

His contact in the Met got back to him overnight. The name Mark Conlon threw up one match—a bank manager from Pontypool who lost his license four years ago for drunk-driving. Five ten. Brown hair. No tattoos. He's not the Crying Man. The plates on the Audi were either stolen or copied. We're back to square one. Maybe Ronnie Cray will have more luck.

We decide to breakfast near Queen's Square in a modern place full of chrome furniture and hissing steam. The waitresses are Romanian girls in short black skirts, who slip outside for cigarettes while it's quiet. Ruiz orders a fried egg and bacon sandwich ("On proper bread not that sourdough shit"). He flicks through the paper. The Novak Brennan trial is still page one.

Marco Kostin will resume giving evidence today. I can picture him in the witness box with hyper-real clarity, every tremor and blink and turn of his head. The cross-examination is still to come and three barristers will be queuing up to pick holes in his story.

The door opens. A tangle-footed teenager comes in wearing cycling gear. Multicolored. A courier. He talks to a Romanian waitress. Kisses her lips. Young love.

"I got a strange feeling about yesterday," says Ruiz.

"Which bit of yesterday are we talking about?"

"When I was following the freak with the tattoos, I stayed well behind him. I wanted to make sure he didn't know he was being tailed. When he dropped off the pavement princess. When he picked her up. When he went to the shithole hotel. I stayed out of sight."

"What's so strange about that?"

"It's probably nothing." Ruiz shrugs. "I just got an impression that maybe he knew I was there. Once or twice he seemed to slow down, like he didn't want the lights to change and for me to miss them."

"He *knew* he was being followed?"

"That's what it seemed like." Ruiz pushes his plate away. "Maybe we should check out his gaff before we talk to Cray. We could take a run over to the hotel; have ourselves a sticky."

"What about the trial?"

"It's not going to end today."

On the street outside, Ruiz drops a coin into a busker's hat and keeps walking, crossing the pedestrian precinct. We pull out of the underground car park, passing over the floating harbor to Temple Circus where we turn north along Temple Way. Taking the exit at Old Market Street, we pass close by Trinity Road Police Station on our way to Easton.

Stapleton Road has notices stuck to power poles warning against curb crawling and drug dealing. It's early and the crack whores and street dealers are still in their coffins. We park in Belmont Street around the corner from the mosque. A Muslim woman with letterbox eyes waddles past us, pushing a pram. She could be seventeen or seventy-five.

The Royal Hotel is a crumbling three-story building with metal bars on the lower windows. An old black man sits in the sunshine on the front steps. His hands are dotted with liver spots and they shake slightly, not with Parkinson's but some kind of palsy. He's reading a newspaper, holding it at arm's length. An unwrapped sandwich rests half-eaten on a brown paper bag.

"Morning," says Ruiz, "beautiful day."

The cleaner blinks and shields his eyes with a hand. "You right about dat, mon."

"You taking a break?"

"Been cleanin' since first ting."

Ruiz sits on the steps. "I'm Vincent and this is Joe."

The old man nods. "Dey call me Clive."

"Like Clive Lloyd."

"Well, he from Guyana and I'm from Jamaica, but dat's close enough." His chuckle sounds like he's playing a bassoon.

Folding his newspaper casually, he takes another mouthful of his sandwich, wondering why two white men are interested in talking to a hotel cleaner when most people treat him like he's invisible.

Ruiz raises his face to the sun and closes his eyes. "I'm a former police officer, Clive, and we're looking for a man with dark hair, slicked back, and tattoos on his face like he's crying black tears."

The old cleaner reacts as though he's been scalded. He gets up from the steps and shakes his head so that his thin frame quivers.

"Don' talk to me about dis biznezz."

"Why not?"

"The Lord gonna call his chillun home

before dat man bring anyting good to dis world."

"Is he staying here?"

"He's got himself a room. Don' know if he sleeps in it."

"What do you mean?"

"Don' see him much. I mind my own biz-nezz."

"But you clean his room?"

Clive shakes his head. "He don' want no cleaning. He puts a sign on his door says, no cleaning. Suits me. Dem pay me by de hour not de room."

The cleaner taps the newspaper against his thigh. "Well, I better be gettin' back to work."

"The man with the tattoos—do you know his name?"

"No, mon."

"You ever talk to him?"

Clive shakes his head, his forehead full of creases. "Mon like that, don' wanna talk to someone like me. He don' like my color."

"What gave you that impression?"

"Couple of black kids were breaking into his motor. Dey was running away, but he caught dem. Made one of dem boys eat dog shit. Made him kneel on de ground and chow down. Never see dat before. D'other boy won' be eating solids for a while. His mama gonna be feeding him strained bananas."

Swallowing drily, he leans down to rewrap his sandwich, no longer hungry.

"You've been very helpful," says Ruiz, shaking the cleaner's hand. Clive looks at the ten-pound note in his palm. Closes his fingers. Opens them again just to be sure.

"Maybe you could do one more thing for us," says Ruiz. "This guy must have signed something. You could show us the hotel register."

Clive pockets the money, putting it deep inside his jeans, and then glances up and down the street before shepherding us into a tired-looking reception room with faded wallpaper and worn carpet. The register is a long rectangular book with ink stains on the cover. Opening the pages, he runs a knobbly finger down the room numbers.

Room 6. Paid for in cash, a month in advance. A signature rather than a name—but he included the registration number for the Audi.

It doesn't help us.

Clive closes the book, sliding it into a desk drawer. "Well, I got work to do."

"You should clean Room 6," says Ruiz.

The old cleaner looks horrified. "Don' you be tinking like dat."

"Like what?"

"Tinking I'm gonna open up dat mon's room."

Ruiz tilts his chin to the ceiling and sniffs. "You smell that?"

Clive raises his chin. "Don' smell nothing."

"Smoke," says Ruiz.

"There ain't no smoke."

Ruiz vaults up the crazy network of stairs that runs between the floors. He stops on the first landing. "Definitely smoke; coming from one of the rooms. Might be a fire."

The cleaner drags himself up to the same level. Ruiz is outside No. 6.

"I think we should call the fire brigade and evacuate this place."

Clive is shaking his head back and forth. "No, no, no, don't be doing dat, mon."

Ruiz touches the door. "Feels a little warm. Maybe you should open up—just to be sure."

"Get away with you."

"You ever heard of something called probable cause, Clive? It means you have the right to enter if you think there's a good reason."

"But there ain't no fire!"

"You don't know that for certain."

The keys jangle on the cleaner's belt. He looks at us sadly and shakes his head in surrender.

The key turns and the door opens into gloom. Ruiz reaches for the light switch. The bed hasn't been slept in and the curtains are drawn. There's a wardrobe with double doors and a mirror in between. A side table next to the bed, a suitcase pushed under the springs. I can hear a dripping sound, which might be outside the walls or within.

Ruiz is moving through the room, opening the wardrobe and the drawers, peering beneath the bed. There is a strange smell to the place that tightens the nostrils and crimps the lips.

"Ain't nuttin here, mon," says Clive. "Let's go."

Somewhere below I hear a door open. I glance over the railing, down the stairs, but can't see anyone. At that moment a pigeon takes off from the window ledge, battering its wings against the glass. My heart takes off as well.

"Maybe we should leave," I say.

Ruiz has pulled the suitcase from under the bed. He uses a handkerchief on the handle and covers his fingers as he slips each latch, lifting the lid, exposing the contents.

There are folders of newspaper clippings and photographs. Street scenes. Faces. Headlines. I recognize Bristol Crown Court. Protesters are waving placards and banners. Police are shown confronting the crowd, pushing them back. A face is circled with red marker pen: a woman in a gray jacket with an ID card around her neck. Police are allowing her through a checkpoint. I recognize her. Another juror.

Ronnie Cray doesn't want to meet us at Trinity Road. This is unofficial, off the record, deniable. She chooses a snooker club in the old part of the city where the buildings look like compacted teeth and sacks of rubbish have stained the footpaths. The baize tables are upstairs and I can hear balls being racked up and broken.

Cray is waiting at a table in the bar, nursing a cup of tea. She glances at me, then at Ruiz, her eyes neutral, then picks up her cup and takes a sip.

"I thought you'd gone back to London," she says to Ruiz.

"Still sightseeing."

A long bar runs down one side of the room, most of it in darkness except for a plasma TV screen showing sporting highlights. The exposed beams are decorated in old Christmas tinsel and squashed paper bells.

We start at the beginning, telling Cray about seeing the jury foreman being roughed up outside a pub.

"He met with the guy I told you about—the Crying Man—the one who's been sitting in the public gallery during the trial, chaperoning Novak Brennan's sister."

Cray doesn't react. Her short-cropped hair is sprinkled with gray and the lines on her face seem deeper today.

"You approached the foreman of the jury?"

"Yes. No. Not really."

"Do you know how many laws you've broken?"

"We had to be sure."

Somewhere above us a cue ball cannons into the pack. The sound echoes like a shot. Cray looks like she's suddenly developed a toothache.

"Tell me again why you were following this guy?"

"Sienna remembered him. On the night Gordon pimped her out—there was a second man in the car. He drove her to the address."

"You're sure it's the same man?"

"Yes."

"Where does the Hegarty girl come into this?"

"What if she had to sleep with someone involved in the case? She's underage."

"Blackmail?"

"Gordon Ellis and Novak Brennan knew each other in college. They shared a house. They could have stayed in touch."

"Yeah, but Ellis's name has never come up in the intelligence files."

Ruiz interrupts. "He used to call himself Freeman. He took his mother's surname after his first wife disappeared."

Cray grunts dismissively, not convinced. Her eyes come back to mine. "The names and addresses of jurors are kept secret. They're protected and after each trial they're destroyed."

"This wasn't a coincidence."

Her voice drops to a whisper. "So you're saying Brennan rigged the jury ballot?"

"Maybe he got hold of their names or he had them followed home. The trial has been going for weeks."

Cray's forearms are pressed flat on the table. "You're talking about jury tampering. Conspiracy. Bribing an officer of the court. Brennan has been in custody for eight months. Every call and letter is monitored. Even if he got to one juror, it won't do him any good. He needs ten to get an acquittal."

I glance at Ruiz. He pulls a dozen photographs from his jacket. Slides them between her forearms. The DCI doesn't look down. For a brief moment I think she might simply stand and walk out. Her eyes stay fixed on mine, clouding.

Finally she lowers her gaze. Her face remains empty of expression but I see her throat swallow drily and her chest rise briefly against her shirt.

"The red circles identify members of the jury," I say.

Cray's eyes cut sideways to me, her lips parting slightly. "Should I ask how you got these?"

"They were in a suitcase under a bed in a hotel room. The Royal. It's off Stapleton Road. This guy had photographs, a list of witnesses, newspaper cuttings, maps—serious research."

"What guy?"

Ruiz answers: "The Crying Man. He took the room three weeks ago. Paid cash. Signed in under a false name."

Color has died in Cray's cheeks. Her next statement is almost an unintelligible whisper. "Don't tell anyone about this."

"What are you going to do?"

She doesn't answer.

"You have to tell the CPS," says Ruiz.

Anger flares in her eyes. "For starters—I'm *not* taking my orders from you!"

It comes out in a hiss. Pale lumpy faces turn from the TV. Cray pivots forward on her elbows.

"This trial has been a circus. It's cost millions. I'm not just talking about crowd control and protecting witnesses. If it collapses there'll be an absolute shit-storm and I want more than just a few photographs before I light that fuse."

She collects the prints. Straightens the edges. Turns them face down. Already I can see her mind calculating her next move. She's going to either stake out the Royal Hotel or seal it off and send in a SOCO team looking for fingerprints and DNA.

She glances at the red neon clock glowing above the bar: 11:46. It could be a.m. or p.m.

"What about Sienna?"

"We collected her from hospital at nine o'clock this morning. She's being interviewed now."

The DCI raises her cup again, balancing it between the fingers of both hands. Her tea has grown cold.

"Ray Hegarty was a good copper. Maybe he was a lousy father. If that girl killed him, she'll face a jury. Right now I'm giving her the benefit."

43

A buzzer sounds, echoing in the night air, encouraging the audience indoors where students are acting as ushers and handing out programs. The curtains are closed in the auditorium but occasionally the fabric bulges with movement and a face peers through a gap, bright-eyed, excited.

The band are tuning instruments and whispering to one another, while Gordon Ellis moves in the glow of the footlights, issuing last-minute instructions and calming first-night nerves. His face is still swollen, with one eye almost closed, but he's wearing dark glasses and stage makeup to hide the damage.

I shouldn't be here. According to the protection order, I can't go within a thousand yards of Ellis or his wife. But I'm not missing Charlie's big night and I'm not letting that bastard be alone with her.

Peering around a pillar, I can see Julianne in conversation with Harry Veitch. Laughing. Emma is in between them, but keeps crawling onto Julianne's lap to get a better view. I wonder if Julianne realizes that Harry has a lumpy head from this angle. Big *and* lumpy.

The lights are dimming. Voices fade to silence. The band strikes up and the curtain sweeps aside, rattling on rails. The entire cast appears, marching back and forth across the stage, dressed as commuters on a busy New York street. Millie, the small-town girl from Kansas, has arrived in Manhattan.

Although I don't miss a moment of Charlie on stage, the show seems strangely muted compared to the rehearsal I watched three weeks ago. The music and staging are the same, but it doesn't have the same energy or excitement. Maybe Sienna is the missing ingredient.

Nobody else seems to notice. There is a standing ovation and three curtain calls. Two girls drag a reluctant director into the spotlight, tugging at his arms. Reaching the front of the stage, Gordon Ellis bows theatrically, touching the floor with his fingertips, before rising again with his arms outstretched, ushering the cast to join him in another bow. He puts his arms around the nearest two girls. Charlie is one of them. I can taste the bile in the back of my throat.

The curtain slides closed. The auditorium lights come up.

Outside, stepping clear, I look for Julianne. She's chatting to some of the other mothers. Harry is hovering, looking for someone to talk to. I try to avoid his gaze but he's seen me.

"What a show, eh? Utterly brilliant."

He's wearing boating shoes and one of those thermal skiing vests that zip up to his throat.

"It started as a film, you know."

"What did?" I ask.

"*Thoroughly Modern Millie*. Julie Andrews played the lead. It also had Mary Tyler Moore in it. It was nominated for seven Academy Awards and won best musical score."

I should have guessed—Harry is an expert on Hollywood musicals.

"The score was written by Elmer Bernstein, not to be confused with Leonard Bernstein—they weren't even related, but they were given nicknames on Broadway. One of them was West Bernstein and the other East Bernstein."

Harry laughs.

Maybe he's gay.

Having finished his anecdote, he smiles at me. Apparently it's my turn to add something to the conversation but I can't think of anything to say. After a long pause he suggests that we should play a round of golf sometime. I could come to his club.

"I don't play golf," I remind him.

"Of course. Tennis?"

"Not much these days."

Harry tugs at his earlobe. After another long silence he closes the gap between us and whispers, "Do you think the two of us can ever finish up being friends?"

He asks the question so earnestly I feel a pang of sympathy for him.

"I don't think so, Harry."

"Why's that, do you think?"

"Because all we have in common is Julianne and eventually, if we become friends, you'll feel it's all right to talk about her with me and it's one thing to lose her and another thing completely to discuss her like she's a shared interest."

Harry tugs harder at his earlobe. "You made her very sad, you know."

"I also made her happy for twenty years."

"I guess people change."

Jesus wept!

"I'm going to try to make her happy," he announces.

I can feel my arm hairs prickle and a chill run down my spine. Irrespective of his size and physical condition, I want to hit Harry now. I seem to be developing a taste for it.

"I don't want there to be any ill-feeling," he says, completely ignoring all the signs, my body language, my tone of voice, my fingers curling into fists. Then he mentions something about not treading on toes and there being no winners or losers.

A guttural sound springs from my throat.

"Pardon?" he asks.

"I said that's bullshit."

"Oh!"

His eyes widen.

"Let's face it Harry, you don't give a flying fuck about my toes or my feelings." I'm talking through gritted teeth, trying not to attract attention. "You like trophies. You have a trophy house full of trophy cabinets full of your golf trophies and your squash trophies and your framed thank you letter from Margaret Thatcher for donating to the cause. Now you want my wife."

Harry blinks at me, completely lost for words. The color rises from his neck to his face. I want to go on. It takes every bit of my willpower to stop saying what I want to say. I want to tell him that he's not Frank Lloyd Wright or Norman Foster and that designing some telemarketing millionaire's ski chalet at Val d'Isère is not going to get him a knighthood, just like pulling his trousers up high doesn't make him look thinner and gelling his hair doesn't make him look younger and the chunky silver bracelet is gangster chic rather than evidence that he's comfortable wearing jewelry.

I want to tell him these things but I don't, because I'm not even interested in hating Harry the way I should. I'm not truly angry. I'm sad and I'm lonely and I'm fed up with not being able to help people who need me.

Julianne appears beside him.

"Wasn't that terrific?"

"Brilliant," I reply.

Emma lets go of her hand and comes to me.

"I wonder what happened to Annie Robinson," says Julianne, looking at me. "She did all the sets and costumes and didn't turn up."

"Maybe she had something more important," I say, but I can't convince myself.

"Charlie is going to the cast party."

"Will Gordon Ellis be there?"

"It's just for the kids. One of the mothers is getting them pizza. Can you pick her up later?"

She gives me the address. "I told her eleven o'clock. I know she's supposed to be grounded, but she was so good tonight and I don't have the heart to play the bad cop on this one."

"I wanna go with Daddy," announces Emma.

"No, sweetheart, we're going home in Harry's car."

"I want to go home with Daddy."

Julianne tries to convince her that Harry has a really nice car. "It has leather seats and that lovely smell, remember?"

Harry puts his hand on her head. "I'll open the sunroof, if you'd like."

Emma twists away and swings her arm. One of her fists collides with Harry's groin. His body jackknifes and he sucks in a painful breath. Still doubled over, he groans—or at least it sounds like a groan from a distance, but up close he clearly says, "Fuck me!"

Emma hears it too. "Harry said a bad word."

Julianne tells her to apologize.

"But, Mummy, it was a really really bad word."

"Tell Harry you're sorry."

"It was an accident."

"I know it was an accident, but you should still say that you're sorry."

Harry still can't straighten completely. "It's OK. It doesn't matter."

"He said the f-u-c-k word," says Emma.

"Don't you *ever* say that!" responds Julianne.

Emma points at Harry. "What about him?"

"He didn't mean it."

"He should get in trouble too."

Harry interrupts. "Just let her go with her father."

"No," argues Julianne. "This is about setting boundaries. Emma has to learn to do as she's told."

Emma clutches her stomach. "I feel sick. I think I'm going to vomit."

"Nonsense," says Julianne, who is fully aware of Emma's dramatic displays of hypochondria (and even more dramatic feats of projectile vomiting).

"Maybe she should go in Joe's car," says Harry, thinking of the Lexus and his leather seats. "He could drop her home."

Julianne fires a look at him.

Meanwhile, Emma drops to the ground and launches one of her famous "you'll-have-to-drag-me-out-of-here" tantrums. Julianne does her best to ignore her, but Emma's limbs seem to liquefy and she's impossible to pick up.

We're not so much drawing a crowd as dispersing it—driving parents towards their cars.

Julianne looks at me. "Please just leave."

"What have I done?"

"Nothing, but you're making things worse."

The last thing I hear is Harry muttering under his breath. "For fuck's sake, why couldn't she just go with her father"—and seeing Julianne give him her death stare.

I almost feel sorry for him. Harry's chances of getting lucky tonight just disappeared with the flying pigs.

Annie Robinson's mobile is turned off and she isn't answering her landline. I drive the familiar roads, trying to come up with reasons why she would have missed the musical. She should have been on stage, taking her bow.

I try her home number again. After eight rings the answering machine clicks in.

Hi, sorry we missed you. Leave us a message after the beep.

She's a single woman living alone, which explains the "we" and "us."

Beep!

"Annie, it's, Joe. I've been at the school. I thought I'd see you tonight . . ." I pause, hoping that she might pick up. "The show was great . . . really good. And the sets were terrific . . . If you're there, Annie, talk to me . . . I hope everything is all right . . . call me when you get this . . ."

Pulling into Annie's road, I see her car parked in front of her building. She doesn't answer the intercom. I press the buttons on either side but nobody answers. Walking back to the street, I follow the footpath until I find a small alley leading between the houses to the canal. Picking my way along the grassy bank, I count the houses until I come to her walled garden.

Hoisting myself up, I clamber over the

wall, landing heavily on a climbing rose bush. Thorns catch on my clothes and I have to untangle the vines. The blue-and-white tiled table is still on the terrace. The two chairs are tilted so as not to collect rainwater.

Pressing my face to the sliding glass door, I peer into the dark lounge and open-plan kitchen. I can see a neon clock blinking on the oven. The only other light is leaking from beneath Annie's bedroom door. It seems to shimmer and cling to the floor. Why is that? Water. The room is flooded.

I should stay outside. Phone the police. What if Annie has slipped over? She could be hurt or bleeding. I bang on the glass door and shout her name.

This is crazy. I should do something. Picking up the nearest chair, I swing it hard against the door. It doesn't shatter. I try again. Harder. The pane vibrates and disintegrates in a mosaic of crumbling glass.

The living room is undisturbed. An IKEA catalog lies open on the sofa. Annie's shoes are under the coffee table. To the left the kitchen benches are wiped clean. Cups and plates rest on the draining rack. A shiny paper gift bag sits on the counter next to a bottle of wine. Open. Half drunk.

Water covers the floor. It's coming from the bedroom. I knock on the door and call Annie's name. Turning the handle, I push it open. A bedside light is on. Discarded clothes are bunched on the floor beside a wicker basket. A matching set of knickers and bra. Mauve. Fresh clothes are laid out on the bed, chosen for tonight.

I remember the bathroom from my night with Annie. White-tiled, it smells of perfume and potpourri. A frosted glass screen shields the bathtub and running taps. Flower petals have spilled over the edge and blocked the drain on the floor.

Annie is lying in the overflowing tub with one hand draped over the edge and a broken wineglass beneath it. Blood and vomit stain the water.

She's alive. Convulsing.

Hooking my arms beneath hers, I struggle to lift her. Water sloshes over my clothes. I get her to her knees, all the while talking—telling her to hold on. Telling her it will be OK.

Half dragging her to the bed, I lay her on her side, pulling a duvet over her nakedness. Then I call three nines. Ambulance. Police. Name. Address. Number.

"I think she's been poisoned," I tell the dispatcher.

"What did she consume?"

"I don't know. It could have been in the wine."

"Is she inebriated?"

"No . . . I don't think so . . . I'm not sure."

"What is her approximate height and weight?"

"What?"

"Her height and weight."

"Oh, ah, she's five-six. Maybe nine stone."

"Did you have any of the wine, sir?"

"No, I found her."

"Don't touch the container."

I go to the hallway and unlock the front door. Annie's car keys and purse are sitting in a bowl. A light blinks on her answering machine. The counter says "2."

I press "play."

The first message is from a woman.

Hi, dear, it's your mum. I guess you're out! Penny is pregnant again. Isn't she clever? Poor dear is sicker than a parrot. It must be a boy. They always make you suffer. Give her a call and cheer her up.

Clunk!

Message two.

Annie, it's Joe, I've been at the school. I thought I'd see you tonight . . .

I press stop. Silence.

Back in the bedroom, I put my arms around Annie and listen to her shallow breathing. Her eyes are closed. What do I know about poisons? I did three years of medicine, but it wasn't high on the agenda. Never induce vomiting if they're convulsing—I remember that much. Fat lot of good . . .

Annie's eyes are open. The skin around her lips is burned and raw. Her stomach is bloated and hard.

"I knew you'd come back."

44

Just gone ten. Dozens of people are standing on the footpath—residents, neighbors and passersby—wearing dressing gowns, anoraks and woolen hats. A blue flashing light seems to strobe across their faces.

Four police cars are parked outside the

row of terraces, alongside two ambulances and a scene-of-crime van. I'm standing in wet clothes beside one of the squad cars, unwilling to sit inside because it makes me look like a suspect. The detectives told me to wait. A police constable has been assigned to watch me. He is standing less than twenty feet away with his back to the onlookers and his eyes trained on me.

"Why you all wet, petal?" asks a voice. It belongs to a short black woman wearing the dark green uniform of a paramedic. She has a name tag pinned to her chest, "Yvonne."

"I found her in the bath," I say in a daze.

Yvonne raises an eyebrow. "I wouldn't want anyone finding *me* in the bath."

She laughs and her whole body shakes. "She's white, right? You don't live in a place like this unless you're white or you're trying to act white. Know what I'm saying?"

"Not really."

Yvonne tilts her wide shiny face up at me. "Are you OK, petal? You want to sit down? I can get you a blanket. How about some oxygen?" She motions to the ambulance.

"I'm OK."

"Suit yourself." She blows her nose on a

tissue and glances at the onlookers. "You know what they're thinking?" she asks.

"No."

"They're wondering what's happening to the world. That's what they always say when the TV camera is shoved in their faces. 'You just don't expect it, do you? Not where you live. This is a nice neighborhood. It makes you wonder what the world is coming to, blah, blah, blah . . .' Isn't that what they say?"

"Yes."

The front door opens and two paramedics appear wheeling a collapsible metal trolley. Annie is strapped to the frame with an IV in her arm, the bag held above her head.

"That's my ride," says Yvonne. "You take care now."

The trolley slides into the ambulance and the doors close on Annie Robinson. I can smell her on my hands—the sweet-as-sugar school counselor, with her bright red lipstick and her liquid brown eyes. Annie told me that nobody ever thought she was beautiful back in her school days but she'd blossomed into marriage and then become a pretty divorcée.

I wish Ruiz were here . . . or Ronnie

Cray. I left my mobile in my car. It's just down the street. I can call them. Someone has to pick up Charlie.

The sandy-haired constable intercepts me before I reach the Volvo.

"What are you doing, sir?"

"I'm just getting my phone."

"You were told not to move, sir."

"I just need to make a call."

"Step back to the police car, sir."

One hand on his belt, he looks at me with cold indifference.

I adopt a voice that says I'm glad to co-operate in any way I can. I'll write a letter of commendation telling his superiors about his conscientiousness, if he'll just let me get my phone.

Unfortunately, my left arm swings of its own initiative. It looks like a Nazi salute and I have to grab it with my right hand.

"Did you threaten me, sir?"

"No."

"Are you mocking me?"

"No, of course not, I have Parkinson's disease."

The tremors are segueing into jerkiness. My medication is wearing off. Using every bit of my concentration, I make a vain attempt to establish a single constant physical pose.

"I'm Professor Joseph O'Loughlin. I have to call my daughter. I'm supposed to pick her up . . . My phone is in my jacket . . . on the front seat. You can get it for me. Here are the keys."

"Don't approach me, sir. Put your hands down."

"They're just car keys."

The crowd are now focused on us. My apparent innocence has been transformed into suspicion and guilt.

"Just take my keys, get my phone and let me talk to my daughter."

"Take a step back, sir."

He's not going to listen. I try to take a step back, but my neurotransmitters are losing their juice. Instead of retreating, I lurch forwards. In a heartbeat an extendable baton lengthens in the officer's fist. He swings it once. I can hear it whistle through the air. It strikes me across my outstretched arm and my car keys fall.

The pain takes a moment to register. Then it feels as though bones are broken. In almost the same breath, my legs lose contact with the earth and I'm forced to my knees and then onto my chest. His full weight is pressed into my back, forcing my face into the cement.

"Just relax, sir, and you won't get hurt."

With one cheek pressed to the cement, I can see the police cars and forensic vans and the watching crowd. Sideways. The spectators are wondering if I'm the one—the prime suspect. They want to be able to tell their friends tomorrow that they saw me get arrested, how they looked into my eyes and they *knew* I was guilty.

Louis Preston is talking to one of his techs. I shout his name. He turns and blinks.

"Louis, it's me, Joe O'Loughlin."

The constable tells me to be quiet.

"I know Dr. Preston," I mutter. "He's the pathologist."

This time he comes towards us, dressed in his blue overalls. Tilting his head, he looks down at me.

"What are you doing, Professor?"

"I'm being sat on."

"I can see that."

Preston looks at the officer. "Why are you sitting on Professor O'Loughlin?"

"He tried to escape."

"Escape to where exactly?"

The constable takes a moment to recognize the sarcasm.

"Let him up, Officer. He's not going to run away."

I get to my feet, but my legs suddenly lock and I pitch forwards. Mr. Parkinson is assuming control. The pills are in my coat . . . with my phone.

Preston grabs hold of my forearm. "What are you doing here?"

"Annie Robinson is a friend of mine. I called this in."

"When did you see her last?"

"Yesterday. Lunchtime."

Preston looks back towards the terrace. "I have work to do."

"Just get my pills for me and my phone. They're in my coat." I motion towards the car.

Preston takes my keys. When he reaches the Volvo, he snaps on a rubber glove and makes a point of opening the rear door, reaching over the seat to get my coat. The inference is clear.

He brings the bottle to me, but not my mobile.

Taking two pills, I swallow them dry and watch as the two detectives head our way.

One has a haircut where the sides of his head are buzzed almost bald.

Preston peels off the glove. “Be extra careful, Professor, these guys aren’t your friends.”

45

Two detectives, little and large, a Detective Sergeant Stoner and his boss Wickerson who looks like a U.S. Marine. It’s gone eleven. I’m supposed to pick up Charlie but they won’t let me make a call.

“She’s fourteen. She’s waiting for me. If something happens to her I’ll personally make sure you spend the rest of your careers briefing lawyers.”

“Is that a threat, sir?”

“No, I’m way past making threats. I’ve asked you nicely. I’ve begged. I’ve appealed to your common sense. Just let me make a call. She needs to get home.”

Stoner and Wickerson discuss the matter privately. Finally, I’m handed a phone. I call Ruiz.

"Want to hear something interesting?" he says.

"Not now."

"What's wrong?"

"I'm with the police. I need you to pick up Charlie."

I tell him about Annie Robinson and my arrest. "Just get Charlie. Make sure she gets home." I give him the address.

"I'm on it."

Stoner takes the phone and escorts me to an interview room. I'm left there, sitting in my wet clothes, drinking machine coffee that could be reclassified as a form of torture alongside water boarding and sleep deprivation.

My mind keeps drifting back to Annie's flat and the open bottle of wine, the gift bag; the thank you card on the counter. Someone tried to poison her. Why?

Annie knew about Gordon Ellis and Sienna. She was asked to investigate by the school but failed to raise the alarm. Friendship can't explain a decision like that. I think back to Annie's flat—the expensive perfumes and designer handbags in her wardrobe. She complained about getting stitched up in her divorce settlement.

When I asked her how she could afford such a nice flat she told me that she refused to wait for things anymore. Perhaps she'd found a way to supplement her income. Blackmail can turn a profit.

Half twelve and the detectives reappear, offering me their apologies. For a moment I think I'm going to be released but they each take a seat. A tape recorder is switched on. Stoner is wearing braces over his white shirt like some yuppie trader from the eighties.

"Run through the story for us again, Joe," he says, sounding like we're old friends.

I tell them about the school musical and Annie not showing up and how I tried to call her.

"So you went round to her place?"

"Yes. I saw her car. I thought she must be home but she didn't answer the bell."

"So you climbed the back fence?"

"I was worried."

"When my friends aren't home, I don't climb over their fences and smash their patio doors."

"I saw water leaking under her bedroom door."

"You said there were no lights on."

"There was one in the bedroom."

"And you could see water?"

"Yes."

This is how it continues. Every detail is examined and picked over: what rooms I entered, what I touched, when I saw Annie last. Then we go back to the beginning again. Stoner is playing the hard arse while Wickerson wants to be my best friend, smiling, offering me encouragement, winking occasionally. At other times he looks bemused, almost doleful, like he's listening to an impaired person.

Stoner stands and moves behind me so that I have to turn my head to keep eye contact with him. He's not a complex man. Keeps it simple. Talks slowly.

"Tell us again how you know Annie Robinson?"

"She's a friend. She teaches at my daughter's school. We've met a few times socially."

"So she's not your girlfriend?"

"No."

"So you're not sleeping with her?"

"Once."

"Really?"

Stoner makes it sound like a telling confession. They're not listening to me.

"Tell us what you put in the wine."

"I didn't touch it."

"Did she say no to you, Joe? Was it some sort of date-rape drug?"

"No."

"Are we going to find your semen on those bed sheets?"

Wasted words. Wasted time. They should be talking to Gordon Ellis.

After an hour of questioning, the detectives take a break. I'm left in the interview suite trying to put the pieces together. How does Novak Brennan come into this? The trial, the jury, the Crying Man—I have fragments of a story, photographs without a narrative.

There are raised voices in the passageway. Ronnie Cray comes through the door like she wants to widen it with her hips.

"I've got to hand it to you, Professor. When you step in shit, you just put on your wellies and jump right in over your head."

Stoner and Wickerson are behind her, protesting.

Cray looks at me: "Have you made a statement, Professor?"

"Yes."

"Is there anything else you want to add?"

"No."

"Good. Get your coat."

Wickerson is having none of it. "You can't just barge in here. This man is still being questioned."

"Take it up with the Chief Constable," says the DCI. "Give him a call. He loves getting woken at two a.m."

She's walking as she talks, ushering me in the direction of the charge room. Stoner says something under his breath that ends with, "too ugly to get laid."

Cray stops and turns slowly, fixing him with a stare. "Do I know you?"

"No, ma'am." He gives her a mocking smile.

"Sure I do. Derek Stoner. Deadly Derek. You're a ladies' man. You dated one of the WPCs at Trinity Road. Sweet thing. She told me you had a pencil dick and couldn't find a clitoris with a compass and a street directory." Cray pauses and winks at him. "Guess only one of us made her scream."

Moments later we're outside. Monk is behind the wheel.

"Where are we going?" I ask.

"Trinity Road," she answers. "Sienna

Hegarty gave us a statement. We're arresting Gordon Ellis at dawn."

"You're going to charge him?"

"We're going to talk to him, but I wouldn't get my hopes up."

"Why?"

"Ellis has been through this before—the police interviews, the searches, the covert surveillance—when it comes to being a suspect, he's a fucking expert."

46

Sienna is curled up on a camp bed in Cray's office, lying with her head in shadow, covered by a thin blanket. A woman PC watches over her, sitting beneath a reading light, a magazine open on her lap.

"Tell me if she wakes."

A nod. She goes back to reading.

Most of the incident room is in darkness except for a pool of brightness like a spotlight on a stage. Cray hands me a transcript and tapes of Sienna's interview.

"We can't corroborate her story. There are no e-mails, notes or phone calls. Nobody saw them together except for Danny Gardiner, and he only puts them in a car. We've tracked both their mobiles. Apart from at the school, we can't put Sienna and Ellis within fifty yards of each other."

"Gordon made her turn her phone off. What about the chat-room conversations?"

"We're getting the transcripts. Even if they show Sienna was coerced, we still have to prove that Ellis created this 'Rockaboy' persona. We've got a search warrant for his home and office but I doubt if we'll find any computers."

Cray's eyes continue to search my face. "Tell me how Annie Robinson comes into this."

"I think she was blackmailing Gordon Ellis over his affair with Sienna."

"Evidence?"

"Annie knew about the relationship but she didn't tell the school or Sienna's parents."

"She was protecting a colleague."

"It was more than that. She's living beyond her means. Expensive clothes. Shoes.

Her flat. She also lied about dating Gordon Ellis at college."

"And Novak Brennan?"

"He and Ellis shared a house together at university. Brennan was supplying drugs to half the campus, according to Annie. Ellis was one of his dealers."

"That was years ago."

"They say the friends you make at university are the ones you keep for life."

"You think Ellis sent her the wine?"

"I don't know. It seems too clumsy."

"Clumsy?"

"He doesn't make many mistakes."

"Maybe he panicked."

"Somehow I doubt it."

Cray stands, stretches her arms and rolls her head from side to side.

"We're running out of time, Professor. We can't prove that Gordon Ellis groomed Sienna. We can't prove he slept with her. And we can't prove he got her pregnant. Unless Annie Robinson can corroborate Sienna's story, Ellis is going to walk out of here with a spring in his step and a hard-on for more schoolgirls."

I look at the clock. I have just a few

hours to come up with an interview strategy. I need to know everything I can about Gordon Ellis—his history, his friends, his relationships . . . I need to know about his state of mind, his personality, the light and shade of his existence. I have to walk through his mind, see the world through his eyes, discover what excites him and what he fears most.

Finding a quiet corner, I sit down at a desk and begin listening to the tapes of Sienna's police interview. Fast-forwarding and playing excerpts, I listen to Sienna explaining how she was groomed by her favorite teacher, wooed with kindness and compliments. Eventually, the relationship became a physical one and they would rendezvous in Gordon's car after school, parking in lay-bys and quiet lanes, always somewhere different. Occasionally, he took her to cheap motorway hotels or organized for her to stay overnight when she babysat Billy. Gordon would slip into her bed during the night, getting a thrill out of taking her while his wife lay sleeping.

I was worried because I lost an earring. It was Mum's favorite pair. I thought it might have slipped down the sofa or

been in the bed. Gordon got really angry because Natasha found it in the main bedroom and accused him of sleeping with me. She wouldn't let me babysit after that. Mum went crazy looking for the earring. She turned our house upside down. You won't tell her, will you?

Monk tells her no. He asks if she kept any notes, photographs or gifts from Gordon.

He said I couldn't tell anyone.

But you must have kept something—a memento.

What's a memento?

Something to remind you, like a souvenir.

No, not really. I used to write a diary on my computer, but I used different names.

Where is the computer now?

It was stolen . . . when Daddy got . . . when he died.

The interview switched to the day of Ray Hegarty's murder. After Danny Gardiner dropped Sienna on a street corner in Bath she waited for Gordon Ellis. He arrived with another man and they made her lie down on the backseat.

What did the other man look like?

I wasn't supposed to see his face.

But you did.

Yes. He had black tears coming from his eyes.

Tattoos?

Yes.

Do you know his name?

No.

What did Gordon tell you?

Sienna hesitates. Faltering. *He said I had to have sex with someone. I asked him why and he said I had to prove how much I loved him.*

"But you know I love you," I said.

"Prove it one more time."

"What if I don't want to?"

"You'll do it anyway."

"What if he's ugly?"

"Close your eyes and think of me."

Monk asks her about the drive, which took longer than fifteen minutes but less than an hour, according to Sienna. When the car pulled up, Gordon told her to brush her hair and put on fresh makeup. She was wearing her black flapper dress from the musical.

Gordon took me to the door and knocked. A man answered.

What did he look like?

Old—maybe fifty—he had a red face.

What color hair?

He didn't have much hair. He offered me a glass of champagne. I made a mistake and told him I was too young. Then I remembered that Gordon had said I wasn't to tell him my age. "How young?" the man asked. I lied and said I was eighteen.

"You're shivering. Are you cold?"

"No."

"Have you done this before?"

"No."

Then he put his hands on my shoulders and pushed my dress down my arms. I tried to cover myself, but he said I shouldn't be ashamed . . .

Sienna began to weep and Monk suspended the interview, announcing the time. There is a pause in the recording and I hear his voice again—commencing a new session.

At that moment I catch a movement out of the corner of my eye. Sienna is awake. Sleepy.

"What are you listening to?" she asks.

"Your interview."

She lowers her eyes. Embarrassed.

"How are you feeling?"

"Like an elephant sat on my chest."

I pull up a chair. She hugs her knees. "Pretty stupid, huh?"

"Don't be too hard on yourself."

"Are they going to arrest him?"

"Yes."

The WPC brings her a cup of tea. Sienna nurses it in both hands, warming her fingers. I can barely recognize the girl I first met. Her sassy, in-your-face attitude and confidence have been stripped away.

How will she recover from this? It's possible. She's intelligent and sensitive. With the right role models and advice she can still make something of her life. Otherwise she's going to end up in the arms of some wife beater or abuser who will recognize that Ray Hegarty and Gordon Ellis have done all the hard work in breaking her spirit.

I ask her about the house she visited. The man she had to sleep with. She hesitates, not wanting to go over it again.

"Remember what we did before? If you don't want to answer a question, all you have to do is raise your right hand, just your fingers. It's our special signal."

Sienna nods.

"What do you remember about the house?"

"It had lots of old stuff. Furniture. Antiques, maybe. And one of those big clocks that bongs every hour. It was bonging when he was . . . when he was . . . you know."

"He took you upstairs?"

"Yes."

"Were there paintings on the walls?"

"Dead people in frames."

"What was he wearing?"

"A dressing gown. And he had on a pair of those half slippers like my granddad wears. They flap up and down when you walk."

"Did he say anything?"

"He was nice. He asked my name. When I told him he said, 'I don't suppose that's your real name.' I knew I should have made one up."

"Did he tell you his name?"

"No."

Sienna is looking at me, gauging my reaction, wanting to know whether I think less of her now.

"At first I thought he was just lonely, you know, like old and on his own, but then I found out he was married."

"How?"

"I opened one of the wardrobes. I saw dresses and shoes. And I think he might have had a daughter my age because once he called me by a different name."

"What name?"

"Megan."

I know I could get more details from Sienna if I took her back to that night and did a proper cognitive interview, getting her to concentrate on the sounds, the smells, the images. But what would it cost her? I'd risk traumatizing a girl who had been through enough.

Instead I choose another event: her weekend away with Gordon Ellis. It was in the autumn, not long after they went back to school.

"Danny picked me up from school and dropped me at a lay-by on the A26. Gordon wanted to make sure nobody saw us together, so he made me lie down in the backseat under a blanket."

"Where was Billy?"

"He was next to me in his booster seat. He thought it was a game, like peekaboo."

"Did Gordon say where you were going?"

"To the seaside; I think he said the caravan was in Cornwall."

"That's a long way."

Sienna shrugs.

I quiz her about the drive, but she can't remember any road signs or place names. At one point Gordon said he was hungry and they stopped for fish and chips. He made Sienna wait in the car and took Billy with him.

"I want you to close your eyes and think back. You're in the car alone. Remember how it smelled and what you were wearing. You were excited. Anxious. Nervous perhaps. Gordon has gone to get the fish and chips. You're waiting. What can you remember?"

"There was a Lily Allen song on the radio."

"That's good."

"And I forgot to tell Gordon to get me ketchup. I don't like vinegar on my chips."

"Did you go and tell him?"

"No. He told me to stay in the car."

"What about your mobile?"

"He made me turn it off."

"What did you see outside?"

"A picture-framing shop . . . another place with salamis in the window."

"What else?"

"There was a pub over the road with a sign outside. It said, 'Dogs Welcome.' I laughed and showed it to Gordon because I kept thinking of these dogs going in and ordering drinks at the bar." She opens her eyes and looks at me. "I don't suppose that's much use."

"You'd be surprised."

I take her over the rest of the journey, plucking out small, often random details. She recalls certain songs on the radio and a billboard advertising a golf course and the smell of a poultry farm.

"After that I guess I just fell asleep."

"For how long?"

She screws up her face in concentration. "Gordon said I had food poisoning."

"You must have woken up at some point."

"Gordon said I'd been sick on my clothes, which is why he took them off. 'I brought pajamas,' I told him, but he said I was sick on those too."

"You were naked?"

Sienna blushes and the details turn to dust in my mouth.

"Tell me about the caravan?"

Her forehead furrows. "It had a bed and a little sink and a table that folded away."

"Did it have curtains?"

"They were black and they were taped down."

"Did you ever manage to look outside?"

"I woke up during the night. I was *so* thirsty. At first I was frightened because I couldn't remember where I was and it was so dark."

"Where was Gordon?"

"He must have gone out. My head was really heavy. I hooked my fingers beneath the tape on the windows and lifted a corner. I could see colored lights and hear music. Kids were yelling. It was a fairground. It made me think of when I was eleven and we went to Blackpool. Lance won me a panda on the shooting gallery and I kissed a boy from Maidstone who Mum said was my cousin but he was just a friend of the family."

Sienna smiles shyly.

"This fairground, what rides could you see?"

"I think it had a merry-go-round. I could see the colored lights on the canopy. Is that important?"

"It might be."

47

The first pale suggestion of dawn has appeared on the horizon as a faint gray smudge. F. Scott Fitzgerald wrote that the real dark night of the soul is always three o'clock in the morning, but that's not right. The darkest part of the night is just before dawn when we wake and peer through the curtains and wonder where the world has gone.

Headlights appear and disappear on the M32. A rubbish truck is reversing into an alley. A shift worker hurries along the footpath. The day begins.

Visiting the bathroom, I squeeze the last urine from my bladder and take another few pills, before going in search of Ronnie Cray. I find her pacing the vehicle lockup with an unlit cigarette in her lips. Like an obsessive compulsive, she is full of tics and routines. She taps the cigarette against her wrist and sucks it again.

The Novak Brennan trial resumes this morning. I haven't asked her what she's going to do about the photographs and the jury foreman.

"So what have you got?" she asks expectantly. I feel an acid surge in my stomach.

"Ellis isn't going to crack. He's been here before—in police custody, under suspicion, interrogated—he won't be tricked into making admissions. He believes he got away with murdering his first wife, which makes him cleverer than the police."

I glance at my notes. Scrawled at the top of the page I have the name: Gordon Ellis Freeman.

Age: thirty-six.

Above average intelligence.

Forensically aware.

Technologically confident.

A practiced manipulator and predator who uses a high degree of planning and has the ability to execute those plans.

His motivation isn't particularly sexual. His satisfaction comes from the hunt rather than the conquest. Bending a young girl to his will. Having her fall in love with him. Offering herself to him unconditionally.

Cray is opening the hinged lid of her lighter and shutting it with a flick of her wrist.

"You can call Ellis a nonce or a pervert or a pedophile, but that doesn't explain him. Unless you can grasp the intense pleasure he gets from taking an underage girl and using her as the culmination of his fantasies, you'll never understand him. Sienna was the punctuation mark for a perfect statement."

I pause and wait. The detective is still listening.

"You have to explore his account of events in fine detail. Don't let him waffle or prevaricate. Ask direct questions; seek times, dates and places. Woven together in the right way, he might slip up."

"But you don't believe he will?"

"No."

"Tell me when the good news is coming," she mutters.

"Sienna is his weak link—the one element he can't control. Right now, Ellis thinks nobody will believe Sienna because she's a murder suspect and she's only fourteen, but he's worried. That's why he tried to silence her.

"Remember the caravan? When his wife disappeared the police couldn't find it. Ellis told them he'd lost it in a poker game, but that's not true. He hid it from them or he's managed to get another one."

"Why does he need a van?"

"He needs somewhere isolated, somewhere he can be alone with his victims so he can savor the experience and make it last. Sienna went with him willingly, yet he still drugged her because he didn't want her knowing the location. He also wanted to do things to her against her will."

A vein in Cray's temple is pulsing with her heartbeat. "You think he took souvenirs?"

"Photographs. Maybe videos. He blacked out the windows of the van, which suggests he could have a darkroom."

The DCI splays open her hand and wipes dirt off the heel of her palm with the tips of her fingers.

"How do we find it?"

"We don't."

"I don't understand."

"We have to convince Gordon that we're getting close. Make him believe we're unlocking his secret. He can't afford to have us find the caravan. He'll have to act."

For the next fifteen minutes I outline a plan—just the bare bones. Most of the decisions can't be made until I see how Ellis reacts. The more pressure he's put under, the more likely he is to make a mistake.

"I want you to tip off the media," I tell Cray. "Turn his arrest into a public event. A schoolteacher arrested over sex abuse allegations—the tabloids will be baying for his blood."

"He'll accuse us of victimizing him."

"Let him complain. Bring him through the front doors in the full glare of the TV lights. Make him run the gauntlet. Show him how society reacts to child molesters."

"Then what?"

"Take him through Sienna's statement. Every time, date and place. The one thing you *don't* mention is the caravan. Leave it out completely. He's going to wonder how you can have so much detail—but not that one."

"And then what?"

"Leave the rest to me."

The arrest warrant is served at 6 a.m. by a dozen detectives who push past Natasha Ellis and move quickly through the house. Gordon is made to wait in his underwear, shivering in a hallway. An hour later he's handcuffed and led outside to a police car in front of his neighbors.

The siren sounds all the way to Trinity Road where a crowd of photographers, reporters and TV crews record his arrival. Blinking into the bright lights and flashguns, Gordon looks stunned by the speed of his changing circumstances.

They say a cruel story runs on wheels and this one has every hand oiling them as they turn. The arrest makes all the morning news bulletins on TV and radio, destined to be the defining story of the day, triggering talkback phone-ins and coffee-room discussions.

Gordon Ellis is told to stand in front of a height chart holding a whiteboard with his name and date of birth.

"Look up."

He raises his eyes and the flashgun fires.

"Turn to the right."

Pulling his shoulders back, he lifts one hand and smoothes down his hair. The camera flashes again. His stitches are barely visible beneath his hairline, but one of his eyes is bruised and yellow.

Ellis was given time to dress before he left the house. The schoolteacher chose carefully—aware of what impression he wanted to make: spectacles instead of contacts, a business shirt, blue blazer and jeans. Smart casual. Studious. Relaxed.

The formal interviews begin just before nine. Ronnie Cray and Safari Roy enter the room with a dozen ring-bound folders. Ellis had wanted a lawyer from Scotland but was told to find someone closer. He settled on a short, stocky solicitor with the sort of nonchalant smile and cocky demeanor that irritates detectives.

Throughout the early exchanges, Ellis seems to be enjoying the attention. This is a game and he's playing it like a professional who's been forced to compete in the lower leagues.

"Sienna Hegarty says you slept with her," says Cray.

"She's lying."

"Why would she lie?"

Ellis sighs wearily and shakes his head. "She's trying to punish me. Can't you see that? She thinks I shunned her. She mistook my kindness for something more and now she wants to destroy me."

"We're going to find her DNA in your home and your car."

"She babysat my boy. I drove her home."

"You had sex with her."

"She tried to kiss me and I pushed her away. Hurt her feelings."

Cray consults her notes. "Is that why you told Professor O'Loughlin that you 'fucked her every which way'?"

Ellis laughs acidly. "And you believe him! The man who did this to me." He pulls back his fringe, showing the bloody criss-cross pattern of stitches on his scalp.

"He calls himself a psychologist but his mind is in the sewer. Let me tell you what he does—he looks in his *own* head and his *own* heart and he sees perversion and sickness. Then he claims *other* people think like he does."

The tone has suddenly changed. Instead of belligerence and sarcasm, Ellis adopts a whining tone, demanding that his interrogators see things his way. It's like watching an illegal arrival trying to talk his way through Immigration without the language to explain himself. He groans. He grimaces. He puffs out his cheeks.

Partly this is feigned, but some of his persecution complex is genuine. Like many men who abuse their power over women, Ellis seems to carry some ancient sense that he's the *real* victim. He's been misunderstood. Led astray. Others are to blame.

"Why did you kill Ray Hegarty?"

"You must be joking."

"He saw you and Sienna together."

"He was sexually abusing his daughter. I was trying to help her."

"How exactly were you doing that?"

"I took her to see a therapist. She didn't want her parents knowing."

"Why you?"

"I know this may surprise you, Detective, but I'm a caring, committed teacher. The only mistake I made was caring too much. I should have recognized the signs. I should have seen she was developing a crush on me."

"You groomed her."

"No."

"You drugged her."

"No."

The lawyer interrupts. "My client has answered these questions."

"Your client is so full of shit his eyes are brown." Cray changes tack. "Annie Robinson knew you were having an affair?"

Ellis hesitates. "What's she got to do with this?"

"She knew the truth."

Ellis reacts, stabbing his finger across the table. "What has that bitch said to you?"

"I'm asking the questions, Mr. Ellis."

"She's lying. She threatened to destroy my career unless . . ."

"Unless what?"

"Unless I gave her ten thousand pounds."

The lawyer puts a hand on Ellis's shoulder, wanting him to stop. They whisper. Nod. Ellis composes himself, sitting straighter.

Cray asks him the question again. "Why did you pay Annie Robinson ten thousand pounds?"

"She was blackmailing me."

"If you weren't having an affair with Sienna Hegarty, why did you pay her a thing?"

"Because I knew she could ruin me.

Even without proof she could have me investigated and suspended."

"So you poisoned her?"

"What?"

"You put antifreeze in a bottle of wine and tried to kill her."

Anger turns to outright surprise. Ellis looks at Cray and Safari Roy and then his lawyer. "What are these clowns talking about?"

His lawyer wants the interview suspended. Ellis shouts over him, "What do you mean, antifreeze? What's happened to her? Where is she?"

Cray continues, "When did you last see Annie Robinson?"

"I want to know what's happened to her."

"Answer my question, Mr. Ellis."

"Sunday."

"Have you ever been to her apartment?"

Gordon stares past her, his mind in flux, racing through the possibilities. Now less sure of himself, he hesitates over his answers, fighting to keep his voice neutral.

"My client needs to use the bathroom."

"Your client can hold it in," says Cray.

"I want it to be noted that he was denied a toilet break."

"Noted."

Ellis is slowing down his answers, giving himself time. This is what makes him so difficult to pin down. He adapts to different circumstances, changing the tempo and elements of his personality to suit the occasion. Ronnie Cray has to stay on the subject of Annie, but she's running out of questions.

"You knew Annie Robinson at university."

"Yes."

"And you also knew Novak Brennan."

A grin tugs at the corners of the teacher's mouth. The spell has been broken. He's on firm ground again. "We shared a house together for a while."

"When was the last time you spoke to him?"

"I don't remember."

"Was it this week?"

"I don't remember."

"When did you last see him?"

"I don't remember."

"In the past month? Six months? Year?"

"I don't remember."

Cray glances over her shoulder towards the observation window. Ellis is going to stonewall now. Every answer will be the same.

Time is called. The tape stopped. Cray emerges and walks past me. I find her outside in the secure parking lot, sitting on the steps in the sunshine.

"This is the smoker's corner—want to join? We're the cool group."

"No thanks."

"We're getting nowhere."

"You shook him up."

"He stuck to his script."

"Except when you mentioned Annie Robinson."

"You don't think he knew?"

"No."

Someone like Gordon Ellis is almost defined by his sense of superiority and control. His whole persona is an act, concealing a warped but calculating mind, but for just a moment when he heard about Annie Robinson the artifice and game-playing vanished. He was out of his comfort zone.

"I still can't understand him," says Cray. "He's got a beautiful young wife at home. Money. Looks. He could have any woman he wanted."

"He doesn't want just *any* woman. Underneath his pretty-boy looks, Gordon is still an ugly, overweight kid who wears glasses and can't get a girlfriend. He transformed himself. He exercised. Lost the weight. Went to the gym. Took vitamins. Got an education, but he never forgot how those girls belittled him at school. The pretty, confident ones. The untouchables.

"Ellis is a narcissist, which is why he gets intensely angry if you suggest that he has a flaw. He cares about his appearance and the impression he makes. He used to hate looking at himself in the mirror, but now he does it automatically, compulsively. And he strains every fiber of his being to meet his own flawless image of himself, demeaning and seeking to destroy anyone who casts doubts on the way he sees himself."

The DCI nods and glances at her polished shoes. "I'm running out of questions."

"That's OK. Keep pushing him. I noticed a few things. When he lies he looks directly at you like he's gazing into a camera. And when he gets nervous he puts his left hand in his pocket as if reaching for something. I think he normally carries some sort of lucky charm or talisman, which he keeps in that pocket. Check out the personal effects log—see what they took off him."

Cray has forgotten to ash her cigarette, which hangs from the corner of her mouth.

"How in glory's name do you know shit like that?"

"I watch people."

"Do me a favor. Don't ever go looking at me. Don't go thinking about me. Don't watch what I do."

"You worried?"

She brushes fallen ash from her coat.

"You're a clever bastard, Professor, but there's something you should know about menopausal women. We can experience insomnia, depression, hot flushes, fluid retention and constant PMS. It's best not to piss us off."

Upstairs, I take Sienna to an interview room. She's dressed in jeans, a sweatshirt and Converse trainers that squeak on the polished floor.

"Does he know I'm here?"

"He probably suspects."

She takes a deep breath and holds it for a moment. "Is he going to hate me?"

"What he did was wrong—you have nothing to be ashamed of."

DS Abbott arrives with a folder of photographs. I spread them on the table—images of caravan parks and aerial photographs of the Somerset and Cornish coastline. I take the best of the prints and put them on a white board. Sienna sits watching me.

"Remember what we said?"

She nods.

"This is just like being an actress. You're my leading lady."

"I know."

"Don't be scared."

"I'm not."

I look into her eyes.

"I don't hate him, you know. Even if he doesn't love me anymore."

Along the corridor, Ronnie Cray leaves the interview room. Gordon Ellis is led back to a holding cell—his lawyer at his side, whispering instructions.

Sienna rubs a lock of hair between her forefinger and thumb. Gordon has reached the door.

"So from the caravan you could see a fairground?"

"Yes," says Sienna.

"What could you see?"

"The top of a merry-go-round with lots of colored lights . . . and I could hear music and people laughing."

"What else?"

"The sea."

"Could you see the beach?"

"Yes."

"Would you recognize it again?"

"Sure."

Sienna is standing at a whiteboard, pointing to a photograph.

Gordon Ellis has stopped in the passageway, waiting for Roy to unlock the next door. He hears Sienna's voice and turns, taking in the maps and photographs. His pale eyes swim with loathing. Roy nudges him forward. The door closes.

Sienna takes a deep breath.

"Did I do OK?"

"You were a star."

48

His name is Carl Guilfoyle," says Cray, staring from her window, watching people dodge through the rain. "He's originally from Belfast, although he's spent half his life in the States—including a dozen years in prison in Arizona for attempted murder."

A bus rumbles by, sending up a flurry of spray.

"We pulled his prints from the room at the Royal Hotel. He tried to wipe it clean, but we got two partials from the suitcase."

She opens a folder on her desk. It contains a handful of photographs of Carl Guilfoyle—most of them police mugshots. The earliest, taken in his teens, shows him clear-skinned, with dark hair and a crooked mouth.

"When was this taken?"

"He was seventeen. He glassed a guy in a bar-fight. When the Arizona police picked him up he had a fake ID. A judge remanded him to an adult prison. That night one of the older cons tried to take advantage of a young white Irish boy in the shower block. Big mistake. They found the con in a shower stall choking on his own blood. Swallowed his tongue. To be more exact—they found it in his stomach."

"What happened to Guilfoyle?"

"He got twelve years for the glassing."

"He was a juvenile."

"Doesn't make much difference in the States."

I study each of the photographs. It's like watching a Hollywood makeup artist transform an actor, putting on a prosthetic mask, altering their age and features. Only Guilfoyle's eyes have stayed the same, rimmed with a quivering energy. I remember how he looked at Sienna's photograph, committing her face, her hair, her budding body to memory. I could smell his aftershave and something else, crawling beneath.

"Ever heard of the Aryan Brotherhood?"

"The white prison gang."

"They make up one percent of the U.S. prison population and they commit nearly a quarter of the prison murders. That's where Guilfoyle got his tattoos—the teardrops are supposed to signify a kill."

"Who?"

"A black guy called Walter Baylor. Carl shanked him in a meal queue in front of a hundred and forty-seven witnesses—and nobody saw a thing. That's the thing with the Brotherhood. People seem to suffer collective amnesia and mass blindness whenever anything happens inside."

"Are there any links between Guilfoyle and the men on trial?"

"The Aryan Brotherhood has been associated with Combat 18, the armed wing of a British neo-Nazi organization called Blood and Honor. The eighteen comes from the first and eighth letters of the alphabet: Adolf Hitler's initials. C18 was formed in the early nineties as a breakaway group from the BNP after certain members became disillusioned with the party going soft on the armed struggle and focusing instead on politics.

"This breakaway group launched a string of attacks on immigrants and ethnic minorities, but most of the ringleaders were rounded up a decade ago during an undercover operation by Scotland Yard and MI5. Some of them were serving British soldiers.

"Tony Scott was a member of Combat 18. When it was broken up in the nineties it fractured into splinter groups, but managed to survive, linking itself with racist organizations in Russia, Germany and America."

"Groups like the Aryan Brotherhood?"

"Exactly. They also set up chapters in cities like Belfast where some of the former Loyalist paramilitaries were quite sympathetic to the racist agenda."

"Brennan grew up in Belfast."

"He and Guilfoyle lived only a few streets from each other."

Cray closes the folder and locks it in her filing cabinet.

"So they could have known each other?"

"MI5 has run a check on Guilfoyle. He and Brennan were on the streets of Belfast at roughly the same time, but they were never arrested together or linked."

A WPC knocks on the office door and hands Cray a DVD. Putting the disk into a machine, the DCI presses a remote and a TV screen illuminates. She hits fast-forward. Stop. Play.

"This was taken outside Annie Robinson's place."

The time code on screen says 15.24.07. The blurred figure in the frame is wearing a hooded sweatshirt or a parka, walking away from the camera. It could be a man or a woman. Carrying something.

Thirty yards along the road, the person climbs three steps and presses a buzzer. What button? Lower half. Nothing clearer. The door unlocks. Someone must have released it.

Cray presses fast-forward again. The time code says 15.26.02. The same person on the street again, head bowed, this time walking towards the camera. I can only see the hood and empty hands.

"That's what I hate about the morons who install security cameras," says Cray. "They get the angles all wrong. This is next to useless."

Rewinding, she runs through the footage again. A left hand reaches out for the buzzer. The right hand holds a waxed paper bag.

"How far off the ground is that intercom panel?" I ask.

"Standard height."

"How tall does that make him?"

"It depends on the focal length of the lens and how far they're standing from the wall. A photographer could tell us."

Pressing fast-forward, the DCI advances to the second lot of footage, taken by a different CCTV camera.

"This was taken two blocks away on Warminster Road."

A silver Ford Focus is on screen, heading away from the camera.

"We can't get a number—the plates are obscured."

She presses eject and glances at her watch. It's one o'clock.

"How's Sienna?"

"Holding up."

Cray turns back to the window. An unlit cigarette dangles from her fingers.

"I want to take Sienna out of here. We'll sneak her into the Crown Court. Quietly. Let her see the jury foreman."

"And then what?"

The detective doesn't answer. Maybe she doesn't know. Shifting slowly, she grabs her coat and opens her office door.

"First we have to cut Gordon Ellis loose. See where the rabbit runs."

The hospital receptionist has a voice like an automated message.

"Are you family?"

"No, I'm a friend."

"Details are only available to family."

"I just want to know if she's OK."

"What is the patient's name?"

"Annie Robinson. She was brought in last night."

"Her condition is listed as stable."

I stop her before she hangs up. "Does she have any family?"

"Excuse me?"

"Is there anyone with her?"

The receptionist makes a decision and her tone softens. "Her mother and father arrived a while back. They're with her now."

"Thank you."

Hanging up, I feel a mixture of relief and guilt. Everything I do nowadays seems to have untoward consequences. I expect my bad decisions to have downsides but even my good calls are starting to look shaky. Small things, details I pick up almost instinctively, are beginning to elude me. I should have recognized Sienna's vulnerability. I should have warned Annie about Gordon Ellis.

Next I call Julianne.

"Is everything OK?" she asks.

"Fine."

"Charlie said Vincent had to bring her home."

"I got held up. Annie Robinson is in hospital . . . it's a long story."

There is a pause. I want her to say something, to tell me what she's thinking. Instead she says, "I have to go. I'm due in court."

I have time to make one more call. Ruiz rattles off twenty questions, talking in a kind of police shorthand.

"Is the dyke looking after you?"

"She's on our side. I need another favor."

"How many you got left?"

"Keep an eye on Julianne. She's in court today."

"What about the Crying Man?"

"His name is Carl Guilfoyle. They've just issued a warrant for his arrest."

The footpath outside Trinity Road has become a makeshift media center for dozens of photographers, reporters and TV crews. There are outside broadcast vans parked in the street and takeaway coffee cups lying crumpled in the gutter.

I'm halfway across the foyer when Natasha Ellis appears in front of me. Dressed in black, her lips bloodless and thin, she looks like a legal secretary with her hair pulled back severely and her eyebrows arching in complaint.

"Why are you doing this to us?" she demands, hatred filling her tiny frame.

I try to step around her. She moves with me.

"That little bitch is lying. Gordon never touched her."

"Don't make things worse, Natasha. I know what Gordon did to you."

"You know nothing about me."

Twisted in anger, her face no longer pretty or pleasant.

"I know that he groomed you as a schoolgirl. I know that he got rid of his first wife so he could marry you. I think you know it too."

"How dare you patronize me!"

"I apologize if I gave that impression."

"It's not an impression."

"I'm sorry just the same."

"Fuck you!"

She turns, stumbling on her high heels, before correcting herself. I have no antidote for her distress. Her life is crumbling around her and she can't do anything except watch.

Moments later, Gordon appears, flanked by his lawyer. Natasha throws her arms around her husband's neck and he peels them away. They have reached the main doors. The lawyer tries to cover Gordon with a coat, but the schoolteacher brushes it aside.

"I've got nothing to hide," he mutters.

More than thirty reporters, photographers and television crews are waiting outside. Clicking shutters and camera flashes greet Gordon's every footstep, gesture and facial expression. When he brushes his fringe from his eyes, when he tries to smile, when he puts his arm around Natasha.

Beyond the media scrum, I see a separate crowd of bystanders who have come to watch, having heard the news on TV or radio or Twitter. Among them are girls in school uniforms. Gordon takes a piece of paper from his pocket, smoothing it between his fingers. Clearing his throat, he smiles with a boyish shyness. The cameras respond with a fuselage of clicks and whirs.

"Firstly I want to say that I have devoted nearly fifteen years of my life to teaching and I cherish every child that I have taught.

I am being victimized here. I am being hounded. I am being punished for caring too much." He pauses, composing himself. "I have a lovely wife and a son. I would never do anything to embarrass them or hurt them."

The quake in his voice, his sense of disbelief, the hurt in his eyes, all seem genuine.

A reporter yells a question: "Did you sexually assault a student?"

"No."

"Why has she made a complaint?"

"I think she has been coerced and coached by a psychologist who recently assaulted me and has been charged by the police. Professor Joseph O'Loughlin has launched a vendetta against me. He has threatened and harassed my wife."

"Why would he do that?" asks a reporter.

"You should ask him that."

Another journalist shouts louder than the rest. "Are you standing by your husband, Mrs. Ellis?"

Natasha nods.

"So you're saying this girl is lying?"

Gordon answers. "The girl who has made these allegations is a very troubled teenager with a history of cutting herself. She is also accused of a serious crime and could be trying to deflect attention from herself."

"Why would she blame you?"

"She developed an infatuation. She stalked me."

More questions are shouted. "Was she your babysitter?" "Did she ever travel in your car?" "Were you ever alone with her?"

A female reporter yells, "Is it true she was pregnant?"

Gordon stammers.

"Did you try to arrange an abortion for her?"

The atmosphere has subtly altered and Gordon's contrived façade is beginning to crack. This has become a blood sport and the hounds are baying.

A photograph appears in his hand. "This is my son, Billy. He's my joy. I love children. I would never do anything to hurt a child."

It's an appeal for understanding rather than a defense. In the beat of silence that follows it's clear he hasn't swayed his audience. His lawyer tries to intervene but the questions keep coming.

"What happened to your first wife, Mr. Ellis?"

"Were you suspected of her murder?"

"Why did you change your name?"

Gordon blinks at the cameras—out of words. Pushing past the photographers and reporters, he manages to cross the flagged concrete path to a waiting car. The crowd has swelled, almost blocking the road.

"We love you, Mr. Ellis!" yells one of the teenage girls, triggering a chorus. "We believe you."

Gordon stops, squares his shoulders and gives them a grateful smile. The girls squeal as though acknowledged by a film star.

The car pulls away. Photographers run alongside, shooting through the tinted windows. Natasha Ellis has covered her face. Gordon defiantly sticks out his jaw.

Ronnie Cray appears alongside me, lighting a cigarette and exhaling.

"He acted like a rock star and they treated him like a scumbag. That's how life balances itself out."

"You briefed the reporters."

"I couldn't possibly comment."

49

There are three unmarked cars and two motorcycles following Gordon Ellis. Neither too old nor too new, the vehicles blend in with the traffic and constantly change positions.

Safari Roy is two-up in the lead vehicle, dressed like a businessman on his way home from work. Car two is a Land Rover Discovery, half a block behind, driven by a woman officer who looks like a typical mother on a school run. There is also a tradesman's van, a motorcycle courier and a minibus.

Gordon Ellis will expect the police to follow him, but this fact won't ease his anxiety. He'll still look over his shoulder and study the vehicles and faces of the drivers. Each time he'll see a different car and a different face. Nobody familiar. Nothing out of place.

"It's costing a fortune," says Cray, as she watches colored dots on a computer screen—each one representing a different surveillance team. "I have to swap vehicles and personnel every twelve hours."

"How long have you been given?"

"Forty-eight hours. He has to make a move by then."

"He will."

We're being driven down Newgate Street past Castle Park. The narrow harbor slides by, sluggish and brown. A handful of boats are tied up along a dock, most of them moored permanently and painted with advertising.

Sienna is next to me, wearing a baseball cap pulled low over her eyes. Leaning her head against the window, she watches joggers dressed in Lycra circling the paths and mothers pushing children on tricycles with handles. Most are wrapped in waterproof jackets and look tired of waiting for the warmer weather to arrive. That's the way it is with Bristol. In winter it's full of weary, pinch-faced urbanites, but come the summer they grow a smile.

The car pauses at a police checkpoint and we wait for the plastic barricade to be pulled aside. The Crown Court precinct is quiet. Most of the protesters have dispersed but a token few are sitting on the steps of the Guildhall, outnumbered by police officers.

We walk Sienna through the main entrance and the security screening. The clock in the foyer has just gone two. Court One is due back in session.

Taking Sienna upstairs, we push through the doors. She slides onto a bench seat in the public gallery. Her baseball cap is pulled even lower. Rita Brennan is two rows in front of us. Ruiz is off to the side. He glances at me and barely nods.

In the main body of the courtroom, Novak Brennan, Gary Dobson and Tony Scott are sitting in silence in the dock. Julianne waits at her microphone and Judge Spencer has his head down, tapping the keys of a laptop. His silver horsehair wig gleams under the hanging lights.

A door opens at the side of the court. The jury enters in single file, moving to their usual seats. The foreman sits nearest the judge.

Cray whispers to Sienna. "Tell me if you recognize any of them."

Sienna raises her eyes, looking from face to face. She shakes her head.

"What about the guy in the front row, far left?"

She leans forward. Studies him. Shakes her head again.

"Are you sure?"

A nod.

Cray looks at me.

Marco Kostin is being recalled to the witness box. He shuffles this time, less confident than I remember. Diminished. The light has washed out of his eyes and his skin is blotchy and damp.

Novak Brennan's barrister, Mr. Hurst, QC, has a narrow, choleric face with small busy eyes. Pacing back and forth in front of the jury box, he makes eye contact with individual jurors who seem to look down or away. He turns to the witness box.

"Before the break, Mr. Kostin, you were describing the house. You said you were sleeping when you heard the sound of glass breaking. Is that correct?"

Julianne translates the question.

Marco nods and answers in a hoarse voice.

"If you were sleeping, how are you certain it was glass breaking that woke you?"

"I heard it more than once."

"How many times did you hear it?"

"I'm not sure."

"You're not sure. I see." Mr. Hurst exchanges a look with the jury. "Are you sure you went to the window?"

"Yes."

"From the second floor you claim to have seen my client sitting behind the wheel of a van. How far do you think that was?"

Marco looks from Julianne to Mr. Hurst. He doesn't understand the question.

"What was the distance between you and the van? Fifty feet . . . a hundred feet . . . more?"

Marco blinks and his mouth flexes uncertainly.

Mr. Hurst: "Perhaps you'd prefer to use meters?"

"From the second floors," says Marco. "I don't know how far this is—maybe ninety feets."

"Ninety. You don't seem very sure."

"I did not measure it."

There is a sprinkling of laughter in the courtroom. Mr. Hurst allows himself a brief smile.

"It was dark—after midnight, in fact. You must have remarkable eyesight."

"I see OK."

"You told the police that you couldn't see the number plate on the van because it was too dark."

Marco hesitates. "I don't understand?"

"Did you tell police it was too dark to see the number plate?"

"It was in shadow."

"It was too dark—yes or no?"

"Yes."

"Yet you could see my client through a dirty second-floor window from ninety feet away in the dead of night?"

"There was a light inside the van when the door opened."

"You told police there were three men?"

"Yes."

"Why couldn't you identify the others?"

"I did not see them clearly."

"Because it was dark?"

"Yes."

Mr. Hurst exchanges another look with the jury.

"Had you seen Mr. Brennan anywhere before?"

"I had seen his picture."

"Where was that?"

"In the newspaper."

"During the council elections. You probably saw his campaign posters and his leaflets."

"Yes."

"Is that why you picked him out of a police lineup?"

"I recognized him, yes."

"You don't agree with his politics or his policies, so you decided to punish him."

"No."

"Who told you to identify him?"

Marco looks at Julianne, not understanding. She explains the question. He shakes his head.

Mr. Hurst braces both his hands on the bar table on either side of a legal pad. "You came to this country as an asylum seeker, is that correct?"

"We applied for asylum."

"Yes, but when you first arrived you told immigration officers that you were tourists."

"Yes."

"And that was a lie."

Marco looks at Julianne and then at the judge. Mr. Hurst prompts him again.

"You lied to immigration officers?"

"I did as my father told me."

"Have you been promised anything for testifying at this trial?"

"Promised?"

"What is your immigration status now?"

"I have been allowed to remain here for four years."

"So you can stay?"

"Yes."

"Isn't it also true that you've been approached by a newspaper and offered money for your story."

"Objection!" says Miss Scriber, quick to her feet. "Mr. Hurst has already suggested Mr. Kostin's immigration status has influenced his evidence. Now he's suggesting that he's seeking to profit from these circumstances."

Mr. Hurst looks affronted. "I'm simply trying to establish whether this witness has any ulterior motives that may influence his testimony."

Marco's eyes move back and forth, trying to follow their arguments.

Judge Spencer intervenes. "Unless you intend to introduce evidence of a conspiracy, Mr. Hurst, you're on very shaky ground. Perhaps you should choose another line of questioning."

Sitting next to me, I feel Sienna suddenly stiffen. Her fists are clenched and the muscles in her jaw, shoulders and her arms have seized up, locking her into a statue-like pose. She's not even blinking. Nothing moves except for the fingers of her right hand, which flutter up and down on her thigh. It's our signal.

Slowly her head turns and her eyes meet mine. Wide. Scared. She turns back to the courtroom and I follow her gaze across the bar table to the lone bewigged figure sitting above everyone else, tapping at his laptop.

Ronnie Cray pulls Sienna outside and into a consulting room, almost kicking the door open and leaning hard against it, making sure it's closed.

"You're sure?"

Sienna nods.

Cray's lips peel back. "Shit!"

Sienna flinches.

"It's not you," I tell her. "You've done nothing wrong."

"Shit! Shit! Shit!"

The DCI wants to pace but the room isn't big enough. She wants to smoke. She wants to dump this box of vipers on someone else.

Pulling me aside, she whispers angrily. "What in glory's name do I do? Who do I tell? He's a Crown Court judge!"

"You have to stop the trial."

"Only *he* can do that!" Cursing, she spins away and tries to pace again. "I need to think. I need to talk to some people. Take advice. A judge! A fucking judge!"

She looks at Sienna. "You *have* to be sure, one hundred percent, do you understand?"

Sienna nods.

Cray opens her mobile and shuts it again. "Come on—I've got to get out of here."

Too agitated to wait for the lift, she walks down the curving staircase. Ruiz intercepts me on the landing.

"What's wrong?"

"I can't talk. Wait for me."

Minutes later we're outside. Monk is behind the wheel. Cray doesn't say a word to him. She's trying to work out what to do . . . where to go . . . what happens next.

Opening her mobile, she stares at the screen. It can't be in a phone call. It's not secure enough. She flips it closed.

"I'm going to Portishead," she says. "I need to see the Chief Constable."

She looks at Sienna. "You need to tell him everything." Then she addresses me. "Don't breathe a word of this to anyone. Not a word."

"What about Ellis?"

"He's our problem now."

50

Ruiz is sitting quietly, letting me talk. We're sharing a wooden bench in Castle Park, overlooking the upper reaches of the floating harbor. Ducks and gulls dot the water, waiting to be fed by toddlers in pushchairs and older siblings who wobble on training wheels.

The Old Brewery rises abruptly from the opposite bank. The weathered brick walls are stained with bird shit and soot, yet are still preferable to modern glass and concrete. Somewhere nearer the cathedral a busker plucks the strings of a banjo and a flower seller with a brightly colored cabin is setting out buckets of blooms, tulips and daffodils.

Ruiz hasn't said a word. The sun radiates through a thin mesh of clouds, highlighting the gray in his hair and making him squint when he raises his eyes. His hands are big and square, no longer calloused. A boiled sweet rattles against his teeth.

"What would you do?" I ask.

"Nothing."

"Why?"

"You have a suicidal schoolgirl who has been sexually abused claiming that she slept with a County Court judge. She doesn't know his name. She can't remember the address. She's also facing a murder charge. You have no forensic evidence or corroboration."

"She recognized him."

"You can't stop a trial and destroy a man's career on that sort of evidence."

"So what's Cray going to do?"

"She's going to commit professional suicide."

A gust of wind ripples the water and topples the tulips and daffodils in their buckets.

Ruiz continues: "My guess is she'll go to the Director of Public Prosecutions, who'll shit himself and call the Attorney General. There'll be a full judicial inquiry, which is rare, and unless the investigation finds corroboration, Ronnie Cray can kiss her career goodbye."

"And the trial?"

"They're not going to stop an expensive, high-profile murder trial on the word of a fourteen-year-old schoolgirl."

"But the photographs in the suitcase . . . ?"

"Someone took pictures of jurors—it's not enough. You need evidence of a juror being approached or intimidated. Payments. Threats. Admissions . . ."

Ruiz stands and works the stiffness out of his back. His body looks too big for his clothes.

"So there's nothing we can do?"

"Not without evidence."

His eyes hold mine for a long time, blue-gray and uncomplicated. They seem to belong in the face of a younger man—a police constable who began his career more than thirty years ago, full of expectation and civic pride. A lot of water has passed under that bridge—violence, corruption, scandal, banalities, mediocrities, absurdities, insanities, hawks, doves, cowards, traitors, sell-outs, hypocrites and screaming nut-jobs—but Ruiz has never lost his faith in humanity.

I'm tired. Dirty. Weary of talking. My mind is full of fragments of broken lives—Ray Hegarty's, Sienna's, Annie Robinson's . . . I want to go home. I want a shower. I want to sleep. I want to put my arms around my daughters. I want to feel normal for a few hours.

Ruiz drops me at the terrace and turns off the engine of the Merc, listening to the afternoon quiet and the ticking sound of the motor cooling. Ugly dark clouds are rolling in from the west, moving too quickly to bring rain.

"I thought maybe I'd head back to London," he says. "Water the plants."

"You don't have any plants."

"Perhaps I'll take up gardening. Grow my own vegetables."

"You don't like vegetables."

"I love a good Cornish pasty."

Wrinkles are etched around his eyes and his slight jowls move with his jaw.

I ask him to hang around for another

day—just to see what happens. Maybe I'm being selfish, but I like having him here. With Ruiz what you see is what you get. He's a man of few contradictions except for his gruff exterior and gentle center.

Ever since I was diagnosed and moved out of London, I seem to have lost touch with most of my longtime friends. They call less often. Send fewer e-mails. Ruiz is different. He has only known me with Parkinson's. He has seen me at my lowest, sobbing at my kitchen table after Charlie was abducted and Julianne walked out on me. And I have seen him shot up, lying in a hospital bed, unable to remember what happened yesterday.

As I get older, friendships become harder to cultivate. I don't know why that is. Perhaps by middle age most people have enough friends. We have a quota and when it's filled we have to wait for someone to die or retire to get on the list.

Glancing at his watch Ruiz suggests it might be "beer o'clock." He waits while I shower and change before we walk as far as the Fox and Badger where I leave him with his elbows on the bar, gazing at a pint of Guinness turning from a muddy white to a dark brown.

Emma is due out of school. Standing on my own I watch the mothers and grandmothers arrive.

"Billy wasn't at school today," says Emma, when she falls into step beside me. "I think he was sick." Then she adds, "I think I should be allowed more sick days, otherwise it isn't fair."

"You shouldn't *want* to be sick."

"I don't want to be sick. I just want the sick days."

Charlie gets home just after four. She doesn't mention Gordon Ellis but I know his arrest must have been texted, tweeted and talked about at school. She makes herself toast and jam for afternoon tea.

"How are you?"

"Fine."

"You want to talk about anything?"

"Nope."

"Are you sure?"

She rolls her eyes and goes upstairs.

At six o'clock I walk the girls down to the cottage. Julianne is home. She's showered and changed and is cooking dinner. Her wet hair hangs out over her dressing gown.

"I saw you today," she says. "What was Sienna doing in court?"

I don't know how much I should tell her. Nothing is probably safest.

"Ronnie Cray wanted to show her something."

"What?"

"I can't really tell you."

Julianne gives me one of her looks. It reminds me of how much she hates secrets. Then she shakes it off, refusing to let me spoil her good mood.

"Well, my job is done," she says, sounding pleased. "Marco finished testifying. He was amazing. They threw everything at him. They tried to confuse him and trick him and say he was lying. It was horrible. I hope the jury saw it. I hope they *hated* that lawyer for what he did."

"He was doing his job."

"Don't defend him, Joe. I know you're a pragmatist, but don't defend someone like that."

She takes Emma's schoolbag from me. I'm standing in the kitchen, which seems to lurch suddenly and I stagger sideways. Julianne grabs me and I straighten.

"Are you all right?"

"I'm fine. I haven't slept."

Mr. Parkinson is shape-shifting on me, messing up my reactions to the medications. The segues between being "on" and "off" my meds have become shorter.

Julianne makes me sit down and begins scolding me about not taking care of myself. At the same time she fills the kettle and makes me a cup of tea.

Wanting to change the subject, I tell her about Annie Robinson, keeping one eye on the stairs in case Charlie overhears me. At six o'clock we turn on the TV to watch Gordon Ellis answering questions on the steps of Trinity Road.

"I can't believe he really did it," says Julianne. "And I let Charlie babysit for him."

"You weren't to know."

She shivers slightly and her shoulder brushes mine.

"Can I ask you something?" I ask.

"What's that?"

"Judge Spencer—what's he been like?"

She looks at me oddly. "Where did that come from?"

"Do you think he's favoring one side or the other?"

"Why?"

"It's just a question."

She studies me momentarily, knowing that I'm holding something back.

"He's a grumpy old sod, but he seems pretty fair. He's very nice to the jury. I think he feels sorry for them. It's a pretty horrible case . . . seeing those photographs of burnt bodies."

"Has he disallowed any evidence?"

"I don't get to hear the legal arguments."

"What happens now?"

"The prosecution has finished. The defense begins calling witnesses tomorrow." Julianne turns down the volume. "I just hope they get found guilty and Marco can get on with the rest of his life."

"What is he going to do?"

"He wants to go to London. Friends have offered to put him up and help find him a job. He's applied for university but that's not until the autumn."

For a few moments we sit in silence. Julianne picks at lint from the sleeve of her sweater.

"Would you like to have dinner with us?" she asks. "Or maybe you'd prefer to go home and sleep?"

"No."

She stands and pirouettes away from me before I try to read anything into the invitation. Summoning the girls, she serves dinner and we sit together at the table like a proper family, or like proper families in TV commercials for Bisto and frozen vegetables. It feels familiar. The familiar is what I crave.

It cannot last, of course. Charlie has homework. Emma has bedtime. Julianne says I can read Emma a story but I fall asleep halfway through it. An hour later, Julianne shakes me awake, holding her finger to my lips.

The dishwasher is humming as I come downstairs. The TV turned down low.

"I've been thinking about what you said about the divorce," I say.

Julianne closes her eyes and opens them again, looking in an entirely different direction. She elevates her face. "And?"

"I think *you* think it's going to change things, but you don't get rid of baggage, you take more on."

"You might be right." She doesn't want an argument.

"Do you want to remarry?"

"No."

"So why?"

"I don't feel married anymore."

"I do."

Julianne pushes bracelets up her forearm. "Do you know your problem, Joe?"

I know she's going to tell me.

"You want everything to *seem* perfect and to *seem* happy and you're willing to let 'seem' equal 'be.' "

Her admonishment is intimate and so laced with melancholy it leaves me nothing to say.

"You don't have to go home," she says. "You can sleep on the sofa."

"Why?"

"Because you're exhausted and some nights I get a little scared on my own."

"Scared?"

She slips her hand down my forearm and hooks her fingers under my palm. "I can have bad dreams too."

My head is vibrating. The sensation comes and goes every few seconds. Opening my eyes, it takes me a moment to recognize my surroundings. I am on the sofa in the cottage.

I remember Julianne giving me a pillow

and blankets, watching the news and feeling a sense of helplessness. Problems in Gaza, global warming, the credit crisis, ozone holes, soaring unemployment, casualties in Iraq and Afghanistan . . .

I don't remember turning off the TV or the hallway light. Julianne must have decided not to wake me. I *do* remember dreaming of Annie Robinson's breasts encased in a lace bra.

The vibrations begin again. My mobile phone is wedged between my head and the armrest of the sofa.

I press green. It's Ronnie Cray.

"Where are you?"

"What is it?"

"Ellis is on the move."

My mind is issuing orders. My feet take a little longer to obey. Navigating through the darkened house, splashing water on my face, lacing my shoes. Suddenly, all thumbs, I can't make the loops and knot the laces.

Julianne appears at the top of the stairs in a thin cotton nightdress. The light behind her paints her body in a silhouette that would make a bishop break his vows.

"What is it?" she asks.

"Go back to bed. I have to go."

"This is what I don't like, Joe."

"I know."

Two unmarked police cars are waiting outside. Monk holds open a rear door. Ronnie Cray is inside, talking on her mobile. She hasn't been to sleep since yesterday.

We travel in silence along Wellow Road towards Radstock and then take a series of B-roads heading west. Kieran the tech is sitting in the front passenger seat, fiddling with an earpiece and tapping on a keyboard. The surveillance vehicles are color-coded dots on a satellite map displayed on a laptop screen.

Safari Roy over the two-way: "Mobile One: We're two back, keeping visual. He's indicating right . . . turning onto the B3135."

"Copy that."

Another voice: "Mobile Three: I'm two miles ahead on the A39. I can take over at Green Ore."

Sunrise is an hour away. Cray looks at her watch. "How soon can we get a chopper in the air?"

"Forty minutes," says Kieran.

We push on through the ink-dark night, listening to the radio chatter and watching the grid lights of larger towns that dot the landscape. Still heading roughly west, we pass through Cheddar and Axbridge and dozens of small villages that appear and disappear, each looking the same.

Gordon Ellis is heading for the North Somerset coast. Every so often he pulls over and waits or doubles back for several miles before turning and resuming his journey. He's making sure that he's not being followed, perhaps checking number plates. Safari Roy gets worried and drops back further. A tracking device on the Ford Focus will keep us in touch as long as Ellis stays with the vehicle.

The eastern horizon is now a yellow slash and the treetops on the high ground are changing color. The helicopter is in the air but still half an hour away. It's another call-sign in the chorus of chatter and static on the radio.

Ellis seems to be slowing down, still turning at every roundabout and doubling back. He's on the A38, passing under the M5. At the next roundabout he takes the second exit onto Bridgewater Road and after half a mile turns left towards Berrow and the coast. The landscape is flat and windswept, broken only by occasional villages and the Mendip Hills in the south.

Kieran points to a satellite image that shows clusters of white boxes along a six-mile beach stretching from Burnham-on-Sea to Brean Down. Caravan sites, chalet parks and holiday cabins are like miniature communities set out in grid pattern with narrow tarmac roads dividing the squares.

The tailing cars are all within a mile of each other as we follow the Coast Road through small villages touched now by a morning sun that paints the cottages in pastel colors and turns fields a brighter green.

There are caravan parks on both sides of the road, along the beachfront and spread in neat rows across fields that were once farmland. Some of the caravans have small gardens, washing lines and faded awnings. Others look closed up and packed away for the winter.

"Is there a fairground near any of them?" asks Cray.

"Brean Leisure Park." Kieran points to the satellite image on screen, which shows up as a series of circles, spiders and snake-like rides, flattened of perspective by the angle of the camera.

The green dot on the screen continues along the Coast Road for another five hundred yards before turning left into a shopping center. Ellis slowly circles the deserted car park and pulls up near a pathway leading from the shops to the beach.

He waits, sitting behind the wheel, watching the entrance. A motorbike passes and disappears along the road. One of ours. The other surveillance teams are hanging back.

The sun has risen above a torn ridge of clouds, bleaching the whitecaps. We've stopped moving and parked at the entrance to the fairground, where the rides are tethered and silent. I can hear flags and canvas beating out a rhythm in the breeze.

Minutes pass. The engine ticks over. Cray's nerves are like guitar strings. I want to ask her about the court case. What did she decide to do? It's not a subject we can talk about openly.

A woman is walking towards us with her dog. She has tight pink leggings and a mass of dyed black hair that matches the color of her poodle. Crossing the road, she looks at us suspiciously.

Safari Roy on radio:

"Target's moving. He's out of the car. Taking something from the boot . . . It's a petrol container. He's on foot."

"Where?"

"Heading down the beach track."

"Stay put. He could double back."

"Mobile Two: I have visual contact."

"Don't get too close."

Cray is sick of looking at dots on a screen. She wants to be outside, on foot, closer.

"Mobile One: Target's on the beach."

"Mobile Two: I've lost visual . . . no, I see him again."

"Copy that."

"Mobile Three: I'm staying at the car."

"Where's the chopper?" asks Cray.

Kieran answers, "Eight minutes away."

"You still with him, Roy?"

"I got him."

"What's he doing?"

"He's cutting over the dunes, back towards the road. You should see him in about ten . . . five . . ."

"Mobile Two: He's walking between vans."

Cray over the radio: "Nobody move until he identifies the van." Then she taps Monk on the shoulder. "Get us closer."

Pulling onto the Coast Road, we travel a

hundred yards and turn into a driveway. The other cars are closing in, sealing off the entrances to the caravan park. I catch a brief glimpse of Ellis about sixty yards away, walking between caravans. A hooded sweatshirt covers his head. One hand is in the pocket of his dark jeans. The other holds an orange petrol container. He stops, crouching on his haunches, scanning the park, but his gaze returns to a particular van.

Cray has an earpiece nestled in the shell of her ear. "Wait for my word."

I can feel the tightness in my scalp . . . in my bladder. Cray is out of the car, making a scuttling dash to a low brick wall. She peers over the top.

For ten minutes nobody moves. I keep trying to fit Sienna's recollections into the real world. She could see the canopy of a merry-go-round, yet the leisure park is a hundred yards away.

Ellis straightens and reaches into his pocket. Something's wrong. It's too easy.

"It's not the van," I whisper to Cray.

She looks at me.

"It's not in the right place. Sienna's statement."

"Maybe he moved it."

"Or he knows you're here."

"Bullshit! We were careful."

"Sienna didn't see Billy that night she woke. Ellis could have a second van. He's going to lead you to the wrong one."

The DCI is staring at me. "I can't let him get inside. What if he has a weapon? I can't risk a siege situation."

Ellis is only feet away from the door of the van.

"It's not the one."

I can hear Cray grinding her teeth. She presses her radio. "Hold your positions. Nobody move."

Ellis has reached the door. He motions to put a key in the lock and then turns, skipping across the narrow tarmac road, disappearing from view.

Safari Roy: "Mobile One, I've lost visual contact."

"Mobile Two, I can't see target."

"Does anyone have a visual?" asks Cray, growing agitated.

The answers come back negative. Cursing, she makes a decision. She wants the park sealed off, locked down, nobody in or out.

Running in a low crouch, I return to the

car and ask Kieran to bring up the satellite image again. Studying the layout, I run my finger in a rough circle around the screen.

"Where are you going?" asks Kieran.

"For a walk."

My left leg is jerking and my arms don't swing in unison, but it's good to be outside, moving. Following the main road, I walk past Brean Leisure Park and then vault a low brick wall, heading in the direction of the beach. There are caravans on either side of the narrow road and more down cross-streets. Occasionally, I turn and look for the canopy of the merry-go-round.

I take out my mobile and punch Cray's number. Almost in the same heartbeat, I see Gordon Ellis emerge from a row of trees about forty yards away. In a half-run he disappears behind a shower block and emerges again, stopping at the last caravan.

Without waiting, he unscrews the lid from the petrol can and begins dousing the walls and windows, swinging the plastic container in long arcs that send liquid as high as the roof.

"Hello, Gordon."

He turns, holding the petrol can at arm's

length. His other hand reaches behind his back and produces a pistol from beneath his sweatshirt. It must have been tucked into his belt, nestled against his spine.

"I assume you're not alone," he says.

"No."

"So you brought the police."

"You did that all by yourself."

I can see him calculating the odds, pondering an escape route. There is a movement in the scrubby hedge behind him. Safari Roy is hunkered down, talking on his radio, summoning backup.

"You're different from the others," says Ellis.

"What others?"

"The police. They want to know how, but you want to know why. You're desperate to know. You want to know if I was abused as a child; if I was buggered by some uncle or the Parish priest. Did I lose my mother? Did I wet the bed? Did she make me sleep in soiled sheets? You think there has to be cause and effect—and that's your weakness. There's nothing to understand. I'm a hunter. It's how we all started. It's how we all survived. It's how we evolved."

"Some of us have evolved a bit further

than others." I want to keep moving to stop my legs from locking up. "Tell me something, Gordon. Were you grooming Charlie?"

He gives me a crocodile smile. "What did you do to that poor girl? She's a timid little kitten."

"She's had a rough few years."

He nods. "I can tell. I thought somebody had got to her first."

That same smile again. He's goading me.

Almost in the same breath, I hear Cray's voice over a megaphone, demanding that he put the gun down and raise his hands above his head. Ellis swings around and hurls the petrol container in my direction, where it bounces end over end.

He turns and puts a key into the lock. Behind him I can see Safari Roy emerge from cover, running hard, his gun drawn. Cray is yelling, "Move! Move!"

The van door swings open and the air seems to wobble like God is shaking the camera. I see a puff of dirty smoke, gray like the sea, and then feel the pressure wave created by the bomb. Gordon Ellis is blown backwards, like the scene is playing in reverse, speeded up.

The caravan disintegrates from within—windows shooting outwards, the roof lifting off, walls splintering into a jigsaw of flying debris—a sink, a toilet, cupboard doors, plastic, stainless steel, reels, spindles—blasting across the park, tumbling to earth.

A hail of metal fragments, nails or ball bearings that must have been packed around the explosives, are sent hurtling outwards, punching holes through fiberglass and flesh.

Knocked from her feet, Ronnie Cray picks herself up. Running. Her hair wet with blood. A nail embedded in her shoulder. She yells into her radio, deafened by the blast and unable to moderate her voice. She wants paramedics.

Ellis had a darkroom. The explosion has ignited the chemicals on the inside and the petrol on the outside creating an orange ball that boils up and evaporates in a wave of smoke and debris. Scraps of photographs, torn paper, twisted negatives and scorched contact sheets are carried by the breeze, clinging to branches and shrubs, skipping across the grass.

Two caravans are burning—one on its side and the other pocked like a Swiss cheese. Roy is lying between them. Monk gets to him first. He signals to me. The front of Roy's shirt is soaked in blood. I rip it off and see half a dozen puncture wounds. Two of the nails are still embedded in his chest.

Someone hands me a first-aid kit. I pull out bandages and dressing, instructing Monk what to do. Roy is conscious and cracking jokes to Ronnie Cray.

"Hey, boss, I'm taking a few weeks off. I'm going to buy ten boxes of condoms and work my way through them."

"You'd be better off buying ten lottery tickets," she replies.

"You think I'm that lucky?"

"I think you're that *unlucky*."

Crouching next to me, she pulls the nail from her shoulder and squeezes a bandage beneath her bra strap.

"He should be OK," I say, looking around for more wounded. The nearest caravan has had its side ripped away. Gordon Ellis is lying in the wreckage. One arm is reaching out for something while the other is only a spike of bone jammed into a wall.

The skin on his face has been peeled away and one eye is a bloody hole. I look at his chest, which has been crushed by the blast. He's dying. He can go in seconds or a few hours, but he's going.

I tell him to hold on, the paramedics are coming, a helicopter . . .

His one good eye is staring at me and words bubble in his throat. "You have a fatal curiosity."

"I'm not the one who's dying."

His tongue appears, licking at the blood on his lips. Can he taste death?

"Who did this?"

He sucks in a ragged breath and coughs. "I wasn't useful anymore."

He's talking about Novak Brennan.

"Why were you helping him?"

"Novak collects people."

"He blackmails them?"

"He's a hard man to refuse."

Ellis grimaces. His teeth are like pieces of broken ceramic sticking from his gums.

"What about Ray Hegarty?"

"The girl must have killed him."

"No. There was someone else in the house that night waiting for Sienna. You wanted to silence her."

"Why would I bother? I *owned* her."

I can hear sirens in the distance, getting

closer. His blood is running between my fingers, over my hands. Ebbing away.

Something brushes my shoulder—a scorched photograph, blown by the breeze from the roof of the caravan. A black-and-white image of a naked girl, snap-frozen, my daughter's best friend, with her arms bound to her ankles and her body, arched backwards. Exposed. Obscene. Unconscious.

I look at Ellis.

I look at my hands.

I walk away.

Rotors flash in the sunshine, beating the air, pushing it aside. Faces appear at the windows of the air ambulance. A door slides open and paramedics sprint across the swirling sand, their hair flattened by the downdraft.

Ronnie Cray is yelling orders and barking into her mobile. Scotland Yard is sending a team from Counter Terrorism Command and the Bomb Squad, while Louis Preston has also been summoned.

The blades of the chopper are spinning more slowly. Safari Roy and Gordon Ellis are strapped to litters and I watch them being carried to the helicopter. There's room for one more. Cray looks nervously at the rumbling chopper. "You go with them. I hate those things."

"What about your shoulder?"

"I'm fine. I'm needed here."

The last of the litters is lifted into the chopper.

"Why booby-trap the van?" she asks.

"Ellis had become a liability. He was attracting too much unwanted attention."

"So Brennan ordered this?"

"He's tying up loose ends."

"Did Ellis say anything about Ray Hegarty?"

"He says he didn't kill him."

Cray doesn't look at me, but I know what she's thinking.

"What about the trial? Are you going to stop it?"

"That's not your concern."

"Ruiz says it could cost you your career."

"It might not come to that."

She pauses and gazes past me along the beach to where a wooden lighthouse on stilts seems to be trapped between the waves and the shore. The daylight is behind her.

"Do you have a lot of friends, Professor?"

"Not too many. How about you?"

"Same. Why do you think that is?"

"I know too much about people."

"And you don't like what you see?"

"Not a lot."

She nods judiciously. "Decency is badly undersold." Her eyes are jittering with light and her lips move uncertainly. "I went to see Judge Spencer last night. I showed him a photograph of Sienna. I was sure he was going to deny it. I thought that underneath the robes and wig he'd prove to be just another lawyer who knows how to play the game—deny, deny, deny or say nothing at all."

Cray runs a hand through her bristled hair. Dust and debris cling to her palm.

"What did he say?"

"He said he didn't know she was only fourteen. He uses an escort agency occasionally when his wife is away. Same old story—lust, desire and the lure of forbidden fruit."

"What's he going to do?"

She shakes her head. "Hopefully, the right thing."

She points towards the chopper. The

engines are revving and the rotors accelerating. A helmeted copilot gives a thumbs-up.

"You'd better go."

Fine sand blasts against my trousers and my face as I run in a crouch and hoist myself on board. Seconds later my stomach lurches and the tail of the helicopter lifts. We leave the earth and swiftly rise, watching caravans shrink to the size of toy building blocks and the roads become black ribbons.

Higher still, we're above the whitecaps and rocky shore, higher than the Mendip Hills and the patchwork fields, where everything is bathed in lustrous sunshine that makes a mockery of all that is dark about the day.

51

Frenchay Hospital on the northern outskirts of Bristol was built in the grounds of a former Georgian mansion, a sanatorium for children with TB back in the 1920s, when lung diseases were as Welsh as male voice choirs.

Little of the old seems to remain. The A&E is decorated in primary colors with modular furniture, cushions and even beanbags. The Intensive Care Unit is on the ground floor, along a wide corridor that squeaks beneath the rubbersoled shoes of the nurses.

There have been too many hospitals lately and the smell seems to stick to the inside of my nostrils, reminding me of my childhood. I grew up around places like this, one of a long line of surgeons until I broke the mold and quit medicine in my third year. My father, God's-personal-physician-in-waiting, has only just forgiven me.

The metal doors swing open and a small Asian woman appears. Dressed in green surgical scrubs, she has short hair, a round face and teeth as white as brand-new. Her name is Dr. Chou and she has a Birmingham accent and honey-colored eyes.

"The detective is out of any danger. We removed fragments from his bowel, but his other major organs seem to have escaped serious damage. We're going to X-ray him again to make sure we haven't missed any shrapnel."

She consults a clipboard. “I can’t give you similar news about Gordon Ellis.”

She begins listing the extent of his injuries, but most of the details wash over me except for her final statement: “Basically we can’t stop the bleeding. X-rays also show there is a nail embedded in his spine and he has no sensation below the neck.”

She pauses, wanting to be sure that I understand what she’s saying.

“Right now he’s on life support and receiving constant blood transfusions. We’re going to wait for his wife to get here before we turn off the machines.”

A rotund priest with a shining dome emerges from the ICU, searching for someone to comfort. He spies a T-shirted teenager in the corner who holds up a magazine as if he wishes it were a force field. Elsewhere, a waiflike couple huddle together as if conserving body heat. The boy has a ring through his eyebrow and the girl has a dozen studs in her ears.

“I’d like to see him,” I say.

“Mr. Ellis won’t be able to speak to you.”

“I know.”

After scrubbing my hands, I follow Dr. Chou through a heavy noiseless door. My eyes take a moment to adjust to the semi-darkness. Only the beds are brightly lit, as though under interrogation by the machines. Gordon Ellis lies on a trolley bed with metal sides. His eyes are bandaged over and his mouth and nose are hidden beneath a mask. Blood is leaking through the bandages on his chest and arms.

For a moment I think he might already be dead, but I see his chest move and the mask fog with condensation and then clear again.

Dr. Chou lays a cool finger on my wrist. She has to leave. I stand away from the bed, not wanting to move any closer. Machines hum. Blood circulates. Tubes, wires and probes snake across the sheets and twist above his body leading to plastic pouches or monitors.

An intensive care nurse is perched on a padded stool amid the machines. She regards me with genial acquiescence, wondering why I'm standing in the half-darkness. She doesn't understand what I've witnessed or comprehend the questions I still have.

Novak Brennan must have known about Gordon's fondness for underage girls and his ability to groom them. He also may have known about the caravan—Ellis's perverted chamber of secrets.

Blackmailing Ellis was the easy part. Corrupting a County Court judge was more challenging. Court appointments are published in advance of a trial, which gave Novak time to investigate Judge David Spencer and discover his penchant for prostitutes, particularly young, innocent-looking, fresh-faced girls. Sienna Hegarty fitted the bill—she was underage, a schoolgirl. Gordon could provide her.

There were thousands of photographs amid the wreckage of the caravan, mostly of young girls, bound and gagged, suffering various indignities. How many other victims were there? Perhaps Natasha was one of them. And what of Caro Regan? Coop and Philippa may never learn the truth of their daughter's fate unless the wreckage of the caravan yields some clues.

The ICU nurse speaks to me. "You can sit down if you'd like."

She has a northern accent and eyes that shine green, reflecting the neon display panels at her fingertips.

"I didn't really know him," I reply.

I wished him dead. I almost killed him.

"I don't know any of them," she says, "but I keep talking. I tell them about the weather and what's on TV. Sometimes I read to them." She holds up a tattered romance novel.

"I'm sure you have a nice reading voice."

"Thank you."

She moves around the bed and reattaches the piece of tape holding a tube against Gordon's forearm. "Was he a good man?"

"Does it matter?"

"I guess not." She blinks at him sadly. "Sometimes I wonder how much control we have over what happens to us, or if our lives are simply a chain reaction. One crash after another."

Walking along the corridor, I push through the doors into the A&E department. A handful of people are standing below a TV on a pillar. I catch a glimpse of the news banner rolling across the lower screen: "RACE HATE TRIAL ABANDONED."

A reporter is standing outside Bristol Crown Court.

The trial of Novak Brennan, Gary

Dobson and Tony Scott was abandoned in controversial circumstances today amid allegations of jury tampering and corruption.

In a morning of high drama, Judge David Spencer told the court that a member of the jury had complained of being approached and threatened by a third party outside the court. Judge Spencer announced that the risk of intimidation was too great for him to ignore. He excused the five women and seven men of the jury, before ordering that the three defendants be retried at a later date.

Lawyers for Novak Brennan and his fellow accused immediately applied for bail, arguing their clients had already spent eight months in custody . . .

My mobile is vibrating.

"Did you hear the news?" asks Julianne. She's speaking from somewhere outdoors.

"I just heard."

"Poor Marco."

"Have you talked to him?"

"I'm meeting him in a few minutes. I'm taking him shopping before he catches the train to London."

"How is he?"

"I don't think he really understands. I thought jury tampering only happened in the movies."

"You'll have to explain it to him."

"Maybe you can help me."

I hesitate and she picks up something in my voice. "You knew! That's why you asked me about the judge."

I don't reply, which simply confirms her suspicions.

"What happened, Joe?"

"I can't tell you."

Before she can ask me another question she interrupts herself: "There's Marco. I'd better go."

I don't get a chance to say goodbye. I want to ring straight back and hear her sweet voice.

A cab has pulled up outside the main doors. Natasha Ellis emerges, clutching Billy's hand. The young boy is wearing his school uniform and has Tigger tucked under his arm. Natasha doesn't acknowledge the cab driver as she pays. Her eyes are bloodshot and she seems to be moving from memory, unable to process what's happened.

Dr. Chou collects her while a nurse takes

Billy to a play area with toys and coloring books. I stand for a long while watching him leaning over a drawing, furiously moving his pencil.

Twenty minutes later Natasha reappears, wiping her eyes and struggling to focus. Billy begins telling her about the drawing. She nods and tries to listen but struggles to hold on to his words. She sees me and a new emotion ignites within her.

Spinning to confront me, her left hand swings from the waist, striking me across the face, raking her nails across my cheek. The slap echoes through the waiting room and my eyes swim.

Her face contorts in grief and rage. "You did this!"

I touch my cheek where her nails have broken the skin. My thumb and forefinger slide together, lubricated by a droplet of blood.

She tries to hit me again, but this time I catch her by the wrist and hold her until I feel her energy dissipate and her shoulders sag. Having surrendered, she lets me take her to a chair where she stares blankly at the far wall, taking short, sharp breaths.

"Is there someone I can call?" I ask. "What about your parents?"

Natasha shakes her head.

"I can get a victim support officer."

She doesn't reply.

"Or I could call a friend . . . You really shouldn't be alone right now."

Taking a deep breath, she looks at me imploringly.

"Why couldn't you leave us alone? We were fine. Happy. Don't you see it was her fault? She was to blame."

I don't reply and hatred blooms in her chest again. "You're no different from Gordon—he was besotted with that little slut. She fooled everybody, but not me. I found her earring in the bedroom. Gordon tried to lie about it, but I'm not stupid. I knew what he was doing with her.

"I followed them one day. Gordon borrowed my car and picked her up after school. He took her to Bradford-on-Avon and bought her an ice cream. They were sitting by the river. I watched him feed it to her. She opened her mouth and he teased her, pulling the spoon away from her lips and offering it again."

Natasha wipes her eyes. "Gordon said I

was being paranoid about Sienna. He said my jealousy made me ugly. He said he still loved me but I had to stop smothering him . . . If that little tart hadn't tried to steal him . . ."

The moment passes and she shrinks away, diminished.

"What happened to his first wife?"

Natasha doesn't look at me. "She ran away."

"Do you believe that?"

"Gordon said he wouldn't lie to me."

"You've seen what he's done."

Her eyes meet mine, clouding.

"He's not a monster. He loved me."

52

Outside in the weak sunshine, looking across the hospital grounds, I watch a mower creating verdant strips of green on the turf, light green and dark green. A curtain of rain is hanging above the horizon as though unsure whether to spoil the day. It creates a strange light that might please a painter or a photographer, but there's nothing I find comforting or appealing about the scene.

I touch my cheek again. The scratches are weeping. Natasha Ellis struck me with her left hand, unleashing all her grief and fury. She has lost her husband. Lost the life she fought so hard to protect. This is the detail I failed to notice. I didn't comprehend how far she'd go to save her marriage. The sins she'd overlook. The risks she'd take.

I have a missed call on my mobile. Ruiz. I call him back.

"Have you heard?" he asks. "They abandoned the trial."

"I just saw the news on TV."

"Looks like Ronnie Cray pulled it off. Does she still have a job?"

"Far as I know."

He asks about last night and why I didn't come back to the terrace.

"I stayed with Julianne."

"Really?"

"Nothing happened. I slept on the sofa."

"Maybe she wanted you to storm her bedroom and ravish her."

Do people "ravish" each other anymore?

I tell him about the booby-trapped caravan and my helicopter flight to the hospital with Gordon Ellis.

"So he's dead?"

"Yes."

"What about Caro Regan?"

"Maybe the debris will yield some clues."

Ruiz is silent for a time, thinking about Coop and Philippa Regan and their mausoleum-like flat in Edinburgh and their funereal existence, wondering what happened to their daughter.

"Where are you now?" he asks.

"Frenchay Hospital."

"You need a lift?"

"If you're offering."

"I should have been a minicab driver."

"More money."

"Better hours."

He hangs up and I walk across the road, feeling the turf beneath my shoes. I am closer to understanding things now. I know why Ray Hegarty was murdered, why Annie Robinson was poisoned and why Sienna was framed.

Not everything makes sense. If there's an exception to every rule, then that rule itself must have an exception. Novak Brennan tried to corrupt a judge. Sway a jury. Secure a verdict. Yet so much of it depended upon factors that he could never fully control. A majority verdict to acquit required ten jurors—a huge ask. By blackmailing a judge the only thing he could completely guarantee was the collapse of the hearing and a retrial with a new jury and a new judge. Novak must have known this.

I glance towards the hospital and see my reflection cast back at me from the doors. I am a man standing alone in a field. Some things we have to do alone. Birth. Death. Sitting in a witness box . . .

Uneasiness washes over me, inching upwards, lodging in my throat. Fumbling for my phone I call Julianne. Her number is engaged. I start over. This time she answers.

"Where's Marco?" I ask.

"He went to buy me a present."

"Does he have a number?"

"He doesn't have a phone."

She's at Broadmead Shopping Centre, which is fifteen minutes away.

Julianne senses my fear. "What's wrong?"

"You have to find him. Get him out of there."

"Why?"

"It's not safe. Find him and call me."

Ruiz has pulled up outside the hospital. I try to run but suddenly freeze and stare helplessly at my legs, telling them to move. I direct all of my concentration to just my left leg, telling it to step forward. It must be like watching a man step over an invisible obstacle. Once I get a degree of momentum, I'll be fine. One leg will follow the other. Walk and then run.

I pull open the passenger door and tumble inside, telling Ruiz to drive, telling him that Julianne's in danger. Without hesitation, he accelerates, weaving between cars, demanding answers.

We're on the M32. Middle lane. Passing the concrete towers, shuttered shops, factories, pawnshops and "For Lease" signs. There are hookers walking up and down Fishponds Road: women who are women and men who are women and crackheads who will be anything you want.

"When you were following Carl Guilfoyle—you said it was strange, you said he seemed to know he was being tailed. Maybe we were *meant* to find the photographs."

Ruiz looks at me askance and back to the road.

"Why?"

"Novak couldn't guarantee an acquittal, but he could guarantee what happened today."

"You're saying he *wanted* the trial abandoned?"

"He needed more time."

"More time for what?"

"To silence Marco Kostin."

"I thought he was under police guard."

"He was until this morning."

Traffic lights. Amber then red. Ruiz brakes heavily.

My mobile chirrups. Julianne.

"I've seen him."

"Marco?"

"No, the man with the black tears."

My heart lurches.

"I saw him outside WH Smith."

"Was he following you?"

"I don't know. I can't find Marco."

I tell her to stay calm. "I'm going to hang up now and call the police."

"What should I do?"

"Where were you going to meet Marco?"

"At Brasserie Blanc."

"Go there. Sit outside. Somewhere public."

My heart is banging in my ribs. Cray's number is engaged. I try again. Monk answers. I tell him to get the boss. It's an emergency.

The DCI replaces him.

"Carl Guilfoyle is going after Marco Kostin. They're both at Broadmead Shopping Centre."

"Is anyone with Marco?"

"Julianne is looking for him. We're almost there."

"Don't approach Guilfoyle. Get them out of there."

The lights are green. Ruiz accelerates. Seventy miles an hour. Chasing taillights and leaving them behind.

My mind is zigzagging ahead, like a small furry creature darting through undergrowth, following a scent, switching direction, moving away from me. We're going too slowly.

Ruiz leans on the horn as we get caught in traffic on the Old Market Roundabout. He swings across two lanes, braking hard, the tires screeching. We almost sideswipe a lorry and he wrenches the wheel, correcting twice. The pine-scented air-freshener swings violently from the mirror.

We're in Quakers Friars. Ruiz pulls over. Hazard lights flashing. I'm already out the door and running across the flagstones, dodging pedestrians, shoppers, office workers.

Julianne is standing alone outside the restaurant in her buttoned-up trench coat and the boots she bought in Milan. Nearby there are children running in and out of water jets that spout like molten silver from the slick pavers.

"We were supposed to meet here," she says, wide-eyed, anxious.

"Where did you see him last?"

"In Merchant Street."

"How long ago?"

"He should have been back by now."

Ruiz arrives. We'll split up and search. Somebody should stay here in case Marco turns up: Julianne.

"Call if you see him."

I start moving, my scalp itchy and damp. There are hundreds of shops over almost six blocks and three levels—department stores, boutiques, specialty shops, restaurants and cafés—the biggest retail center in Bristol. As long as Marco stays somewhere public. As long as he's in the open . . .

Weaving through the crowd, I keep looking at the faces, expecting to see Marco or Carl Guilfoyle. There are too many people. He could walk right past me and I might not see him.

Pushing through the doors of BHS, I jog up the escalator and weave between racks of clothes. The window overlooks the intersection of Broadmead and Merchant Street.

I scan the crowd. Young mums with prams, joggers in Lycra shorts, a hooded youth with a skateboard, an elderly couple, hunched arthritically, moving in slow motion. A juggler in a clown's hat has drawn an audience by tossing colored balls in the air and bouncing them off the pavement.

There are so many people, a sea of moving heads. That's when I see Marco on the edge of the crowd watching the juggler. He's wearing a red baseball cap and carrying a glossy carrier bag.

Retreating down the escalator, through the automatic doors, I emerge on street level. A toddler runs under my feet. Half catching him as I fall, I bounce up and spin around, planting the boy on his feet. His mother gives me a foul-mouthed tirade, but I'm looking past her for Marco.

I can't see him. He was on the far side of the square. Pushing through the crowd, I look for his red baseball cap. In the periphery of my vision I catch sight of Julianne. What's she doing? She must have seen Marco too.

Suddenly, someone collides with me from the front on my right side and continues walking. I glimpse his features—the marks on his cheeks, more like scars than tattoos, as though his face has been sewn together from discarded pieces of skin.

I can hear my breath escaping as I watch his right hand slip into his coat pocket. He moves away. I know I have to chase him. Stop him. Instead I feel an overwhelming sense of fatigue. One step. Two steps. Three steps. What's happening?

I glance down. A red plume spreads out from my ribs down to my trousers. The blade slipped in so easily that I didn't feel it enter beneath my ribs, rising towards my heart and into my lungs.

I'm staggering, falling to my knees, frantically trying to stay upright. My head keeps bobbing and weaving but it's not one of Mr. Parkinson's cruel jokes. The pain has arrived, a dull throbbing, growing in intensity, screaming at me to stop. It's as if someone has driven a heated metal rod into my chest and is jerking it from side to side.

My shirt is sodden, sticking to my body. I look up and around, frightened. Through the forest of legs, I can't see Marco. Maybe he's gone. Maybe he's running. Julianne must be close. I see her first. They're together.

In that instant, I recognize Guilfoyle's hooded sweatshirt. His right hand comes out of his pocket. The blade is flush against his forearm. He's moving at pace through the crowd.

I try to yell, but it comes out as a groan. Guilfoyle is only a few paces away, passing Marco on his knife-hand side, his arm in motion, using his momentum to drive the blade beneath his ribs, aiming for the heart.

At that moment a girl in a pink skirt and candy-striped leggings loses her helium balloon. Marco spins on one foot and tries to catch the trailing string. The blade slides through his shirt and into his flesh, but the angle is wrong. Guilfoyle knows it. The speed of the thrust has carried him two paces from Marco and he turns. Julianne has seen him. She screams, openmouthed, terrified. Head down, hands in his pockets, Guilfoyle carries on, pushing through the crowd.

Marco drops to his knees, holding his side. I can't see him anymore. People are stepping around me and over me. A woman trips over my legs and almost falls. She has tight blue jeans and a huge arse. Another face, upside down. Her husband—he's wearing an AC/DC T-shirt.

"Are you all right?" he asks.

I can't answer.

"That's blood!" says his wife.

"He's been shot," says someone else.

"Do you want me to call an ambulance?"

"Who shot him?" asks another voice.

"It could have been a sniper."

"A sniper! Where?"

"There's a sniper!"

It's like watching a rock being thrown into a tranquil pond, rippling outwards. People scatter. Yelling. Running. Falling down. Dragging children. Fighting to get away. There are cries and yells and scuffles.

Now I see Julianne clearly. She's safe. I feel a quickening torque of my heart. She takes off Marco's shirt. Blood is leaking over the waistband of his underwear and jeans.

At the far end of Merchant Street a black Range Rover pulls up. Carl Guilfoyle jumps into the passenger seat. I glimpse a woman behind the wheel. Rita Brennan.

Ruiz is charging after them. He runs like a front-rower with his head down and knees lifting, everything happening below the waist. He grabs the driver's door and pulls it open. Rita Brennan accelerates and the door swings out and back in again. Ruiz grabs at the wheel and wrenches it down. Moments later I hear the crunch of metal on metal but can't see what happened.

There are police sirens. Growing louder.

The pain in my chest is overtaking every other sense. My fingers are cold, my skin clammy. Nothing feels like it is happening to bring help. Where are the paramedics? Someone get a doctor.

Julianne looks up and sees me. I wish I could smile bravely, but I'm scared and I'm shaking.

She's with me now. Kneeling.

"Where?"

I lift my arm. She can see the puncture wound below my rib cage. The hole seems to be breathing. She takes off her trenchcoat and presses it to the spot.

"That's going to stain," I tell her.

"I'll soak it."

Straddling me, she presses her fingers against my ribs, keeping pressure on the wound. Her eyes are shining. She's not supposed to cry.

"I need you to stay awake, Joe."

"I'm just closing my eyes for a second."

"No, you stay awake."

"You were right," I tell her. "I should have protected you and Charlie."

She shakes her head as a signal that I'm not supposed to talk about this now.

"How's Marco?"

"He's going to be OK."

My heart is no longer battering. It's slowing down.

"I'm just going to have a little rest."

"Don't! Please."

"Sorry."

Julianne lowers her head to my chest and it feels like we've slipped back through the years since we separated and she's listening to the same heartbeat that serenaded her to sleep for twenty years.

"Don't be angry with me," she whispers.

"I'm not angry."

My lips are pressed into her dark hair.

I remember the last time we made love. I had come home late and Julianne was asleep or only half awake. Naked. She rolled on top of me in the darkness, performing the ritual half-blind, but practiced. Rising and descending inch by inch, accepting my surrender. I thought at the time that it didn't feel like make-up sex or new-beginning sex. It was goodbye sex, a dying sigh drawing color from the embers.

If that has to be the last time then I can live with that, I think, opening my eyes again.

"Charlie is going to be OK," I say.

Julianne raises her face to look at me. "I know. It just makes me a little sad because you two are so alike."

"You think she's like me?"

"I know you both too well."

She runs her finger down my right cheek, tracing the scratches.

"Who did this to you?"

"The woman who killed Ray Hegarty."

"It wasn't Sienna."

"No."

EPILOGUE

I have a student waiting to see me outside my office. His name is Milo Coleman and I'm supposed to be overseeing his psychology thesis, which would be a lot easier if I had something to oversee.

Milo, one of my brighter students, has spent the past four months trying to decide the subject of his thesis. His most recent suggestion was to pose the question whether loud music in bars increased alcohol consumption. This only slightly bettered a proposal that he study whether alcohol made a woman more or less likely to have sex on a first date.

I told him that while I appreciated how diligently he would research such a subject, I doubted if I could get it past the university's board of governors.

Opening my office door, I don't find him waiting on the row of chairs in the corridor. Instead he's chatting to Chloe, an undergrad student who answers the phones in the psychology department. Milo is dressed in a James Dean T-shirt, low-slung jeans and Nike trainers. Chloe likes him. Her body language says so—the way her shoulders pull back and she plays with her hair.

"When you're ready, Milo," I announce.

Chloe gives him a look that says, Next time.

"Professor O'Loughlin, how's it hanging?"

"It's hanging just fine."

"I heard about you being stabbed and I was, like, shocked, you know. I mean, that's a heavy scene."

"Yes, Milo, very heavy."

He takes a seat opposite my desk, leans forward, elbows on his knees. A long fringe of hair falls across one eye. He brushes it aside, tucking it girlishly behind his ear. Smiling quietly. Beaming.

"I think I've got it: the big idea."

"Hit me with it."

"Well, I went to see a comedy night last week and I was watching this black dude telling jokes, really edgy stuff, racist, you know. He's telling nigger jokes and all these white people in the audience are laughing and cheering. I got to wondering what effect racial humor has on prejudice."

Milo looks at me nervously. Expectantly. Hopefully.

"I think it's a great idea."

"Really?"

"Yes, really. How are you going to do it?"

Milo gets to his feet, pacing the room while he lays out his ideas for a cognitive study involving an audience and a series of questions. He's energized. Animated.

"So how long do I have?"

"Start work now and you can update me at the end of November."

He cocks his head, looking at me with one eye. Milo often looks at me sideways so I never see both his eyes at the same time.

"That's only two months."

"Sufficient time."

"But I got to work out questions. Parameters. Study groups . . ."

This is the other side of Milo's personality—making excuses, questioning the work involved.

"Two months is plenty of time. Show me too little and I'll mark you down as being lazy. Show me too much and I'll think you're sucking up to me."

"Are you serious?"

"You tell me."

"Huh?"

"You've spent four years studying human behavior. Decide if I'm lying."

Milo pushes back his fringe. Frowns. Wants to argue.

"I know what you're like, Milo. You cruise. You coast. You wear that earring and that T-shirt because you see yourself as a rebel without a cause, channeling the spirit of James Dean. But let me tell you something about Dean. He was the son of a dental technician from Indiana, where he went to a posh school and studied violin and tap dancing."

Milo looks completely bemused. I put my hand on his shoulder. Lead him to the door. "Start your thesis. No more excuses. Show me something by November."

I watch him disappear along the corridor with his exaggerated slope-shouldered walk. My old headmaster at prep school, Mr. Swanson (who looked like God with long white curly hair) would have barked at him, "It took a million years for humans to learn to walk upright, Coleman, and you're taking us back to the trees."

Coop Regan is sitting nervously on a chair. Dressed in a coat and tie, he has combed his oiled hair across his head and buttoned his jacket as though waiting for a job interview.

This is a completely different man to the one I met four months ago in Edinburgh, hiding away in a dark lounge watching old home movies of his missing daughter. Now clear-eyed and sober, he stands and shakes my hand firmly, holding my gaze.

"Ah'm sorry to bother you," he says, in a voice ravaged by years of smoking. "Ah know you're a busy man."

"That's OK."

"We couldn't go home without saying goodbye."

"Where's Philippa?"

He motions outside. "Billy wanted to play. It's a long old drive home."

Glancing out the window, I see a young boy running through the trees, being chased by a large woman in a bright green cardigan who is shaped like a fireplug. Philippa has no chance of catching Billy, but she'll keep on chasing as long as he keeps laughing.

"Vincent brought us to see you," says Coop.

Then I notice Ruiz standing beneath a tree, which has blooms as big as his fists. Billy runs towards him and hides behind him for a moment as though his legs are tree trunks.

"We're going to have to watch that one—he's cheeky like his ma used to be."

"You'll do fine."

Coop's chest expands and he stares at his polished shoes. "Ah said some things to you before, when you came to see us. Ah blamed Caro for making us love her so much. Ah was going off my head."

"I understand."

Coop nods. "Aye, Ah think you do."

He pulls me into a hug. I can smell his

aftershave and the dry-cleaning fluid on his jacket.

Releasing me, he turns and wipes his eyes. I walk him downstairs and say goodbye to Philippa, who is pink-faced and breathless, ten years younger than I remember with her bright red hair pulled back from her round face.

They wave and toot their horn, taking their grandson home. Ruiz lets his eyes wander across the grass to a group of pretty students having a picnic in the shade. For a fleeting moment I glimpse a yearning in him—a longing to be young again—but he's not a man to look over his shoulder or contemplate what might have been.

It has been two months since I left hospital and three months since the stabbing. The stiletto blade entered beneath my ribs and traveled upwards through my spleen, aiming at my heart. Narrowly missing the chambers and aorta, it punctured my left lung, which slowly collapsed. The slenderness of the blade limited blood loss externally but filled my chest cavity. I needed three blood transfusions and two operations.

I came out of hospital on the same day

that Natasha Ellis appeared in Bristol Crown Court charged with the murder of Ray Hegarty and attempted murder of Annie Robinson. These were crimes of passion and crimes of revenge. Natasha thought she was losing Gordon to another schoolgirl lover—someone just like her.

At first she denied the allegations and then tried to strike a deal after Louis Preston found her DNA on a hand towel at the murder scene.

On that Tuesday evening, Natasha let herself into the Hegartys' house using a key that she copied from Sienna. She hid behind the teenager's bedroom door, looking at the reflection in the mirror so she knew exactly what moment to strike.

She was expecting Sienna, but Ray Hegarty arrived home instead. He must have heard a sound and walked upstairs into Sienna's room. Perhaps he saw Natasha at the last moment as the hockey stick was falling.

She couldn't risk being recognized or identified so she silenced him, cutting his throat, right to left.

Ronnie Cray said it on that first day—it had to have been someone small to hide behind the door. Somebody left-handed. Somebody who neatly folded the hand towel in the bathroom.

The amount of blood must have surprised Natasha—how fast it flowed, how far it sprayed, covering her hands and her clothes. Minutes later Sienna came home and saw her father's bag. She crept quietly up the stairs, wanting to avoid him, but heard a tap running in the bathroom and a toilet flushing.

Running the final steps, desperate to get into her room, Sienna tripped over her father's body and screamed, scrambling up, leaving her handprint on his shirt. Natasha didn't react quickly enough to stop Sienna fleeing. However, she quickly saw another way to get rid of her rival. She dropped the Stanley knife into the river close to where Sienna was discovered that night.

Did Gordon know what she'd done? Perhaps. Surely, he suspected, but in a perverse twist the crime reinforced his bond with Natasha because each had to provide an alibi for the other.

Annie Robinson proved to be another hidden danger. She was blackmailing Gordon over his affair with Sienna, extorting money and threatening to destroy his career. Natasha had killed to protect her marriage and wouldn't hesitate to do it again. Spiking a bottle of wine with antifreeze, she delivered it to Annie's flat with a gift card from a grateful cast.

Annie phoned me on the day I got out of hospital. She said that I sounded different.

"How do I sound?"

"Like maybe you could forgive me one day."

She laughed nervously and kept talking.

"I wanted to come and see you, but I didn't know how you'd react or what your wife would say. I did a very bad thing, asking Gordon for money. I should have protected Sienna. I should have stopped it."

There was a long pause. Maybe Annie expected me to disagree or wanted me to make her feel better. I couldn't do it.

Then she told me about her plans to take long service leave and travel to Vietnam, Laos and Cambodia. She might even get to Australia.

"I think I might like Australian men. They're not so buttoned up."

"You think I'm buttoned up?"

"No, you're just in love with your ex."

Novak Brennan and his co-accused go on trial next week at the Old Bailey. The hearing has been transferred to London for security reasons and the Attorney General has promised greater protection for jurors and witnesses.

Marco Kostin will be the star witness again. Julianne visited him twice in hospital before he was taken to a safe house. I don't know if they're going to offer him a new identity after the trial, but I wouldn't blame him for going back to Kiev or trying to start a new life somewhere else.

I have my own court date to contend with. Not as a defendant, thank goodness, the charges against me were dropped. Instead I'm to give evidence against Carl Guilfoyle, who faces two counts of attempted murder, as well as perverting the course of justice and jury tampering. Rita Brennan will be tried alongside him as an accomplice.

The murder of Gordon Ellis is still an ongoing investigation, but Ronnie Cray has Guilfoyle in her sights. She has recommended Safari Roy for a Police Bravery Award, but refused to accept a nomination for herself. The scar on her shoulder will serve as a trophy.

Meanwhile, Judge David Spencer stepped down from the bench very quietly during the summer. There was a paragraph in *The Times* Law Reports and a small article in the *Guardian,* but no judicial inquiry or police investigation. He retired with his reputation and pension intact, although a separate diary entry mentioned that he'd separated from his wife of forty years. That can be punishment enough.

The collapse of the so-called race-hate trial was a big news story for a week as the experts and commentators debated again whether trial by jury is an outdated system, akin to asking the ignorant to understand the incomprehensible and decide the unknowable.

I don't know the answer, but if I were on trial for my life, I would rather put my fate in the hands of twelve people too stupid to get out of jury duty than one judge who may have an agenda. Jurors can be colossally ignorant and easily bewildered by the sophistry of lawyers, but I'll take my chances with the ordinary man and woman because they can tell the difference between justice and the law.

I see Helen Hegarty occasionally in the village, but she still keeps to herself, rarely smiling. She no longer works nights and Zoe has moved home, deferring her university course for a year. Sienna has started at a new school in Bath, but she and Charlie still see each other, one of them struggling to reclaim her childhood while the other is desperate to grow out of hers.

I used to want to stop Charlie growing up. I sought to hold on to the girl who watched *Lord of the Rings* with me and liked her pizza with extra pepperoni and made fun of the fact that Julianne couldn't catch a ball. Now I have a more realistic vision of the future, one that isn't based on a pathological desire to protect my children from people like Gideon Tyler and Gordon Ellis and Liam Baker; as well as bad boyfriends, ignorant bosses, cruel comments, drunk maniacs and intolerant bigots.

Parenthood is a lot like being a trapeze artist, knowing when to let go and watch your child tumble away in midair, reaching out for the next rung, testing herself. My job is to be here when she swings back, ready to catch her and to launch her into the world again.

Lately, I've become more optimistic that Charlie will be OK. She'll weather adolescence and a divorce (if it comes to that), and I'll be around to see her graduate from university, collect the Nobel Prize, fall in love, marry and be blissfully happy.

When I lie awake in the morning, inventorying my tics and twitches, waiting for my medication to click in, I sometimes think of all the things I haven't done yet. I haven't slept with a movie star or climbed Kilimanjaro or learned a language other than schoolboy French. I haven't written a book or run a marathon or swum with dolphins.

Mr. Parkinson will not kill me, but I will die with him unless the race for a cure beats his unrelenting progress. Some people think news like this would change their attitude towards life. They have fantasies of self-transformation, of climbing mountains or jumping out of planes.

Not me. You won't catch me running with the bulls in Pamplona or searching for the source of the Amazon. I'd rather a mundane end than a gloriously brave or stupid one.

In the meantime, I am going to tremble and twitch and spasm into middle age. It's not that I don't feel the aching pain of loss. When I see footage of myself from six years ago, standing tall, fighting fit—images of a younger, healthier me—I do feel angry. My strength, balance and dexterity have been compromised. I am half the man I was, searching for the rest.

Maybe I'll move back to London. Maybe I'll learn to dance. Maybe I'll be the guy I dream of being, holding the line on the life that I promised myself.

Some nights I still sit outside the cottage, watching over my family, seeing their shadows behind the curtains—it's the best show in town and I still have a pretty good seat.

Raising children, I've decided, is a lot sadder than I expected. Seeing them grow up brightly and vividly is tempered by the knowledge that each year brings another share of lasts. The last time I push my daughter on a swing. The last time I play the Tooth Fairy or Santa Claus. The last time I read a bedtime story.

If I could give my daughters one piece of advice I would tell them to make the most of the first times—their first kiss, their first date, their first love, the first smile of their first child . . .

There can be only one.

ACKNOWLEDGMENTS

Writing might be regarded as a solitary profession, but publishing certainly is not. I am indebted to many people without whom I couldn't have written this novel and would have been forced to find a proper job.

Firstly I must thank my agents Mark Lucas and Richard Pine, whose thoughts and notes on the manuscript improved it immeasurably. The same can also be said of my publishers Ursula Mackenzie and David Young and their very talented and professional teams, in particular my editors David Shelley and John Schoenfelder.

For their friendship and hospitality, I

thank Mark and Sara Derry, Richard and Emma Honey and Martyn Forrester, who know how much I hate hotel rooms and how much I enjoy their company.

For their patience and love, I will always be indebted to my three daughters, Alex, Charlotte and Bella, who put up with my highs and lows, laughing at my eccentricities. Thankfully, they take after their mother, who keeps my feet on the ground so I can live with my head in the clouds.

Finally I make special mention of Annie Robinson, whose name appears in *Bleed for Me.* Although Annie didn't get the chance to read about her namesake, I know that she's partying with the angels and living in our hearts.

Michael Robotham began his career as an investigative journalist in Australia and Britain. He later became a ghostwriter, collaborating on more than a dozen bestselling autobiographies for pop stars, actors, decorated soldiers and politicians.

Michael's first psychological thriller *Suspect* sold more than a million copies around the world. His second novel *Lost* won the Ned Kelly Award for Australia's best crime novel in 2005—an award he won again in 2008 with *Shatter.* He has twice been shortlisted for the UK Steel Dagger Award in 2007 (*The Night Ferry*) and 2008 (*Shatter*).

Michael currently lives in Sydney with his wife and three daughters.

His website is www.michaelrobotham.com.